About the author

David C. Ayre was trained as an electronics engineer at Loughborough University and has worked in the electronic field most of his life, later concentrating more on software. He was born in Hertfordshire but has lived in North Yorkshire for the last forty-seven years where he enjoys walking in the wilder parts of the county as well as the Lake District with his wife, Muriel. He has a son and a daughter and two step-daughters, four grandchildren and one step-grandson. He is also very keen on painting and drawing and has been very involved with amateur theatre for many years. He has written several books for teenagers as well as several pantomimes and screen plays.

THE DOOMSDAY MACHINE

David C. Ayre

THE DOOMSDAY MACHINE

Vanguard Press

VANGUARD PAPERBACK

© Copyright 2018
David C. Ayre

A CIP catalogue record for this title is
available from the British Library.

ISBN 978 1 784654 78 8

Vanguard Press is an imprint of
Pegasus Elliot MacKenzie Publishers Ltd.
www.pegasuspublishers.com

First Published in 2018

Vanguard Press
Sheraton House Castle Park
Cambridge England

Printed & Bound in Great Britain

To my wife, Muriel, who has read the work as I have progressed and pointed out any errors, of which there were quite a few. (Big fingers, small keys!)

Acknowledgments

I would like to thank all at Pegasus Elliot Mackenzie
Publishers for all their help and advice in getting this
book into print.

One

It was a bright sunny morning in early summer, as Alan Westbrook trudged along the stony path that led up onto the moors. He had parked the camper-van in a lay-by, put on his boots, slung the small rucksack over his shoulder and set off on a little-used path. He was happier than he had been for a long time. A cool breeze wafted through the heather, a lark was singing nearby and in the distance he could hear the call of a curlew as it flew low across the moor. Not a soul was in sight, and that was how he liked it. He had a pet hate of 'walkers' with all the gear – socks rolled down over their boots, large rucksacks containing everything to cover all eventualities from a grazed knee to a nuclear strike. They would each be armed with at least one ski pole, without which they seemed unable to walk. He used to ask them what the skiing was like and was rewarded with blank expressions. But really his worst hate was the folded map in a plastic wallet hung around their necks. He really didn't think these people should be let out on their own.

Once he was walking in the Lakes and was wearing a pair of chunky sandals, which had commando soles. They were very light and comfortable and his feet didn't overheat in them, but the looks he got from the 'walkers' were unbelievable. One even commented on them and asked if he didn't stub his toes. He replied that if people went about stubbing their toes they would be likely to end up hurtling down the mountainside head first.

But today seemed clear of people and he was able to enjoy his own company and watch and listen to nature all about him as he made his way up the winding path to the high moorland beyond. He was surprised when a brace of grouse broke cover, way over to his right, and sped off down the valley. He couldn't see what had disturbed them, as he wasn't high enough to see over the ridge, but it could have been anything. *Maybe a stoat*, he thought.

At the top of the climb he decided to sit among the rocks for a while and have a snack from his rucksack. He found a nice sheltered spot among the rocks and selected a comfortable looking flat surface to sit on. From his perch, he could look out over the valley. He could see the little lane where he had parked the camper and the sun glinting off its roof. About half a mile further down the lane, he caught sight of another car that was parked just off the road. His heart sank to think that he didn't have the place entirely to himself. But perhaps they had gone the other way. He hoped so.

After a while he set off again and was soon walking along the flat rocky surface above a steep cliff with a sheer drop of over a hundred feet onto the scree below. The height didn't bother him as the surface was flat and firm and there was no danger of accidentally walking over the edge.

He stopped suddenly. His sharp ears had picked out a sound amongst all the other sounds, which alerted him to company. It was the sound of a boot scrunching on loose gravel. Someone was approaching from his left, a little behind him. He chose to ignore them and walked on.

"Peter! Where are you going?" It was a woman's voice. He carried on walking, as he had no desire for company today.

"Peter! Wait for me, please." The sound of footsteps speeded up into a run. Perhaps she would head off down the slope the way he had come up.

But that was not to be. She was getting nearer and he could hear her panting breath. *What was this woman thinking, running along the edge of this cliff?*

"Peter, will you wait for me please." It was a command. Alan looked about him to see where this Peter was and why he wasn't waiting for this noisy woman. She was almost behind him now, so he stepped off the path to let her through, and as he turned, she stopped dead in her tracks, mouth open in surprise. She was a small, quite attractive woman in her late fifties or early sixties, he guessed, wearing a bright orange anorak with a pair of binoculars hanging around her neck. She wore a tweed skirt above long socks and lightweight boots. In her hand she had a lightweight haversack that appeared to be almost empty. She stood, panting from the exertion.

"Oh, I am sorry," she said. "From a distance you looked just like my husband."

"Oh, I see," said Alan. "Sorry."

"Same anorak, same rucksack, same trousers… well almost, and the same grey hair with the bald patch on the top." Alan grimaced.

"Oh, I'm sorry," she said, looking embarrassed. "I didn't mean to be rude about your hair."

"Or lack of it," said Alan. "You can't be rude if it's true."

"Well, that's kind of you," she said. "You haven't seen someone who looks a bit like you, have you?"

"Sorry, no," he replied. "You're the first person I've seen today. But I think there might have been someone up here a bit earlier. I saw a couple of grouse take off in alarm from a bit further along this ridge. What was he doing?"

"He went off on his own and left me to have a rest and a bite to eat," she said. "He wasn't very hungry and was keen to see if he could see the peregrines."

"Peregrines?"

"Peregrine falcons."

"Yes, I know what they are," said Alan. "But I didn't know there were any round here."

"Perhaps there aren't," she said. "But he had been told that there was a nest in the cliffs along here and he wanted to see them."

"Keen twitcher, is he?"

"Not as such, but we both like watching birds. We don't really know the names of most of them, but we like to see them in their natural habitat."

"If there are any," said Alan, "they'll be along here. I'm going that way so I'll walk with you, if you like."

"Thank you," she said, smiling. "Very kind of you." They set off along the path in single file with Alan in the lead.

"I saw a curlew a bit earlier," said Alan.

"Did you?" she replied. "I'm told they are returning to the moors again."

"I believe so."

The ground rose steeply and they had to concentrate on what they were doing. It wouldn't be a good thing to slip here.

At the top, Alan waited and held out a hand to help his companion up the last bit of the ascent.

"I'm sorry," said Alan suddenly, "but I didn't introduce myself. My name is Alan Westbrook."

"Maggie Finch," she replied. "My husband is Peter. I'll introduce you when we find him."

"A very appropriate name."

"Maggie?"

"No, Finch," said Alan with a grin. "Bird watchers?"

"Oh, I see what you mean," she replied. "That has been said before."

"The old ones are the best."

"Are you on your own up here?" she asked, changing the subject.

"Yes."

"Doesn't your wife like walking?"

"Divorced."

"Oh, I'm sorry." She looked a bit embarrassed.

"I'm not," he said. "I'm quite enjoying the freedom."

"Aren't you lonely?"

"Sometimes, yes," he said. "But overall it's worth it."

He stopped suddenly, causing Maggie to walk into him. She started to apologise but then, following his gaze, saw what had caused him to stop. Down below them on the scree was a figure lying head-first down the slope.

"Oh no," she gasped.

"I'll ring for help," he said, taking out his mobile phone and switching it on. "I hope the battery's OK. I don't use this thing much."

He found that it had enough charge in it to make the call and alerted the police and ambulance services.

"I must get down to him," said Maggie, moving to the edge of the cliff.

"Not that way," said Alan. "There's a steep way down just along here, but I think we ought to go round the long way. It's less dangerous."

"No. I'm not doddery yet, thank you. Show me the steep way."

Alan led the way, further along the cliff path, until they came to a cleft which looked too steep to get down, but he shuffled his way down on his backside until he was almost out of sight. Maggie followed as best she could and found him waiting just round the corner on firmer ground. She looked down and grabbed his arm.

"You'll be OK," he said. "Just follow me and keep close into the cliff face."

The path was barely more than a broken ledge with a long drop to one side. Alan began to wonder if it had been such a good idea to bring Maggie down this way. He turned to see that she was all right and saw the terror in her face as she gripped the rock for all she was worth.

"Perhaps we should go the other way?" said Alan.

"It's all right," she said, looking anything but all right. "Just keep going. I'm right behind you."

Alan moved a step further on and a handful of pebbles went cascading down the side of the cliff, bouncing out and onto the scree below.

"A bit of loose ground here," he said. "Go carefully."

"I am going very carefully, I can assure you."

After about twenty yards of painfully slow progress, the path improved slightly. It was still narrow but firmer underfoot. By the time they were halfway down, Maggie was moving more easily and progress became better.

"I think I'm getting the hang of this now," she said.

"Don't get carried away," he replied. "It's still a nasty drop to the bottom."

There was the sound of a vehicle moving slowly down the road below.

"That was quick," said Alan. "I thought they would take much longer to get here."

"It's not the ambulance," said Maggie. "There's a black car going down the lane at the bottom."

"I thought that was your car," he said.

"No. We came by bus and walked up from the other side."

"I didn't see anyone up here," said Alan. "I wonder where they were."

"I hope they don't meet the ambulance on that narrow lane," said Maggie. "They'll never get past each other."

"I think the ambulance will come from the other direction."

They were almost at the bottom of the steep part. In another few minutes they had reached the scree, which consisted of loose rock and shingle that sloped down to the level ground below. They needed to make their way back along the top of the scree, but found this too difficult as they kept sliding down the slope.

"It's no use," said Alan. "We'll have to go down and walk along the bottom and then climb up again further along. The thing with scree is to go with it. Don't hold back. Stride out."

He set off down the scree, taking large strides, and was soon at the bottom. Maggie tried to emulate his action but ended up slithering on her backside. She got to her feet and tried again and had soon made it to the bottom.

"Are you OK?" he asked.

"A few scratches, I think, but nothing much really."

It was much easier going at the bottom, though they did have to skirt some gorse bushes at one point.

As they came round the outcrop that had been obscuring their view, they could see that the ambulance had just arrived, two men had leapt out and they were making their way across the rough ground to the foot of the scree, carrying what looked like a stretcher. Just behind them, two other cars had pulled up. One was a police car and the other, Alan assumed, was the paramedics. There were six of them in all.

Alan and Maggie arrived at the foot of the scree just after the ambulance men had started to climb up to the prostrate body lying on the scree above them.

"He hasn't moved," said Maggie.

"Are you the people who called us?" said one of the policemen, walking towards them.

"I rang you," said Alan.

"Perhaps you could wait here until the medics assess the situation."

"Is he all right?" asked Maggie, getting quite agitated.

"We'll know that when they have had a look at him. Constable Jones will look after you."

Constable Jones turned out to be a policewoman who came over when called by her superior officer. She was quite young but of very stocky build. She ushered them to one side, out of the way of the paramedics and ambulance men.

They seemed to take an age up there and didn't appear to be doing anything.

"What are they doing?" asked Maggie, getting more agitated by the minute.

"They have to assess the damage before moving him, and it isn't easy on this loose stuff. Moving an injured man can do more damage than the original fall," said the constable taking out a notebook and pencil. "Now perhaps I could take a few details. You are?" She was looking at Maggie.

"Margaret Finch."

"So you'll be Mr. Finch, I presume?"

"No. I'm Alan Westbrook. That is Mr. Finch up there."

"Is he a relative?"

"No relation at all," said Alan. "Mrs. Finch was looking for her husband when she met me. We were up there."

"Where were you when Mr. Finch fell?"

"I didn't see him fall," said Alan, "but I started from the road down there and came up the slope onto the top. You can't see the path from here. It's round the corner. I did see some startled grouse fly off from somewhere round here though. That would have been about an hour ago."

"And you, Mrs. Finch? What were you doing?"

"I had stayed at our picnic spot to eat my sandwiches," she said. "Peter, that's my husband, Peter wanted to see if he could see the peregrines and went off in this direction. When I had finished my sandwiches, I packed up my things and set off to find him. When I got near the cliff, I thought I saw him walking along the cliff path and chased after him, but it turned out to be Mr. Westbrook."

"Yes, I can see why you thought that. They do look similar."

"Then Mr. Westbrook said he'd accompany me along the cliff path because it could be dangerous, and then we saw Peter... lying down there. He must have slipped as he tried to see the birds."

"That's when you called us, is it?"

"I rang you," said Alan. "Then we went to find a way down. There is a steep path down, back there. Mrs. Finch said that she could manage it, so we came down that way."

"You seem to have cut yourself, Mrs. Finch," said the policewoman. "I'll get the paramedics to take a look at you before they go."

"Oh, it's nothing," she said.

"Better not risk it."

The ambulance men had manoeuvred the injured man onto the stretcher and were lowering him down the scree. Maggie made to move towards them but the policewoman held her arm to restrain her.

"I want to see him," she pleaded.

"Wait until they are on the level ground and one of the medics will put you in the picture."

It was a slow process bringing a stretcher down the scree, as the whole surface moved with them, but eventually they had arrived at the bottom and placed the stretcher on the ground. One of the paramedics was talking to the policeman who turned and indicated Maggie. The constable nodded and walked over to her.

"I'm sorry, but it's bad news I'm afraid," he said. "He must have died instantly. There was absolutely nothing that could be done for him."

"My deepest condolences, Mrs. Finch," he said. "He'll be taken back to Skipton for the post-mortem but we would like you to accompany us to the station to fill in the details. We'll need to speak to you too, Mr. Westbrook. Do you both have transport?"

"I have my camper-van," said Alan. "I believe Mrs. Finch travelled here by bus."

"In that case, sir, Mrs. Finch can travel in the police car and Constable Jones will travel with you," he said. "She can show you the way."

"I think I can find my own way, thanks."

"No trouble at all, sir," he said. "Just procedure."

The ambulance men had reached the ambulance with the stretcher and were loading it when they set off towards the road.

"But I haven't had a chance to say goodbye to him," Maggie said to Alan, who was walking beside her.

"Probably for the best," said the policeman. "You'll be able to do that in the chapel of rest, eventually. He'll look more presentable by then."

He said goodbye to Maggie, who was escorted off towards the police car, while Alan, escorted by Constable Jones, headed further up the road to where his camper-van was parked. It was over half a mile and as they walked, Alan asked her name.

"Pam," she said frostily.

"I see," said Alan, realising that he must be a suspect, "and you think I might have had something to do with it, do you?"

"I don't, personally," she said, "but, at this stage of an investigation, anyone involved must be classed as a suspect until eliminated."

"What do you mean, investigation?"

"When someone dies in unexplained circumstances, there has to be a coroner's investigation. We need to establish what happened and what part everyone involved played in his demise."

"And all I wanted was a quiet walk on my own."

"Do you usually leave the door of your van open?" It was a surprise change of subject and it took Alan a few seconds to realise what she was asking him.

"No, I don't," he said, and broke into a run, with Constable Jones close behind him.

"Be careful," she said. "There may be someone still in there."

They arrived at the camper-van and Alan looked through the windows to check before going inside. There was no one there so he climbed in to be met by utter turmoil. The place had been thoroughly turned over. Things were lying everywhere.

"Good God," he said.

"Bit of a mess," said Constable Jones. "Anything missing?"

"I don't know. They don't seem to have been interested in money. They've left a twenty-pound note that I kept in the drawer. I can't see my laptop anywhere, can you?"

"No," he said, "just the laptop as far as I can see."

"Was it valuable?"

"No. It was quite old," he replied. "I used to use it to demonstrate software to prospective customers, but I don't use it much these days. I don't like the things."

"Computers?"

"No, just laptops. I like a proper-sized keyboard and a proper mouse."

"So you have a desktop computer, then?" she asked.

"Oh, yes," he replied. "It's built into the van. I use a cordless keyboard and mouse to operate it." He lifted the top of one of the bench seats and pointed at what looked like a lot of old computer junk. Then he lifted the table-top from its folded position and swivelled it round to reveal a flat screen attached to the back. "Voilà!"

"Why did you conceal it like that?"

"I didn't do it to hide it," he said. "When you travel about in your home, you have to have things secured or they end up flying about and smashing into things. So it's best to fix everything down and arrange it so that it can be folded neatly away when not in use."

"It would appear that whoever broke in here was looking for something," said Constable Jones. "They didn't take the money but they did take your old laptop. Now why would that be?"

"I do some work for the government," he said. "Maybe they were after that."

"You mean you keep sensitive government information in your camper-van?"

"Of course not," he said, "but whoever broke in here must think that it was a possibility."

"Who would want to get hold of government data?" she asked.

"You tell me," he said. "It could have been anyone. Not just your casual burglar. More likely agents of a foreign power."

"Russians?"

"More likely the Americans," he said.

"But they are on our side," she said.

"Oh no," he replied. "The Americans are on their own side. They are just friendly with us when it suits them."

"But surely they wouldn't try to steal government secrets, would they?"

"You can't rule anything out," said Alan.

They set off towards Skipton and a long and tedious session of questioning. The day had been a complete disaster. He had hoped for a pleasant solitary walk on the moors and had ended up being taken to Skipton Police Station for questioning as a murder suspect, and on top of that, his van had been broken into and wrecked.

*****

Two

The prime minister was sitting at his desk, looking worried, as he waited for his visitor to be shown in. He found himself staring at the oak panelling on the opposite wall. This was his sanctuary – a place he could disappear into when things got too much for him, and now this objectionable American had demanded to see him immediately and was in the lift heading his way at that very moment. He didn't like Walter Greenbank. He made him feel uneasy. Walter worked for the CIA in a very senior position and he spoke with the authority of the president himself. The prime minister knew what Greenbank wanted and knew that he couldn't give it to him. He didn't know how the Americans had got wind of Project Genesis, but somehow they had, and now they wanted to take control of it. It had all started as a very low-key research project, but after they had recruited the help of freelance engineer, Alan Westbrook, many other possibilities had arisen, and now the Americans were hell-bent on getting it for themselves.

There was a knock at the door and his private secretary, John Marshall, came into the room.

"Mr Greenbank is here to see you, sir," he said.

"Show him in," said the prime minister, and sat back in his chair. He would normally have stood up to receive guests, but in this case, he didn't feel inclined to.

A short, rather overweight man entered. He was well dressed, if rather casually. There was a glint of perspiration on his forehead, which he mopped with his handkerchief as he sat down without being asked.

"Please be seated," the prime minister said pointedly.

"I guess you know why I'm here, George?"

"I have a shrewd idea, Mr. Greenbank," he replied. "But I'm sure you'll tell me."

"Project Genesis," said Walter Greenbank.

"What about Project Genesis?"

"We can't allow you to carry on with it in the way you are at present. The president demands that it be handed over into our control immediately. It is just too dangerous to leave in the hands of people who do not take the threat of terrorism seriously."

"That is something we do take seriously," said the prime minister. "Very seriously indeed. We now find ourselves the target of terrorist attacks, thanks to my predecessor giving in to American pressure and joining you in your ill-conceived invasion of Iraq."

"It was the only course of action we could take. We had a duty to give democracy to the people of Iraq."

"Whether they wanted it or not," said the prime minister. "Didn't it ever occur to you that they didn't want your interference? Anyway, that's water under the bridge now and we're stuck with the consequences. So why does your president feel that it's his duty to relieve us of the responsibility of handling our own project?"

"Do you realise what would happen if this project got into unscrupulous hands?"

"I realise very well what would happen. That's why you're not getting it."

"Your predecessor acceded to our request for assistance in Iraq because he knew that it was better to be for us than against us. Perhaps you should think carefully about exactly where you stand before making your decision."

"I've made my decision."

Walter Greenbank stood up, looked as if he were about to say something, and then turned and left the room, slamming the door as he left.

"Temper!" said the prime minister.

Three

When they arrived at the police station, Alan was shown into an interview room, so he didn't see Maggie as he had hoped. He supposed that was normal procedure; otherwise they could have concocted a story between them, if they had had anything to hide, that is.

A young police constable came into the room with a mug of tea, which he put down in front of Alan.

"Hope you take sugar," he said.

"No, I don't, actually."

"Sorry." He sat down opposite Alan and said nothing.

"What happens now?" asked Alan.

"We wait for DI Wilson."

DI Wilson took quite a long time, and Alan passed that time sipping his very sweet tea. He assumed this was all part of the procedure to soften up the villains. He wasn't feeling particularly worried, at this stage, just a little irritated. Eventually, the door opened and a senior looking man in plain clothes came in and sat down next to the constable.

"Sorry to keep you waiting, sir," he said. He obviously wasn't at all sorry. "I'm DI Wilson and this is Constable Briant."

"We've met," said Alan.

"I see we have a comedian," said Wilson. He then switched on the tape recorder and told it who was there and what they were doing. He also told it the date and time.

"You can get those now," said Alan, "that add date and time automatically."

"Can you really, sir?" said Wilson. "You're into that sort of thing, are you?"

"I'm an electronics engineer," said Alan. "But I work more in software these days."

"I thought you had to be young to understand computers?"

"I was when I started."

"I see." Wilson sat and looked at him for what seemed an age. "Have you known Mrs. Finch long, then?"

"No. As I told the officer out on the moors, I had just met her today."

"Can you prove that, sir?"

"Well I can't prove that I hadn't met her before, as it's not possible to prove that something hasn't happened. However, I'm sure that if you ask all her friends, there won't be one who knows me."

"I'll take that as a no then, shall I?"

"Why does it matter if I knew Mrs. Finch previously?" asked Alan impatiently.

"Well, sir. You see, if you'd known each other for some time, and were, perhaps, on more intimate terms, then it might just be possible that you colluded with Mrs. Finch to give her husband a helping hand over the cliff, if you see what I mean."

"Well, I suppose you have to look at all possible scenarios," said Alan. "But that was not the situation at all, and in fact, I'm more worried about who broke into my camper-van."

"Nothing of value taken, was there, sir?"

"Only my laptop computer," said Alan. "Not worth much in itself, but they didn't seem to be interested in value. They left cash, my hi-fi, a television and a DVD recorder, so why do you think they were interested in an old laptop?"

"What could be on a computer that would interest them, then?"

"Software," said Alan. "I am doing some work for a government department that could interest certain parties."

"And what was the nature of this software?"

"I'm afraid I'm not at liberty to divulge that," said Alan, feeling a bit smug. "Official Secrets Act, and all that."

"So who should I contact to corroborate this story?"

"The Unit Manager at Blakely House," said Alan. "It's under the control of Porton Down. I can give you a telephone number."

"OK. So what's your story then?"

"Well I've told you what I was doing," said Alan. "Though you seem to prefer a more imaginative version. Anyway, as I was walking up the path from my van onto the moor, I saw that another car was parked just down the road from my van. It was black, but I couldn't see what type it was. I didn't think much about it, but just hoped I wasn't going to have to share my solitary walk with a noisy crowd of walkers."

"Did you see anyone?"

"No. But I did see a pair of grouse rise from over in that direction," said Alan. "Something must have disturbed them, but I didn't think much of it at the time. When I got to the top,

I sat on a rock and ate my sandwiches and had a cup of tea from my flask."

"And you still hadn't seen anyone?"

"No one at all. It was very pleasant, and it was lucky for me that I'd decided to stop for a while. You see, I think those people in the car were after me."

"What makes you think that?"

"Well," he continued. "It was a coincidence that Mr. Finch had been wearing very similar clothes to mine, and he would have arrived at the top of the cliffs at about the time I would have been there had I kept walking. All I can think is that they caught him and, maybe, tried to get him to tell them where he kept the software. He wouldn't have known what they were on about and when he couldn't tell them what they wanted to know, they threw him off the cliff."

"What makes you think he was thrown off the cliff?"

"I thought that was what you thought," said Alan, "except that you think I did it. No, what made me think he was pushed or thrown off is the way he had landed... head first. If he had slipped, he would have been facing the cliff and would have fallen feet first facing the cliff. And if he had turned in the air to land head first, he would have been on his back. The way he landed, he was either pushed or he jumped."

"That was my thought too," said Wilson. "You realise we have to consider every possibility, and the simplest one is the one we came up with first. We won't make any decision until we have more evidence. My gut feeling is that it wasn't you that pushed him, but I do find your explanation a trifle difficult to accept. So, what sort of people would want to get their hands on your work?"

"Could be any number of groups," said Alan. "The green groups would certainly want it stopping and would probably feel quite justified in terminating my existence in the process."

"Any group in particular?"

"Well, Green World would be very much against anything involving genetic engineering," said Alan.

"So that's what you're into, is it?"

"Not exactly," he replied. "I'm working on software used to specify genetic codes, but that isn't the aspect that bothers them."

"Anyone else?"

"I would think that most terrorist groups would like to get their hands on it, but they would want me alive to show them how to use it. Then there're the Americans."

"Americans? How do they come into it?"

"They feel they should have control of the project, for safety reasons you understand. But the PM isn't having any. Normally they can apply pressure whenever there is anything they want, but good old George has dug his heels in."

Wilson looked surprised. "You're on first name terms with the PM?" he said.

"No. I've never actually met him," said Alan, "but my boss has, many times."

"Well I think that's about as far as we can go at the moment," said Wilson, closing his file and switching off the tape recorder.

"So I can go now?"

"Yes, but we'll need to know where we can contact you."

"I park my van at a site near Harrogate, but I'll give you my e-mail address and mobile number. I don't leave my mobile on most of the time, but I check for messages every now and again."

They went out into the reception area and Alan noticed Maggie sitting in the waiting area.

"Hello again," he said. "How are you getting home?"

"They said that someone would take me," she replied. "But it could be quite a while before anyone is free."

"Where do you live?" he asked.

"Knaresborough."

"Well that's not far from me. I could offer you a lift in my van if you like."

"Thank you. That would be most kind."

Four

They didn't say much on the way home. For one thing it was a bit noisy in the van, and Maggie was still in shock from the events of the day, which to Alan had seemed most unreal. But now, as he sat driving the camper-van, it began to dawn on him that this was very real and very dangerous. Good God, someone had tried to kill him and had turned his van inside out. But how did they know about him? He wasn't a well-known figure and the work he was doing was supposed to be secret. But, it seemed, they did know about him. Maybe it was time for him to disappear into the sunset in his camper-van. But they knew about the van, so what now?

But then, as far as they knew, he was dead, unless there should be any publicity. He'd have to make sure that a stop was put on any word of this getting out, then he could feel safe. He'd have to sell the van though. His mind was in a whirl. He wondered how long he had before they'd be after him again.

As they approached Knaresborough, Alan decided to tell Maggie what he thought had happened.

"At first they thought we were responsible for what happened to Peter," he said. "Look, I'm sorry if this seems indelicate. I know you must be devastated by all this but I thought you ought to know what I think."

"It's OK, Alan," she said. "Yes, obviously it's been a great shock, and I know this sounds awful, but Peter and I weren't that close. In fact, I had been thinking of asking him for a divorce. Nothing had been going on, either with him or with me, but we had just grown apart. He had his interests and I have mine. So it's rather like hearing that your next door neighbour has been killed in an accident, and yes it was more of a shock to find that the police were thinking along those lines. But I suppose they get like that, doing the job they do. Still, I suppose they have to ask the questions if only to rule it out. I think they're quite happy it was an accident now."

"I'm not so sure." said Alan. "About it being an accident, I mean. I am beginning to think that someone killed Peter thinking he was me."

Maggie looked shocked. "Who would want to kill you?"

"I don't have any idea," he said. "But there's a possibility that an extremist environmental group might have found that I am involved with some secret work for the government involving genetic engineering. They broke into my van while we were up there and took a laptop computer."

"So they got want they wanted, then?"

"Oh no," he said. "It was an old one and didn't have anything of use on it."

"So they'll still be after you, then?"

"Not if they think it was me they killed. But I'll have to get rid of the camper-van as soon as possible and find somewhere else to live."

"Another camper-van, perhaps?" she said.

"I don't think so," he replied. "I'll have to find somewhere more permanent, nearer to my work."

"That'll take some time," she said. "Won't you be in danger until then?"

"It depends how long it is before they find out that it wasn't me. And then the other factor is that they didn't get what they wanted, so they might have another go at the van."

"Turn left here," she said and directed him down a narrow lane with fields on either side.

"Where on earth do you live?" he said. "We seem to be in the middle of nowhere."

"That's right," she said. "That's exactly where I live – the middle of nowhere. A non-life for a non-person in the middle of nowhere. Turn in here."

There was a gap in the hedge leading on to what looked like a cart track. The van creaked and rocked as he drove carefully down the track. At the end was a cottage with some outbuildings and a yard, which he pulled into.

"It used to be a smallholding," she said. "But most of the land was sold off. It may look quaint, but it's cold and draughty and very isolated."

"You don't think I could park here until I can find something more permanent, do you?" he asked, not expecting her to agree. "Being so hidden from view, it couldn't be better."

"You know, that would be very nice," she said.

"Really?"

"I was dreading coming back to this place all on my own," she said. "It's quite a spooky place at night. Come in and I'll make us something to eat."

"Oh, I don't want to be a nuisance."

"No. I would welcome the company."

They went into the house, which seemed rather cold and bleak. It was rather like an old farmhouse, with a stone floor and mats here and there. There was an old kitchen table made of pine with a drawer at each end. The top was scrubbed board.

"We used to have one of these when I was little," said Alan, running his fingers over the surface.

"Peter liked that sort of thing," she said. "The whole place is a bit like that. Full of ancient tatty old stuff. He said it had character."

"But you don't agree?"

"Well this sort of thing is fine when you visit an old place kept by the National Trust. But it's hell to live in. Tea or coffee?"

"Coffee please," he said.

She went over to an old built-in cupboard and took out two mugs, put a spoonful of instant coffee into each and carried them over to the table. "Milk?"

"Please."

She went to the fridge, which was also very ancient, and took out a bottle of milk and put it on the table. She then went over to the range, took a kettle off the top, carried it over to the table, poured hot water into the two cups and sat down in one of the chairs that were pushed under the table.

"Most people would think this an idyllic life," said Alan.

"Well, most people don't have to put up with it, all weathers, year in, year out, do they?"

"It's better than a camper-van," he said.

"Yes, I suppose it is," she said. "Why on earth do you live in one?"

"Long story," he said.

"I'm not going anywhere."

"Well, if you're interested," he said. "A few years ago, I got divorced and only had enough money to move into my old camper-van. I also thought it would give me some sort of freedom and a bit of peace and quiet."

"And did it?"

"Not really," he said. "But it did allow me to move around a bit which was quite useful in my work."

"Didn't you miss your friends?" she asked.

"Not really," he replied, "I had been away a lot, in Scotland mostly, on business. I had this old campervan which I stayed in. it was better than spending good money on hotel accommodation, so most of our friends were more friends of my wife's."

"You sound bitter."

"Not really," he said smiling. "We'd been drifting apart for years; she had her interests and I had mine. People change over the years. None of us is the same person we were in our youth. I've come to terms with it now and I actually feel a lot more tranquil than I ever did before. Well I did until today.

"Yes, indeed," she said.

"Oh, I'm sorry," he said. "That was thoughtless of me. You must be feeling dreadful."

"Surprisingly not," she said. "Shocked, yes, and I know it sounds dreadful, but somehow relieved; as if a huge burden has been lifted."

"Life was that bad?"

"I think it must have been, though you sometimes don't realise how good or bad things are until they change."

"I suppose that's how it was with me," he said. "We'd led almost separate lives for the last few years of our marriage, though we were never at odds with each other, and it wasn't until the children had left home and I hit fifty, that it struck me that I hadn't had a life at all, so I thought it best to call it a day."

"How did your wife react to that?"

"She agreed with me," he said. "I told her she could have everything, and she said that was only fair, as she didn't see why she should have to suffer because I wanted out. We're still on good terms, though we don't see each other very often."

"So what did you do then?"

"I moved into the campervan with some sort of idea of driving off into the sunset," he said. "I don't know where I thought I was going to go, but just about then I had this enquiry from the Ministry of Defence. I'd done a few jobs for them over the years and knew a few people, RAF, Home Office, Porton Down, places like that." "So what did they want you to do?"

"Nothing much, to start with," he continued. "I'd done some work in nano-engineering and a few years ago I built an interface for an electron microscope so that analysis work could be automated. I wrote the software for it too. That was one of my strengths as well, which was very unusual. I was a design engineer who could write software. This time they wanted me to write a DNA database coupled to the electron microscope. Anyway, I won't bore you with all that."

"It's not boring," she said. "It's quite fascinating, actually. Now, what would you like to eat?"

She set to work preparing a meal while he used the telephone to ring Sir Malcolm Birch, Head of Research at Porton Down. It was lucky he had his home number, but he'd had to call him several times in the past for one reason or another.

Sir Malcolm sounded perturbed at what Alan had to tell him. "They didn't get hold of anything, did they?"

"Oh no, sir," said Alan. "I don't leave sensitive material lying about."

"Just as well," said Sir Malcolm. "I've just had the PM on about this project again. It seems he is under pressure from the states to hand it over to them. Worried about terrorists it seems, or at least that's their excuse."

"I think the greens are more of a worry, myself."

"Look," said Sir Malcolm. "I think it would be better if you got rid of that van of yours and found somewhere to keep your head down. In the meantime, I'll organise for the police to release news of your untimely death up on the moors. No mention of the break in, of course. It was just an accident while out walking. Now, can you find somewhere to stay for a while?"

"I think I already have," he replied. "I can carry on working from here for the time being."

"We'll need you down here in the next few weeks to set up the next batch of tests. Can you manage that OK?"

"Yes, no problem," said Alan. "I'll arrange the sale of the van and get a car to replace it."

"Don't get the car from the same place that takes the van, will you?" said Sir Malcolm. "I don't want you to be traced by anyone and it would be better if they came to a dead end when they traced the van."

After they had eaten, they went through to the living room and Maggie lit the fire, which was already set in the grate.

"I hope you don't mind me camping in your yard for a while," said Alan. "I'll have to get rid of the van as soon as I can find somewhere more permanent to stay."

"I told you," she replied, "I am happy to have the company."

"I'll be quite comfortable in the van," he said. "After all, I have lived in it for a couple of years now." So after she had made him a cup of coffee, he went out to the van to settle in for the night.

The next day he went into the house for his breakfast when he saw signs of life in the kitchen.

"Could I move all my gear into the house?" he asked. "I'll have to sell the van so I need to clear it out first."

"Of course you can," she said. "Just put it all in the spare room. I'll give you a hand if you like."

So after they had had their breakfast they set about emptying the van. There was quite a lot of rubbish that Alan was quite happy to consign to the bin. In fact he realised how little of any importance he had accumulated since his divorce. There was a box of old photos from years ago, which he had managed to salvage before his wife had taken everything. He had a small portable TV, a tape player and radio and a couple of cameras that he used for his work occasionally.

It took several days to clear out the van completely, and that night he found it a bit eerie sleeping in the empty van and couldn't get to sleep at all. At about two in the morning, he got up and made himself a cup of tea with the few things left in the kitchen. There was no milk, so he decided he would have to drink it black. The kettle had just boiled when he heard a quiet knock at the door, which startled him, but when he looked out he realised that it was Maggie wrapped in a large woollen rug.

He opened the door and she peeped out of the folds of the rug, shivering.

"It must be cold out here," she said. "Why not come inside and get warm?"

He felt a bit flustered, but switched off the kettle and followed her into the house.

"I couldn't sleep," he said.

"Nor could I," she replied, "so I thought we might as well do it together." He wasn't sure if she was being suggestive, but smiled and took the steaming cup that she offered him.

"I've slept in that van for about two years," he said, "and have always felt quite comfortable there. But now it is virtually empty it seems a bit unnerving."

"I just found it difficult to sleep knowing that you were just out here on your own. It seemed so daft." He still wasn't sure what she was suggesting, but he had been on his own for so long he was a bit slow off the mark.

After they had finished their coffee, she took his cup and leaned over and gave him a light kiss on the cheek.

"I'll never sleep after that coffee," he said.

"Good," she replied and led him up to her room.

Five

In the next few days, Alan managed to sell his camper-van, though he didn't get a good price for it, and buy a second-hand Citroen C3. Maggie used the ancient Ford, which they had kept in the barn and used very infrequently, to run Alan around while he got organised. But now he had his own car, he had to think about going down to Blakely House as he had been instructed.

He had stripped all his computer equipment out of the van before he sold it and had set it up in his room where he worked for several hours each day. At dinner that evening, he told Maggie that he would have to leave for Blakely House the following morning.

"Will you be gone long?" she asked him.

"I'll probably need an overnight stop there," he said, "but it shouldn't take longer than that. I should be back late afternoon the next day."

"It'll be strange being alone in the house," she said.

"Will you be OK? I can leave it a bit longer if you prefer?"

"No, I'll be OK," she said. "After all it's only for one night. I'm sure I'll survive."

"If you're sure?" he said. "It's just that they're ready to run another analysis and they need my software to run it."

"Don't they have a copy?" she asked in surprise.

"Oh no," he said with a grin. "I've been caught like that before."

"Oh?"

"Yes," he said. "It was about twenty years ago when I was much younger and more trusting."

"What happened?" she said. "It sounds intriguing."

"Well, I was into manufacturing in those days and we were making radio signal synthesisers."

She looked puzzled.

"Sorry," he said. "A bit technical. They produced a very accurate frequency radio signal, which was used for testing radio systems. Anyway the RAF tried one at one of their satellite communication stations and asked us if we could make a special plug-in module for their system, so I went down and had a look and got all the details and some of their metalwork and went back to design the module they wanted. It took a couple of months to make the prototype and then I arranged to go down and try it.

"When I got there, there was one of their boffins waiting to test it. It was a bit nerve-racking – a bit like waiting to start your driving test. Anyway, we plugged the module in and set it up and waited for the system to lock on.

"Well, this chap did his tests in silence, then finally turned round to face me and told me that he had said that it was impossible, but that I had proved him wrong."

"So, what was the problem?" asked Maggie, looking puzzled.

"Well, there didn't seem to be any problem at that point. They ordered eight units there and then at a very good price, but he then told us that there was a slight problem in that they couldn't buy from a non-approved supplier, and we weren't approved. But they could buy from us if we were a sub-contractor for the supplier of the main satellite equipment. That entailed handing copies of all our drawings over to the main supplier. I told them I wasn't happy giving our detailed design drawings to a competitor, but he said that they wouldn't be interested, as the quantities were too small.

"So, we supplied the first batch of eight units and all was fine. They said they might order some more shortly but that there were talks going on with the army and navy as they had similar requirements. I thought that sounded good. Maybe we would end up supplying several dozen units.

"Then there was talk of a full development contract and the numbers started to run away. This was going to be big. We went away and did all the sums and put forward a proposal, and then it all went quiet and after a while we got a letter telling us that the project had been dropped."

"Why was that?" asked Maggie. "If it was so important."

"Because it was now of interest to the main supplier, and all I can surmise is that they decided to do it themselves. I can't prove anything, but I'm sure that's what happened."

"That's awful."

"Yes, but that's what happens to the small fry when the big fish scent big profit. So after that they don't even get a look at the details. No, I keep all my software in this." He took a small key fob from his pocket. "That contains all my software and I just have to plug this into a computer and I can run it and not leave a trace on the computer after I've finished."

"But what happens if you lose that?" she asked. "Or break it?"

"I keep a backup on the internet on one of my websites. Which reminds me. Is there broadband in this district?"

"We're lucky to have a telephone."

"Right. Well I'll just have to call in at an internet café tomorrow and upload it."

"How does that work?" asked Maggie.

"I have a website," he replied, "and I just send the contents of this memory stick to the website. It's another computer, could be anywhere in the world, and you have to know the password to get access to it. It isn't impossible, but it's not easy, and they have to know where to look first."

"What happens if they get hold of that stick thing?"

"The memory stick? Well that's protected too. If they don't use the right passwords in the right order, it erases everything on it and then trashes their computer."

"You seem to have thought of everything," she said.

"I hope so."

Six

It was a long and tedious drive down to Blakely House, but Alan took a break on the way and found a local library with internet facilities.

Blakely House had been a stately home at one time and still looked the part. There were no Ministry of Defence signs at the gate so you had to be in the know to find it.

He drove through the wrought iron gates, which he had previously opened using his mobile phone, and they closed behind him. The tyres scrunched over the gravel drive, and rabbits hopped out of his way. It seemed just like a rural idyll.

At the top of the drive there was a circular lawn in front of the main door of the house, but he veered off to the right just before that and drove into what looked like a farm's stock yard, which is what it once had been. But now there were no animals and a very modern looking building nestled behind the old barn structures.

He parked alongside the other cars that were parked there, got out, and walked to the glass door in the new building. He had to use a pass card to get in, along with a voice recognition system. It was a bit like saying 'open sesame' and the door slid silently back.

Inside was a corridor going straight ahead, and another door to his right, but he walked down the corridor, through another door at the end and up some stairs to a narrow landing in the old building behind. At the end of this landing was another door with a brass plate on it, saying 'Unit Manager'.

He knocked and went in. John Palmer, the Unit Manager, was sitting behind a huge walnut desk which had virtually nothing on it except a blotting pad, a stand for his pens, which were neatly arranged in it, and a framed photo of his wife and two children.

He didn't look up immediately, but continued writing on a sheet of paper that he had taken from a folder that was open in front of him.

"Sit down," he said without looking up. Alan sat down and waited. He didn't like John Palmer, particularly. He was a typical bureaucrat who didn't understand the work that was being done in his department, but tried to make out that he was superior to menial scientists and engineers.

He finished writing, put the sheet of paper back into the folder, closed it and looked up at Alan.

"Glad you could make it," he said with a trace of sarcasm in his voice.

"No trouble at all," said Alan, not rising to the bait. "Now, what's to be done?"

"We're doing a run on the new strain and need to get the data for analysis," he said, pretending he knew what he was talking about. "Dr. Stanley is waiting for you in room seventeen."

"Right," said Alan. "I'd better not keep him waiting." He stood up to leave.

"Just before you go," said Palmer, "I've had Sir Malcolm on the phone. He was rather concerned about the security of the project."

"Yes, I've spoken to him about it and I think we have it covered now. Thanks for your concern." He turned and strode over to the door and left before any more could be said. It was one of the anomalies in this country, putting people who knew nothing about anything and had no brain in charge of the people who had the knowledge and ability, and paying them much more than the people who mattered. If there was any chance of you getting your hands dirty it made you the lowest of the low. He wondered why he hadn't moved abroad where they treat engineers and scientists a lot better. He had had the opportunity many years ago when he was head-hunted by a firm in Madrid. Name your own salary, they had said, all expenses paid. Now Madrid was fine for the six weeks he had worked there, but he couldn't see himself living there for a prolonged stint, so he had turned it down. He didn't know whether he had done the right thing or not, but it was too late now to worry about it.

Jim was leaning over a piece of apparatus and frowning. As Alan entered, he straightened up and smiled warmly. "Good to see you," he said. "Now you can sort out this little beast."

The little beast in question was made up of a stainless-steel cylinder with an assortment of plastic tubes emerging from it and a great bunch of cables that went off in all directions, mostly towards a computer on the bench nearby.

"You have to speak nicely to her," said Alan. "She's very temperamental, Jim. I think you upset her."

"Most likely," said Jim. "Now, can we get moving? I've had Palmer on my back the whole time. Doesn't he know you can't rush these things?"

"I doubt it," said Alan. "Now, let's get the computer fired up." He took the memory stick out of his pocket and plugged it into the socket at the front of the computer, and hit a few keys.

"I could do with one of those," said Jim.

"I know," said Alan, "but I'm afraid this is my insurance policy. Once I hand this over, I'm finished here."

"Surely not."

"Most definitely," said Alan. "And on top of that, someone tried to kill me the other week. If you'd read our local paper you'd have seen my obituary. Not very flattering, but it did the trick."

"I don't think I follow you."

"We thought that if I was reported as being dead, whoever it was that was after me would think he had succeeded and give up. They trashed the camper-van too."

"But why? Why should anyone want this software, other than me, that is?"

"Why do you think?" said Alan. These pure scientists really did live in a world of their own.

"I haven't the faintest idea," said Jim, shaking his head. "I wouldn't have thought that DNA mapping was of much interest to anyone else."

"That's just part of it," said Alan. "It's what you can do with it when you have it mapped."

"Still don't follow."

"If you have the DNA map in the computer," said Alan speaking very slowly, "you can modify it as you wish."

"True." He still looked blank.

"Well, what the powers that be would like is to be able to use that to modify real DNA and create bespoke viruses."

"Yes, I know that," said Jim. "By matching a new virus to a natural one, you can use it to fight pandemics or cure difficult infections. There was a case once of someone having a kidney disease that they couldn't cure. It was eating away at her kidneys and her parents were told that she wouldn't see double figures. Then she caught diphtheria, which she survived and there was no more kidney disease. No one linked the two at the time, but we think the diphtheria killed the kidney virus. So, if we can make the right virus that won't hurt us but will attack a particular natural virus, we have the cure-all that the medics are looking for."

"Yes, very noble," said Alan. "But what do you think the MoD would do with such technology?"

"No, they wouldn't, would they?"

"Well it's crossed their minds," said Alan, "but the Yanks are even more interested, firstly because they see it as a weapon of selective mass destruction which they feel they should be in charge of, and secondly, they are scared stiff of it getting into the wrong hands."

"Personally, I think their hands are entirely the wrong hands," said Jim. "There's nothing worse than someone who thinks he's the good guy and wants to sort out the problems of the world, mostly to his own benefit."

"Precisely," said Alan. "Now, I think we're ready to run this next sample."

They set to work and carried on until dusk.

Seven

Alan stayed for three days and had just about finished the run of tests. The computer was almost bursting with data from the tests. That was left on the computer for Jim to work with, but the software that had done all the work was kept on the memory stick that Alan kept with him at all times.

Margaret had told him not to worry about staying away, but he knew she wasn't happy, so he rang her twice a day to make sure that she was all right. It was strange, really. He had only known her for a short time and felt, in fact, no more than a lodger, but was actually much closer to her than that. He hadn't felt this close to anyone in his life, especially his ex-wife who had always been rather distant. Due to this, he had tended to keep people at arm's length so as not to get hurt again. But in Margaret's case, he had inadvertently lowered his guard, probably because he had not seen her as a possible close relationship.

On the last day before he left, he was in the laboratory with Jim, tidying up the results and doing some printouts when he was called into Palmer's office. He assumed it was just because the officious little man had some paperwork for him to sign.

"I'll be back in a minute," he said, and made his way to the office. When he got there, he was surprised to find two security guards there also. Then he realised that the person behind the desk wasn't Palmer but Sir Malcolm Birch. Alan closed the door behind him and stood waiting for Sir Malcolm to speak.

Without looking up he said, "Sit down Alan." Alan sat. "I gather that the project is virtually finished now?"

"Well, we have all the data," said Alan. "Now we have to analyse it and do the modifications."

"Dr. Stanley will be quite capable of doing that I suppose?" said Sir Malcolm looking up and staring Alan in the eye.

"Not really, said Alan, "Not without my software."

"Of course," said Sir Malcolm. "We would like to buy the full rights to your software."

"I have never believed in selling the rights to my work," said Alan. "I usually work on some sort of licence agreement."

"But in this case it has to be a total purchase of all the rights," said Sir Malcolm. "You see, the MoD has decided, that for security reasons, we should have complete control of the project. You will be amply rewarded for your contribution and then we must sever all connections with you. I'm sorry, but that's how it is." He opened a folder and handed Alan a cheque for £250,000.

"I think you have grossly undervalued my software," said Alan. "I think the licence income from such a project would be far in excess of this."

"You are welcome to your opinion, but that is what I've been authorised to give you so now we must bid you farewell."

"And what if I don't accept this?" said Alan, angrily.

"As I see it," said Sir Malcolm, "you can leave either with or without that cheque, but the software stays with us, and that's final."

"In that case I may have to consider legal action," said Alan.

"I think you would find that rather difficult," said Sir Malcolm, "considering that you're officially dead."

"But that was just a ruse to get the pressure groups off my back."

"Of course," said Sir Malcolm. "But to make it convincing, the body that was cremated after that nasty accident was one Alan Westbrook. There is a death certificate to prove it, so you are now dead, and dead men don't sue. You are now Mr. Peter Finch, and I don't think we have ever done business with a Mr. Peter Finch. So I will have to bid you goodbye, Mr. Finch. Close the door after you." He turned to the two guards. "See Mr Finch off the premises, would you? I wouldn't like him to get lost."

The two guards strode over to Alan and each took one of his arms, not very gently.

"OK, OK," said Alan. "You win. I'll go quietly."

Outside in the car park the guards left him by his car and waited for him to get in and drive off. It was no use trying to get back in because they didn't seem the type of people you would want to trifle with. He thought about coming back later, but realised that his card key would have been deactivated. *Still*, he thought, *they don't know that my software is password protected. As soon as they close the programme at the end of the day, they'll need a password to get in again, and if they use the wrong one, the programme will be wiped and so will the contents of the computer they are using.* Jim had always let Alan open his programme and may not have realised that he had used a password to open it, or at least, he hadn't made it obvious that he had. Anyway, what did it matter? It required a different password each day, so if he had managed to see what was typed in to open the programme, it wouldn't work the next day.

It was quite simple really. He had used a little rhyme:

Monday's child is fair of face,

Tuesday's child is full of grace,

Wednesday's child is full of woe,

Thursday's child has far to go,

Friday's child is loving and giving,

Saturday's child works hard for his living,

And the child that is born on the Sabbath day

Is bonny and blithe, and good and gay.

So, on Mondays, the password was 'fairofface' and on Tuesdays it was 'fullofgrace' and so on. So if Jim had seen what he had typed in this morning, he would think that the password was 'lovingandgiving', the Friday password, and that would work today, but tomorrow is another day, he thought. Just to add another safeguard, he appended the number of the month as well, so that in May, he would add 05 to the daily password.

He had also made it difficult to copy the programme to another machine. Again, a password was needed in conjunction with a special copying programme on the memory stick. Alan used this to copy his work to his secret website where he kept his backup. Any attempt to copy it by other means would wipe it completely.

Yes, he felt quite smug that he'd fooled them, then it occurred to him that when they lost their software they might just come after him. But what could they do? They couldn't just kill him. That would be counter-productive. Perhaps they would torture him? Surely not in this day and age? He wasn't too sure that he was convincing himself. Perhaps it was time to disappear. After all, he was officially dead, and he was now having other thoughts about who had been responsible for the attempt on his life.

Eight

He had decided not to mention any of this to Maggie, but when he got back, she could tell by his demeanour that all was not well. But he said it was just that he was tired after the long journey and she let it go for the time being.

The next morning he was still very thoughtful and she pressed him again for some enlightenment and he gave in and told her the full story.

"Surely they can't do that?" she said indignantly.

"It seems they have," he said, "and I'm officially dead."

"But what about the cheque?" she asked. "Who is that made out to?"

"Oh my God," he said, fumbling in his pockets. "It didn't occur to me."

The cheque was made out to Alan Westbrook. "I wonder if the bank knows I'm dead."

"Perhaps not yet," she said. "Probate usually takes months and I don't suppose anyone has started things moving yet anyway."

"I need a new identity, pronto," he said. "How do you get a new identity?"

"Well this isn't something that happens often, is it?" she said. "But hasn't it crossed your mind that there's an identity going begging right here?"

Alan looked puzzled. "How do you mean?" Then he remembered what Sir Malcolm had called him as he left.

"Well think," she said. "You're alive but there's a death certificate that says you're not, and Peter is dead and cremated but there's no death certificate to say so."

"When I left Blakely House, that was what Sir Malcolm called me. It didn't register at the time," he said. "No, I couldn't possibly. I'm sure you wouldn't want that, would you?"

"Why not?" she said. "I've been closer to you in the few weeks I've known you than I ever was to Peter." Alan's head was spinning. On the one hand he could have shouted for joy, but on the other, something was holding him back.

"But it could be dangerous, you realise."

"Surely the authorities won't do anything to hurt you, will they?" she said. "And any other organisation thinks that you're dead now, and anyway, if they found out that you're still alive, they'll also know that you're no longer involved in all this molecular stuff any more."

"I don't know," he said thoughtfully. "A few years ago, I would have thought it impossible for our country to invade one that we were not at war with. Now I know differently."

"But didn't we have good reason to do it?"

"Iraq had a leader that ordered troops to attack and kill other groups of people," he said. "They were thought to have weapons of mass destruction that might possibly be used against us. How many other countries can you think of that meet those criteria? Don't you think that we might fit that description, and that goes for the Americans tenfold."

"I hadn't thought of it like that."

"The thing is," he continued, "that it is OK to do anything you like nowadays, as long as you can justify it in some way, even if it is just to think that we are the good guys so it must be right. That's what worries me. If they can think up a scenario where I am the bad guy and they are the good ones, who knows what they might do?"

"Well," she said. "If you're in danger then I'm not going to throw you out just to save my own skin. I'll stick with you whatever happens."

"But I feel responsible," he said. "I just can't let you put yourself in danger for me. You've done more than enough for me already. Now it's up to me."

"Well if that's how you feel," she said. "I wouldn't like to force you to stick around if you so desperately want to get away."

"That's not what I said or meant," he said. "There's nothing I'd like more than to stick around with you. I think we get on very well, and anyway, I've grown very fond of you."

"Very fond?"

"I'm an engineer," he said, "and that is very flowery language for an engineer."

"Well, in that case, stay. I'm sure with two of us working against them we stand a lot more chance of succeeding."

"I don't know what to say," he said.

"Then say nothing," she said getting up from the table and kissing him on the cheek. When he looked surprised she said, "It's quite all right. After all, we are married, and I have a marriage certificate to prove it."

She picked up the teapot and took it over to the kettle where she refilled it and brought it back to the table.

"I don't think I could answer to the name 'Peter', though," he said.

"No problem," she said. "Peter's middle name was Albert, Peter A. Finch. So we could say your middle name was Alan and that's the name you use now. You could be P. Alan Finch."

"I suppose that would work," he said. "But I don't really see myself as a Finch, either."

"Well, that you will have to put up with," she said with a laugh. "Anyway, a change of image might be useful in throwing them off the scent."

"OK, I give in," he said. "But we can't stay here. They know I'm staying with you, so it wouldn't be difficult for them to find out where you're living."

"Right. Well, let's sell up and move away, somewhere no one will think of looking for us."

"We could go up to Scotland," said Alan. "I like it up there. Maybe the isles, somewhere remote."

"Very nice," said Maggie, "but I don't think that'd work. We would stand out like a sore thumb up there. No, the place to lose someone is in a city, amongst the crowds. After all, the Home Office has lost hundreds of thousands of illegal immigrants, and where do you think they are? Not on remote islands in Scotland. You'd soon see them there. No, they'll all be in the big cities. We'll have to get a flat in one of the cities. Maybe Leeds or Bradford."

"Don't like Leeds," said Alan. "York's OK though. We could look for somewhere in York. But first I'll have to get this cheque into my old account and then close it and take out a banker's draft to bearer. Then I'll put it into Peter's account."

"It's a joint account, actually."

"Even better. You can do it and then I won't need to sign anything," he said. "Then perhaps we should open another account in a different bank and close the old one, or at least take everything out of it. Then I can use my own signature."

"You'll have to start practising your new signature," she said. "P. A. Finch."

"I suppose I will."

Nine

Dr. Jim Stanley arrived early at the laboratory on Monday morning, and went straight to the computer. He was quite excited about his new position. Sir Malcolm had put him in sole charge of the project, answering directly to him. No more having to justify himself to Palmer.

He slipped his hand into his pocket and found the memory stick, which he had taken from the computer before the weekend. He had been waiting all weekend for this moment and his hand trembled as he fumbled for the USB socket on the computer. He had felt rather guilty about looking over Alan's shoulder on Friday morning as he entered the password, but it had to be done. It had been explained to him that for such important information to be in the sole possession of someone outside the MoD was madness. National security demanded that it should be taken into secure custody where terrorists and other undesirables could not get hold of it.

He'd come to like Alan during the weeks that they had worked together, and he still felt a bit guilty about his part in removing Alan from the project, but Sir Malcolm had said that Alan would be well rewarded for his work, so Jim told himself that all was well and that he had done the right thing. He just hoped that he could handle the software all right without

Alan's help. It was strange, though, that Alan hadn't come back to say goodbye.

He took out the piece of paper on which he had written the password. He didn't really need the paper as he had thought of nothing else since he had written it down. It was a strange password, 'lovingandgiving05'. He wondered what significance it might have. Usually people used names of family or friends or even pets so that they were easier to remember, but this one was nothing like that. Perhaps it was so that no one could guess it, but surely it must have some significance. Anyway, the computer was now asking him for the password so he would have to key it in.

Very, very carefully, he typed it in, then hit the return key and waited. A message box appeared asking him to wait while it set up the programme. The hard disk was whirring so it must be loading all right, but it did seem to be taking quite a long time. Then the message box disappeared and a new one appeared in its place. This one said, in red lettering, that the password was incorrect and all data had been erased. Jim panicked.

"Oh my God," he said to himself looking around to see if anyone else was about. "What's happened?"

He opened up 'Explorer' and found that his data appeared to have disappeared, and when he went to the memory stick, that was empty. "Oh my God," he repeated. What was he to do now? He had just been given an enormous promotion with a substantial pay rise on the basis that he would be able to do amazing things with this software, and now it was gone.

He couldn't go to Palmer. He could just see his expression when he found out. No, Palmer wasn't to know. What about

Sir Malcolm? No, that would be no good either. It would be the end of his very short career. No, he would have to get in touch with Alan. After all, he had been paid handsomely for his work. He'd be able to help. He reached into his jacket pocket and took out his wallet, which was full of slips of paper with little memos on. He fumbled through them until he found the one with Alan's mobile number on it. Quickly, he picked up his mobile and dialled the number. It wasn't answered, but went through to the messaging service where a pre-recorded voice spoke to him telling him that unfortunately Mr. Alan Westbrook had passed away but if he would leave a message, someone else would get back to him.

His jaw dropped. Dead? How could Alan Westbrook be dead? He was here on Friday in very good health. Perhaps he had had an accident on his way home. Oh no. What was he to do now? If he went to his home, perhaps someone would let him look at Alan's computer. Was he married? He'd never mentioned a wife, but that didn't mean he wasn't married. Mind you, he'd lived in that camper-van thing, and Jim couldn't imagine any self-respecting wife putting up with that for long.

Now he parked the thing in a caravan park in Yorkshire, somewhere. What on earth was the place called? He had it written down somewhere. He fumbled through the bits of folded paper until he found the one he was looking for. Ah, yes. He remembered now. It was near Harrogate. He'd go there immediately. He didn't have to get permission from Palmer now. He could just go. He'd leave a message at the desk telling them that he'd had to go out and would be back in tomorrow; he fervently hoped so.

He switched off the computer, pocketed the memory stick and headed for reception. A few minutes later he was in his car heading for Yorkshire. That wild untamed place in the distant north that he had heard about, but never visited, where everyone had whippets and wore cloth caps, and there were twenty-foot-deep snow drifts in winter. He was glad it wasn't winter.

Ten

Walter Greenbank was sitting in his hotel room talking on the telephone.

"That's right, sir," he said. "Alan Westbrook is dead. An accident on the Yorkshire moors, or something... Yes, that's right. The project is now in the hands of a Dr. James Stanley. I've got an agent keeping an eye on him. I believe that Westbrook was relieved of his responsibilities just before his death. I'm told that Sir Malcolm gave him the push and kept his software... No, sir. No joy from the PM. D'ya want me to go ahead with phase two? Right, will do."

He put the telephone down and then picked it up again and rang a mobile number.

Eleven

Jim Stanley was surprised to find that Yorkshire was not only quite civilised but that it had some beautiful countryside as well. There wasn't a whippet in sight and the sun was shining and the birds were singing. It was, in fact, quite delightful.

He drove into the caravan park and parked outside what seemed to be the office. He got out and went inside, but there was no one there, so he went outside again. There were quite a few caravans parked around the site, though it didn't seem to be the height of the season and it looked as if most of the caravans were unoccupied.

"You won't find him here." Jim spun round to see who had spoken, only to see that a rather dirty old fellow had appeared from apparently nowhere.

"What?"

"I said you won't find him here," he repeated.

"Who?" asked Jim, wondering what the old fellow was going on about.

"Old Bill," the old fellow said, shuffling closer. Jim backed away. "'Appen he'll be in the pub by now."

"I was hoping he'd know about a friend of mine," said Jim.

"Oh, an' who'd that be, then?" he said, almost menacingly.

"A friend of mine," repeated Jim. "His name is Alan Westbrook."

"Was," said the old fellow.

"What?"

"He's dead. Didn't you know?"

"Well, yes," said Jim, "but I was trying to find someone who was with him when he died."

"Oh. I wouldn't be knowin' anything about that."

"Well, do you know who would?" asked Jim, getting a little impatient.

"I might. If someone was to cover my expenses, so to speak."

"Your expenses?" said Jim, baffled.

"Aye, 'appen. I got overheads just like anyone else."

"Overheads?"

"Twenty pounds should cover it."

"Twenty pounds?" said Jim as the light began to dawn on him. "You want twenty pounds to tell me who can give me the information I want?"

"That's right."

"Don't you think that's a bit steep?" said Jim. "How about five pounds?"

"Can't be very important then can it?" He turned and started to walk away.

"OK. Twenty pounds it is then," said Jim taking out his wallet and handing a twenty-pound note to the tramp, who folded it carefully and slipped it in his pocket.

"Better go to Skipton, then. They'd know."

"Who would know?"

"Gawd 'elp us. The police of course. Who else?"

"Do you mean to tell me that I have just paid you twenty pounds, just to be told to go to the police?"

"In Skipton," said the tramp. "You could have been searching for weeks without that information. I call it a bargain."

"Maybe."

Jim got hurriedly into his car. Perhaps what he had heard about Yorkshire was true after all. The tramp was grinning broadly as Jim drove out of the caravan park.

It was a pleasant ride over to Skipton, which turned out to be quite a busy little town, so he parked in the big car park and walked into the town to find somewhere to eat before finding his way to the police station. He sat in the cosy little café, near the window, and watched people walking past. They didn't seem too different from the people he saw down south. In fact, you couldn't really tell that you weren't actually in the south.

There was a market in the high street so he decided to stroll along and see what was on offer. He was looking at a vast array of cheeses when he noticed a man looking at the next stall. He looked familiar, but there would be no one up here that he knew. Then it came to him. He'd seen this chap walk past the café. In fact, he'd gone past several times. Perhaps he was filling in time while he waited for his wife, or something.

He found the market quite interesting and when he got to the end of it, he continued on to the police station.

It took a while before someone came to the counter.

"I'll like to speak to someone concerning an accident that happened to a friend of mine, recently," he said.

"Name?"

"I'm Dr. Stanley," said Jim.

"No, sir. I meant what was the name of your friend, please?"

"Mr. Alan Westbrook," said Jim and he felt sure the officer looked surprised.

"Wait here please," said the officer and disappeared from sight. There was a further very long wait before the officer appeared again. "DI Wilson will see you in the interview room. Down the corridor on the right."

Jim walked down the corridor and a door opened at the end and a middle-aged man in plain clothes appeared. "Would you come in here, please?" Jim followed him in and sat down opposite the officer. It felt as if he had been taken in for questioning. "Now, sir," said DI Wilson, "How can I help you?"

"A friend of mine was killed in an accident recently," said Jim, "and I believe someone was there, as a witness, and I wondered if you could tell me who it was as I would like to get in touch with them."

"And what was the name of this friend of yours?"

"Alan Westbrook."

"Perhaps you could tell me how you knew Mr. Westbrook, sir?"

"I worked with him at the MoD," said Jim.

"Oh, I see," said Wilson. "Perhaps you could wait here for a few minutes while I just go and look into it." He left Jim and went off down the corridor. After a while he could hear the sound of voices but couldn't make out what they were saying. Then there was the sound of footsteps returning and DI Wilson came into the room again.

"Sorry about the delay, sir," he said, "but I just had to check with the MoD. Security, you see, sir."

"Oh," said Jim. "I didn't realise there would be any problem with security."

"Just routine with people involved in official secrets and so forth. Anyway, it seems there's no problem in your case so here are the details you require." He handed Jim a sheet of paper, which was obviously a photocopy of an official document.

"Thank you," said Jim, standing up. "That is most helpful."

The address was in the Knaresborough area, but he would have to get a local map to be able to find it. But it was getting a bit late now so he decided to find somewhere to stay in Harrogate for the night, then get a map the following morning. The fact that the policeman had had to contact the MoD bothered him a little. He had hoped that they wouldn't find out about his little trip, but now questions would be asked. Still, if the worst came to the worst he'd just have to come clean and tell them what had happened.

He found a nice little hotel and booked in for the night. Luckily, they had some local maps on the table in the hallway so he took one to study in his room.

Twelve

The next morning Jim Stanley checked out of his hotel and set off for Knaresborough. It was only a short drive, though the roads were quite busy. The address he had was at the other side of Knaresborough, on a little country road. It was quite a secluded spot.

He drove into the driveway and up to the house. All seemed quiet, so he got out of the car and walked over to the front door and knocked. He waited. There was no reply. *Just my luck*, he thought and decided to walk round to the back of the house. The garden was a bit wild but reasonably well kept.

He knocked on the back door and waited, but there was no sound of movement from inside so he peered through the window. There wasn't much to see, so he walked back round to the front. There were a couple of old outbuildings opposite the house, so he went to investigate. One was a sort of tool shed, fairly full of tools of all sorts, but very neatly arranged. The other had been used as a garage though it was empty now. It had an earth floor, which showed the impression of the tyre marks of the vehicle that was stored there. It was probably a small family car, though there were also some other marks, as if a larger vehicle had been there.

He was about to leave the garage when he heard a car coming down the gravel drive. He didn't really want to be caught nosing around their sheds, but what else was he to do? He waited until the car had stopped and peeped out through a small gap in the boarding to see a large black car parked right behind his own. All four doors opened and four quite burly men in dark suits got out and looked around. Surely these can't be the people who lived here? That was when he knocked against a pile of oil drums and knocked them over.

He jumped away from the door and stood waiting as he heard footsteps running towards the shed. The doors burst open and two dark shapes filled the doorway, each holding a gun. Jim put up his hands and stuttered an apology for being in their shed.

"I was just looking to see if anyone was out here," he said. "I couldn't make anyone hear."

The other two men had now joined the first two; one of them looking a bit more important than the others, so Jim guessed that he must be in charge.

"Dr. Stanley, I presume?" he said with a pronounced American accent.

"An American with a sense of humour," said Jim. "That's a novelty."

"What's he on about?" said the American, apparently to his accomplices. "What're you on about?"

"Sorry," said Jim. "I thought that was supposed to be a joke."

"I don't see what's so funny about asking you if you're Dr. Stanley."

"Well," said Jim thinking he should explain, "when Stanley met Livingstone in Africa, he said 'Dr. Livingstone, I presume,' and I thought you were doing a skit on that, or something." The American looked blank. "Perhaps I was right first time about Americans having no sense of humour."

"Is, or is not, your name Dr. Stanley?"

"Yes, it is. Who wants to know?"

"I'm Walter Greenbank, CIA," he said. "I have it on good authority that you have some highly confidential software, and I would like you to hand it over immediately."

"What software would that be, then?"

"You know what software," said Greenbank, looking threatening. "Now just hand it over. These three aren't just here for the ride, and those aren't water pistols they're holding. Now gimme." He held out his hand and two of the gorillas raised their guns to point at Jim. Jim fumbled in his pocket, brought out the memory stick and handed it to Greenbank.

"I think you ought to know that it's password protected," said Jim.

"OK," said Greenbank. "So, what's the password?"

"I have no idea," said Jim. "I tried what I thought it was and it wiped my computer."

"We could try persuasion," said Greenbank.

"I told you. I don't know. That's why I'm here. I believe that my colleague, Alan Westbrook might have it somewhere among his possessions. This was the password I copied down." He handed a piece of paper to Greenbank.

"Westbrook's dead."

"So I heard," said Jim. "I was trying to trace the people who witnessed his accident. I think they live here."

"Doesn't seem to be any sign of life here now," said Greenbank turning to his assistants. "Take a look." Two of the thugs walked off in the direction of the house. "And why do you think they can help you?"

"They might know what happened to his camper-van," said Jim.

"And you think there could be some clue in the van to this password?"

"Where else do you suggest looking?" said Jim. "He lived in the thing full time, as far as I know. Everything he had has to be in that van."

"Well, you can leave it to us now," said Greenbank turning to see the two heavies coming back from the house. "Well?"

"No one there, sir," said the smaller of the two. "Looks as if they're away on holiday. Not much sign of life there."

"OK, Stanley," said Greenbank. "You can leave it to us now. You'd better get back to your lab. They're probably missing you by now."

"But what am I supposed to tell my boss?"

"Tell him the project is in safe hands now, unlike when he was in charge." He turned and walked to his car, tossing the memory stick into the air and catching it as he went. They got into the car, turned and drove off down the drive.

"Now what am I to do?" said Jim to himself.

Thirteen

There was nothing he could do now. He couldn't wait here until the occupants returned. They could be away for weeks. But on the other hand, it wasn't much good his going back to the lab. What could he do there without the software? And worse than that, what would Palmer say? He could just visualise the gloating face. The pompous little twit. And Sir Malcolm would not be too pleased either. It was doubtful whether he still had a job to return to. Perhaps he should have a quick look inside the house. Who knows, there might be a clue in there, and, anyway, he didn't have anything else to do at this precise moment.

The back door had been forced by the American heavies, but not badly damaged, so he opened it cautiously and went in to find himself in a neat farmhouse kitchen. It certainly had the air of a house left temporarily empty. Everything had been put away in the cupboards, but strangely, there was milk in the fridge. They couldn't be expecting to be away for long, then.

Then a thought struck him. Why not stay here until they returned? They might be upset to find him in their house, but he could always use the 'National Interest' ploy. It would be much cheaper than staying in a hotel, probably more comfortable and he would be on hand when they returned.

So he put the kettle on and made himself a cup of coffee. There was food in the freezer, so he wouldn't have to go out to the shops. This was ideal.

After drinking his coffee and eating a couple of their digestive biscuits, he decided to explore the house. There were three bedrooms, all quite large, and one was obviously the main bedroom. While the beds in the other rooms were made up, they looked as if they were only used for guests. So, as he considered himself a guest, he chose the more comfortable of the two, went down to the car and brought his belongings up to the room.

He parked the car in the barn so as not to arouse too much interest and settled down to watch television while he ate the sausages and beans he had cooked for himself. He was very tired and fell asleep in the chair, but woke, stiff and aching, at about eleven o'clock.

Time for bed, he thought. So he made sure the back door was secure and went up to bed.

He stayed at the house for three days before anyone came near the place. It was on the morning of the fourth day that he was awoken by a noise downstairs. He looked at his watch to find that it was half past nine and there was someone moving around downstairs. He looked around for something heavy, but decided that he wouldn't be any use at violent stuff so decided to bluff it out.

He quickly pulled on his clothes and crept out onto the landing. No one was in sight, so he crept down the stairs.

The person was in the living room. He could hear them moving about. The door was slightly ajar so Jim went up to it and peered through. There was a man in a suit. Jim didn't like men in suits, but this one looked quite harmless. He seemed to be measuring the room. An estate agent! God, they're selling the house. I've been wasting my time here.

He pushed open the door and walked into the room. The man looked startled.

"Oh, I'm sorry," he said, staring at Jim. "I thought the house was empty. Mrs. Finch said it was OK for me to come and measure up."

"Oh, that's all right," said Jim. "I'm her brother. She wasn't expecting me. I thought I'd give her a surprise, but found they were away, so I let myself in and decided to wait for them to return."

"I wasn't aware that they intended to return," said the estate agent.

"Oh, I think they will," said Jim. "You can't just move without telling anyone. Anyway, they've got to collect all their stuff. Perhaps you could let them know I'm here when you next speak to them."

"I expect them to phone me this afternoon," he said. "So I'll tell them you're here. What name is it?"

"Just tell them Jim is here." He went into the kitchen to get himself some breakfast while the estate agent finished his measuring up. After he'd gone, he thought it might be a good idea to have a more thorough look round before they came back. There wasn't a lot out of the ordinary. He found photos of the couple at various ages. It seemed that the husband was into birdwatching. She was called Margaret Finch, which he already knew and he was called Peter.

He wondered if he was doing the right thing. Perhaps these people knew nothing about Alan, but then again, what was he doing with them when he had his accident? At least they should be able to tell him where to find the camper van.

This was all very confusing. Jim was a pretty straightforward sort of a man. He had got on with his work to the best of his ability and assumed that if he did well he'd be rewarded. Now it wasn't so clear. Alan had always seemed straightforward too, and now he was dead. He was told it was an accident, but after Jim's brush with the Americans he was beginning to wonder what he had got himself into. Also, he hadn't liked being told to get the password for the software by watching Alan key it in. It all seemed a bit underhand. Maybe it would be better to cut his losses and go back to the lab and come clean. Surely they couldn't blame it all on him. It wasn't his fault, he kept telling himself.

Maybe he would wait a little longer and see if the Finches could help, and if not, then he'd go back.

Fourteen

The following day, nothing happened until late in the evening. Jim was sitting in the living room, watching the television, when he heard tyres scrunching on the gravel drive. Quickly he turned off the television and the light and peeked through the edge of the curtain. There was a car outside and two people had just got out. At least it wasn't the Americans again. There was a man and a woman. It had to be the Finches.

He felt awkward standing there in a stranger's house waiting for them to come in and find him, but he strengthened his resolve and waited.

The front door opened and he heard feet being wiped on the doormat. Then the living room door opened and someone switched on the light. Jim was momentarily dazzled. Margaret screamed and Jim stepped back in alarm, nearly falling over the coffee table. His eyes had now adjusted to the light and he was amazed to see Alan standing there.

"Alan?" he gasped. "It can't be."

"What on earth do you want?" snapped Alan. "And how did you find us here?"

"Who is it?" asked Margaret. "What does he want?"

"A good question," said Alan. "This is Dr. James Stanley. The rat who conspired with Sir Malcolm Birch to steal my software."

"I did not," said Jim. "I knew nothing about it."

"Then why did you copy down my password? Did you think I hadn't seen you?"

"Palmer asked me to get the password," said Jim defensively, "just for security reasons. He said that you were going to sell them the rights."

"Never," said Alan indignantly. "I've told you that I never sell the rights to my software."

"I assumed you'd changed your mind."

"No."

"So what happened, then, and why was I told you were dead?"

"All down to our good friend Sir Malcolm Birch," said Alan. "But it's a long story. It was Margaret's husband that died. Look, sit down. I'm ready for a coffee, or something stronger. I'll tell you the whole story."

They sat down with their drinks and Alan told Jim all that had happened.

"So you are officially dead, then?" asked Jim.

"So it would seem," said Alan. "So now I am Peter Finch. But how did you find me? I'd hoped that with a new identity and the news that Alan Westbrook was dead, no one would be able to find me. I hope you weren't followed."

Jim looked a bit sheepish. "Some Yanks found me here and took the memory stick."

"Well, that's no loss. It would be empty after you tried to use it," said Alan. "It doesn't matter what they try to do with it, it's empty. But your computer isn't. If you reboot it, you'll find everything is still there. I should have made it do what it said in the message box."

"Well, that's something," said Jim, looking relieved. "At least all our analysis work is safe."

"But that's not necessarily a good thing," said Alan thoughtfully. "It's not much use without the software, but eventually someone will manage to write a similar programme to mine and be able to use the data. I need you to go back to the lab and delete the lot. Then you can tell Sir Malcolm that the software was booby-trapped and it is all lost. They can't blame you for that."

"Me?" exclaimed Jim. "You want me to delete all our work?"

"Yes," said Alan. "And the sooner the better. It is more dangerous than you can imagine."

"I would have thought it would be safe enough in the hands of the MoD."

"So would I, once," said Alan. "But after what has happened to me, I have serious doubts."

"I don't follow you."

"Look, Jim," said Alan. "For a PhD, MSc and God knows whatever other qualifications you have, you're remarkably thick. At first, I admit, I thought that the people who tried to kill me and then broke into my van were members of some 'Green' group or, at worst, members of a terrorist organisation. I must admit that I was slightly surprised when Sir Malcolm agreed to cover up the fact that I was still alive, but I was grateful to have the killers off my back for a while. Then, when he forced me to sell the rights to my software, and got you to pinch the password, I realised that he could have been behind the whole thing."

"What? Sir Malcolm?" exclaimed Jim.

"Yes, Sir Malcolm," replied Alan. "He was desperate to gain control of the software and resented the fact that I had control of it."

"I would have thought that he could have got it using some sort of compulsory purchase – Official Secrets and all that?" said Jim.

"So would I," said Alan. "That still puzzles me. But the thing that worries me most is that if someone like him actually gets control of it, where would they stop?"

"I'm sure he's a man of integrity," said Jim. "I can't see him doing anything underhand."

"Well, he has already."

"You don't actually know that," said Margaret.

"No," said Alan. "But everything points that way. I feel responsible for this and now that I can see what could be done with it, I want to stop anyone getting hold of it."

"But you said that someone else might develop something similar," said Margaret. "Then it would be out of your hands."

"I know," said Alan. "But that could take some time, and I don't see why I should give them a start by handing them a full set of data on a plate. Analysing the data structure could give them just the help they need to write the software. No, the data must go, and Jim is the only person who has access to it."

"Do I have to?" said Jim.

"Absolutely," said Alan. "I know this is hard and that you will be out of a job, but you should be out of harm's way as well. Unlike us. We'll just have to try and disappear from sight and hope they forget all about us. Look, I'll give you our new address in York, and when you've got rid of the data you can come and stay with us until it all dies down. But don't, whatever you do, let anyone have our address, and make sure you aren't followed this time. I would imagine your car has a tracker fixed to it. I'll have a look in the morning and remove it for you. But to be on the safe side, when you return, come by train."

"By the way," said Jim. "Why didn't that password work? I'm sure I copied it correctly."

"I'm sure you did," said Alan. "But there's a different one for each day of the week. You copied Friday's and used it on Monday."

"Oh," said Jim.

Fifteen

The next morning, Alan removed the bug from Jim's car and he set off back to Blakely House. Alan and Margaret collected more of their smaller possessions, which they loaded into the car before setting off back to York.

They had found a small two-roomed flat for which they had been able to obtain a short-term lease to allow them to find somewhere more permanent. Neither of them had any reason to stay in the area, so they could move to anywhere that took their fancy. They had decided that the more sparsely populated areas would be a bad thing, as they would stand out like a sore thumb. But then again, they didn't like big cities. At least they could look at their leisure and leave this place at almost a moment's notice.

They had had an offer on the old farmhouse, which was encouraging. Moving house was difficult at the best of times, and it was even worse when you had to leave it in the hands of an agent and hope for the best. At least they could start looking for somewhere else, that is if they could decide where to start looking.

"How about a rural setting?" said Margaret. "A small town or large village, maybe. Somewhere where we wouldn't look like foreigners. Somewhere near here, perhaps?"

"I like the idea of that," said Alan. "Did you have anywhere in mind?"

"Somewhere in the Dales," said Margaret. "Or even the North York Moors. I'm sure we could find somewhere nice where we wouldn't stand out too much."

"It's very lucky neither of us has anyone we need to keep in touch with," said Alan.

"Yes," said Margaret. "Peter's brother lives in Canada and we haven't heard from him for years. The only relatives I have are distant cousins and I haven't been in touch with them for ages either."

"I suppose my divorce was quite fortuitous," said Alan. "None of my old friends wanted to know me after that. My parents are both dead and I have two cousins who live in America, but they don't ever contact me. Not even a Christmas card."

"We sound a very sad pair, don't we?" said Margaret. "Perhaps it's just as well."

"Maybe we should have a drive out into the Dales and see if there's anything on the market that will suit us, and suit our budget," said Alan. "We've got my cheque from the MoD, and whatever we make on the farm house."

"Don't we need to keep a fair bit back to live on?" said Margaret. "After all, we don't know whether you'll be able to get any more software work. I don't suppose you'll be able to use any of your old contacts now."

"No," said Alan. "Word will be out now that I'm dead, so I'll have to start afresh. Mind you, I've never had any problems getting work, and the beauty of software work is that you can do it anywhere that has an internet connection."

So the next day they set off into the Dales and headed up Wharfedale to see what they could find. Alan wasn't too hopeful, as properties in the Dales had become very rare or very expensive. The locals were completely against property being sold to absentee owners, but this could work in their favour as they would be living there.

It was a beautiful day with a few fluffy clouds and a light breeze as they made their way up the windy road towards upper Wharfedale. They stopped in Kettlewell for a coffee before moving on up the dale, and bought a local paper to see if there were any properties for sale in the area. There was one that looked interesting, a little further up the dale, so they headed off to have a look. The agent was in Skipton, so it would take too long to go and see them and get a proper viewing, but it would be worth having a quick look first.

It was in a fairly remote area, down an unmade track, off the main road.

"This is a bit like where I used to live," said Margaret. "I thought we were going to get lost in a small town."

"Yes, I agree," said Alan, "but this is rather nice. Let's have a look anyway. We don't have to have it if we don't like it."

It did look rather idyllic as they drove up the track and stopped outside the cottage. An old man was leaning on the gate and he gave them a suspicious look.

They got out and walked over to him.

"We saw this property in the paper," said Alan, "and thought we might have a look at it."

"Did you now?" said the man. "Looking for a holiday cottage, are you?"

"No," said Alan. "We're looking for somewhere to live."

"Permanent?"

"Yes."

"Well in that case come in and have a look." He turned and walked back towards the house. There wasn't much of a garden, and what there was seemed a little neglected. The cottage was built of local stone, and on closer inspection, required quite a lot of work.

Inside it was very basic, like going back to the nineteenth century or even earlier. Today was warm, but there was a chill in the air inside the house.

After looking round, they thanked the old man and drove off down the drive.

"I think that would be ideal," said Alan enthusiastically.

"What?" exclaimed Margaret, a look of horror on her face. "There was no gas or electricity, and the water came from the well down the garden, and I dread to think what the septic tank was like."

"Just joking," laughed Alan. "No, I think our earlier idea of a small town was better."

They set off back down the dale and stopped off at a little pub for lunch. It was a beautiful spot, and all the problems surrounding them seemed to drift far away. With the sun shining on the nearby hills, the birds singing, the sheep bleating and the little stream that ran past the pub making a soothing sound, they could have stayed there and forgotten about the world outside. However, that couldn't be, as they had to get back to reality. If they stayed there the outside world would soon come and find them.

It had been a very pleasant day out and both of them had managed to forget about their present problems for a bit. Back in York, they made their way back to the hired flat and parked outside in the road. There was some activity two doors along. There was an ambulance outside, a paramedic's car and two police cars.

"Wonder what that's all about," said Alan.

"Looks as if someone's been taken ill," said Margaret. "Shall I go and see?"

"Better not," said Alan. "We're supposed to be keeping our heads down. The last thing we want is for the police to be asking our names and address."

"Maybe you're right."

They locked the car and went into their flat and set about getting something to eat. They had had lunch out but the fresh air had given them an appetite.

That evening they settled down in front of the television and were surprised that their street featured on the local news. It seemed that an elderly couple, living two doors away, had been murdered in their home. The police were quite baffled as the couple had no known connections with organised crime and nothing seemed to have been taken, even though the flat was turned upside down.

Alan and Margaret looked at each other, each knowing what the other was thinking.

"But why them?" said Margaret. "They couldn't have mistaken them for us, could they? Anyway, no one knows we're here."

"Other than Jim Stanley," said Alan. "Even so, why did they go to that flat and not ours? It doesn't make sense."

"Perhaps it's just a coincidence," said Margaret.

"Some coincidence," said Alan.

The next day it was all over the papers. Alan scanned the articles for any further information but not much more was forthcoming.

"It says here that they were at number thirty-eight," said Alan. "I thought this was number thirty-eight."

"No, this is thirty-four," said Margaret.

"Oh my God," said Alan. "I told Jim it was thirty-eight."

"So when he told whoever it was where we were staying, he told them number thirty-eight," said Margaret. "So it was our fault those people died."

"If it was anybody's fault," said Alan, "it was mine. Though the fault really lies with whoever is trying to kill us."

"Who would Jim talk to?" asked Margaret.

"Well, anyone at Blakely House," said Alan. "He has also talked to the Yanks. Perhaps they're keeping tabs on him. Or it could be someone we have no knowledge of. I hope he doesn't come back here. Anyone could be tracking him."

"But you told him to come back here."

"I know," said Alan. "And now I wish I hadn't. Mind you, he'll go to number thirty-eight, not here."

"And then the police will want to know all about him and why he was going there," said Margaret.

"We'll have to stop him," said Alan.

"I don't think so," said Margaret. "I think we should get out of here as soon as possible."

"Maybe you're right," said Alan. "We're paid up here until the end of the month so it won't matter if we leave early. I think you're right about Jim. We just can't afford to stay in

contact with him any more. He's caused us enough trouble as
it is, not to mention the people down the road. Better start
packing."

Sixteen

Sir Malcolm was sitting, looking through some papers that he had taken from a folder which lay on his desk. A cup of coffee stood on the desk next to him, going cold. The telephone rang and he picked it up with a look of annoyance.

"What?" he barked at the phone. "Oh, yes. Better send him in." He replaced the telephone and carefully gathered up the papers and put them back into the folder, which he then placed neatly at the side of his desk. He picked up his coffee and took a sip, grimaced, and put it down again.

There was a knock at the door.

"Come," he shouted.

The door opened and Roger Stacey entered. He was a weaselly little man with a mouth that had a permanent sneer.

"Well?" said Sir Malcolm. "I assume everything went to plan?"

"Of course, sir," said Stacey. "Doesn't it always? After all, I am a professional."

"I hope so," said Sir Malcolm, "for your sake. You see, if anything should go wrong, you're on your own."

"I understand that. Nothing can go wrong," said Stacey. "They can't trace anything back to me."

"I certainly hope not," said Sir Malcolm. "But if they do, it will be you who takes the rap."

"Of course."

Sir Malcolm opened a drawer in his desk, took out a bulging envelope and handed it to Stacey, who took it and looked inside.

"You don't need to count it," said Sir Malcolm. "It's the amount we agreed."

"Well it's been good doing business with you, sir," said Stacey. "You know where to find me if you need me again?"

"Indeed we do, Stacey," said Sir Malcolm with a smile. "Indeed we do."

Stacey tucked the envelope into his inside pocket and left.

Sir Malcolm's grin broadened. "Indeed we do, Stacey."

*****

John Palmer was sitting in his office with a large spreadsheet in front of him. He was puzzling over the figures, as he was not very good with this sort of thing and it had put him in a bad mood, when the door burst open and Jim Stanley burst in.

"Good grief man," shouted Palmer. "Don't you know how to knock? What is it?"

"Something terrible has happened, sir," spluttered Jim. "I can't believe it."

"Well, out with it, man. What is the cause of this hysteria?"

"The software, sir. It's gone."

"Gone?" snapped Palmer. "What on earth do you mean?"

"Gone," repeated Jim. "It was OK yesterday, but when I tried to log in today it was gone. Software, data, the lot, gone."

"What have you done?" said Palmer. "You can't have deleted everything. Even you can't be that inept."

"I didn't delete it," said Jim. "I put in the password and a message came up saying that the memory had been wiped. I checked it and it has all gone."

"Haven't we got people who can restore deleted data?" asked Palmer as if talking to an errant schoolboy. "Get IT on to it."

"Oh. Right, sir," said Jim. "I'll do that right away."

"And I assume you have backups of the data?" said Palmer.

"Well, no, actually," said Jim rather sheepishly.

"Well let's hope the IT people can restore it for you, then, as I wouldn't like to be in your shoes when Sir Malcolm finds out."

*****

Alan had left Maggie packing their things into the two cases that held all the possessions they had taken with them, while he went to the local supermarket to stock up with food. He walked across the car park, pushing his trolley as quickly as he could without drawing attention to himself. He quickly unloaded the bulging bags into his car boot and then took the trolley back to the rack where they were kept.

He took out his mobile phone, switched it on and called Maggie.

"Just finished the shopping," he said. "I'll be back in about ten minutes. Love you."

He switched off the phone and put it back in his pocket and walked back to his car and got in. To his horror, he found that someone was sitting in the passenger seat.

"Who are you?" he snapped. "What are you doing in my car?"

The interloper was of Asian origin and didn't seem inclined to answer questions. "Just drive," he said.

"Get out of my car," said Alan getting alarmed, "or I'll call the police."

"I said drive," said the man in the passenger seat raising his hand to display an evil looking handgun. Alan couldn't tell if it was real or not but he thought it best to take no risks.

"Where to?" Alan asked as he pulled out of the car park. The Asian passenger gave him curt instructions from time to time until, at last, they drove into a business park and stopped outside some sort of warehouse that looked rather unused. Alan was made to get out and was led into the building. It appeared even more unused inside. Dust and cobwebs were everywhere.

He was ushered down a dark corridor to a small room at the end. There was a solitary chair in the centre of the room, which Alan was made to sit on. The Asian gentleman then tied him to the chair.

"What is the purpose of all this?" asked Alan. "It's no use trying to get a ransom for me. I haven't any money." The Asian said nothing, but continued making sure that Alan was securely tied to the chair. Then, without saying anything, he left.

Alan tugged at his bonds, but only succeeded in taking the skin off his wrists. He hadn't a clue who had captured him, but as his captor had been Asian, perhaps it could be a terrorist organisation, which was rather disconcerting. If it had been the MoD, he would probably be dead by now, unless they had found that the software had been destroyed and wanted to get any remaining copies from him. That didn't seem very good as he didn't know how far they would go to get what they wanted. If it were the MoD, he thought, that wouldn't be so bad. If he let them have the software, at least it would be in safe hands. Or would it?

Who else would have been able to find him? He didn't think the Americans would have been able to trace him, but who could tell where they had contacts?

By the time it started to get dark, he wondered whether they were just going to leave him there to starve. It was getting cold, he couldn't move very much to keep warm and his legs were beginning to cramp.

As the evening wore on and it got dark, it got colder until Alan was shivering uncontrollably. Still no one came. It must have been after midnight when Alan thought he heard a sound outside. Could it be someone parking a car? He called out, but his mouth was so dry he could hardly make a sound. Then he heard a door open and slam closed again. Someone was coming into the building. Footsteps could be heard in the corridor outside the room where he was held prisoner. It was them coming back. Fear mingled with hope. Was it help coming or was it his captors coming to torture him until he gave them what they wanted?

The door opened and light flooded into the room, dazzling him. It hurt if he opened his eyes. But by squinting, he could make out someone in the doorway.

"So, Mr. Westbrook," said a voice with an American accent. "You really are a slippery customer."

"I don't know what you're talking about," said Alan. "My name is Peter Finch."

"Tell that to the marines. Do I look stupid?" the American voice said. "My name is Walter Greenbank. We got your memory stick from that wet friend of yours, Stanley. It was empty."

"Of course it was," said Alan. "He used the wrong password and it wiped itself."

"Fine," said Greenbank. "So now we need a new one, and that's where you come in."

Alan's eyesight was now returning and he could see a rather overweight, though short, man in a casual jacket with two rather tough-looking accomplices standing just behind him.

"Don't look at me," said Alan. "The MoD paid me off and took my software, so you'd better talk to them."

"According to your friend Stanley," continued Greenbank, "they haven't got it. Apparently they think they have but he hasn't told them yet. That's why they've been trying to get rid of you. Lucky you gave your friend the wrong address."

"What do you mean?"

"They got the wrong people, didn't they?" said Greenbank. "Lucky for us. So we thought we'd better look after you for a bit. We couldn't have anyone bumping you off, could we?"

"Who are you, anyway?"

"Oh, just some good friends and allies from across the water. Now, about that software. Just tell us where it is and we'll go get it. End of problem."

"I told you I haven't got another copy," said Alan, trying to sound convincing.

"That's not what your friend thinks."

"I wish you'd stop calling him my friend," said Alan. "He's no such thing, and I certainly wouldn't tell him if I had another copy."

"Of course you wouldn't," said Greenbank. "But you have, haven't you? This was your baby, this project, wasn't it? You wouldn't password protect it so that it would self-destruct if you hadn't another copy."

"Well, I haven't," said Alan emphatically. "I used to have, but I haven't now. I thought it would be too dangerous to keep."

"Oh dear," he replied. "Now that's a pity because it could have saved you so much pain and distress. I have some very ingenious colleagues who I might have to let loose on you. I don't think you'd like that."

"You can do your worst. It won't make any difference. I still haven't got the software."

"We shall see." He turned and went to the door. Two heavies came in looking eager to set to work on him.

At the door, Greenbank stopped and looked back. "Perhaps we'll give you a little more time to think about it," he said. "See you later." To Alan's horror, he left the two heavies with him.

He didn't know what to do for the best. If he gave them the software, would he be released or just killed out of hand?

If he held out, it would give him more time, but he wasn't sure how long he could stand whatever it was they had in store for him. After all, he had never been tortured before and he wasn't sure that he wouldn't crack as soon as they started. If that were the case, what would be the point of resisting?

Seventeen

Sir Malcolm was sitting in Palmer's office, sipping a cup of coffee, while Palmer fidgeted with some papers on his desk. There was a tentative knock on the door.

"Come in," called Palmer. The door opened and Jim Stanley entered.

"You sent for me, sir?"

"This is very disturbing news," said Sir Malcolm, placing his coffee cup back onto the saucer. "Very disturbing. You have a backup of the software, I take it?"

"No, sir," he replied. "I didn't have time. I used the password that I saw Alan keying in and it wiped the lot."

"But we still have the data?"

Jim looked perplexed. "No, sir. Unfortunately, it wiped my whole hard drive. The IT team tried to restore it, but the disk was clean."

"This is outrageous," barked Sir Malcolm. "Why wasn't I told sooner?"

"I tried to catch up with Alan and get another copy."

"Too late for that," said Sir Malcolm. "He's dead."

"I know, officially, yes. But not actually," said Jim. "I've caught up with him since then."

"That's as maybe," said Sir Malcolm. "But now, I'm afraid he actually is dead. So now we have to find out where he hid the backup copy. Didn't he tell you anything?"

"No, sir. Nothing at all."

"We'd better start with the memory stick, then," said Sir Malcolm, scratching his chin. "It may be possible to retrieve the data from it. You'd better let me have it."

"Well. . ."

"Good God," exclaimed Sir Malcolm. "Don't tell me you've lost that too?"

"Well, not exactly," spluttered Jim. "The Americans got it. I was trying to track down Alan Westbrook and they must have followed me. They took the memory stick. There was nothing I could do about it. Anyway, it was empty."

"Well I know that the programme had been erased, but it might have been possible to recover it," said Sir Malcolm, as if he were talking to a five-year-old.

"Well, when I tried to open the programme, it wiped my computer and itself," said Jim. "The IT people had a go at my computer and the data had been completely erased and couldn't be restored. I assume the same will have been done to the memory stick. Alan was no fool."

"Unlike you, it would seem. You had better go and have a look around that flat he was living in. See if you can't find something. The police will have finished there by now.

"Police?"

"Yes," said Sir Malcolm. "When he, and that Mrs. Finch he was living with, were murdered, the police moved in to gather forensic evidence. They will have finished by now."

Jim's face went ashen. He gasped. "That was them? I saw the story but didn't realise it was them."

"Well, it was," said Sir Malcolm emphatically. "Someone must have given away their new address and it got into the wrong hands."

"But I think I was the only one to know his address," said Jim, "and the only person I told was you."

Sir Malcolm glared at him. "Well I didn't kill them, did I? He must have told someone else, or maybe he was followed. How would I know? Now, I want you to go back to the flat and see if you can find a copy of the software. It might be on a memory stick, or it might be on a computer or laptop, or even a mobile phone or iPad. Just find it."

*****

Margaret was getting worried. It was two hours since Alan had rung and there was still no sign of him. She went to the door and looked out to see if she could see him anywhere. She knew it was stupid but she had to do something. Just down the road, a car was pulling up and parking and she thought for a moment it was Alan's. They had bought a new car when they had sold the camper-van, and she still wasn't too sure what the new one looked like.

The car door opened and someone got out. It wasn't Alan, but he looked familiar. Then she realised who it was. It was that Jim that he worked with. Alan had told him to come back and hide out with them when he had deleted all the data on his computer, but after the murder two doors up, she had assumed that they wouldn't see him again. He had obviously given away their new address, or at least the address he had thought was theirs.

He walked over to number thirty-eight, which was the flat where the murder had taken place, and walked up the path to the front door.

"Wrong house," she shouted, and Jim spun round to see who was shouting. When he saw her, his jaw dropped and he mouthed something incoherent. Turning, he hurried back down the path and round to where she was standing.

"I thought you and Alan were dead," he said.

"Not so loud," she said. "Quickly, come inside."

They went in and shut the door. "So what happened?" he asked. "I was told that you had been killed."

"Well, luckily for us, and unluckily for our neighbours, Alan gave you the wrong address. Whoever you gave our address to must have sent someone to kill us."

"Oh my God. I am sorry," said Jim, "but I only told Sir Malcolm, and it can't have been him."

"Can't it?"

"Of course not," he said. "Can it?"

"I can't be sure of anything now," she said. "I seem to have been dropped into a most mysterious world of politics and intrigue. I used to have such a dull and uninteresting life, before I met Alan, and I often wished for something more exciting to happen."

"You should be careful what you wish for," said Jim.

"Don't I know it? Now, why are you here?"

"I've done what Alan asked me. Deleted all the data on my computer. But I'm under pressure from Sir Malcolm to get a copy of the software." He looked around. "Is Alan in?"

"No," she said. "He just popped out to get some bits and pieces from the supermarket. He rang about two hours ago and said he'd be back in ten minutes. I don't know where he could have got to. I'm worried sick."

"He'll be OK," said Jim. "No one knows he's alive, do they?"

"I don't know what to believe any more."

There was a loud knock at the door and they both jumped.

"That'll be him now," she said. "I wish he'd remember to take his key with him."

She went to the door, opened it and a small Asian pushed his way in, holding a gun. Margaret screamed.

"Be quiet and move over there," said the Asian, indicating the settee.

Margaret gasped. "What do you want?"

"Two birds with one stone," said the newcomer. "Very good. Now I will tell you what I want. You are both to come with me."

"What do you want with us?" pleaded Margaret. "We haven't anything of value."

"No, but a friend of yours has. You will persuade him to help us."

"No. I won't do it," said Margaret, desperately. "What have you done with Alan?"

"He is being looked after as we speak. You will help us, as I said. You have no choice. Now, whose car is that outside?"

"Mine," said Jim.

"Good. We'll go in that. You will drive and I will sit in the back with Mrs. Finch."

He motioned them to the door and opened it. "Now, no sudden movements or you will die. Just walk normally to the car and get in. I am right behind you."

They walked down to the car, Jim unlocked it and they got in.

"Now drive," said the Asian. "I will direct you."

*****

The door of the warehouse room was flung open and Jim and Margaret were pushed into the room and the door slammed behind them. They found Alan slumped in a chair, to which he was still tied, semi-conscious.

"Alan!" screamed Margaret. "What have they done to you?" She rushed over to him and started undoing the tape around his wrists and ankles. Jim came over and helped. As the bonds were untied, Alan fell out of the chair and Jim caught him and helped lower him to the floor. Alan started to regain consciousness and groaned. "Alan, it's me. Wake up." Margaret sobbed, hugging him.

Alan gasped. "Don't squeeze, please, I'm a bit sore."

"What happened to you? Who brought you here? What do they want?"

"They got rough," replied Alan. "The Yanks, and they want my software."

"The Americans?" said Margaret, surprised. "I thought they were on our side."

"Think again," said Alan. "No, they're on their own side, and when they think they're in the right, they'll do anything and think it's OK."

"We've got to get out of here," said Margaret, looking around the room.

"Easier said than done," said Jim, who had also been looking around the room.

"What're you doing here?" snapped Alan. "Haven't you done enough damage?"

"What do you mean?" said Jim, walking over to where Alan was sitting. "I've done what you wanted."

"And who did you give our address to?"

"No one," said Jim indignantly. "Well, only Sir Malcolm. He was concerned."

"Yes," said Alan. "Concerned enough to have us killed. Unfortunately for our neighbours I gave you the wrong address. Our dear Sir Malcolm sent someone to kill us, only they went to the wrong flat."

"Oh my God," said Margaret. "Those poor people. This must stop now. For heaven's sake, give them the software and let that be an end to it."

"But it won't be an end to it," said Alan. "It'll just be a beginning. Once they have the software, they'll need me to build the synthesiser, and I think that's why you're here."

"I can't do anything," said Margaret. "Why would they want me?"

"As leverage," said Alan. "If they can't break me with torture, they'll make you suffer. They think I'll give them what they want if they threaten you."

"Oh my God. No," said Margaret.

*****

106

Sir Malcolm was pacing up and down his office, while one of his heavies stood to one side.

"So where are they now?" asked Sir Malcolm.

"They've got them in a disused factory near York."

"I want them getting out as soon as possible," said Sir Malcolm. "We can't risk Greenbank getting that software. Who knows what he'll do with it. How long will it take to get a unit up there?"

"They are waiting near the warehouse for your orders right now, sir."

"Do it," said Sir Malcolm. "But be careful. I don't want to be held responsible for an international incident. Take them to unit thirty-five. I'll have the gear transported there immediately."

"Right away, sir." He left hurriedly.

*****

Alan was massaging his legs as he tried to walk about. Jim had continued to probe the walls for any sign of weakness.

"Unless we can force the door," said Jim, "we're stuck here."

There was the sound of a door opening and footsteps coming down the corridor.

"Sounds as if they're back," said Alan. I'm sorry I got you into this, Maggie."

"Can't be helped," she said, trying to sound brave.

The door opened and Greenbank strode in, followed by two of his muscular-looking assistants.

"So," he said. "It seems as if we have a full house now, so perhaps we could start again, Mr Westbrook."

"How can I give you what I haven't got?"

"Well if you haven't got the software in reality," said Greenbank, "it will be very unfortunate for you all, starting with this lovely lady here." He grabbed her by the arm and pulled her towards Alan. "Now how would you feel about being responsible for the most unpleasant things that might happen to your lady, here? I'm sure that you, being an English gentleman, wouldn't wish to be the cause of any distress that might be inflicted upon her."

"Leave her alone," said Alan.

"Certainly," said Greenback with an unpleasant smile. "As soon as you give me the software."

"How many times do I have to tell you?" said Alan, "I haven't got it any more."

"That's all right," said Greenbank with a smile. "It's surprising how things can change when a little pain is inflicted. Perhaps we should start with the lady."

"You can't do this to us," shouted Alan in desperation. "We are British citizens."

"Very touching," said Greenbank. "In here you are nothing and no one and we can do whatever we like. So, where shall we start? We could alter the lady's pretty face to start with."

"No," sobbed Margaret.

"Oh yes," said Greenbank.

Suddenly the door burst open and three men in army combat jackets poured into the room. Each had an automatic weapon which they pointed at the three Americans, who in turn pointed firearms at the newcomers.

"Now," said Greenbank, "we don't want to have an international incident, do we? If anyone gets shot, there will be some awkward questions to answer, for you and your prime minister."

The three squaddies glanced at each other, then threw down their rifles and pitched in with their fists.

Jim and Margaret helped Alan over to the side of the room, away from the action, as quickly as they could.

"Quick," said Alan, "get me through that door." With Jim holding one arm and Margaret the other, they sidled through the door. "Now slide the bolts before they realise we've gone." Jim slid the bolts home as fast as he could manage. The door had obviously been built to keep people in and was very sturdy.

Outside in the parking area, Jim's car stood next to Alan's. Luckily neither had been relieved of its keys.

"Jim, you go in your car," said Alan. "Go back to Blakely House. You were brought here by the Americans, so no one from our lot will be aware that you were here. By the way, why are you here?"

"Sir Malcolm sent me to see if I could find a copy of the software."

"Well, you can tell him from me that there isn't another copy," said Alan. "I'm sorry if you lose your job over this, but you're probably better out of it. Now go."

Jim got into his car and drove off. Alan and Margaret got into their car and set off also.

"Is everything packed?" asked Alan as they drove.

"Yes," said Margaret. "I had just finished when Jim arrived, followed closely by that Asian fellow."

"Good," said Alan. "We daren't stop there for more than a few minutes. We'll just pick up the bags and go."

"Where will we go?" asked Margaret.

"Who knows?" said Alan. "Who cares, as long as it is to somewhere they won't find us."

*****

About half an hour later, Sir Malcolm Birch arrived at the warehouse in a black limousine, accompanied by three burly assistants from a special army unit. They got out of the car, leaving it in the parking area outside. They entered the building and made their way down the corridor to the bolted door at the end.

"What the hell?" exclaimed Sir Malcolm. "How in hell did they manage to lock the door from inside?" He slid the bolts back and opened the door, to be confronted by an array of firearms pointed in his direction. He stood, taking in the scene. "So what is all this, then?" he asked no one in particular.

One of his troops stepped forward and saluted. "We had a problem with this lot, sir," he said.

"So I see," said Sir Malcolm. "And where is our friend Westbrook, or should I say Finch?"

"They managed to slip out when we were involved trying to overcome the opposition," he said.

"Oh well done," he said sarcastically. "And what do you think you're doing abducting one of our people, Greenbank? I was under the impression that the prime minister had instructed you to butt out."

"I'm sorry," said Greenbank, "but I don't take orders from your prime minister."

"Well, thanks to you," said Sir Malcolm, "we have both lost the only man who can restore that software into safe hands. You realise, of course, that if a terrorist group gets their hands on him and he gives them the software, the problems that would cause both of us?"

"Well it just proves what we have been trying to get into your prime minister's thick head." said Greenbank. "You lot aren't safe to be in charge of such a project. It should have been handed over to us from the start."

"You have a misplaced sense of confidence in your superiors back home," said Sir Malcolm. "And you would be well advised to keep out of this from now on."

"We'll see," snapped Greenbank, making for the door, closely followed by his two heavies. "Goddam amateurs." The door slammed behind him and there was the sound of bolts being slid home.

"The stupid idiot!" exclaimed Sir Malcolm. "I suppose he thinks that's funny." He turned to the senior of his accomplices. "Get onto the local base and get someone over here sharpish to open that door." The sergeant took a mobile phone from his pocket and made the call. Ten minutes later, the bolts were being slid back and the whole party trooped out into the parking area.

"Right," said Sir Malcolm. "Back to the depot immediately. We must put out an alert for Westbrook as soon as possible. We can't afford to let them loose for too long. The whole security of the realm depends upon it." He got into his car with his three accomplices and drove off.

The others piled into the army vehicle. "Pompous oaf," said one of them as he climbed in.

Eighteen

After stopping long enough to load their luggage, Alan and Margaret set off in a westerly direction, not knowing exactly where they were going. They just wanted to get as far away from York as they could. They now had the Americans after them as well as their own military, and who knew who else would like to get their hands on them. They would just have to disappear, and to do that they would have to keep on the move. It wasn't the retirement Alan had foreseen for himself.

Going west from Harrogate took them towards Skipton, over some higher ground. As they went further west, the sky clouded over and it grew darker. By the time they reached Bolton Abbey, it had started to rain quite heavily. There was quite a lot of traffic heading in both directions, so progress was not too fast, but that did not matter.

They bypassed Skipton, and at the large roundabout just beyond the town, they had a choice of route – go further west to Clitheroe, Nelson or Colne, or fork right towards the Lake District, which was the option Alan took.

"Where are we heading?" asked Margaret, getting out the AA book.

"Hadn't really thought," said Alan. "We'll just keep going until we find somewhere that seems a good place to stop. We ought to get rid of this car as soon as we can. I'm sure they must have a note of it by now."

"I hadn't thought of that," said Margaret. "Do you think they would involve the police in their search for us?"

"Not sure," said Alan. "Let's hope not."

They stopped at Settle for some petrol and a bite to eat. The rain had eased up and it was looking a bit brighter, which made them feel less gloomy.

After a light meal they set off again. Soon they found themselves passing through Kirkby Lonsdale.

"They hold an annual horse fair here," said Alan. "But I don't think it is on at the moment. We'll carry on a bit further."

Rather than carry on to the Lake District, Alan decided that it might be better to get off the beaten track for a bit. Although he knew the main road quite well, he was venturing into new territory now. The lanes were narrow and winding, but the scenery was astounding.

"Perhaps we could find a bed and breakfast place to stop," said Margaret.

"Probably be a good idea until we get organised," said Alan. "I'm not sure if we'll find anything up here, though."

They carried on, slowly wondering if it had been such a good idea to set off into the unknown like this.

"At least," said Alan, "if we don't know where we are, I don't see how anyone else can." Then, as they reached the top of a long slow climb, a stunning view opened up before them of a deep narrow valley with a stream winding its way along the bottom.

"Seems to be quite deserted," said Alan.

They started down the winding road into the valley, and about half way down, a small group of farm buildings came into view nestled among the trees at the side of the valley.

"Perhaps we could ask here if they know of anywhere to stay," said Margaret.

"Don't suppose it would hurt," said Alan.

When they reached the farm it was even more run down than it had looked from further up the hill. Alan pulled into the farmyard and stopped near the house. There didn't seem to be any livestock about, which was strange.

"Maybe they keep sheep," said Alan. "They would all be out on the hillside somewhere."

An old sheepdog came ambling out of a nearby barn towards them, wagging its tail.

"Looks friendly enough," said Alan. "Let's see if we can find its owner." He opened the door and made a fuss of the dog, which seemed to enjoy the attention. Alan walked over to the house, knocked on the door and waited, but there was no reply.

"No one there," he said, walking back to the car. "Perhaps they're in the barn where the dog came from."

"Better have a look, then," said Margaret, walking towards the barn. Alan followed with the dog.

It was dark in the barn. Margaret walked in, then stopped, staring at something.

"What is it?" asked Alan walking up behind her. She didn't need to reply as it was obvious that Alan could see what she was looking at.

"It's a bus!" exclaimed Alan. "What on earth is a bus doing in here?" He walked closer to examine it. "It's been converted as a living van."

"So it has," said Margaret. "You know, that would be ideal for us, wouldn't it?"

"Depends on the state of it inside," said Alan. "Could be full of mice and muck."

"Well it ain't," said a voice behind them. They spun round, feeling as if they were children caught doing something they shouldn't be doing.

"Sorry," said Alan. "We were just looking for whoever lived here to ask if there was a bed and breakfast anywhere near here and found your bus."

"There's nowhere up here to stay," said the man. "Anyway, come inside the house. I'm ready for a cuppa." He turned and walked towards the house. Alan and Margaret hurried after him. He was youngish and slightly built with a mop of tousled hair. He was wearing dungarees and looked rather like a hillbilly.

"Beautiful dog you've got," said Margaret. "Is he your guard dog?"

"He might lick you to death," he said. "Otherwise he's harmless."

They reached the house and the man opened the door. He went in, leaving it open behind him. They followed him in and were surprised to find that in the old traditional farm kitchen there was an easel with a picture on it, and other paintings stacked all around. The table was covered with tubes of paint and jars of brushes. There was a strong smell of linseed oil pervading the air, mixed with old frying smells. They both stood open-mouthed.

"Make yourselves at home," he said. "I'm Josh and this is my studio."

"Hello, Josh," said Alan. "I'm Alan and this is Maggie. I take it you're an artist."

"I like to paint," said Josh, "but I don't know about artist though. You tell me."

Alan looked at the painting on the stand. "I would say you were an artist."

"Well thank you for that," said Josh. "Do you know about painting?"

"I've not been to art school," said Alan, "but I have done a bit of painting, some watercolours and some acrylics."

Josh poured the tea and brought it over to them.

"Would you like anything to eat?" he asked.

"That's very kind of you," said Margaret. "But we don't want to be a nuisance."

"Think nothing of it," said Josh. "It's a bit lonely out here and it's nice to have the company. In fact, you said you were looking for somewhere to stay. If you're not too fussy about the accommodation, you're welcome to stay here for a while."

"If you're sure," said Alan, "that would be very nice. I hope we won't be interrupting your work."

"Why don't you have a go too?" said Josh. "You said you used to paint. I've got plenty of stuff here. What do you fancy?"

*****

They stayed for a couple of weeks. Alan enjoyed himself painting with Josh, while Maggie went out for walks in the hills round about. She enjoyed the freedom, walking wherever the urge took her. She took her binoculars with her and watched the wildlife for hours.

One evening, after going to their room to sleep, they got to discussing their future plans.

"I really like it here," said Maggie. "I can't think of anywhere better to hide out and not be found."

"I know what you mean," said Alan, "but we can't take advantage of Josh's generosity for ever."

"We could offer to pay him," said Maggie.

"Yes," said Alan. "I'd always intended to pay for our keep. The trouble is that I'd have to go to a hole-in-the-wall for some cash."

"So?"

"Well, if I do that, they would be able to trace us from our bank records."

"Would they do that?" asked Maggie.

"Who knows?" said Alan. "They seemed very keen on getting hold of us again so I think they would do whatever it took, and they have the ability. If we leave any traceable evidence, we'd have to move on straight away. Perhaps we should confide in Josh."

"Do you think that wise? How do we know we can trust him?"

"We don't," said Alan. "But what has he to gain by shopping us? He hasn't asked for payment for stopping here and he doesn't seem the type who would do anything just for the money."

"But you never can tell, can you?" said Maggie. "If he thought we were criminals, or something like that, running away from the law, he might feel he had to tell the authorities."

"Well, we'll have to make sure he understands the situation completely, then," said Alan. "Tell him virtually everything."

"But suppose he was one of those green types?" said Margaret. "He might think that we should be stopped because your software was too dangerous. Who knows what these green fanatics might do?"

"He doesn't seem the fanatical type," said Alan.

"No, but his friends might be. After all, you originally thought it might have been a green group who was after you."

Nineteen

Sir Malcolm was sitting in his office, waiting for his visitor. He had put out feelers among his informants and had sent out minions to try and find some information about the whereabouts of Westbrook and his new wife. *Damn the man*, he thought, *we should have acted earlier to take control of the project*. Now, God alone knew where he and his software were and whether they had fallen into other hands – hands he would not want them to fall into. He had one option he had been leaving until all else faiied. But first he would hear the latest report on the hunt for Westbrook.

There was a knock at the door.

"Come in," he shouted impatiently. The door opened, a nondescript man entered and he handed a folder to Sir Malcolm. "Thank you. Tell him I'll be in touch if there's anything else I want him to do."

"Yes, sir," said the minion turning and leaving.

Sir Malcolm opened the folder and thumbed through it. Why did these people have to wrap everything up in verbose wording? Basically, they could have it done in three words, 'can't find him'. There were some items that could be useful though. He was still driving the car he was last known to have, but who could tell for how long? But it might be a possible start. The bank hadn't seen any movement in his account, so he had either taken enough cash to last him for a while, or he had opened an account in another name. He was beginning to have a great deal of respect for Alan Westbrook, but then you would expect someone of his ability to think of most things. But he was on new territory now, out of his comfort zone, as they say. Perhaps he would make a mistake, allowing them to pounce. *Let's hope no one else gets to him first*, he thought.

His telephone rang and he grabbed it. "Yes?" He listened for a few seconds then snapped, "Well send him in immediately." He put the phone down and tidied the folder on his desk. The door opened and small weaselly man entered. "Don't you ever knock?"

"No," said the newcomer. "You were expecting me, so what would be the point?" He was middle-aged, slightly balding and he walked with a slight limp. He was dressed in a pair of old jeans, a checked shirt and an old grey tank top pullover. On his feet he wore a pair of nondescript trainers, just visible beneath his jeans, which were rather long. His hands were short and stubby with well-chewed fingernails.

He walked up to the desk, sat on the wooden chair that had been placed in front of it and looked at Sir Malcolm.

"I have a special job for you," said Sir Malcolm.

"Why else would you ask to see me?"

"I didn't ask to see you," said Sir Malcolm sharply. "I command and you obey."

"Whatever," said Weasel, which was how he was known. He never used his real name and even Sir Malcolm didn't know what it was.

"I do hate that expression," said Sir Malcolm. Weasel shrugged but said nothing. "I am looking for this man," he said, passing a photograph to Weasel. "His real name is Alan Westbrook, but due to circumstances which needn't bother you, he is now known as Peter Finch. He has taken off in this car with his wife, Margaret." He slid two more photographs across the desk. "This is the folder containing everything we know about him. It's not much to go on, but we need him finding as quickly as possible. He mustn't fall into the hands of any other organisation whatsoever, and he mustn't be harmed. I need him healthy and able to carry out some work for me."

"Which, I assume, he doesn't want to do?"

"He can be persuaded," said Sir Malcolm. "I can be very persuasive. Now on your way before the tracks grow too cold. Report to me daily whether you have made progress or not. I will have other people out there keeping an eye out for them, so they need to be kept up to date."

Weasel nodded, picked up the bundle of papers and left the office. As the door closed, Sir Malcolm picked up the telephone again.

As soon as he was outside the building, Weasel got into his car and set off towards York, where Alan had last been seen. That was the only place to start. Then he would have a word with that boffin type from Blakely House. Surely he must have some idea where Westbrook would go.

*****

121

Walter Greenbank was sitting in the passenger seat of the dark-coloured car in the car park outside Sir Malcolm's office. When Weasel appeared, he nudged the driver and pointed.

"That's the one," he said. "I want you to follow him wherever he goes and keep me informed of his movements."

"Sure thing, sir," said the driver, starting the engine.

"And don't let him know he's being followed."

Walter Greenbank quickly got out of the car, which moved off in pursuit of Weasel, and walked over to another car which was waiting for him at the other end of the car park. As he approached, the driver got out and opened the rear door for him to get in. The driver returned to his seat and the car slowly edged out of the car park, entering the continuous stream of traffic passing the entrance.

Sir Malcolm stood at his window, watching them as he spoke into his mobile phone. Another car slid slowly from the car park and joined the traffic a few cars behind the one in which Walter Greenbank was sitting, lighting a new cigar.

Twenty

Alan and Margaret had just come in after their short walk, up the hill behind the farm.

"Just timed it right," shouted Josh from the kitchen. "Dinner is just about ready."

"I'll help you carry it through," said Margaret, hurrying through into the kitchen while Alan hung up their coats. "There's a chilly breeze up there."

"Yes," said Josh. "We're quite sheltered down here." He handed her one of the steaming dishes, picked up another himself and followed her through to the dining room. Josh had decided that he should be a little more formal, as he had guests. Normally, he would have simply cooked something, slid it onto a plate and sat in his comfy chair in front of the television.

When they had carried everything through and sat down, Alan broached the subject of payment.

"We have taken advantage of your generosity far too long now," said Alan. "I feel we should offer you some sort of payment."

"It's only fair," said Margaret.

"Well, I've enjoyed the company," said Josh. "But I admit a little financial help would be appreciated if you plan to stay a little longer. Don't get me wrong. I enjoy your company and you can stay as long as you like."

"The problem," said Alan, "is that if I withdraw money from my account, we will have to move on immediately. Don't look so alarmed, we're not on the run from the police, but we would rather no one was able to trace us here."

"Sounds intriguing," said Josh. "I don't mean to pry, but I'd appreciate an explanation so that I know what I'm getting involved with."

"We're in a difficult situation," said Alan. "I have done some work for the MoD and there are people who would like to get their hands on it, and we certainly don't want to get anyone else involved in our predicament."

"Are these people dangerous?" asked Josh, feeling a little perturbed by what he was hearing.

"I don't know quite how dangerous," said Alan. "But I wouldn't like to put anyone else at risk just in case."

"Well I don't think anyone would be able to trace you here if you stay put and no one sees you," said Josh. "You don't seem to be the sort of people who would do anything untoward. How long do you think you will have to hide?"

"I really don't know," said Alan.

"The more I think about it," said Margaret, "the more I think we should move on. It isn't fair on Josh to get him involved, and now that we've told him, I think we should leave as soon as possible. We don't want anyone coming here asking questions."

"No," said Alan realising Margaret was referring to the people who had come to grief in York. "We'll set off tomorrow morning, and when we are far enough away, we'll withdraw some money and send it to you. You have done more than enough to help us already."

"A few years ago," said Josh, "I decided to opt out of the rat race and disappear. That was when I bought that old bus you were admiring in the barn when you first arrived. I joined a group of new-age travellers and toured the country going to horse fairs and pop festivals and the like. I used to keep in touch with the real world via an old friend in the art community and one day I heard that a solicitor was trying to contact me. I thought it must be someone trying to sue me for something, though I didn't know what. Eventually I rang him and found that an old relative had died and left me his farm. I wasn't a farmer, so my first thought was to sell it, but when I came here to have a look at my inheritance, I realised that it was just what I wanted. A retreat where I could hide away from the world and do my painting. I have an agent down in London who sells my paintings for me, but he doesn't know where I live. What I'm getting round to is that you can stay. Forget about the money. Perhaps we could sell some of your paintings, they're really quite good, and you could do some jobs around the farm. I'd like that."

"Sounds an attractive proposition to me," said Alan. "But we still don't know if they will find us here, and if they did, we wouldn't want to put you in any danger."

"I'll take my chances," said Josh, "but I would like to know a bit more about what it is they want from you."

"Probably best you don't know the details," said Alan, "but I did some software work for them and they decided that they would take charge of it themselves and give me the push."

"They stole your work?" Josh asked incredulously.

"Well, not exactly," said Alan. "They paid me for it but I had no choice in the situation. They gave me a cheque and escorted me from the building."

"So what's the problem?"

"They thought they had the password to access the software," said Alan, "but they didn't have the full story. There was a different password for each day of the week."

"Couldn't they have just waited until the same day the next week and had another go at it?"

"That wouldn't have been any good either," said Alan. They would have had to add the day number as well. But when the password failed, the programme wiped everything on the memory stick, including the programme itself. So, you see, they are after another copy. I don't think they would harm me for fear of never being able to get their hands on the software. But that doesn't mean they wouldn't hurt anyone else who got in their way."

"So who, exactly, is after you?

"Firstly, the MoD," said Alan.

"Firstly?" said Josh. "You mean there are others after it as well?"

"Yep. Secondly, there's the CIA," said Alan. "I don't know if there is anyone else, but there could be terrorist groups and possibly any of the 'green' groups who take exception to anything they don't understand."

"Why would terrorists and green groups be interested?"

"The terrorists might think that they could use it in germ warfare and the greens might think it had something to do with genetic engineering and was going to kill us all."

"And would it?" said Josh looking a little perturbed.

"Not on its own," said Alan. "The software enables us to obtain an exact model of a genetic structure. The initial idea was to obtain the structure of a virus and then synthesise a variant designed to attack it, or perhaps a cancer cell. As you can see our – or at least my – intentions were honourable. What I hadn't realised was that other people may have had other uses for the technology."

Josh gasped. "That's awful."

"But it would need more work doing to achieve the final part," said Alan. "That's also why they would need me."

"But you wouldn't do it, would you?" said Josh. "Surely not."

"I wouldn't choose to," said Alan. "But who knows what any of us would do if the appropriate pressure were applied?"

"Then wouldn't it be better to destroy the software so that no one can use it?" asked Josh.

"Maybe," said Alan. "But I have spent a lot of time on this and I would still like to use it for its original purpose."

"I really think that is too dangerous," said Josh. "Please think about it."

"I have thought of little else ever since they took it off me and I have been on the run."

"Have you got it with you?" asked Josh.

"Of course not," said Alan. "It's somewhere safe. In some ways, its existence makes me feel safer."

"It scares the hell out of me," said Josh. "How about you, Maggie? Don't you feel threatened by this?"

"Of course," she said. "But I trust Alan knows what's best."

"But suppose they use you to persuade him to give them what they want?"

"They've already threatened that," said Margaret. "And of course I'm scared, but I think Alan is right. He has to keep the software safe. If he destroyed it, they wouldn't hesitate to kill us both so that we didn't spill the story to the papers."

"Would you like us to go now you know the full story?" said Alan. "I wouldn't blame you if you did."

"I said you could stay," said Josh, "and I stand by that. Stay as long as you want. You are welcome."

Twenty-one

Walter Greenbank got out of the car and walked over to the front door of the building, followed by two of his heavily built minions.

"This the place?" he asked.

"Yes, sir," replied one of the heavies. "Lives here on his own."

"Good," said Greenbank. "Knock."

One of the heavies knocked. After a few moments, footsteps could be heard in the hallway and the door opened. Dr Jim Stanley peered out.

"So, Mr Stanley," said Greenbank. "We meet again."

"What do you want this time?"

"Just a few words," said Greenbank. "So good of you to ask us in." One of the heavies pushed him back into the hallway and stepped in, followed in turn by the other heavy and finally Walter Greenbank himself. They pushed him though into his own living room and stood holding an arm each until Greenbank entered.

"Please be seated," said Greenbank, and the two heavies threw him heavily onto the settee.

"What do you want?" squeaked Jim. "I've told you all I know."

"Perhaps not," said Greenbank. "We would like another word with your friend Westbrook, and would like you to tell us where he is."

"I have no idea," said Jim. "When he left York, even he didn't know where he would be going."

"Then perhaps you could hazard a guess or two," said Greenbank. "After all, you do know him quite well. Now tell us all about him. What he likes to do in his spare time. The sort of places he might like to go. Anything at all, however trivial."

"I really don't know."

"Now look, Dr Stanley," said Greenbank, "we are prepared to be quite civilised about this if you are prepared to co-operate. However, if you're not then you might find the next hour or two quite unpleasant."

Jim shuddered. "OK," he said. "I'll tell you all I know. But it really isn't much."

"I'll be the judge of that," said Greenbank sitting in the chair opposite Jim. "So let's start, shall we?"

*****

The car pulled up behind the one that Walter Greenbank had just got out of. The driver turned off the engine and sat back to listen to the radio, after first making a short phone call to the office. It was a quiet road with little traffic. A woman pushed a pram past with a toddler complaining beside her and trying to keep up. An elderly man came past with a dog. An amorous pigeon was bothering two female pigeons who were having none of it.

"You and me both," said the man in the car. It was a boring job, but well paid. *James Bond*, he thought, *never had to do this sort of thing.* Why did people think it was a glamorous job? Sitting in a cold car for hours on end, watching people walking past was no fun at all, and he daren't nod off for a few minutes, however tempting the thought. It would be more than his job was worth. He wondered how long they were going to be in there. Perhaps quite a while. He opened the plastic box on the passenger seat and took out the pork pie wrapped in foil, unwrapped it and took a large bite. He had thought about leaving it until later so that he had something to look forward to, but had decided on the spur of the moment that he would enjoy it now.

He had just finished his pie, when someone walked up to the front door that he had been watching, and knocked. He waited for a while and then knocked again but no one answered the door. The man looked a bit perplexed but walked away, looking back once as he reached the pavement. The man in the car made a note.

Another half hour had passed when the door opened and Walter Greenbank came out, followed by two heavies. They got into their car and drove off. The man in the car made another note. He watched the car disappearing into the distance before getting out and walking over to the door and knocking.

*****

About an hour later, the man who had knocked on the door earlier and had got no reply came back again. He knocked on the door and stood back and waited. Nothing happened. He tried again, and again he got no reply so he walked over to the window and peered in. He then went to the narrow passage that ran down the side of the building. A few minutes later he appeared again, looking rather flustered. He looked up and down the road, but there was no one in sight so he took out his mobile phone and made a call.

When he had finished speaking on the phone, he started pacing back and forth in front of the house until a police car screeched to a halt outside. The doors flew open and four policemen leapt out and surrounded the man.

"In there," he said pointing at the house. They went up to the front door, but found it locked.

"How did you get in?" asked the senior officer.

"I didn't," said the man. "I came round because we were supposed to be going down to the pub for a game of pool, but I got no answer. So I went away. But I came back a bit later and there was still no reply so I went round the back to see if I could see if he was in. I looked through the back window and could see a leg poking out from behind one of the armchairs. It looked as if he had fallen. I assumed he must have had a heart attack or something, so I called you."

"Did you call the ambulance as well?"

"Yes."

"They should be here any time now then," said the officer. "You go round the back and see if you can force the back door." Two of the men ran off down the passage. After a few minutes, the front door opened and the two officers appeared. At that moment the ambulance arrived and the paramedics got out and approached the police officers.

"It would appear to be too late," said the officer in charge. He had just been speaking to the two officers that had broken in. "This is also now a crime scene."

*****

Weasel had arrived in York, and having found nothing of significance, had decided to head west. He knew that Alan Westbrook had previously stayed in Knaresborough for a while after camping in his van near Ripley. He would try those places first. He had very little to go on, but he was used to challenges so wasn't particularly worried. They would be seen eventually and news would get back to him as soon as they were. He had a wide band of undesirables who were quite happy to give him information for a fee. He knew he could rely on them as they knew what would happen if they tried to deceive him.

He drove up to the farmhouse where Margaret had lived and Alan had stayed for a while. It looked as if the place was newly inhabited. They must have sold the place then.

He walked up to the front door and knocked. The door was opened by an elderly man, and Weasel could see a woman just behind him peering out of the gloom in the hallway.

"Yes," said the man. "Can I help you?"

"I hope so," said Weasel. "A friend of mine used to live here and it seems he thinks he might have left some of his things here. He asked me if I could pop in and ask you if you had found anything."

"And what was your friend's name, may I ask?" said the man.

"Yes, what was his name?" repeated the woman.

Weasel thought for a moment. He couldn't use the name Westbrook, because he would have been using a different name when he was here. Now what the hell was it? A bird?

"They were called Mr and Mrs Finch," said Weasel.

"That's right," said the man. "And what's your name then?"

"I don't see that that is relevant," said Weasel, "but if it is important to you, my name is Williams. John Williams. "I live in Harrogate."

"Well, as it happens," said the man opening the door a bit wider, "he did leave his rucksack here. Go and get it Doris."

"Oh good," said Weasel. "Was that all?"

"As far as I know," said the man. "I've not been up in the attic, but there was nothing else down here."

The woman appeared again with the rucksack and handed it to the man.

"I want a receipt for this though," said the man.

"If you would like to write one out," said Weasel, "I'll sign it for you with pleasure."

They did that and Weasel put the rucksack into his car and then drove off down the drive.

"Funny sort of bloke, that," said the man.

"Yes," said his wife. "Funny. Very funny. I didn't like him. Do you think we did right giving him the rucksack?"

"Don't suppose it matters," said the man, closing the door.

Weasel drove off down the drive and into the lane. When he found a spot to pull in, he parked and emptied the contents of the rucksack onto the passenger seat. There was an empty plastic container, a compass, a packet of first aid plasters and a collection of maps. He picked up the maps and looked at them closely. There was one of the local area and several of the Lake District. It would seem that Westbrook liked walking, so that was a start. He also seemed to favour the Lakes which gave him a direction in which to start looking. He didn't think that he would go to the most popular parts of the Lakes, but maybe somewhere on the edge.

He put the things back into the rucksack and headed towards the caravan site where Alan had stayed recently.

*****

Things seemed a little tense at the farm after Alan had told Josh his situation. Josh had said that it was all right and that they could stay, but it seemed that maybe he had thought about it a little more and was having reservations. Also, Alan was thinking that it might not be such a good idea to hang around the same location for too long as it gave whoever was looking for him more time to close in. He couldn't think how they would be able to follow him here. As far as he knew no one other than Josh knew they were here. But had Josh told anyone? He had to go out occasionally to get fresh supplies and it would be so easy to let slip that he wasn't alone at the farm. And even if he didn't say anything, people might notice that he was buying far more supplies than he had been before they arrived. Perhaps they should move on. At breakfast the next morning, Alan put it to Josh.

"I think it would be for the best," he said. "We are very grateful for your help and hospitality, but we really don't want to put you in any danger."

"I've told you," said Josh, "that it's OK. I really don't mind. Just stay a little longer. I like the company."

They left it at that for the time being, but Alan really didn't want to stay any longer. Anyway, it was getting boring. He picked up the paper that Josh had bought at the next village and glanced through it. There was nothing of much interest until he saw a headline that made him sit up. It said, "Government Scientist Found Dead." He read the article, which wasn't too long, looking for the name of the government scientist, but it wasn't given. Maybe it was nothing to do with him, but he felt very uneasy about it and he said nothing to the others, at least not for the moment. He would see if there was any more news tomorrow. He didn't see why it would be Jim Stanley, but he couldn't get the thought out of his head. If it were Jim, there was nothing he could have told them. He didn't know where they had gone as he hadn't known himself, when he and Margaret had set off from York.

The following day he couldn't find any follow up article on the government scientist, but it still gave him a very bad feeling. It was no use, they would have to leave. He discussed it with Margaret that evening, and she agreed with him that it would be for the best. So at breakfast he broke the news to Josh.

"But where will you go?" asked Josh. "I'm sure you would be safer here than driving around the country in that car of yours. Why did you get a white one? It stands out a mile."

"Had to change my last one in a hurry and had to take what was available," said Alan. "And as to where? I don't know. We'll just follow our nose. Perhaps become new-age travellers."

"I don't think you'd look the part in that car though," said Josh. "Look, why don't you take that old bus of mine and leave your car here. We can hide it in the barn under a pile of hay. And when this is all over you can come back for it."

"What about tax and insurance for the bus?" said Alan. If I tax and insure it, it will be traceable."

"No problem," said Josh. "I had to tax and insure it recently as I use it occasionally to transport stuff. You can take my documentation and pretend that you're me, if you like."

"Is it habitable?" said Margaret.

"It would be luxury to a new age traveller," said Josh. "Just needs a bit of a sweep out maybe. I'll help you if you like and you could be off by this afternoon."

Twenty-two

The bus turned out to be excellent for their requirements. It had been converted into a type of camper-van with a built-in kitchen and lounge-cum-bedroom. There wasn't much room for storage, but they hadn't much to store, so that was all right. There was half a tank of diesel, so they wouldn't need to stop to refuel for quite a while. They planned to draw as much money as they could from the bank, send some back to Josh in payment for his help and keep the rest to pay for things such as food and fuel.

After backing the bus out of the barn, Alan drove his car in and parked it as far back as he could manage. Then they set to, forking hay over it. Then they piled some hay bales in front of it until you wouldn't believe there was anything there other than hay.

They thanked Josh again for all his help, promised to take care of the bus, and told him they would send some money to pay for his extra costs while they had been staying there. They got into the bus, and after a few moments adjusting the seats, set off up the lane back towards civilisation.

About a mile up the road, they had to pull in to let a rusty old banger get by. The driver didn't look too pleased, but that didn't bother them. They wouldn't be seeing him again.

When they reached the main road, they decided to head north to see if they could find one of the horse fairs that were popular in the region. Perhaps if they mixed in with one of the travelling groups they might go unnoticed by the community at large, and they assumed that the travelling fraternity were unlikely to say anything to anybody.

"Perhaps," said Alan, "if we find somewhere to withdraw some cash fairly soon, we could drive further north and then fill up with diesel. If anyone is able to trace us to those two events they will think we are heading north. Then we get onto the M6 and promptly head south."

"What about linking up with the travellers?" asked Margaret. "I thought we were going to travel with them."

"We don't have to travel with them, exactly," said Alan. "If we find any up here, we could find out where the next meeting place is going to be. If we have no luck there, we could drive down to Glastonbury and mingle with the festival crowd."

"I don't really see myself as a hippie," said Margaret, "rolling half naked in mud."

"Neither do I," said Alan. "I think the rolling in mud and drug-taking is optional. But where better to hide than somewhere no one would expect us to be?"

As it turned out, they didn't find a group of travellers, so carried on to the M6 and then headed south towards Glastonbury. They stopped overnight at a caravan site where they received some sideways glances, so they decided that the next time they would either stop in a secluded place off the motorway, or find a travellers' site at the edge of a town. They would just have to play it by ear.

*****

Weasel had travelled up the road towards the Lake District and had stopped at every filling station he had passed. Of course no one could remember the white Citroen driven by the man in the photograph that he had taken from the folder Sir Malcolm had given him. That was until he stopped at the filling station where they had, in fact, stopped for fuel. At least they had passed this way, so his hunch that they were heading for the Lakes had been right. How predictable people were. Even intelligent people like Westbrook. Time to call in some help. He had a few contacts in this area who could be alerted to look out for the white car. It was a pity he didn't have the registration number, but you can't have everything you would like.

He made a few calls on his mobile phone, then drove to the next village and pulled into the car park beside a nice little country pub where he had arranged to meet his friends, if they could in fact be called friends. Business colleagues perhaps. Then he went into the pub, ordered a pint of the local ale and found a secluded corner to sit in and wait.

The first to arrive went by the name of Knuckles to his friends. He had, at one time, been a bare-knuckle boxer. Of course that was illegal, but what did he care? It had made him quite a lot of money and more than a few enemies. He was quite heavily built, had a broken nose and several old scars were visible on his face. He bought himself a pint and sat down in the corner with Weasel. Neither said anything.

Shortly an old rattle trap of a car staggered into the car park.

"That'll be Old Albert," said Knuckles. "He's still got that old wreck of a car. It's not as if he can't afford something better."

"Would never put his hand in his pocket," said Weasel. "The old skinflint."

Albert shambled in, looked around, then seeing Weasel and Knuckles, walked over and sat down. He looked pointedly at the glass in Weasel's hand, but said nothing.

"Would you like a drink?" asked Weasel with a resigned expression on his face.

"Very kind," said Albert. He was a small, shifty-looking man with a permanently grumpy expression on his face. He shuffled about in his seat as if he had livestock in his pants. Knuckles thought he probably had.

Weasel went to the bar, bought another pint and carried it back to the table.

"So," said Albert. "What's on?"

"I'm trying to track someone down," said Weasel. "Well, two people to be precise. A man and a woman travelling together in a white Citroen." He took out a small bundle of papers and pulled out some photographs and laid them on the table. "They came through here five days ago. I think they may be heading for the Lake District."

"Why not get the cops onto it?" asked Albert. "They could have the whole area covered."

"Too sensitive," said Weasel. "This is a matter of national security."

"Then it'll pay very well?" said Albert.

"Possibly," said Weasel.

"How well?" asked Knuckles.

"There'll be a grand in it for the one who finds them."

"And what do you want doing with them?" asked Albert. "It'll cost a lot more than a grand if they're to be got rid of."

"Oh, nothing like that," said Weasel. "Just let me know where they are and you'll get your money as soon as we have them. They seemed to be heading for the Lake District, so that would be the direction to start looking. However, they may have turned off anywhere between here and the Lakes, so if you find no trace further on you had better backtrack and try the smaller roads."

*****

Alan and Margaret were getting quite used to living in their newly-acquired bus, and were now chugging along a country road in Worcestershire. They had stopped at one or two camping sites on the way, but due to some curious looks they had received from the other campers, had decided to keep clear of those in future. They had found that it was possible to do what many of the old travellers do and pull up at the roadside and stay there until someone complained. Usually, they hadn't waited long enough for people to complain. Now they were heading for a large wooded area where they might be able to stop for quite a while. Alan had thought he might set up in the forest as a bodger. That was something he had always felt he would like to do, and it would also be a way of making a bit of untraceable money.

A bodger is someone who makes furniture and other things out of unseasoned wood that they take from the forest. It is actually an ancient craft and is quite skilled. Alan thought that he would have to practise for quite a bit before he was good enough to sell anything. But he had seen a TV programme about just such a person and thought that if he could track him down he might be able to set up with him and learn the trade from an expert. They were heading for the Forest of Dean.

Alan wasn't able to use his mobile phone or a WiFi connection to his laptop, but he had been able to use internet cafés, on their way down. He had been able to find the location of the bodger in the woods, and had programmed the ancient satnav that Josh had fitted in the bus to take them there, avoiding all the major roads. It had been quite an experience being directed down some tracks that were hardly suitable for a car, let alone a bus.

Now they were on a windy but wider country lane, running through the edge of the forest. Suddenly the satnav gave an instruction to turn left onto a forest track. At first this was hard to see, as it was so overgrown that Alan didn't think he could get the bus onto the narrow track. But, after quite a lot of reversing, he managed to drive onto it. After the first fifty yards, the track became easier, though it was very uneven and Alan wondered if the bus's suspension could take all the jolting.

The sun was getting quite low in the sky and so only filtered through when the forest canopy thinned out. It gave everything a mystical feeling. Alan remembered when he was small and his father had taken them to the woods. They had pretended that the place was enchanted. As they drove along, Alan half-expected a group of elves to step out in front of them.

"I've always liked woodland," said Alan.

"It certainly has an atmosphere of its own," said Margaret. "But I think I prefer the open country more."

"Don't you like the world of elves and trolls?" he joked.

"No I don't," she replied. "And this place is creepy enough without you adding trolls and monsters. Especially as it's getting dark."

At that moment the forest opened up into a more sparsely wooded area. At the far side of the cleared area was an old caravan, next to a sort of timber enclosure with a thatched roof. A little way from the caravan was a fire with a pot hanging over it, but there was no other sign of life.

Alan drove the bus over to a space near the caravan and turned the engine off.

"I don't think I like this," said Margaret.

"It's OK," said Alan. "I'll go and find him. What was his name again?"

"Walter Watkins, I think," said Margaret.

Alan climbed down from the bus and walked over to the camp fire. *There must be someone around*, he thought. *They wouldn't leave a fire burning unattended.* He walked over to the caravan and called out, but no one appeared. When he turned to walk back to the fire, he saw the silhouette of a man standing in front of the flames, holding what looked alarmingly like a gun.

"Walter Watkins?" asked Alan.

"Who wants to know?"

"My name is Alan Finch," he said, moving towards the figure by the fire.

"Stay where you are," said the figure, making a small gesture with the gun. "What do you want?"

"We were hoping that we could stay here for a while," said Alan, "and learn some of the wood-craft that I have heard you are so good at."

"We?"

"My wife and I," said Alan, pointing at the bus.

"And why would you want to do that?"

It's something I have always fancied doing," said Alan. "But now we just want to get away from all the hassle of the world for a while. A sort of holiday, if you know what I mean."

"Better bring your wife over here then," he said, putting the gun down and sitting on a log by the fire. Alan called to Margaret to come over.

"I used to have groups of people come out here to learn bodging, at one time," he said. "But I got fed up with all these townies thinking they were God's gift to country pursuits, while all the time they were complete idiots. So I gave it up and I haven't seen anyone out here for ages. Prefer it on my own, but you don't seem the same as all those Hooray Henrys that used to come out here. Must admit I made quite a bit of money out of them. But then I don't need much money out here. I'm almost self-sufficient."

"Almost?" said Margaret.

"Well there are things you can't find in the forest," he said. "Such as toilet paper. There are things you can use instead, but some of the benefits of civilisation are worth having. And yes, I am Walter Watkins."

"You didn't seem too pleased to see us when we first arrived," said Alan, glancing at the gun propped against the log.

"Well, what did you expect?" he said, sitting down on the log. "You come rumbling through the forest in that bus of yours, and that's not something I see every day, thank goodness."

"You don't like buses?"

"Buses as such are OK, but a converted bus like that usually travels in convoys full of disorderly young people who seem to have the idea that they have a right to everyone else's property. I had visions of being overrun by hordes of hippies, or suchlike."

"I see your point," said Alan. "I never thought of that. But are you OK with the two of us and our bus on our own?"

"For a while, maybe," said Walter. "Why have you come here?"

Alan gave him the story they had prepared about wanting to get away from the rat-race and get back to nature. "I've always fancied trying my hand at bodging," he said. "I was hoping you could give me some lessons."

Walter looked a bit doubtful, but said nothing.

Margaret fetched some food from the bus and the three of them sat round the fire eating while the sun went down. After they had eaten, Alan and Margaret went back to their bus while Walter remained by the fire. They didn't know how long he had stayed there, but he had gone in the morning.

Twenty-three

Weasel continued on to the Lake District while Albert and Knuckles searched the local area. When Weasel reached Kendal and had found no trace of the fugitives, he decided to head back to see what the other two had discovered, if anything. He was getting rather worried by this time, as he felt he might lose his rather remunerative position with Sir Malcolm. But not only that, it was well known that once you had done work of a certain nature for Sir Malcolm, it was not a good career move to hand in your notice. You didn't retire from that sort of work. You were retired, permanently, so that you would not be a worry to Sir Malcolm. So it was important to get some results, quickly.

When he reached the little country pub where they had all met up previously, he found them waiting for him in the secluded corner by the window. Weasel bought himself a pint at the bar and walked over to the corner and sat himself down.

"So?" he said.

"Nothing, Guv," said Albert.

"Nothing?" said Weasel.

"Not a bleedin' thing," said Knuckles. "Been up all the side lanes that go to nowhere. Nothing up there and no one's seen anything."

"There's an artist bloke that lives at a remote farm," said Albert. "Thought he might have seen them. It was just the sort of place they might have hidden out, but he said he hadn't seen anyone recently."

"Did you believe him?" asked Weasel, leaning forward.

"Why would he lie?"

"Maybe they spun him a line, or something, and he took them in, and when they had been there for a while he felt he had to protect them," said Weasel.

"Well there was no sign of the car," said Albert. "But we didn't look in the barns. Didn't think anyone would hide them."

"That's the trouble," said Weasel. "You didn't think. Perhaps we should go back there tonight and have a look in the barns."

"I'm not going up there after dark," said Knuckles with a shudder. "Bloody spooky up there it is."

"God, am I employing kids?" said Weasel. "Tonight at eleven we set off from here and we search the barns. I won't be satisfied until we have found that car or proved that it isn't there. Now one more drink, then you can go home, put on some dark-coloured clothes and be back here by eleven. I'll meet you in the car park. We'll go in my car, and by the way, bring a torch that works."

*****

It was getting on for midnight when they pulled off the road near the farm. It was very dark as the sky was overcast. A light rain was falling and there was a blustery wind. In fact, the conditions couldn't have been better, as any noise they made would be masked by the noise of the wind, or so they hoped.

"I don't like this," said Knuckles.

"Keep it down," whispered Weasel. "Now not another sound." They headed off into the farmyard, which was rather muddy underfoot. Knuckles slipped and nearly fell, but was caught by Albert. "Right," whispered Weasel, "I'll take that barn over there. Albert, you look in that one, and Knuckles, you take that one."

"What?" said Knuckles with a look of panic. "On my own?"

"Of course on your bloody own," snapped Weasel. "Now go, and meet back here in five minutes."

They went off to their appointed barns and disappeared inside as quietly as they could, with the exception of Knuckles, who found to his relief that the door was locked with a large padlock, so he stood outside looking furtively around until the others reappeared.

"Nothing in there," said Albert.

"Nothing in mine either," said Weasel. "How about you, Knuckles?"

"Didn't see anything."

"Perhaps we'd all better have a look then," said Weasel.

"What's the matter?" said Knuckles. "Don't you trust me?"

"In a word, no," said Weasel and headed off to the locked barn. "So you couldn't see anything?"

"No."

"Well, if you didn't get in, I don't suppose you would," said Weasel. "Now make yourself useful and go and get the

bolt cutters from the boot of my car. And don't slam it shut."
Knuckles disappeared into the gloom. Eventually he returned
with the bolt cutters, which Weasel snatched from him and set
about cutting the chain securing the door of the barn. It didn't
take more than a few seconds to cut through the chain securing
the door, which then swung open, creaking.

"Quiet," said Weasel in a loud whisper. "Quick, inside."

It was dark inside, but Weasel took out his little torch and
switched it on. The sudden light made them all screw up their
eyes until they adapted to it.

"Nothing here," said Knuckles, starting towards the door.

"Not so fast," said Weasel. "What's under that straw?"

"More straw I should think," said Albert.

"Well, I think we should have a look," said Weasel. "So
shift it."

"What, us?"

"Who else?"

"What was that?" said Knuckles, backing towards the
door.

They all stopped and listened. "I can't hear anything," said
Weasel. "So get on with it."

"I think I heard something too," said Albert. They all
stopped and listened, and sure enough there was a sound that
made their blood run cold. It was a deep throated growl
coming from the shadows in the corner. Weasel pointed his
torch and all they could see was a dark mass of straw with two
luminous points of light looking back at them.

With a strangled scream, Knuckles made a dash for the
door. The panic being infectious, he was followed seconds
later by Albert and Weasel, fighting each other to get out first.

As they came out into the yard, they ran into Knuckles, who had skidded to a halt, staring at something in the gloom. The others stopped, following his gaze, and saw a dark figure standing facing them. The moon had momentarily come out from behind the clouds and the moonlight glinted off the barrels of what looked like a twelve-bore shotgun.

With another screech, Knuckles was off again at a speed that was surprising for someone his age. Albert was nearly knocked off his feet as Weasel took off at a sprint. By the time he reached the gate, Knuckles was nowhere to be seen, but the clatter of his boots could be heard as he disappeared up the road.

There were two deafening explosions as the dark figure emptied both barrels into the backside of the retreating Albert. Weasel reached the car, clambered into the driving seat and started the engine as fast as he could. He jammed it into gear, and with wheel spinning, slithered out into the road, where the door was wrenched open and Albert threw himself into the passenger seat, slamming the door shut as the car sped off up the road. It was quite a way up the road before Knuckles appeared in their headlights, still running for all he was worth. They skidded to a halt just in front of him and he scrambled into the back seat. "Told you it was a bad idea," he said, gasping.

Albert just groaned.

"I hope you aren't bleeding all over my seat," said Weasel.

"Serves you right if I am," said Albert. "You'd better get me to a hospital before I bleed to death."

"Don't be stupid," said Weasel. "How're you going to explain that?"

"I'll say I was shot," said Albert. "But I think they might guess anyway."

"No," said Weasel. "I'll take you back to Knuckles' gaff. You can have a pleasant evening relaxing on the bed while Knuckles goes to work with the tweezers."

"If I get blood poisoning and die, I'll sue you," said Albert, but didn't argue further.

*****

Weasel had booked a room at the pub, and so went straight to his room to get some sleep before the morning. At breakfast, he got talking with the landlord, who had lived in the area for years, and knew all about the artist who lived a reclusive life at the old farm up the dale.

"Does he welcome visitors?" asked Weasel. "I'm quite interested in art."

"Don't suppose he'd mind," said the landlord. "He has to make a living, doesn't he? I wonder if he still has that old bus."

"Bus?"

"Yes," said the landlord. "He used to live in it and travel around the country in it. He arrived here in it a few years ago before he moved into the farm."

"Maybe I'll take a ride up there this morning."

"Well it looks as if the weather should stay fine today," said the landlord. "Will you be staying another night?"

"No," said Weasel. "I'll have to get back, but I've had a nice break up here."

So, after checking out, he got into his car and headed back up the dale to the old farm. It looked a lot more friendly with the sun shining, and after the recent rain, everything was a clean fresh green. This time he drove straight into the farmyard and parked outside the farmhouse. The place looked deserted, but as he got out of his car, the door of the farmhouse opened and a youngish man appeared, dressed in denims with what looked like a potter's apron liberally covered in paint of many colours.

"Can I help you?" he asked, amiably.

"I was told that an artist lived and worked up here and I was interested to meet him." Weasel grinned. "And by your apron, I assume you must be he?"

"I dabble a bit," said Josh. "What is your interest?"

"Quite keen on watercolours," said Weasel, having heard the term but not really knowing what it was.

"I used to do quite a bit at one time," said Josh. "But I prefer acrylics or oils now."

"Well, you have some marvellous scenery up here. Do you do landscapes?"

"I do a bit of everything. Come inside and I'll show you some of my work."

At that moment, the old sheepdog came ambling out and walked over to them. It went over to Weasel and sniffed him, as dogs do, and then growled.

"That's strange," said Josh. "He's usually friendly with everyone. I usually joke that he would lick any intruder to death."

"Well, he doesn't seem to like the smell of me for some reason," said Weasel.

"Perhaps he's still a bit upset," said Josh. "We had intruders last night and they broke into the barn where Leonardo usually sleeps."

"Leonardo?"

"Just my jokey name for him, after the artist."

"But why would anyone want to break in there?"

"After farm machinery, I would think," said Josh. "It's worth a lot of money these days, but they were unlucky as I haven't any. Anyway, they must have heard Leonardo growling and left in a hurry."

"Chap at the pub said you had a bus," said Weasel. "Would that be worth anything?"

"Doubt it," said Josh. "Anyway, I got rid of that ages ago."

Weasel had the feeling that he was lying about that, by the way he said it, but decided there was no point in pursuing it further. So after having a quick look at some of the paintings he set off back to Porton Down.

*****

Sir Malcolm was sitting in his office, looking through some papers when Weasel arrived.

"So you have some news for me, I hope?" said Sir Malcolm, without looking up.

"Yes and no," said Weasel.

"And what is that supposed to mean?"

"Well," said Weasel, "It hasn't been that easy finding him."

"That's why I gave you the job," said Sir Malcolm, looking him in the eye. "You are supposed to be the best. So where is he?"

"Can't tell you that, exactly," said Weasel. "He went to ground for a while at a farm in the wilds near the Lakes, but when we found the place, he had gone."

"So you haven't found him."

"He must have abandoned his car somewhere up there, but it seems the chap at the farm used to have a bus that he travelled around in, like a new-age traveller, and I think that our man is travelling in this bus."

"So?"

"So it would be useful if you could alert your people to look out for such a bus," said Weasel as if talking to a backward five-year-old. "In the meantime I'll follow up any leads we have as to the whereabouts of the bus. I think it likely that he will be going to the sort of places that a new-age traveller might go to. I have someone making out a list of possibilities. I'll keep you informed."

"Yes you will," said Sir Malcolm with an icy glare.

It was obvious that the interview was over, so Weasel left the office and went back to his car, which was parked in the car park at the front of the building.

He sat there for a minute or two to collect his thoughts. He hadn't actually got anyone making out a list for him but he thought it might be a good idea, so he rang Albert who was not too pleased to hear from him.

"Look Albert," said Weasel. "It's not as if you can go out in your tender condition. Get on the internet and make me that list. Any folk festivals, new-age travellers' meetings. He must be trying to hide himself among a group of them. He would stand out like a sore thumb on his own. So, as soon as you can."

"It's all right for you," said Albert. "But I'm in a lot of pain here."

"Nothing to the pain you'll be in if I don't get that list ASAP."

*****

A few days later, Albert had a list of possible places to start the search, mostly pop festivals or horse fairs. He was able to move around a bit more now the tenderness had subsided a little, so was able to answer the door when someone knocked loudly that afternoon.

"I'm looking for a Mr. Albert Birch." It was Walter Greenbank, and behind him stood two heavily built men in suits. Albert didn't like the look of them.

"And who might be looking for him?" said Albert, trying to look unconcerned, at which one of the heavies stepped forward, grabbed Albert by the collar and pushed him back into the house, followed closely by the other two.

"We are," said Greenbank in a quiet voice that froze the blood. "I assume that you are the guy we're looking for?"

"My name is Albert Birch, as it happens," said Albert. "How can I help you?"

"We work for the government of the U S of A," said Greenbank. "And our masters are really keen to have words with a Mr. Alan Westbrook."

"Never heard of him," said Albert.

"But you might know him as Peter Finch," said Greenbank. "Or perhaps he still uses his first name of Alan. Whatever he calls himself, we want to have a word with him, and we know you are on his track, so perhaps you could share your knowledge with us?"

"Well, if I am 'on his track' as you say," said Albert, trying to put a brave face on it, "I'll be working for Her Majesty's Government and therefore cannot divulge any information that I might possess."

"Perhaps you don't understand the seriousness of the situation," said Greenbank. "It doesn't matter whether you think your bosses are more important than ours or not, there's three of us and one of you, so I should think very carefully."

"OK," said Albert. "I am looking for him, but as yet have not got very far."

"So how far have you got? You seem to have quite a lot of paper scattered around the table over there. Perhaps we'll start looking there." He walked over to the table and glanced through the sheets of paper.

"So you're looking for him at pop festivals and horse fairs. Why is that?"

"We think he's in a bus," said Albert.

"Bus?"

"Yes. It's a converted bus for living in."

"Well thank you very much, Mr Birch," said Greenbank, walking towards the door. "You have been very helpful. You two, thank Mr Birch properly, will you?" He walked out into the front garden and headed for the gate, stopping momentarily when he heard a shout from inside. Then it was quiet and the two heavies came out and closed the door.

"Can't you two do anything right?" asked Greenbank.

"Sorry, Boss," said one of the heavies. "But he was as slippery as an eel."

Twenty-four

Three weeks had passed since Alan and Maggie had arrived in the forest, and Alan was quite enjoying the life. However, Maggie had become very bored with the forest, and was also getting quite jumpy, thinking that they would be found any time now.

Walter had been enjoying having an enthusiastic pupil again, but was beginning to wonder how long they would be staying. Most normal people would be getting back to their everyday lives after two or three weeks at the most, but Alan showed no signs of finishing their visit, and Walter was beginning to be a bit suspicious. Perhaps this wasn't just a holiday. Perhaps they were hiding from something or someone, and that made Walter uneasy. The last thing he wanted was to have strangers descending upon him and upsetting his tranquil life of seclusion. And even if no one came, he was beginning to feel that he would like to have the place to himself again. Perhaps he should say something. He would have a word with Maggie. She looked as if she had had enough of the forest life.

That evening, after their usual supper round the fire, Alan got up to go back to the bus, but Maggie remained seated.

"You go on," she said. "I'll be in in a few minutes."

"OK," he said. "Don't be too long."

After he had gone, she and Walter sat in silence for a few minutes. Walter was wondering just how to broach the subject of their leaving when Maggie saved him the trouble.

"You must think we're never going," she said.

"Well I did wonder," he replied. "I have enjoyed having you here for the last few weeks, but I would really like to get back to normal now."

"I'll have a word with Alan," she said. "To tell you the truth I would like to be moving on myself. Don't get me wrong. I have enjoyed our stay and you have been very kind, but three weeks in the woods is more than enough for me."

"Thank you for being so understanding," said Walter.

Maggie got up and made her way to the bus where she found Alan already in bed. She sat down on the end of the bed.

"What was that all about?" he asked.

"I think it is time that we moved on," she said, "and I think Walter would like to get back to his solitary life without us being under his feet all the time."

"Did he say that?"

"Not in so many words. He's enjoyed having us here, but I think we've outstayed our welcome."

"I thought we had found a good place to hide out," said Alan.

"We can't stay here for ever," she snapped. "I'd go out of my mind, and anyway they would be sure to find us eventually."

"So where do we go next, then?" said Alan.

"I don't know," said Maggie. "All I know is that I've had enough of this existence, on the run all the time. I thought I could do it, but now I know I can't. I want to go back to normality. I want you to give them what they want so that we can settle down to a normal life."

"You know I can't do that."

"Then you're on your own. I want out. I'm sorry, Alan, but I want you to drop me off at the nearest railway station."

"But why?" said Alan. "I thought we were getting on OK."

"I lived with Peter for over thirty years, and I was sick to death of his boring life, which made mine boring too. And when he fell off that cliff I was horrified but also relieved to be free of his boring ways. Free to do whatever I liked. And you seemed different, exciting, and for a while you were. But now you seem to be turning into Peter and becoming boring. But not just boring, dangerous as well, and not in an exciting sort of way. A worrying sort of way, and I've had enough."

"But you would be safer with me," said Alan. "They're looking for both of us, not just me."

"I'll take my chances. If we split up now, they won't know that I'm not with you and will go on looking for the pair of us. That'll make it safer for you as well, and they won't know where to start looking for me. I don't know myself where I'll go."

"I wish you would stay," said Alan. "I've got rather used to you."

"That's the trouble," said Maggie. "You're used to me, and I'm used to you. It was all a big mistake and I want to go my own way now. I'm sorry."

"So am I," said Alan. "We'll leave in the morning."

Walter was pleased when he received the news the following morning, though also a little sad. He hadn't realised it, but he had enjoyed the company. However, he valued his solitary existence more, so he cheerfully waved them off as the old bus trundled off down the forest track.

*****

When they were clear of the forest, Alan headed the bus for Bristol. He hadn't a clue where he would go after he had dropped Maggie at the station. He pulled up in the station car park and carried Maggie's cases for her as they walked into the station.

"Let me buy you a coffee before you go," said Alan, hoping that he could make her change her mind.

"OK then," she said. "But then I'll have to go."

They walked into the café and Maggie sat down while Alan went to get the coffees. There was a bit of a queue and the service was a bit slow, but eventually he had the two lattes he had ordered. When he turned towards the table where he had left Maggie, he saw to his dismay that she had gone. He put the coffees on the table and dashed out towards the platforms, but she was nowhere to be seen. So he walked dejectedly back into the café and sat down to drink his own coffee before setting off again.

He had just started to drink his coffee, when someone pulled back the chair beside him and sat down. To his amazement he found that it was Maggie.

Alan gasped. "I thought you had gone."

"Just had to answer an urgent call of nature," she said.

"Have you thought where you will go?"

"Not entirely," she said. "But I know where I shall go first. Then I'll decide what to do next."

"And where will you go first?"

"It's best you don't know," she said. "If these people catch up with you, and I hope they don't, I don't want you to be able to tell them where I am."

"Why would they want to know that if they have me?"

"I don't know," she said, "but I don't want to take the risk."

They sat in silence while they finished their drinks. Alan was wondering how he could persuade her to stay with him, or whether he should. After all, she would be in danger if she stayed with him. But if they went their separate ways, where would he go now? He had talked about going to pop festivals and getting lost in the crowds. But he didn't like pop festivals or the mud or the discomfort. He could join a band of new-age travellers, but he didn't know where he would find any. Perhaps he should go abroad? But that idea didn't appeal to him.

"Look," he said, "why don't we arrange a rendezvous for, say, midsummer next year? If we have both decided that we would like to meet up again, we'll go, and if not we won't. Easy as that."

"All right," she said. "I don't see why not. Where do you suggest?"

"I don't know," said Alan. "How about the top of Blackpool tower at midday on the twenty-first of June?"

"That sounds as good as anything," she said. "Maybe we'll meet again, maybe not."

Finally, they said their goodbyes. Maggie walked off to buy her ticket and Alan strolled aimlessly back to his bus. As he turned the corner into the car park, he stopped short when he saw that there was someone inspecting his bus. It didn't seem to be an official. Perhaps it was just someone interested in unusual vehicles. He waited for a few minutes, but the fellow didn't seem to be thinking of going away. There was nothing for it but to see what he wanted, so he walked purposefully into the car park and up to the bus.

"Can I help you?" he asked the stranger.

"Sorry?" came the reply.

"You seem to be very interested in my bus."

"Oh," he said. "Yes, it is an interesting conversion. Did you do it yourself?"

"No," said Alan. "I have borrowed it from a friend for a bit of a touring holiday." It was the first thing that came into his mind.

The stranger was about his age and there was something vaguely familiar about him. He seemed quite ordinary. He wore an old sports jacket and had rather baggy trousers. His shirt was open at the top button and he wore an old-fashioned raincoat which was unbuttoned and flapped about as he moved. His hair was unkempt and blew this way and that in the breeze.

"Do I know you?" asked Alan.

"Shouldn't think so," came the reply. "Williams is the name. Justin Williams. Professor Justin Williams to be precise. And I do like to be precise. Don't you?"

"Well, yes actually," said Alan. "It's a bit of a coincidence, but I used to work with someone called Justin Williams, many, many years ago. He was an electronics nut."

"I still am."

"Good grief," said Alan. "How amazing that after all these years we should bump into each other in a station car park."

"Yes, it is rather amazing," said Justin.

"Do you live in Bristol?"

"No," said Justin. "I have been down to a symposium at the university. I'm about to catch a train back to Yorkshire."

"I could give you a lift back," said Alan. "I have had enough of touring and I thought I'd make my way back up north. Mind you, it won't be as comfortable as the train, nor as quick, but I would enjoy the company."

"Well, I'm in no particular hurry to get back," said Justin. "I'd love to drive back with you."

Alan climbed into the bus and shifted some stuff about to make room for Justin to sit at the front so they could talk. It seemed that Justin was travelling light and had just his briefcase with him. As soon as he had settled himself, Alan started the engine and drove out into the traffic. Justin said very little as they found their way through the traffic and headed out towards the motorway. Once on the M5, they settled to a steady speed of sixty miles an hour in the inside lane.

"If I remember rightly," said Justin, "you were into computers and the like. What are you doing now?"

Alan wasn't sure how much he should say, but thought it wouldn't hurt to talk in vague terms. "Yes," he said, "I'm still doing a bit."

"Freelance?"

"Something like that," said Alan. "Nothing on at the moment though."

"I seem to remember you were trying to link your software to various sensing devices. I seem to remember you thought you could read atomic structures using an electron microscope. I don't suppose that was successful?"

"Depends what you mean by successful," said Alan.

"Well, did it work?"

"I did get some good results," said Alan, trying to be a bit evasive, "but I dropped that line of research a while ago. Thought it might be a bit dangerous."

"Dangerous? How do you mean?"

"Well, being able to read DNA sequences is one thing, but what happens if someone tries to synthesise DNA from a modified sequence? Mind you, I don't think that would be possible anyway."

"Oh, I think it might," said Justin. "Just think of the benefits it would bring to medicine. You could create viruses to target cancer cells, or other viruses. You could fight almost any disease."

"Yes, I used to think that," said Alan. "But what if the technology got into the hands of the wrong people? Think what they could do with it."

"Well, maybe we should keep it from those people."

"Easier said than done," said Alan. "I'm not religious, but it seems to go against anything that religion teaches. It doesn't seem right to interfere with God's creations."

"You don't believe all that, do you?"

"I really don't know what I believe," said Alan.

"Well, if there is a god," said Justin, "why would he be in the form that the various religions portray him? If you go by the scriptures, he is a male mammal. Not a furry one scuttling about in the long grass, but a magic one that you can't see. Then, what sort of god is he? Apparently he created the world and covered it with beautiful plants. A really idyllic place. Then, not happy with that, he creates a load of animals to eat the plants. Then, still not happy with that, he creates a load of carnivores to eat the plant eaters. Quite a sense of humour, eh?"

"I don't think you are meant to take it that literally," said Alan.

"Oh, I think you are," said Justin. "After all, he was invented by Bronze Age Man, and in those days people would believe anything. Only they didn't think it through properly."

"Well, I don't think any amount of argument or discussion will determine anything. You either believe or you don't, and belief doesn't have to be in the form it is written down in ancient writings."

"The thing is," said Justin, "that whatever you may believe, you have to accept that work of this sort could benefit mankind tremendously."

"I agree," said Alan. "That's why I started this work in the first place."

"So what made you change your mind?"

"I did some work for the authorities," said Alan. "And they did the dirty on me. They tried to get the software for themselves and push me out of the equation."

"So it's personal," said Justin.

"Well there is an element of that," said Alan. "But it showed me what might happen in the hands of people like that. So I opted out altogether."

"A bit defeatist, don't you think?"

"Not really. These people can be really dangerous."

"So that's the reason why you're chugging around the country in a converted bus?"

"Yes."

"I have a private research lab, up in Yorkshire, hidden away where no one can find it," said Justin. "I do all my research up there out of the way of politicians and people who think they know better. Why don't you come and join me? They would never find you there."

"Sounds tempting," said Alan. "But I don't have the facilities for synthesising molecules, and I don't think anyone else does either. Thanks anyway, but I don't think it would work."

"Well, the offer is there," said Justin.

They continued their journey in silence, but the idea kept running through Alan's brain. It would be good to have somewhere to hide out, and it would be good to get back to work. He had actually been missing it quite a lot, but he was still torn between completing what he originally set out to do and keeping the whole thing safe from the people who were after him.

Twenty-five

Weasel sat nervously in the foyer of Sir Malcolm's office, waiting to be called in. Things hadn't gone to plan. It should have been easy to track Westbrook down, but he had managed to give them the slip. Weasel didn't even know who had done it or why. And now he had to explain it all to Sir Malcolm, and he wasn't looking forward to it. Sir Malcolm was not one to be crossed, as Weasel had found to his cost in the past. Although Sir Malcolm was working for a government department, Weasel thought that he had agendas of his own. What they were he didn't know, but it meant that he didn't work by the book, and this frightened Weasel. He would much rather face an opponent with a knife than not know what someone like Sir Malcolm had in store for him.

The lift doors opened and a slim, dark-haired secretary came out and walked towards Weasel.

"You can go up now," she said.

"Thanks," said Weasel and walked towards the lift.

"The stairs," said the girl bluntly.

So it was like that. Only favoured visitors used the lift. He had used it last time he was here, but it would seem that he was definitely out of favour this time.

There were three flights of stairs and Weasel was puffing when he got to the dark wooden door that led into Sir Malcolm's office. He knocked and waited. There was no response, so he waited for a while then knocked again. This time a voice boomed out, "Come." So he opened the door and went in.

Sir Malcolm was sitting behind his desk with a folder open in front of him. A smart-looking, blonde was sitting opposite him.

As Weasel entered, Sir Malcolm closed the folder and handed it to the woman, who stood up and turned to leave.

"Keep me informed," said Sir Malcolm.

"Of course," she said and walked purposefully to the door. She had such an air of authority about her that Weasel opened the door for her. She walked out without a glance at Weasel, who closed the door behind her. He walked over to the desk and stood waiting, but he wasn't invited to sit.

"Well," said Sir Malcolm, "what do you have to say for yourself?"

"We're still looking for him…"

"So I imagine," cut in Sir Malcolm. "But with no success it would seem.

"Well yes, but you didn't tell…"

"I didn't tell you it was urgent? I didn't tell you it was dangerous? These are things you should know, that's why I hired you."

"I'm sorry," said Weasel. "We'll do better next time."

"Next time?" snapped Sir Malcolm. "There won't be a next time. You're fired."

"What about my fee? My expenses?"

"No result, no pay. Now go." Weasel went, and as he closed the door behind him, the side door into the office opened and a man in a smart suit entered. "There are some loose ends to tidy up," said Sir Malcolm. The man didn't answer but gave a slight nod of the head and headed for the door that Weasel had left by.

*****

Alan had decided, as he hadn't anywhere in particular to go, that he would take Justin all the way to his final destination at the edge of the North York Moors. They left the main road before they got to Pickering and took a narrow lane that headed up, but before they reached the steep climb up onto the moor, they came to a run-down looking set of farm buildings.

"Just pull in here," said Justin.

"Here?"

"Yes, this is it. My own private little kingdom."

"Not my idea of a high-tech lab."

"Exactly," said Justin. "I'll show you round if you like, unless you're in a hurry to be elsewhere."

"I would like that very much," said Alan. "I must admit that I'm intrigued."

They got out of the bus and Justin led them to the old farm cottage and unlocked the front door.

"Please come in," he said, leading the way. Inside it was quite cosy and very rustic. Justin put a match to the fire that had already been set in the wood-burning stove. "We'll leave this to warm up while I show you the lab, if you'd like to follow me through here."

They went through a door at the back of the room which led into an old farmhouse kitchen. Beyond that was a utility room and scullery leading into a store room at the back.

"Don't tell me this is your lab?" said Alan, looking around. There were some old bits of scientific equipment on shelves at the side.

"Good grief, no," said Justin, going to the back of the store room and dragging a sack of potatoes away from the wall. Alan looked puzzled. Justin then went to an old mangle and started to turn the handle.

"What are you doing?" said Alan, thinking that Justin must be off his head and starting to feel rather uneasy. But as he watched, he realised that a section of the wall was sliding to the side to expose a tunnel into the hillside that rose steeply behind the house. "Well, this is very James Bond."

"I got the idea from 'The Man From U.N.C.L.E.'" said Justin. "It amused me but has turned out to be very practical. Do come in."

They went through the opening, into the tunnel and Justin pressed a button to close the door behind them. Although the tunnel was fairly roughly cut out of the rock, there were lights that came on as they walked through. Also it seemed quite dry. After about fifty yards they came to another door, which was more like a bulkhead in a submarine. Justin took out a pen-like object and pointed it at the door.

"Sonic screwdriver?" said Alan.

"Not quite," said Justin. "This is similar to the key fob you use to open your car doors, but more sophisticated." He clicked something on the pen and a light came on in the middle of the door. He clicked something else and the door swung open. "Pretty well bomb-proof."

"So it would seem," said Alan, following Justin into the laboratory, which seemed packed with all the latest equipment. "How on earth do you fund all this?"

"Freelance development projects, mostly," said Justin. "I have an office in York where I can communicate with potential customers. They don't need to know where the work is done."

"What about workers?" said Alan. "Won't they talk to friends?"

"No one else works here. I have other more public labs in other locations and I ship the equipment out there as required. This is my own private kingdom, all paid for by big corporations and universities. I do all the design work here and the development and other donkey work is done by employees at the other sites."

"So you have a company that does the business?"

"That's right," said Justin. "The Cymru Corporation. Being a Williams, I use my Welsh heritage as a corporate image. Fancy joining the gang?"

"Doing what?"

"Well you could work with me here, carrying on with the work you have been doing with no one to bother you. Wouldn't you fancy that?"

"Yes," said Alan. "But what's in it for you?"

"My corporation would offer our services to medicine to produce the genetically created products to fight diseases and other illnesses. In that way we can retain control of the technology and make sure it is only used for good. You would receive a salary, of course. I wouldn't want you to work for nothing."

"I never sell my code or copyright, you realise," said Alan. "That would have to be agreed from the start."

"Perfectly reasonable," said Justin. "As long as the corporation can have use of it to carry out its work. Look, why don't you sleep on it and let me know tomorrow what you have decided? You can stay here if you like."

"I really must get the bus back to its actual owner," said Alan. "So I'll take it back to him this evening and collect my own car and come back tomorrow morning if that is all right by you."

"I don't see why not," said Justin. "But I must ask you to swear not to tell anyone about this place. You are the only person other than myself who knows about it."

"Of course," said Alan. "But what about the people who built it?"

"It was originally a Ministry of Defence bunker, but they abandoned it years ago. As far as they know it was filled in. I managed to get hold of it before they actually destroyed it and got it converted for use as a warehouse. At least, that is what the contractors thought it was for. I got some local people to make the work benches and shelves etc. and I installed them all myself."

"Quite an undertaking for one man," said Alan, looking around.

"I didn't do it all at once. I got a couple of benches to start with, and added more as time went on, so it wasn't too difficult. I did all the wiring myself. That was easy enough. The plumbing was a bit of a problem. I had to learn about that from scratch, but it was easy enough when I learnt how to do it. I had a few leaks in the early days but I'm quite expert at it now. The gas cylinders are a bit of a problem. Rather heavy to move about, but I made a special wheeled rack for them and that works fine. I told the suppliers that I did a bit of hobby silversmithing work to explain the hydrogen and oxygen cylinders. I don't know what they think the nitrogen is for. They've never asked. I've got a little silversmith's workshop in the barn outside. That's where they deliver the cylinders. I think they think I'm just a harmless eccentric.

"Anyway, you take your bus back to its owner and I'll see you tomorrow."

*****

It was dark when Alan drove the bus into the farmyard. Josh was just walking across the yard from the barn and stopped in his tracks when he saw his bus driving in. Alan leaned out as he brought it to a halt next to Josh.

"Thought it was about time that I brought her back," he said.

"Better put her in the barn," said Josh. "I'll open the doors for you."

After they had put the bus into the barn, they went into the house.

"Wasn't sure if I'd see her again," said Josh.

"Nor was I, but I seem to have avoided being found, so far. Have you had any trouble?"

"A bit," he said. "But I sent them packing. One of them got a backside full of lead shot. They've not been back since."

"Sorry about that," said Alan. "I had hoped they would never think of looking here."

"No harm done. Where's Maggie?"

"We parted company," said Alan. "She had had enough of travelling about with the constant worry about being found. So she went her own way. I must say I miss her."

"Where did she go?"

"Don't know. I don't think she did either, and she didn't know where I was going because I hadn't made up my mind what I was going to do when we parted."

"So what now?"

"Could I possibly stay here tonight? I'll leave in the morning and take my own car. I'm sure they will have stopped looking for that ages ago."

"No problem," said Josh. "Have you eaten?"

"Well no, actually."

"Beans on toast be OK?"

"Sounds great."

Alan still wasn't sure whether he should take up Justin's offer. It all sounded too good to be true, but he couldn't think of a better place to hide out. If he didn't take up the offer, where would he go? He could go abroad, but to do that he would have to pass through customs. He could disappear into the wilds of Scotland or Wales, or maybe the remote islands in the north. But what would he do? How would he make a living? The more he thought about it the better the offer sounded.

*****

The next morning found Alan driving into Justin's yard and pulling up outside the cottage. The door opened and Justin appeared with a broad smile on his face.

"So you've decided?" said Justin. "You won't be sorry."

"I hope not," said Alan. "Where shall I put my stuff?"

"I've got a room prepared for you just along from the lab. You'll be safe there from prying eyes, and it is really quite comfortable."

Justin picked up Alan's suitcase. "God, what have you got in here?"

"Let me take it." Alan took the case and followed Justin into the underground complex.

"I'm not sure that I will like living underground."

"Wait 'til you see it. You may be surprised."

And he was surprised. They entered the flat via a spacious hallway which had several doors leading off it. Apparently there were two bedrooms, and a bathroom. The door they took led into a large living room which was luxuriously appointed, with wide-screen television, a massive hi-fi system, a pool table in a large alcove and what looked like a large window looking out onto the moor.

"I thought we were underground?" said Alan, walking over to the window.

"We are," said Justin. That is an HD TV screen. The camera is on the moor about a hundred feet above our heads. Good, isn't it?"

"It certainly is."

"Anyway, I'll leave you to settle in. I'll come and fetch you for something to eat at twelve thirty."

"Thanks. That would be great."

Alan fetched the rest of his meagre possessions into his new flat and set up his computer in the little office that was tucked into another alcove off the living room. He found that he had broadband piped in so he was all set to start. This man had thought of everything. It was a bit daunting and more than a little bit strange. How could he afford all this? He must be doing very well in whatever he did to make money. Alan had never found that doing clever things made you much money. It was the non-technical people who made the money. Perhaps Justin had partners who made the money for him. Well he would just have to accept it for now, but he would keep alert for any signs of betrayal.

Twenty-six

Weasel didn't have much chance of getting back into Sir Malcolm's good books, but he thought that if he could track down Westbrook he might manage it. So he decided to call on Albert to see if he had got anywhere with his investigation. He didn't hold out much hope but thought it worth a try. When he arrived at Albert's and got no reply to his hammering at the door, he went round the back and forced his way in. The scene that met him made his blood run cold. Was this the work of Sir Malcolm? He knew the man had no qualms about ridding himself of embarrassing situations. He didn't do it himself, of course, but there was always someone willing to do it for him. After all, he had done so in the past, himself, for the right sort of fee. The trouble was, that with that sort of work, that once you had done it they had control of you. There was no retiring. But why bother about poor old Albert? He was just a minion and knew nothing. Maybe it wasn't Sir Malcolm. Then who? Who else was interested in Westbrook? The Americans, obviously, but would they go to such lengths? Quite possibly. Perhaps he could find out more and get back into Sir Malcolm's good books. But where would he start? Maybe they would be staying locally. It would be easy to ask around at the pubs and small hotels to see if they had any American guests.

So Weasel set off on a tour of the local hostelries in search of American guests. Most tourists would be staying at the larger centres like Kendal and the Lake District and not in little hotels around this area. His first port of call was his own local where he met up with his team of local spies, as he liked to think of them. Most would call them riff-raff and be closer to the point. He sat in his usual corner with a pint of his favourite beer and sent text messages to his little team. It wasn't long before they were all seated round the table in the corner, each with a pint of the same brew.

*****

The next day, Alan was introduced to his new lab. It was vastly better than the one he had had at Blakely House. What's more it was full of devices that he hadn't seen before and were obviously developments that Justin had been working on.

First he set about getting his computer in order and installing his software. He still ran it from a memory stick that was booby-trapped to stop anyone getting hold of it, with a permanent backup on the web.

At about ten o'clock, Justin appeared with a mug of coffee in each hand.

"I see you've settled in," he said. "Hope I've thought of everything you need."

"And a lot more by the looks of it. What's this thing here?"

"Ah. That's something I've been working on for some time now. It started when I was in nanotechnology and I needed to assemble items on a molecular scale. This is a development of that and can assemble molecules from individual atoms. The first version was manually controlled, but this one can be controlled by a computer, and that's where you come in."

"Quite a challenge," said Alan. "I'll have to study the interface requirements first. Then I'll see how it could interface with my programme."

Justin handed Alan a large folder. "Well, you could start with this. I'll leave you to browse. I've got an appointment in Leeds this afternoon so I'll see you again this evening."

Left to his own devices, Alan took the opportunity to examine everything in the laboratory. He also went online to see what was happening in the world outside. He had been living in virtual isolation for several weeks now and felt it was about time he got back into the real world.

There was a little kitchen attached to his flat, stocked with all sorts of things, from frozen meals for one to fresh fruit and vegetables.

He took one of the prepared meals from the freezer and put it into the microwave. He wasn't sure whether he was going to like this sort of existence, as he preferred the company of others and wasn't really a solitary sort of person, but he could manage for a while.

After he had eaten, he went to explore the rest of the complex. Further into the hillside was a storeroom, a generator room and what looked like some sort of communications room. The corridor continued further into the hillside and finally terminated at the bottom of a stairwell with a spiral metal staircase leading upwards.

Halfway up, he had to stop for a rest. It was like climbing up inside a lighthouse, but much taller. Eventually he made it to the top and found himself inside a small domed room with a single door which was well secured with hefty bolts.

He slid the bolts back, one by one and eventually the door swung open to reveal a view across the open moor. Outside, he pushed the door shut and walked a little way up the hill. When he looked back, he could hardly make out the dome as it was well camouflaged by the heather and the small grassy hummocks. As he was out, and it was a nice day, he thought he would go for a stroll over the moor. The place was deserted except for the grouse and other birds that lived there. There were a few stunted trees at the top so he sat himself down in the shade to enjoy the scenery.

When he returned, he thought at first that he wouldn't be able to find the doorway, but as he got closer, he realised that he recognised the hump in the ground and walked over to it. The door, though, was harder to find. The whole mound was covered in turf and had obviously had plenty of time to settle into a natural looking state. Eventually he managed to find the opening side of the door and pulled it open. Inside, he slid the bolts back into place and headed back down the staircase. It was nice to know that there was a way out in case of an emergency.

*****

It had been a month since Weasel had resumed his search for Alan Westbrook, and he hadn't had much success. He was sitting in the living room of his little cottage, wondering what his next move should be, when there was a knock at the door. Weasel leapt to his feet. No one came knocking at his door at this time in the evening, at least no one he wanted to see. As he stood there wondering if he should make his escape out of the back door, the knocking came again, only louder and more urgent this time. He made up his mind and made a dash for the back door, slid the bolt and slipped silently into the back yard. He moved silently over to the gate and peered out. The coast was clear and he was about to open the gate and disappear into the darkness when something jabbed him in the ribs.

"Going somewhere?" said a gruff voice with a distinctly American accent. Weasel raised his hands.

"OK, inside," said the voice. Weasel turned and walked back to the door, opened it and went inside, followed by the unseen figure behind him. The knocking was still going on.

"Better answer it," said the voice. Weasel turned to see a giant of a man in a suit with his index finger pointed at him.

"You don't have a gun?" asked Weasel.

"Oh, yes I have. But I didn't need to use it this time, did I?"

Weasel went to the door and opened it to come face to face with two more men in suits. The one standing further back was the bigger of the two. The one in the doorway was shorter and fatter.

"Walter Greenbank at your service. May I come in?"

Weasel backed into the living room, followed by Greenbank and his other heavy.

"Sit down, Mr....?"

"Weasel," said Weasel.

"Sit down, Mr Weasel," said Greenbank. Weasel sat.

"What do you want?" asked Weasel, trying to keep his voice steady.

"I believe we have an aim in common, Mr Weasel."

"Weasel. Just Weasel." Greenbank looked puzzled, but continued.

"We are both looking for a Mr Alan Westbrook, sometimes going under the name of Finch."

"Maybe."

"Well it's like this, Mr Weasel." said Greenbank. "If you find him before we do I want you to tell me before you tell anyone else. In fact I don't want you to tell anyone else at all. Got it?"

"Got it," said Weasel.

"Good," said Greenbank. Here is my card. I'll expect to hear from you soon. Very soon." He clicked his fingers and the two heavies went to the door and opened it and Greenbank walked out. Before closing the door again, the second heavy turned and grinned at Weasel.

"Don't try too hard," he said, "'cos it will spoil all our fun."

Weasel sat there as the sound of the door closing reverberated around the cottage. He didn't know who this Greenbank was or why he wanted Westbrook. What should he do? Maybe it would be best to speak to Sir Malcolm. Perhaps he could get some protection, or at least get back into Sir Malcolm's good books for letting him know. But how to do it? It was most likely that his phone would be tapped and his mobile monitored. Who knows what these secret service people got up to? And if he went to see Sir Malcolm in person, how would he know he wasn't being followed?

Weasel didn't like problems.

*****

Alan had been progressing quite well with his work and was very impressed with the equipment that Justin had produced. It was almost as if he had designed it especially for this purpose, but that wasn't possible, as he hadn't known what Alan had been working on. After all, it *was* secret.

He had been working in this underground lab for about six weeks now and he was beginning to feel a bit claustrophobic. It would be nice to get out for a bit. But where could he go? He would quite like to see Josh again, but would that put Josh in danger? He thought probably not as no one had linked him with Josh as yet.

"Do you think it's a good idea, going out where you might be seen?" asked Justin when he met Alan on his way out.

"I need to get outside for a while," said Alan, "before I go completely mad. I'll keep away from the main roads so there shouldn't be any chance of anyone seeing me, unless they already know I'm here and are watching."

"No chance of that," said Justin. "Good luck then. See you later."

Alan kept to his word and took the back lanes across the moors. As he approached Josh's farm he decided to park further up the road and walk across the fields to the farm. That way he would be less likely to be seen.

He found a place where he could pull his car off the road and leave it where it would be unlikely to be noticed, and set off across the fields. He had to climb to the top of a low ridge before dropping down the other side to the field behind the farm.

At the top of the ridge was a small rocky outcrop and a few stunted trees, where he was surprised to see a man sitting on a rock eating a sandwich. He was looking down towards the farm and Alan realised that you could see the entrance to the farm and the road leading down to it from here.

The man had a Thermos flask on the ground beside him and as Alan approached, he bent to pick it up, and that was when he saw Alan. For a moment, Alan thought the man looked startled and a little guilty, as if he had been caught doing something he shouldn't have been doing. But then he smiled.

"Like a cup of coffee?" he asked, pleasantly.

"That would be nice," said Alan. "Thanks very much."

"You gave me a start," he said. "You don't get many people up here."

It was then that Alan noticed the binoculars.

"What are you doing up here?" asked Alan casually.

"Interested in wildlife. This is good place 'cos you can see it all from up here and there's no one to disturb them. I was just watching those red kites up there." He pointed and Alan suddenly realised that there were two large birds circling above them. "They'll be down here when we've gone to see if we've left any scraps for them. Where are you headed?"

"Nowhere in particular," said Alan. "I was driving along the lane back there and thought this might be a good spot for a walk."

"Well you can head down there past the farm and up onto the ridge behind it. Or you can head off that way into the valley. You meet the river about a mile down there."

"That sounds good," said Alan. "I'll bear it in mind for another time, but I'd better get back to the car now." He looked at his watch. "Just had half an hour to fill in, but better get on now. Thanks for the coffee. Nice to meet you."

"And you," said the man.

Alan thought he could feel the stranger's eyes on his back as he walked back down to his car, but managed not to turn round and look. Perhaps he had better leave the visit to Josh for another time. So with a feeling of intense disappointment, he set off back to the lab.

*****

"Are you sure it was him?" asked Weasel.

"As sure as I can be," said Knuckles. "I think he was on his way to the farm but changed his mind when he saw me."

"Pity you couldn't have hidden yourself better, then we could be sure."

"Well how was I to know he'd come that way?"

"OK, so it's not your fault, but what do we do now?"

"Don't ask me," said Knuckles. "You're the boss."

"I'll ring Greenbank and tell him we've tracked him down," said Weasel.

"But we don't know where he is, do we?"

"True," said Weasel, "so we'd better find out where he went." Where does that road lead to?"

"Up onto the moors."

"So he could be anywhere," said Weasel. "It's no good, we'll have to stake out that farm again and watch the approach roads. How many can you rope in to do that?"

"Enough, I should think," said Knuckles. "But it'll cost you."

"Payment on results," said Weasel. Knuckles scowled.

Twenty-seven

Alan was still a little perturbed about his encounter on the moors, but felt sure that he hadn't been followed back to the lab. He had taken a circuitous route and had pulled into lay-bys several times to see if he was being followed. The trouble was, that if the fellow on the moors was watching the farm, he will have realised who he was. It was just surprising that he hadn't been followed. Perhaps they were rather inept. He hoped so. He would have to be more careful next time, if there was to be a next time.

Anyway, another three weeks had elapsed since his unfortunate encounter and he was wondering if he dared risk going out again. If he did, it would have to be in disguise, but that wasn't really his forte. He was certain that the farm was being watched and wasn't sure whether it was worth the risk. On the other hand, life was getting very dull and he was feeling rather lonely and it would be great to be able to talk to someone else. Justin was away most of the time and he was left alone in that great big lab. Alan was quite happy to work alone, but he needed company occasionally. He would have to think of a way to get back to the farm without being recognised. A farm labourer wouldn't look out of place, or perhaps a shepherd.

Where could he get a sheepdog? No it would have to be a farm worker.

He got up out of his comfy armchair and made his way out to the lab. But as he reached the door that divided his quarters from the lab, he thought he saw a movement through the small glass window in the door. But that was ridiculous. Justin was away until the end of the week, and no one else had access to the lab.

He crept up to the door and peeked through the small window that was set high in the door. No, he must have been mistaken. There was no one there, but it was strange that he thought he had seen a movement. He scanned the whole of the lab, but there was no sign of anyone. Perhaps the isolation was getting to him, so after another quick glance around the lab, he pushed the door open and went in. As the door closed silently behind him a figure suddenly rose from behind one of the work benches.

It was a woman with long dark hair dressed in casual clothes. In fact, she looked as if she had just come in from a run.

She had her back to Alan, so was completely unaware of his presence, so he stood stock still to see what she was doing. She had taken a small cash-box out of the cupboard and was in the process of opening it. It didn't seem to be locked and she took a bundle of notes out of it, counted out what she wanted and put the rest back in the tin. Then she disappeared from sight as she returned it to its resting place in the cupboard under the bench.

She stood up again, picked up the notes, which she stuffed in a back pocket of her tightly fitting jeans, and turned to leave. That was when she saw Alan.

"Who the hell are you?" she snapped.

"I might ask you the same question," said Alan. "After all you are in my lab."

"Your lab?"

"Yes this is my lab and I'd like to know what you are doing here."

"I don't believe you," she said. "I'm going to call the police."

"I would rather you didn't as this is a top secret facility, and you would certainly be arrested."

"Rubbish," she said. "This is my Uncle Justin's lab. So what are you doing here?"

"I am working on a project with him, but no one else is supposed to know about this place. There are people out there who would stop at nothing to get hold of my work."

"Well to be truthful, Uncle Justin doesn't know that I know how to get in here, but I've been coming in here for ages. I keep things in here that I don't want other people to get their hands on."

"I see," said Alan. "What sort of things?"

"Just things," she said, evasively.

"Tell you what," said Alan. "Come through to the sitting room. I'll make some coffee and you can tell me all about yourself."

"Why would I want to do that?"

"Then I'll tell you a bit about me. Maybe we can help each other."

She looked a bit dubious but eventually agreed, so they went through to the sitting room. Alan put on the kettle and made coffee.

"Don't you find it a bit lonely here?" she asked.

"More than a bit. Yes. I was just working out how I could get out for a while without being spotted."

"Spotted? Who's looking for you?

"Who isn't?" They sat and drank their coffee and Alan outlined the problems he had had with various organisations, including his own government.

"You mean they actually tried to steal your software?"

"Tried being the operative word," said Alan. "But several people, including some innocent bystanders, have been killed for this project. I just don't know who to trust."

"But you trust Uncle Justin?"

"I think so."

"Well, he has some pretty influential friends, so I'd be a bit careful if I were you."

"You mean this might be a set-up?"

"Could be," she said. "How would I know?"

"Well, I thought you might have some idea about your uncle's friends and business contacts."

"I've met a few," she said. "But no one I can think would be in with any spy organisation."

"It doesn't have to be a spy organisation," said Alan. "It could be someone in the employ of the government. My last boss was Sir Malcolm Birch, and I would have thought he was squeaky-clean until he tried to con me."

"I think I met him once," she said. "By the way, I'm Kirsty."

"Pleased to meet you, Kirsty. I'm Alan. So what do you do?"

"My degree is in genetics," she said, "but I have dabbled in all sorts of things. What do you do exactly?"

"I'm into software, and I'm working on an interface with some of this synthesis equipment."

"Trying to synthesise bugs, are you?"

"That's about the size of it."

"I can see why there is so much interest," she said. "Aren't you tempted to scrap the lot so no one can get their hands on it?"

"Yes, I tried that but it kept niggling at me, and when I met Justin, the opportunity seemed too good to turn down."

"Perhaps it was?"

"Maybe you're right. But I just don't know where to go from here."

"I couldn't say," she said. "Maybe you should just disappear."

"I've tried that. It's quite difficult. Anything you do seems to be logged somewhere. You can't draw money out of your bank account. You can't make a phone call. And then there are people out there looking for me, so I'm at a loss."

"Perhaps I could help you," she said.

"And how would you do that?"

"Not entirely sure at the moment," she said. "Leave it with me. Look I've got to go now, but I'll be back tomorrow."

"OK," said Alan feeling a bit bemused. "See you tomorrow."

Alan thought she would leave via the main door, but he got a surprise when she went to the store cupboard and closed the door behind her. He stood there waiting for her to come out again, wondering why she had gone in there in the first place, and when she hadn't reappeared after a couple of minutes, he went to the cupboard and opened the door expecting to see her standing there, but to his surprise, the cupboard was bare. He stepped inside and looked round for an exit, but there was nothing, just shelves.

He looked more carefully at the shelves and they all seemed to be fitted quite solidly onto the walls. There was no obvious way out.

Puzzled, he went back to his room and sat down. Who was this strange girl, and could he trust her? He wasn't sure of anything any more. However, she was the most interesting thing that had happened in quite a long time, so maybe it was worth a try.

Twenty-eight

The rest of the day passed very slowly. As much as he tried, Alan couldn't concentrate on his work and he kept finding himself thinking about that strange girl who had so suddenly appeared in his laboratory. He was completely smitten with her even though he kept telling himself he was being stupid. He knew nothing about her, and anyway, she was half his age. He was old enough to be her father. The solitude must be getting to him.

The evening passed even more slowly and when he eventually turned in for the night he was unable to sleep. Who was she and could she be trusted? He wanted to trust her. He needed to trust her, but could he? He didn't really have a choice, as she knew he was here, and unless he took off and tried to lose himself somewhere, he would have to trust her. He wanted to trust her but knew he couldn't afford to really.

In the early hours of the morning, he finally drifted off to sleep. He awoke with a start and looked at his bedside clock. It was eight thirty a.m., later than he usually got up, so he crawled out of bed and staggered to the bathroom where he soaked in the shower for quite a while until he had fully woken up. He turned off the water and stepped out of the shower, wiping the water from his eyes with the back of his hands.

"Very nice," said a voice, "But I think you need a bit more exercise."

He removed his hands from his eyes to see Kirsty sitting on his bed grinning at him. Alan made a grab for his towel, which he wrapped rapidly around himself.

"What are you doing here?" he spluttered.

"Thought you might be cooking breakfast," she said. "Oh dear. I do believe you're embarrassed."

"So would you be if I had walked in on you in the shower."

"Maybe. Maybe not. We must try it some time and I'll let you know. Now, are you going to get dressed and make me some breakfast?"

Alan grabbed some clothes, disappeared into the next room and got dressed hastily. By the time he was presentable, he had calmed down a little. There was now an aroma of frying bacon as he walked through into the kitchen-diner.

"Got fed up with waiting for you so I've made a start," she said without looking over her shoulder at him. How do you like your eggs?"

"I don't like eggs. Well, they don't like me actually. That's why I haven't got any."

"Oh. Well, never mind. What have you got?" She turned and looked at him and smiled. "Sorry if I gave you a shock."

"It's OK," he said. "It's just that I've been on my own for so long." She waved the frying pan at him. "In the fridge. Sausages. You've already found the bacon, I see." He opened the fridge and pulled out a packet of sausages and put them on the work surface. "Some cheese as well if you want some."

Eventually they had everything prepared and sat down to eat it.

"I hope you don't mind me coming and going as I like," she said, putting a slice of sausage in her mouth.

"Do I have any choice?"

"Perhaps not," she said. "Never mind. You'll get used to me eventually."

"Maybe."

"You'll have to get some better coffee. This is foul."

"I like it."

"I'll bring you some proper coffee next time." Alan said nothing.

"Have you thought how I can get out of here without being seen?"

"Yep. I'll tell you later. More coffee?" She filled his cup again. Alan wasn't sure if he liked this young lady taking over his life but then he didn't dislike it.

When they had finished eating, they cleared the dishes.

"I'll wash," she said. "You can dry." She threw the tea-towel at him. He said nothing, but dried the dishes as she washed them. It was very domestic and quite pleasant in a way, but he wasn't sure that he wanted to have his life hijacked like this. Maybe it would be easier to go along with it and wait until she got fed up with it and left him alone again.

"You seemed to suggest that I shouldn't trust Justin?" he said as he started drying the dishes. "Was there any particular reason?"

"None at all," she replied. "In fact, I can't imagine him getting involved with any political stuff. He's too interested in his work. If he didn't make a lot of money at it, I'm sure he would do it as a hobby."

"So you think I should trust him, then?"

"I make it a rule not to actually trust anyone," she said, "as you will usually be disappointed."

"Do you trust me, then?"

"I don't mistrust you," she said. "I have an open mind on the subject. Now to change the subject. You said that you wanted to get out of here. Why is that?"

"Well, if you were hidden away in here, day in, day out with no one to talk to, I think you would understand."

"Oh, I see," she said. "Where would you like to go?"

"There's a farm some way away from here where I stayed for a while," he said. "I would quite like to go back and see the chap who lives there. He is an artist, actually, but it seems that there are people watching the place."

"How do you know?"

"I saw one of them last time I went," he said. "I don't know if he recognised me, but he wasn't able to follow me so he still doesn't know where I am."

"Who is he working for?"

"I really don't know," he replied. "It could be the Yanks, or it could be Sir Malcolm. I'm sure he uses freelance agents."

"Perhaps we should go and ask him," she said.

"What?"

"I think it's about time you took the fight to them. You can't keep on running all your life."

"Easier said than done," he said.

"Not necessarily," she replied. "If these people are freelance we might be able to use them to our advantage."

"We?"

"Well you seem in need of help," she said. "So, yes, it's the two of us. We might even get Uncle Justin to help."

"Do you think he would?"

"I'm sure of it. First, let's go and see this fellow who's watching the farm," she said in her business-like fashion. "We'll go in my car as they won't know that. Come on."

She walked over to the locker cupboard and opened it.

"Where are you going?"

"Out," she said. "Follow me." When he reached the cupboard, he realised that she was using the shelves as steps and had almost disappeared. So he started to climb up after her. At the top of the cupboard, the shelves were replaced by iron rungs in the form of a ladder that rose another ten feet or more before it ended and he could climb off it onto a flat surface. It wasn't completely dark, as a little light filtered up from below and there was a glimmer of light at the end of the tunnel, which kept disappearing and returning as Kirsty moved along the tunnel ahead of him.

He scrambled after her, and emerged into a small cave with an iron grille across the entrance, where Kirsty was waiting for him. She was fumbling in a crevice in the rock and pulled out a large key.

"A bit before Yale locks," she said as she opened the gate in the grille. He followed her out into the mouth of the cave and she locked the gate from the outside and slipped the key into another crevice in the rock and placed another rock on top of it.

The entrance to the cave was quite small and almost blocked by brambles, which she squeezed past. Alan followed, to find himself in a small, ancient quarry. They scrambled down to the floor of the quarry, made their way to the edge and followed a narrow sheep track down the slope to the bottom, where her car was parked. It was completely hidden from the road, and Alan wondered why she went to the trouble of hiding it like this and then creeping into the lab through the hidden tunnel.

Her car was a small red Citroen which had seen better days.

"Get in," she said.

"I was waiting for you to unlock it," he said.

"Oh, I don't bother with locking it," she said.

"Why not?"

"Because, firstly, it's not worth pinching, and secondly, there's not much chance of anyone finding it."

They got in and she set off down a narrow track at an alarming speed, winding around boulders and gorse bushes until the track met a better track that obviously led to a farm somewhere.

"Do you always drive like this?" he asked.

"What's wrong with my driving?" she said, narrowly missing a sheep that was crossing the track.

"Absolutely nothing," he said, getting a firmer hold on the seat.

*****

The drive took them about an hour and a half, but would have taken nearer two hours if the speed limits had been observed.

"It would be nice if we didn't draw too much attention to ourselves," he said.

"You mean, you would like me to drive more slowly?"

"Just a bit, yes," he said. "By the way, why do you come and go at the lab through that tunnel?"

"Why not?"

"Well, what's wrong with the front door?"

"Justin doesn't like me being in his precious lab on my own," she said. "So I use the tradesmen's entrance when he's away."

"How did you find out about it?"

"I remember it being there before the place was converted," she said. "It was an old air shaft, I think, and rather than fill it in, they just hid the entrance and put the grille across it."

"Turn left here," said Alan, as they came to a road junction. They were following a narrow winding road across the moors so that they could approach the farm from the side away from the main road. It was the route that Alan had used previously. They followed what seemed to be a single track road for a while until Alan told her to slow down. At the next field entrance, he told her to pull off the road.

"On foot from here," he said, getting out of the car. They climbed the gate and set off across the moor towards a small group of trees on a small rise at the edge of the valley where the farm nestled. It was quite quiet up there with just the whistle of the breeze and the occasional call of a distant curlew. As they approached the trees, Alan stopped.

"I'll go straight on towards that little knoll," he said. "That's where they had someone posted last time. You veer off to the right and hide among the trees. If someone is there, we'll just have to play it by ear." They set off as quietly as they could manage. Alan watched Kirsty disappear into the trees, as he approached from the other side. At first he thought that there was no one there. Perhaps they had moved to a better vantage point, or perhaps they had given up altogether. But as he got closer, he noticed that there was someone sitting on the rocks, almost hidden from his viewpoint, drinking something from a Thermos flask.

At that moment he looked round and saw Alan. At first Alan thought that he had reacted, but then wasn't so sure when the fellow carried on drinking his coffee, or whatever he had in the flask. Alan noticed that he had a pair of binoculars on his lap. Perhaps it was just a bird watcher.

"Hello," said Alan. "Lovely spot, isn't it?"

"What do you want?" said the fellow, gruffly. Not a bird watcher then.

"Have you seen anything interesting then?"

"Mind your own business," said the man, getting up and looking menacing. "What you doing here anyway?"

"Just out walking," said Alan.

"Don't I know you?"

"Shouldn't think so," said Alan. "I don't live around here. I'm just passing through."

The fellow took out a folder from his rucksack, shuffled through it, took out a much-thumbed picture and glanced from it to Alan.

"You're Alan Westbrook, aren't you?"

"Fame at last," said Alan. "Who wants to know?"

"The name's Knuckles," he said, pulling a large knife from his rucksack. "We've been looking for you for ages, and I'm getting fed up with it. So now you can come with me to see my boss."

"I'd love to," said Alan. "By the way, what's his name?"

"Weasel," said Knuckles. "Let's go." But before he could do anything more, his eyes glazed over and he fell face-down at Alan's feet.

"What did you hit him with?" asked Alan, as Kirsty stood grinning.

"Just a bit of wood I found over there," she said. "Better tie him up before he is able to object." She took a roll of adhesive tape from her pocket and started to bind Knuckles' hands behind his back. When he started to come round, they propped him up against a rock so that they could talk to him.

"I don't think your Weasel will be very pleased with you, will he?" said Alan. "And I don't suppose his bosses will be very pleased either."

"They aren't pleased anyway," said Knuckles. "Weasel hoped to get hold of you to get back into their good books."

"And who, exactly, are 'they'?"

"Well, he goes to see someone in London," said Knuckles. "Not sure what they call him. Sir something or other at the Ministry of Defence."

"Sir Malcolm Birch?"

"Yes, I think that was what he was called. And then there's those Yanks. Big blokes in suits. They killed poor Albert."

"Albert?"

"One of my mates. Farmer down there shot him and while he was recovering they came and killed him."

"So who was your Weasel going to hand us over to, then?" said Alan.

"I don't know," said Knuckles. "Yanks, most likely."

"What do you think we should do?" Alan asked Kirsty who had been silent up to now.

"We can't just let him go, can we?" she said. "Better just slit his throat, then we'll track down this Weasel and get rid of him too."

"You can't do that," squeaked Knuckles.

"Why not?" asked Alan. "I can't think of any alternative, can you, Kirsty?"

"Not really," she said. "I can't see this lot shifting sides and working with us, can you?"

"Look," pleaded Knuckles. "Why don't I take you to meet Weasel and the others and we can talk this through?"

"I don't know," said Alan. "What do you think, Kirsty?"

"Well, it would speed up the search for Weasel, wouldn't it?" she said. "Anyway, we could slit his throat later if there are any problems."

"You seem very keen on slitting his throat," said Alan.

"I won't be any trouble," said Knuckles. "Honest."

"Honest is the last thing you are," said Kirsty. "Well, if you don't want your throat slit, you'd better make sure that your friends fall in with us, and no tricks. Are they coming to relieve you on watch here, or are you just going back when it gets dark?"

"Weasel will come out at dusk with my replacement."

"Good," said Alan. "We'll wait for him."

*****

Annabelle Pringle arrived at the headquarters of International Pharmaceuticals in Cardiff, and walked up to the reception desk.

"I have an appointment with Mr. Justin Williams," she announced to the receptionist.

"Please take a seat and I'll inform him that you are here."

She walked over to one of the plush armchairs and settled down to wait. This was a very impressive building. From the outside it appeared to be made totally of dark glass, with wide steps leading up to the glass doors.

Inside, there was a spacious reception area with a marble floor and several marble pillars. The reception desk was rather like the control centre of the Starship Enterprise.

Over to the right hand side was an array of lifts, where lights flashed to show where each lift was at any particular moment. As she watched them, one of the doors opened and a short, plump, very well-dressed girl emerged and headed her way.

"Miss Pringle?" she asked.

"Ms. Pringle. Yes, that's me."

"If you would like to come this way, I'll show you to Mr. Williams's office," she said and headed back towards the lifts. Inside, the girl pressed one of the buttons and the lift took off at an alarming rate, which made Annabelle grab the rail.

"Sorry," said the girl. "I should have warned you. Mr. Williams hates lifts that keep you waiting for ages."

"No problem," said Annabelle. "Just took me by surprise." Within seconds, the lift was slowing to stop at the top floor. The doors opened and the girl led her out into the corridor. She stopped at the end and knocked on a door. A voice answered and she ushered Annabelle into the office.

It was a very large office, taking up most of the end of the building, with glass all the way round looking out over the city. At the far side was a large desk, behind which sat Justin, looking through a folder which he closed and put down on the desk.

"Good morning," he said. "How can I help you? I wasn't aware we were doing any business with the ministry at the moment."

"I have to admit that I may have got to see you on false pretences," she said, brushing her long blonde hair back from her face.

"I hope you're not trying to sell me double glazing," he said, grinning.

"Not at all," she said. "I do work for the ministry, but I also know your niece, Kirsty, or at least I did when we were at university, but we have lost touch since, and I hoped you could give me her new address."

"Why now?" he asked. "And how did you find me?"

"Well, I have been meaning to try and get in touch with her for a while, but there was a technical article I saw recently with your name attached to it so I thought that was a good place to start."

"I believe you work for Sir Malcolm?"

"Not exclusively," she said. "He occasionally asks me to deal with certain aspects of his work, mostly to do with market research, or public relations, but mostly I have nothing to do with him."

"What is your opinion of him?"

"What a funny question," she said, looking puzzled. "Why do you ask?"

"Well, we have to deal with many people in this business, and it's nice to know as much about them as possible."

"I don't deal with him all that much," she replied. "But, to be honest, I don't like him overmuch."

"Why is that?"

"Nothing tangible," she said. "It's just his manner and the way he looks at you. I find him a bit creepy. Don't you trust him either?"

"Not really," he said thoughtfully. "But if I have to do business with him, I want to know what private agendas he might have. I know he is attached to the Ministry of Defence, but that doesn't mean he is trustworthy, and I have my business interests to protect."

"Last time I was in there he had a very disreputable fellow arrive just as I was leaving. Not the sort of person you would expect in an MoD office."

"That's what I mean," he said. "He probably has all sorts of other activities that the Ministry doesn't know about, but he is of such a rank that it would be difficult to get him investigated. Now, if I put you in touch with my niece, I want you to promise me that nothing that is said between you gets back to Sir Malcolm or anyone associated with him. Is that clear?"

"Of course," she said, puzzled. "But why would anything we said be of interest to Sir Malcolm?"

"It might not be," he said. "But my niece is involved in several projects of commercial sensitivity, and it is surprising what people can glean from bits of what seems to be harmless information. For instance, if you were to mention whom she was with, that might lead him to put two and two together and deduct what they were involved with. The thing is that you never know how important a little statement might be to someone else."

"I see what you mean," she said. "I promise never to mention anything in the hearing of anyone at the office."

"Or to anyone who might know someone at the office."

"OK."

"Right, if you can write down a contact telephone number on this pad, I'll tell her and she can ring you if she wants to. Is that all right?"

"Thank you very much," she said, writing down her mobile number. "It is much appreciated."

"And one other thing," he continued. "Don't say anything on the phone of importance, as you never know when your mobile phone is being tapped."

"Good grief," she said. "What a complicated world you live in."

"Isn't it just!"

After Annabelle had left, Justin dialled again, this time to Kirsty but she wasn't available, so he left a message, "Please phone me ASAP."

*****

Kirsty and Alan were still waiting for Weasel to appear. It was about the time that he was expected so they hid among the rocks, leaving Knuckles, still tied up, leaning against another rock where Weasel would see him. It was another ten minutes before they heard the sound of a car pulling up on the road nearby. A door slammed and they waited. Soon two figures appeared, walking across the field in the direction of Knuckles.

"Seen anything?" one of them called as they approached. Knuckles didn't answer as they had gagged him. "What's the matter with you, Knuckles?"

"He's a bit tied up at the moment," shouted Alan from his hiding place. "So put up your hands and turn round. It would be a pity to have to shoot you before we have had a little talk." They raised their hands and turned around.

"What do you want?" asked Weasel.

"Just a little talk," said Alan. "Tie them up, Kirsty. I'll keep them covered."

She climbed out of her hiding place and set to work with her sticky tape.

"Now you can turn round and sit down with your friend here," said Alan, climbing out from behind the rocks. Weasel was a little peeved when he realised that Alan hadn't a gun and was just bluffing. "Now you can tell us why you have been spying on this farm."

"You know damn well why," said Weasel.

"Yes," said Alan. "You were waiting for me, but why? Who is paying you?"

"No one at the moment," said Weasel. "We were hoping to get paid when we found you."

"By whom?"

"All sorts of people."

"Sir Malcolm for one," said Alan. "And what about the Americans?"

"The Americans don't pay for info. They just kill you if you don't come up with the goods."

"And you haven't?"

"No."

"Well, you are in a bit of a fix then, aren't you?"

"Look," said Weasel, "what do you want from us?"

"Well, it doesn't look as if you are going to get paid by Sir Malcolm, does it?" said Alan. "So perhaps we can come to an arrangement where you get paid and certain people don't get to find out where we are."

"What do you suggest?" asked Weasel.

"Forget about Sir Malcolm," said Alan. "But give false information to the Americans. Send them on a wild goose chase to the south of England, or abroad if you like. Just make sure they don't find us."

"That could be dangerous," said Weasel.

"Not helping us could be even more dangerous," said Alan. "What do you think, Kirsty?"

"They'd never be found up here, would they?" she replied.

"OK," said Weasel. "We know when we are beat."

"Pass me his phone, would you, Kirsty?" said Alan. She rummaged in his pockets until she found a mobile phone, and passed it to Alan, who transferred its number to his phone. "Just so that we can stay in touch. By the way, you haven't introduced your friend here."

"Meet Kevin," said Weasel.

"What a name for a secret agent."

"What's wrong with it?" asked Kevin.

"The name's Bond – Kevin Bond," said Alan. "Doesn't have that same ring to it, does it?"

Alan approached Knuckles and took out his knife. Knuckles flinched.

"It's OK," said Alan. "Just going to cut the tape round your wrists." He sliced the tape and Knuckles massaged his wrists to restore the circulation. "We'll leave you to free the others, we'll be on our way and we'll be in touch." He handed Weasel's phone to Knuckles, and they set off across the field.

Do you think they'll play ball?" asked Kirsty as they set off back home.

"Not for one minute," said Alan. "But I think they might lead the Yanks a merry chase. It's in their own best interests to keep them occupied."

Kirsty inspected her phone and found there was a message from Justin which just asked her to phone him. So she did, but he wasn't in his office, so she decided to leave it until they got back to the lab.

*****

"What are we going to do, then?" asked Knuckles as they sat round the corner table in their regular pub.

"Nothing much for the moment," said Weasel. But they offered to pay us to lead the Yanks away from here, so maybe that's the best thing to do. It'll make us a bob or two and keep them off our backs for a while."

"What about Sir Whatsisname?" asked Knuckles.

"We'll wait 'til he contacts us. If he is willing to pay we'll give him whatever info he wants," said Weasel. "Now down to business. We'll have to work out an imaginary route for Westbrook to take, heading down south, and if possible abroad. Anything to keep him out of our hair. This could be a job for Kevin. What do you think, Kevin?"

"Not doing anything better," said Kevin. "What do you want me to do?"

"We'll have to play it by ear," said Weasel. "You set off and stay overnight wherever you end up. Let us know each night where you are and we'll tip them off where you have been seen, but by then, you will have gone. Head generally in a southward direction but zigzag across the country. Go into Wales, for instance, then back over to Norfolk. Play it by ear. Finally, when you get to the south coast, book a place on the cross-channel ferry, but don't go on it. I'll arrange a credit card for you to use and make sure Westbrook keeps it topped up."

"When do I leave?"

"As soon as you like," said Weasel. "And ring me as soon as you are well away from here, and keep us updated daily. OK?"

"OK," said Kevin. "I'll go and pack."

"Good luck!" said Weasel.

Twenty-nine

Alan and Kirsty arrived back at the lab quite late that evening, and Alan set about making them a meal while Kirsty rang her uncle to find out what he wanted.

"Do you know someone called Annabelle Pringle?" asked Justin.

"Yes," said Kirsty. "But I haven't been in touch with her for ages. Why?"

"Well, she came to see me today," he said. "And wanted me to pass on her number so that you could contact her."

"Why would I want to do that?"

"She didn't say," said Justin. "Look, I'm coming up there tomorrow so I'll tell you all about it then."

"OK," said Kirsty. "See you then. I'll be at the lab with Alan."

"Oh! You've met, have you? See you tomorrow then."

"What did he say?" asked Alan, over the noise of sizzling bacon.

"He's coming up tomorrow," she replied. "Seems someone I used to know wants me to get in touch with her."

"Why did she go to Justin?"

"Who knows?" she said. "I am beginning to think that everyone has a secret agenda. Justin said that he would give me the details tomorrow, so I think he thinks there is something odd too."

"Where did you know her?"

"It was when we were at college," said Kirsty. "She wasn't a special friend, but I saw her from time to time about the place. I can't think why she should want to get in touch again. We'll just have to wait until Justin gets here."

*****

Kevin had been travelling for several days under the name of Alan Finch so that he would be easy to follow. He had just booked in at a little bed and breakfast near Snowdon and would be moving on in the morning. He was finding it quite pleasant travelling around the country at someone else's expense. It hadn't yet occurred to him that he could be in danger if the Americans actually caught up with him. The weather was fine, the scenery was stunning, so what could possibly go wrong?

The next day he set off in a southerly direction. He didn't know where he was actually heading, and as far as he was concerned, it didn't really matter. He wasn't in a hurry so was able to enjoy the journey. He would travel all day, stopping for lunch, and then find somewhere to stay overnight.

He rang Weasel each evening to let him know where he was so that he could tell Walter Greenbank, though he would give him two stops previous so that he wouldn't catch up with him. Weasel wondered how long they could get away with this, but hoped for the best.

* * *

The next day Justin arrived back at the lab.

"I see you two have already met," he said, seeing Alan and Kirsty sitting together on the settee in his private quarters.

"Yes, Kirsty introduced herself at a rather inconvenient moment," said Alan.

"That would be about right," said Justin. "If she's on her usual form. Now, about this Annabelle Pringle. She came to my office in Cardiff asking for your telephone number, but I didn't think it was prudent to give out your phone number, so I took hers so that you can contact her if you want to. I can't think what she could want."

"Nor can I, after all this time," said Kirsty. "Perhaps we should meet her somewhere well away from here."

"Seems sensible," said Alan. "I need to see Weasel again, so we could travel over to that pub he frequents. I could meet Weasel and you could meet Annabelle. She wouldn't know that we knew each other and I could keep an eye on you and perhaps get Weasel to put a tail on her. Arrange to meet her at the weekend if you can."

On Saturday, they set off for the pub Weasel used as his base. It was a nice day and quite pleasant for a drive through the hills.

When they arrived, they looked around the car park to see if anyone was waiting there, but it was deserted, so Kirsty got out and went into the pub. Shortly afterwards, Alan got out and wandered in. Weasel was sitting in his usual corner with Knuckles, so Alan walked over to join them. Kirsty was sitting in a seat by the window with a stunning blonde, immaculately dressed.

"I need to keep an eye on the woman sitting with Kirsty," said Alan.

"I bet you do," said Knuckles, grinning stupidly.

"Shut up, Knuckles," said Weasel. "Do you know who that is?"

"No," said Alan, "Should I? All I know is that she is an old friend of Kirsty's who wanted to get in touch. We don't know why."

"Well, last time I saw her," said Weasel, "she was coming out of Sir Malcolm's office, acting as if she owned the place."

"Did she now?" said Alan. "I wonder what her game is. When she leaves, I want you to put a tail on her. I want to know everywhere she goes and who she sees, and if possible what is said."

"Job for you, Knuckles."

"Better than some I've had recently," said Knuckles.

"Of course she could have nothing to do with you," said Weasel.

"Well, I'm taking no chances," said Alan. "Keep me informed, Knuckles."

"OK," said Knuckles, getting up to leave.

"I don't know how Sir Malcolm would associate Kirsty with me," said Alan.

"Could just be coincidence," said Weasel.

"I don't like coincidences," said Alan. "It could just be that Justin is in a similar sort of business, and he may have discovered that he and I knew each other when at college. If so he is grasping at straws. I had forgotten all about Justin before meeting him in that car park."

A couple of drinks later, Annabelle stood up and after they said their goodbyes, left. Alan hoped that Knuckles was ready to follow her. Weasel looked out of the side door to watch her drive off and to make sure that Knuckles was following.

As soon as she had disappeared, they all sat down again together.

"Did you learn anything?" asked Alan.

"Not a lot," said Kirsty. "She was rather evasive and I couldn't really get any clues as to what she was after. So we'll just have to wait and see."

"Weasel says that he met her at Sir Malcolm's office," said Alan.

"She was just leaving as I arrived," said Weasel.

"Are you sure it was her?" asked Kirsty.

"Come on," said Weasel. "She's not someone you're going to forget that quickly, are you?"

"Well, keep us fully informed," said Alan. "We should be getting back now. By the way, where is Kevin now?"

Heading for Cardiff," said Weasel.

"It wouldn't hurt to feed them a few red herrings now and then," said Alan. "Now we'll make our way back. Keep up the good work."

They set off on the road back home as it was getting dark, and about five miles down the road, Alan's phone rang. He frowned and passed it to Kirsty to answer as he certainly didn't want to be pulled over by the police for using his phone while driving.

"It's Knuckles," said Kirsty. "Apparently, Annabelle was waiting for us a mile or two back and is now following us."

"Can't see any car headlights in the mirror."

"No," said Kirsty. "She must have dropped a tracker into my bag and is following at a safe distance. Actually, she could track us all the way home without actually following us. Perhaps she just wants to be sure." Kirsty rummaged in her bag and found the offending article. "Shall I throw it out of the window?"

"Oh no." said Alan. "Keep hold of it. I think we'll have some fun with your friend Annabelle. Tell Knuckles he's done a good job and to go back and finish his drink." Kirsty did so.

"He asks if you really think he would leave a drink unfinished on the table," she said.

"I suppose not," said Alan.

They carried on along the hilly road until they were about three-quarters of the way home, at which point Alan pulled off the main road onto a quarry track.

"Where are we going?" asked Kirsty in surprise.

"You'll see," said Alan as they pulled into a flat area at the base of a steep cliff, and turning off the engine. "I hope you're not wearing high heels."

"Well I wouldn't to impress you," she said. "You never notice."

"Well I did notice, actually," said Alan. "You are wearing a pair of smart trainers. I was only joking about the high heels because I'm sure Annabelle is wearing a very expensive pair of shoes that weren't meant for rock scrambling."

"You're wicked," said Kirsty.

Alan headed for a dark corner of the quarry where, it transpired, there was a ramblers' footpath climbing steeply up the cliff-face. It was difficult going, in the dark, but they managed it quite easily. At the top was the opening to a mining tunnel, where Alan stopped.

"Throw the tracker in there," he said. Kirsty did so. He then continued a bit further up the path, turned and scrambled behind a mass of overhanging creeper which hid another path, which was probably quite visible in daylight. This took them to a shelf almost above the old mine working, where they could wait and observe anyone following them. There was a light breeze blowing, which rustled the undergrowth and the distant call of an owl could be heard as it glided otherwise soundlessly down the valley.

"That can be your reason for coming up here at night," said Alan.

"What can?"

"You've come to see the pair of Himalayan Eagle Owls that have been seen up here recently," said Alan with a grin.

"Don't be daft," said Kirsty. "Who would believe that?"

"That's just the point," said Alan. "Some of the locals, in the pub, try to con the city lads into believing that there is this pair of very rare birds to be seen up here. Annabelle knows that you came up here, so when you speak to her next, spin her that line."

At that moment, the headlights of a car turning into the quarry swept across the hillside. There was the sound of a car door closing, and after a short delay, the sound of someone scrabbling up the footpath below.

In the moonlight they could see that Annabelle was not dressed for this sort of thing. It looked as if her expensive designer shoes were for the waste bin as was her smart coat and dress.

When she reached the mine entrance, she obviously decided she would have to go inside, as that was where the tracker was leading her, so after a bit more scrabbling about, all went quiet.

"Time to go," said Alan and led them further up the slope before descending by another path.

Back at the car, they were about to leave when Alan noticed that Annabelle had left the keys in her car. "You just wouldn't believe it, would you?" He walked over to her car, opened the door and took the keys, then closed the door and locked it. Then he got in his own car and they drove off.

"That was a bit cruel, wasn't it?" said Kirsty.

"If she wants to play with the big boys, that's what she can expect," said Alan. "I would give anything to be a fly on the wall when she tries to explain it to Sir Malcolm." He opened the window, threw Annabelle's car keys out and then closed the window again.

Half an hour later, they arrived back at the lab and drove straight into the farm. Justin was waiting for them, eager to hear their story. There was some supper set on the large dining table in the farmhouse, so they all settled down to eat and recount their evening adventure.

"Lucky your Weasel friend was there," said Justin. "And that he had seen her leaving Sir Malcolm's office. But from what you say, she doesn't seem a very proficient spy. I can't understand why Sir Malcolm would trust her with a job like that. But now I think of it, he has a niece who he helped to finance the start-up of a PR agency."

"Do you know where she's staying?" asked Alan.

"No, she was very evasive," said Kirsty.

"Sounds very fishy," said Justin, sitting down with a steaming cup of coffee. "But I think we'll just have to ignore her until she does anything positive. Even if she links you or me with Alan, she is very unlikely to find this place. It was designed specifically not to be found. Now there's something I need to discuss with you, Alan. My corporation would like to be able to manufacture and distribute vaccines for dangerous illnesses. Now I know that this can be done now, but it takes forever, and by the time it is ready the virus has probably mutated. So we want to be able to do this really quickly. So how far off do you think we are?"

"Well, the analysis part is well under way," said Alan. "Just need a few bits of hardware and we could get results. As far as the synthesis is concerned, the software is complete, with the exception of extensive testing, but there is quite a bit of hardware required."

"Get the drawings done ASAP and let me have them by encoded internet connection, and I will get the hardware made and delivered here. Well, in fact, I'll bring it myself. One of our delivery vans might be too obvious."

"Just a little," said Alan.

*****

The next day Kirsty got a call from Annabelle.

"It was really nice to meet up again after all this time," she said, as if nothing had happened the previous evening.

"Actually," said Kirsty, "after you left, some of the locals got talking and they told me all about a sighting of a pair of Himalayan Eagle Owls at an old quarry, and you would think I had just come out of primary school as I fell for it hook, line and sinker. I felt such a fool when I scrambled down again after finding nothing, only to find a local yokel leaning against his car, grinning." 'Didn't find 'em then', he said. Then he just locked his car and ambled off. Anyway, no harm done other than the fact it'll take some living down."

"Oh you poor thing," said Annabelle, not too convincingly. "I had intended meeting up with you again, but I'm afraid I'll have to head back to the big smoke later today. Still it was nice meeting up again, wasn't it?"

*****

After that, things quietened down a bit and Alan was able to get on with his work undisturbed, other than from Kirsty who was always around. She was extremely inquisitive, always asking questions, but as time went on she began to make useful contributions to the work. She had quite a mathematical mind and could solve some of the most difficult problems.

Justin was very useful, being able to get any sort of mechanical assembly fabricated for them. Of course, the people making the various bits of apparatus didn't know what they were for, and most were given imaginative names to keep people off the scent. Rather like in the First World War when drawings for a novel armoured gun carriage was titled a

'Water Tank'. Of course the name stuck, and all further developments of this vehicle were known as 'tanks'.

When Christmas arrived, Justin invited Alan to spend it with them in the old farmhouse. It was only sensible, as it would have been miserable for him sitting in his little flat, just seventy-five feet from where it was all happening. Kirsty had lived with Justin in the old farmhouse ever since her parents had died in a car crash one wintery November night. Anyway, Justin and Kirsty were glad of the company. Alan managed to get out and do a bit of Christmas shopping, though he wasn't sure what to buy for them. He just used his imagination and hoped for the best.

As it turned out, it was very enjoyable and Alan was quite pleased to have a break from the continual work. He enjoyed the work, but missed the company of other people, so the presence of Kirsty brightened things up quite a bit. She was a strange one, though, he thought. She didn't seem that interested in going out and socialising, though she had always enjoyed any forays out into the wider world with Alan, even though they had to be careful not to draw attention to themselves for fear that they were being watched.

Winter slowly receded and spring crept in. First the snowdrops appeared, then the crocuses, followed by the daffodils. Alan wondered who it was that planted all these flowers along the roadsides. There must be millions of them across the country.

Eventually the time approached when Alan had suggested to Maggie that they met up again at Blackpool Tower. He didn't know why he had suggested Blackpool Tower, but it had been the first thing that had come into his head and was easy to remember.

He had mentioned it to Kirsty, who had prompted him to keep the appointment, though he had been rather reticent.

"What would be the point?" he had replied.

"Well, it's obvious that you still feel some sort of tie to her," said Kirsty. "You say you are married, but that is a complete fiction set up by Sir Malcolm, supposedly to hide your identity, but more likely to get you under his control. That failed, she walked out on you. Anyway, go and meet her and set your mind at rest, once and for all."

"All right," he said at last. "I'll go and meet her, if she comes, and we'll take it from there. Maybe you should come too."

"Me?" she said, surprised. "What on earth for?"

"I would like you to come," he said. "Someone to talk to."

Thirty

They arrived in Blackpool in the late afternoon, so decided to walk along to the amusement park.

"Are you going to take me on the big dipper, or whatever the latest scary ride is called these days?"

"That's not for me," said Alan. "We could go on the big wheel if you like. That's more in my line."

"You're not scared of being turned inside-out and upside-down, are you?" she said mockingly.

"No, not at all," he said. "But I just don't enjoy it. Anyway, look at the queue."

From the top of the big wheel they could see for miles, and the people walking about below looked like small insects. Alan wondered if one of them might be Maggie. He wasn't sure whether he wanted her to turn up or not, but tomorrow would answer that question for him.

When they got off the big wheel, they found a restaurant for their evening meal. The place was quite busy and they said very little while they ate. Kirsty realised that Alan was concerned about the outcome of tomorrow's possible meeting. She didn't know if he hoped she would be there, or hoped she wouldn't show, and he said little to indicate his feelings.

After the meal they walked to the car park, removed their cases and carried them to the hotel Kirsty had booked for them. It was a small place in a back street.

"Very salubrious," said Alan.

"Well, this is Blackpool," said Kirsty. "And it's only for one night."

They were shown to their room, which surprised Alan as it dawned on him that there was, in fact, only the one room booked.

"So you have booked us into a double room?" he said when the landlady had gone.

"It was supposed to be a twin," said Kirsty. "Do you have any problem with sharing?" Alan didn't know what to say. He was meeting his 'wife' the next day, but sharing a bed with an attractive young thing tonight. He didn't know what to think.

"I suppose not," he said, "but it is not how I was brought up."

"You mean that you were repressed as a child?"

"I suppose so," he said. "That's the way it was in those days."

"Never mind," she said. "I'll be gentle with you." She laughed when she saw his expression.

In spite of his unease about the situation, he slept well and woke to the sound of the shower running and realised that Kirsty was up and about. He was even more surprised when she emerged from the shower, drying her hair with a towel. Alan didn't know where to look, so he grabbed his towel and made a dash for the bathroom to the sound of mirth from Kirsty.

At breakfast, he asked her what she proposed to do while he made his trip to the top of the tower. She thought she might do some shopping but would meet him for some lunch at twelve thirty, with or without Maggie. But they had the morning to fill in before that, so decided to take a tram ride along the front.

It was a bright but chilly morning with a cool breeze blowing in off the sea. There was a group of donkeys looking rather fed up with life, and several people walking dogs. Gulls swept in close to them to see if there was anything worth pinching from them, but they weren't eating so they swept away again, voicing their disappointment.

They got off the tram at the far end and decided to walk back. There was a fair amount of traffic on the road and the pavements were getting busier as people emerged from their hotels.

"I'm glad we aren't staying in that hotel again tonight," said Alan.

"Shame," said Kirsty mockingly. "Didn't you like sharing a bed with me then?"

"That's not what I meant," he said. "Actually it was quite pleasant to have company at night. No, it was the fact that the landlady felt it was necessary to put a waterproof under the sheet. What sort of people do they get staying at these places?"

"Don't ask," she replied. "Anyway, I'm glad you didn't find my presence too repelling."

"No, not at all," he said. "It was just a bit odd seeing as I might be meeting my wife today, even if the relationship is only technical."

"I understand perfectly," she said. "I was only pulling your leg."

"The 'Waterloo' is down here somewhere," he said, changing the subject.

"What's that?"

"The Mecca of Crown Green Bowling," he replied. "I've never been there but I've watched on TV occasionally."

"Do you play?"

"Used to," he replied, "but haven't had time recently."

They arrived back at the tower with a little time to spare, so they parted and Alan made his way to the top of the tower to wait. The breeze at the top seemed much colder than at ground level, so he pulled his coat tighter round him and settled down to wait. He could see people walking past below, but no one that looked like Maggie.

After a while he heard the lift coming up and he felt a little shudder of expectation as it stopped and the doors opened. Out came a small group of Japanese tourists, each with the obligatory camera or smartphone. Many photos were taken, including some of himself. *A bit of local interest*, he thought. Then they were gone. Another wait and then a courting couple emerged from the lift and glared at him, obviously hoping to be alone, so he stepped into the lift and descended to ground level again.

He waited at the bottom of the lift for a bit longer, just in case she was late, but she didn't appear. Across the road he noticed a solitary figure sitting on one of the benches, reading a newspaper. He thought that there must be better places to read a paper than on a windy seat. Then he wondered if he was being watched, and this was the watcher trying to look inconspicuous, and in doing so, standing out like a sore thumb – grey trenchcoat with collar turned up, hiding most of his face.

No, he was getting paranoid now. After all, no one knew he was going to be here. So he set off to find Kirsty.

The restaurant was quite busy, so it was lucky that she had got there in good time to be able to claim a table.

"Didn't show, then?" she said, trying not to look too pleased.

"No," he replied. "I didn't really expect her to. It's quite a relief actually."

"Well, at least you can put her out of your mind now," she said, "and get on with your life."

"See that man walking past the window?" said Alan. "He was sitting opposite the tower entrance, pretending to read a newspaper."

"Perhaps he was reading the newspaper."

"Too windy," said Alan. "I felt he was watching someone."

"You?"

"Yes," he said. "And now he is walking past the window."

"Could be a coincidence," she said.

"Well, we must keep our eyes open when we leave."

"If you say so."

They finished their meal and made for the door where they looked both ways to see if they could see the suspicious character, but all seemed normal.

"Well I'm not taking any chances," said Alan. "Follow me." He set off down the street and suddenly took a right-hand turn into a back alley. After about thirty yards, he ducked into an open doorway, followed closely by Kirsty.

"You really have been watching too many thriller films," she said.

"Sssh," he hissed and moved back further out of sight. They could hear footsteps outside as someone passed, walking quickly. As he passed, Alan peeked out to see who it was. "It's that same man we saw walk past the window while we were eating, and the one sitting opposite the entrance to the tower."

As soon as the follower had disappeared round a corner at the end of the alley, they dashed out of their hiding place, hurried back onto the main street and quickly on to their parked car.

"Perhaps you were right," said Kirsty.

"Looks like it," said Alan. "But how did he know I'd be there today?"

"Must have found out from Margaret somehow," said Kirsty. "Anyway, I think we have given them the slip, but maybe we shouldn't go straight home from here."

"What do you mean?"

"Well we're in no hurry," she said. "Let's motor up to the Lakes and spend a night or two there before heading back. That should throw them off the scent."

"I have nothing against that," he said and adjusted his route to take them up the motorway to the Lake District.

They arrived at Grasmere in the late afternoon and set about finding a bed and breakfast place to stay. The smaller ones they tried were already fully booked so they moved on to the larger ones and managed to book a room for the two of them for two nights. Kirsty did the booking and unashamedly asked for a double room, so Alan could do nothing about it without looking stupid. They booked a table for dinner at the hotel as they didn't feel like trudging round the town looking for a restaurant that opened in the evening.

It was a very nice room with a king-size bed, two comfortable armchairs, a dressing table and a wardrobe.

"You really are a wicked woman," said Alan.

"Yes, but you like it," said Kirsty. "Don't deny it."

"I wouldn't dare," said Alan. "So, are we now an 'item' as they say these days?"

"That sounds a bit organised," she said. "I don't like being pigeon-holed."

"Well, we seem to be a bit more than friends to be spending a couple of nights in a hotel," he said.

"You really are a bit old-fashioned," she said. "Lighten up a bit."

"I just like to know where I stand," he said. "Once bitten, twice shy."

"Well I'm not planning to disappear in the morning, leaving you broken-hearted."

"Good," he said. "Now let's go down for dinner. All this cloak and dagger stuff is making me hungry."

It was a very pleasant hotel with an old-fashioned dining room. The waiter showed them to their table in a secluded corner.

"I think he knows we're not married," said Alan.

"I don't suppose he even thought about it," she answered. "They get all sorts in here and no one could care less, as long as you pay your bill."

The food was excellent and they moved into the lounge for their coffee and watched the other guests coming and going.

"I quite like to watch people and see if I can discern their relationships," she said. "That couple over there. I think they are business associates, perhaps boss and his secretary away for a business trip and making the most of it."

"You have an overactive mind," said Alan. "But I see what you mean. I wonder what they make of us."

"I don't think they have even noticed us," she said. "They are too wrapped up in each other. Now that pair over there, they are married and probably have been for about fifty or sixty years. He's busy with his newspaper and she couldn't care less about him. She has that look as if there is an unpleasant smell emanating from somewhere nearby – probably him."

"They are probably very nice people," said Alan. "What about that family over there?" He inclined his head in the direction of a family seated round a table. Both parents had very prominent noses, as did the three children.

"The nose family," said Kirsty as they got up and filed out of the lounge. "Following their noses."

"That's very cruel," said Alan. "Anyway, let's go for a stroll before turning in, shall we?"

"Anything to avoid the inevitable, eh?"

"Not at all," said Alan.

It was a clear evening and the stars shone brightly in the crisp evening sky. They wandered around the town for a while before heading back to the hotel.

"You know," said Alan, "at one time this town would be full of walkers and climbers – people who headed to the hills each day. But now they're all tourists who find it a trek to walk from the car to the pub. If only they knew what delights were in store for them if they put on their walking boots and set off up one of the many mountain paths."

"Perhaps we could do that tomorrow," she replied. "And get away from all these sightseers."

They made their way back to the hotel and went up to their room. Kirsty immediately stripped off and disappeared into the shower. Alan unpacked his things and read the literature left on the dressing table until she emerged, pink and glowing from her shower. She dropped her towel and put her arms round Alan and kissed him, then laughed at his startled expression. Then she climbed into bed.

"Don't be too long," she said. "And if you dare to wear those awful pyjamas, you can sleep on the floor."

*****

The next day they ate a hearty breakfast and then set off for the mountains. On the corner opposite their hotel was a bakery and sandwich shop, so they stopped and bought some provisions for the walk.

They then set off down the road round the side of Grasmere Lake. It was a pleasant morning, ideal for walking. About half a mile down the road they went through a gateway on their right and headed up the lower flanks of the mountain. Soon they left the trees and were on open grassland, sloping steadily upward towards the top of the ridge that skirted

Grasmere village. Alan liked ridge walking, as you could look down on all the countryside round about.

About halfway along the ridge, they stopped to eat their sandwiches and cake, and drink their coffee. They were near the edge of the ridge and there was a steep drop down to the valley below. Alan told Kirsty about his encounter with Maggie on a similar bit of mountain, when they had found Maggie's husband, Peter, who had fallen to his death from such a point.

"I was very lucky," said Alan. "If I hadn't stopped to drink my coffee and gaze out at the rolling scenery, it might have been me lying on that scree slope. It was unfortunate for Peter that he was the same build as me and was wearing a similar anorak. The thugs must have been lying in wait further along the path. They would have seen me pull up, get out of my camper-van and head up the path to the ridge. Then after a short while a figure appeared dressed very like me, so they had no reason to believe it wasn't me. I have had several lucky escapes. Unlucky for others though.

"When Maggie and I were staying in York, I gave my colleague, Jim Stanley, the wrong address, accidentally, and he must have told someone at Blakely House. The couple that lived two doors away were attacked and killed by thugs. One of Weasel's men was killed by the Americans, and I don't know if there was anyone else, but as you can see, I am not a good person to know."

"If you're trying to get rid of me," she said, "it isn't going to work."

"No, that's the last thing I want. But I worry that I am putting you in danger."

"I've always lived dangerously," she said with a grin.

Thirty-one

Sir Malcolm Birch was sitting impatiently at his desk when the door opened and his niece, Annabelle Pringle, entered.

"Don't you ever knock?" snapped Sir Malcolm.

"Sorry Uncle," she said.

"So you have made a complete mess of things," he continued. "I knew it was a mistake to entrust such an important assignment to you. But I suppose it was the fact that you knew her that made it seem feasible."

"I couldn't have known that she would find the tracker," She said indignantly. "I did exactly what you said. How is it my fault that it went wrong?"

"Maybe you're right," he said. "The thing is, how are you going to redeem yourself? If you are to be a successful agent, you have to be resourceful and deal with things as they happen. Now it is imperative that we find Westbrook as soon as possible. We have to get to him before the Americans."

"Perhaps I could find the woman he was with originally, the one whose husband your agents killed accidentally," she said.

"There's no need to bring that up again," he said angrily. "The woman's name is Margaret Finch and she was last seen in the Bristol area. We don't know if she is still there, but that would be a good place to start."

"Leave it to me," she said and made for the door.

"And keep the expenses down," he shouted after her. "This department isn't made of money."

*****

She had been lucky to track down Maggie a couple of weeks earlier. She was a member of a 'Keep Fit' class and Annabelle just happened to pass her as she was going into the community centre to get some information.

"Hello, Maggie," she said. Maggie looked surprised.

"Hello," she replied. "Do I know you?"

"We met some time ago up in Yorkshire," said Annabelle. "Your husband is a keen bird watcher, isn't he?"

"Was," said Maggie. "He was killed in an accident. Fell down a cliff."

"Oh, I am sorry," said Annabelle. "So you're on your own now?"

"I am," she replied. "Unfortunately. I was with someone for a while, but it didn't work out."

"Oh, that's a pity," said Annabelle. "No chance of a reconciliation then?"

"Well, when we split he suggested a rendezvous a year later at Blackpool Tower, of all places. I think it was the first place that came into his mind. But I won't be going."

"That's a pity," said Annabelle.

"Not really," said Maggie. "We were rather thrown together after Peter's death, but it wasn't to be."

"When were you supposed to meet?"

"Very soon, I think," said Maggie, "but to be honest I can't remember. Sometime next week I think. Well it doesn't matter as I'm not going."

"Well good luck for the future," said Annabelle. "It was nice seeing you again."

"Yes it was," said Maggie, still unable to remember seeing her before.

So Annabelle set one of her contacts to watch the Tower at Blackpool for the whole of the following week and then to follow Alan Westbrook to wherever he was living now.

*****

"So you found him, and then lost him again?" said Sir Malcolm.

"I discovered where he would be and set one of your so-called agents to watch for him," she said. "And he found him but then lost him again. However, it would seem that he is with Kirsty Williams, whom I knew at college, as we guessed previously."

"But we don't know where either of them lives," said Sir Malcolm. "So what do you propose doing about it now?"

"Leave it to me," said Annabelle. "I'll think of something."

*****

Alan and Kirsty returned to the hotel exhausted. Kirsty flopped into a chair and Alan headed for the shower. As the heat of the shower seeped into his tired muscles, he began to relax. Then there was a cold draft and he was pushed to one side.

"Don't hog all the hot water," said Kirsty.

Thirty-two

Back at the lab, they found a pile of packing cases in the middle of the floor.

"This must be my new equipment," said Alan. "Here, give us a hand unpacking them."

"You make a start," she said. "I'll make us a cup of coffee."

The equipment was superb. Justin had excelled himself. All he had to do now was set it up and interface it to his computer. It was all theoretical, so he hoped the practical realisation of his ideas would work as required.

They spent the next two weeks rearranging benches so that the equipment could be arranged sensibly with the computer in the middle controlling everything. Much of the time was taken up in getting the computer to actually communicate with all the hardware. Kirsty turned out to be very good with the hardware, seeming to understand exactly what it was required to do, which was very helpful to Alan because he could then concentrate on getting the software going. Finally, it all seemed to be working.

"What are we going to try it on first?" said Kirsty.

"Well we could get it to make a full DNA sequence for either of us," said Alan. "That would check that the hardware is actually working."

So they took a sample of each other's DNA using a mouth swab and Alan set the system in motion.

"It could take some time," said Alan. "It has a lot of calculations to do, and I probably haven't got the algorithm optimised for speed. Accuracy is more important."

So they went and made themselves a meal while the computer crunched away at the numbers.

"So, would you be able to synthesise another me from the DNA data?" asked Kirsty as they ate their meal.

"I suppose it would be theoretically possible," said Alan. "But I'm not sure how I could do it. Anyway, don't you think that one of you is enough? I can just imagine you having an argument with yourself. You would both self-destruct."

"Maybe you're right," she said. "You can have too much of a good thing. Anyway, I don't think you would survive two of me."

"No, one is about the limit," said Alan.

When the computer had finished its work, Kirsty was a bit disappointed. "It's just a lot of numbers," she said.

"I can display it in graphics if you like," said Alan, entering a command into the computer. A multi-coloured display of a double helix appeared on the screen.

"Well that's a bit prettier," she said. "But it doesn't mean a lot."

"It doesn't have to," said Alan. "The figures can now be used to tailor a virus or a vaccine specifically for you."

"I don't like the idea of tailoring a virus for me," said Kirsty.

"Oh, it doesn't have to be a killer," said Alan. "It is possible to design a virus that will attack another virus but be harmless to you."

"So what next?"

"We need to try it out on an actual disease," said Alan. "To make sure it does what it was designed to do. But we will have to try it out on an animal first. We'll have to ask Justin if any of his neighbours have any animals with a malady, preferably one which, if left alone, would mean it has to be put down. TB for instance."

"I'll ask him."

*****

A few weeks later, Justin returned and told Alan that a neighbour had a cow that might have TB and would be happy let them experiment on it. If it was successful, all well and good, but if it was a failure nothing would be lost as the animal would have to be destroyed anyway.

Justin took Alan and Kirsty up to the farm so that they could take the required swabs and blood samples.

"It would be good if you could find a cure for this," said the farmer. "It's such a waste of livestock."

"Let's hope for the best," said Alan. "But if it fails, we will be one step nearer a solution." He took some swabs and then looked dubiously at the syringe.

"Give it to me," said Kirsty and promptly took a blood sample. "There, easy."

"Where did you learn to do that?"

"A woman of mystery, me," she said with a grin.

Back in the lab, Alan set to work preparing the samples for analysis. It was rather a long and drawn out process, had to be done very carefully and would take over a week. He found that Kirsty seemed to understand what he was doing so he left her to do some of the more tedious work.

"What happens if you get it wrong?" she asked.

"Well, hopefully it won't start an epidemic," he said. "Though that is very unlikely as we aren't producing a virus. We are producing an antibody for the virus, so the animal should just get better. However, if we get it wrong, it just won't work and the animal will be destroyed anyway."

"Is it possible to create a virus?" she asked.

"Theoretically yes," he said. "Why do you ask?"

"Just wondering why people were interested in this work," she said. "I suppose the military of any country would be interested in being able to create a pandemic that their own people were immune to. Do you think that is why the Americans are interested?"

"Well, either that," said Alan, "or they are worried about someone else getting hold of it. Our people don't seem to be so worried, other than Sir Malcolm. I don't know why he is so interested."

"Isn't he just the person responsible? I'm sure there are people putting pressure on him to get control of this."

"What I don't understand," said Alan, "is the way he goes about it. I would have expected him to be sending military groups to hunt me down, but he hires people like Weasel. It doesn't make sense, does it? Anyway, if I keep control of it we can produce beneficial products that Justin's organisation can market."

Finally, the finished product was ready and Alan and Kirsty set off to the farm to administer the vaccine.

The cow had been kept isolated from the rest of the herd so as not to pass on its infection, so it was easy to give it the injection.

"When are they coming to do the final checks on this animal?" asked Alan.

"End of the month," was the answer. The farmer wasn't a great conversationalist.

"I'll check in a week's time," said Alan. He received a grunt in acknowledgement.

Back in the lab, Alan decided to check his algorithm to fill in the time until they knew the results. In a programme like this, it was so easy for a simple mistake to creep in; just a plus sign instead of a minus could reverse the whole process.

By the end of the week, he had gone through the code thoroughly and done several runs on test data, and there was one section that he wasn't sure about. If there was an error, that was where it would be.

"Have you found anything?" asked Kirsty.

"I'm not sure," said Alan. "There is one section that could be wrong but I won't know until we get the results from the farm. If there has been no response, there is one line I could change for a second try."

"Well why don't you do a run with the changed programme and produce a new sample? Then if it hasn't worked you could give the new vaccine immediately and perhaps save the cow before the ministry vet comes to do his tests."

"Worth a try," said Alan. The synthesis of the new vaccine only took a day as all the analysis work had been done previously, so when they set out for the farm, Alan had a dose of the new vaccine ready in case the first had failed.

The farmer was as cheerful as ever.

"Don't think it's worked," he said. "Didn't think it would."

"Well, if it hasn't," said Alan, "we have a new one we can try."

"If you think it's worth it," said the farmer. "I think you're wasting your time. If the government vets can't do anything, why do you think you can do better?"

Alan decided it was better not to answer that question.

"Well, we'll give it a go," he said. The previous attempt had obviously failed, though the animal wasn't any worse than before. So Alan administered the new vaccine and told the farmer that he would be back in a week.

"If this doesn't work," said the farmer, "they'll send the animal for slaughter."

"Yes I know," said Alan. "It's a crying shame, so let's hope we've got it right this time."

"Won't hold my breath," said the farmer.

*****

Kevin had reached Southampton and was preparing to take the ferry across to France. The idea was to lay the trail to France, and then disappear, returning to England from another port under his own name. He had just packed his case and was heading down the stairs to pay his bill, which he did in the name of Alan Finch

He then made his way to the car park and put his case in the boot. As he turned, he found two large men in suits standing behind him.

"Mr. Westbrook?" asked one of them.

"No," said Kevin. "I am Kevin Wilson."

"Then why are you signing in at hotels as Alan Finch?"

"Not me," said Kevin. "You must have me confused with someone else. Come to think of it, there was someone called Alan in the bar last night, but I don't know what his surname was. He left first thing this morning. Said he was going to catch the ferry. I'm off home to Hertfordshire."

The two heavies looked at each other then dashed back to their car and sped out of the car park. Kevin grinned to himself, got in his car and set off back to Yorkshire feeling rather pleased with himself. It would be a while before the two heavies got back from France after failing to find Alan on the ferry.

*****

After a phone call from Weasel, Alan and Kirsty drove to meet him in his usual haunt, where they found him sitting in the alcove watching people come and go.

"I think we have lost them for the moment," said Weasel. "Kevin has just returned from the south after the Americans dashed off to catch the ferry to France. What would you like us to do now?"

"Have you had any contact with Sir Malcolm since we spoke last?"

"Not a whisper," said Weasel.

"Well, it would seem that he has a niece called Annabelle Pringle who is trying to be a super sleuth for her uncle," said Alan. "She knew Kirsty at college and got in touch with her to see if she could glean anything about me via her. She was here last time we met, if you remember. You kept an eye on her and let us know that she was following us. We threw her off easily, but we think she got someone to watch me at Blackpool. We lost him too, but she will now know that Kirsty and I are together so will try to track her down in the hope of finding me. I want you to watch out for her and let me know what she is up to."

"Have you got a picture?" asked Weasel. "Not all my people saw her that night."

"This is one I had at college of a group of us," said Kirsty. "It was a poor photo but I did a bit of enhancing on the computer and this is the best I could come up with." She handed Weasel a print of the enlarged photo.

"Not bad, actually," said Weasel. "I'm sure we can use this OK."

"I think she might start from here," said Alan, "but she might also keep a watch on Justin's farm. Justin is Kirsty's uncle. I'll show you on the map." He unfolded the map and pointed out the farm.

"And where do you hang out?" asked Weasel.

"That's still a secret," said Alan. "The fewer that know that the better."

"What are they after you for?" said Weasel. "You never did tell me."

"Also a secret," said Alan.

"A man of mystery," said Weasel. "OK. I'll set them on to it."

*****

At the end of the week, the ministry vet would be coming to test the cow that Alan had treated, so he and Kirsty made their way to the farm to watch the test. They pretended to be farm workers so went in their oldest clothes to try and look the part.

When they arrived, they got a rather odd glance from the farmer.

"You didn't have to dress for the occasion," he said.

"Just wanted to look like two of your workers," said Alan.

"Well you didn't do very well at that," he replied. "If you want to look like a real farm worker, you'd better do a bit of work like a real farm worker. The byre needs mucking out, so you better get to work. Then you can stop when the vet arrives and come over and watch."

Alan had the distinct impression that he was being made fun of and being conned into doing some unpaid work into the bargain. But they thought it best to go along with it.

Mucking out was not only unpleasant, it was hard work, and Alan was glad when the vet arrived. Kirsty seemed unabashed by the experience. "Used to this," she said. "Except with horses. They aren't as bad though."

The vet set to work with his callipers and soon announced that the animal was clear of TB. He looked a little surprised, but filled in the required forms and left.

"Well, I suppose I should thank you for saving my cow, then," the farmer said reluctantly.

"You certainly should," said Alan. "And I think it is certainly worth a cup of coffee."

"I suppose so," said the farmer even more reluctantly, but he trudged off to the farmhouse followed by Alan and Kirsty. "You can take those boots off before you come in here." They did, but noticed that he didn't and the floor couldn't be much dirtier anyway.

The coffee was dire, but they drank it anyway before setting off back to the lab, where Justin was waiting for them.

"So it would seem your vaccine works?" said Justin.

"Just the one test," said Alan. "But the animal passed the ministry tests, so yes, it would seem to be successful."

"So what we need now is a production facility to produce this vaccine," said Justin. "If you could design it, I'll get it built at one of our facilities, and if it is specifically for this vaccine, it won't be possible for anyone to use it for other purposes."

"I can design it so that you can have a preprogrammed plug-in for each product that you might want to produce," said Alan. "You can build several production lines, all identical, and each can have a different programme so that you can use each for a different product."

"Sounds good to me," said Justin. "In the meantime, can you make a couple of dozen doses of the vaccine so that we can carry out proper clinical trials and get the vaccine approved?"

"I'll get on to it," said Alan "And get started on the design of the production equipment."

Thirty-three

Weasel wasted no time in assembling his team. Of course there was Knuckles and Kevin, but they were going to need more manpower than that.

"Anyone got any ideas?" asked Weasel, at a meeting at their usual meeting place and watering-hole.

"There's a group I used to knock about with," said Knuckles. "They call themselves the Cumbrian Angels."

"Not bikers?" said Weasel.

"What's wrong with that?"

"Are they reliable?"

"Sort of,," answered Knuckles. "Specially if they're paid well."

"How many of them are there?"

"Used to be about fifty of them," said Knuckles. "Don't know how many there are now, though."

"How long ago was it that you knew them?"

"Not sure," said Knuckles. "Must be about forty years."

"Good grief," said Weasel. "Are they still alive? Sounds more like Hell's Grannies."

"I'll find out for you," said Knuckles.

"What about you, Kev?"

"Not sure I can help," he said thoughtfully. "Mind you, I know a couple of rough birds who run a riding stable. They could be useful."

"Not sure about that," said Weasel. "Sound them out. On thinking about it, the more unusual they are the less obvious they'll be."

*****

Annabelle had been doing some recruiting of her own. She decided that she wouldn't use any of her uncle's people as they seemed rather useless. She was keen on hunting and shooting, but not fishing, so had quite a few friends from the shooting world who might be recruited. Most of these were based up on the moors, which was useful as she thought that Alan Westbrook must be hiding somewhere up there.

There was a shoot the following day, so she thought that would be a good opportunity to sound out some of her friends. As these people spent a lot of time up here on the moors, they would be ideal lookouts. If Alan Westbrook had a base around here, he must have to come and go occasionally, and that would be when he was most likely to be seen. She had some photos of him, supplied by her uncle, and she also had a photo of Kirsty from her college days. It wasn't very good as it was a group photo, so she had had to do a bit of photoshopping to separate her picture.

The following day, she drove up to the farm on the moors where they were all meeting before the shoot. There were several possible candidates that she had selected. William

Johns was a possibility, usually called Billy by his friends. She cornered him first.

"Sounds exciting," he said.

"Not really," she said. "It's really more observation and reporting to me. All I want to know is where he is and where he goes."

"Well, you can count me in," he said.

"And not a word to anyone," she insisted. "Understand?"

"Message received and understood." She wasn't sure if he was really the right material for this sort of work, but beggars can't be choosers.

The next one she approached was Giles Morgan-Smith. He was a solicitor and really lived in a completely different world.

"Well, I don't come up here all that often," he replied when Annabelle put the idea to him.

"Good," she said. "We need someone to keep an eye open in the town. In fact, I hope to have people spread around a large area. It's no use if they're all in the same place."

"OK," he said. "I'll keep my eyes open and let you know if I see either of them."

"Thank you, Giles," she said. "Much appreciated, and remember, not a word to anyone."

Daphne Morrison owned a boutique and was a bit of an airhead, but thought it would be quite exciting, as did Sophie Reece-Johnson who didn't work because her husband was too well-heeled, and anyway, there was nothing she was able to do. She went here and there as the mood took her, so was in quite a good position to look out for their two fugitives – if she actually remembered.

The last of the group was Major Magnus Worthing, an ex-army man. He was all for it and wanted to set up an army unit and knock them all into shape, as he put it.

"That's not what I want," said Annabelle. "This is more of a covert operation. Totally hush hush."

"Oh, I see," he said, mulling over the possibilities.

"Each of you is to work independently," she said. "And report back to me if you sight either of our targets. Understood?"

"Totally," he said, making it completely clear that he had ideas of his own.

*****

Alan set the rendezvous point for Weasel's new recruits at the quarry where he had led Annabelle a bit of a dance. He didn't think she would be anywhere near there ever again.

He arrived with Kirsty in good time and waited for the others to arrive.

"What do you hope to achieve with this lot?" asked Kirsty.

"Well, not a lot, I suppose," said Alan. "But I thought it useful to have eyes and ears all around the area, especially if they didn't look the part, and I'm sure this lot will not look the part one little bit."

After a while, Weasel drove into the quarry in his battered old pickup truck. Knuckles and Kevin were squeezed into the cab beside him. It looked most uncomfortable.

"The others should be here shortly," said Weasel. "What do you want us all to do?" he asked Alan.

"Basically, it is just to keep your eyes open for Annabelle and find out if she has recruited anyone else to help her look for us. So, the more inconspicuous you all are, the better."

"I'm not sure that inconspicuous is perhaps the right word for this lot," said Weasel. "Anyway, you can judge for yourself, now," said Weasel. "I can hear them coming."

"So can the whole of Yorkshire," said Kirsty.

"Ever heard the term 'hidden in plain sight'?" said Weasel.

"Yes, actually," said Alan. "And I see what you mean."

Three very laid-back motorcycles rolled into the quarry, throwing up a cloud of dust.

"Sorry about that," said the first one, in a voice that really didn't fit the appearance. This was Nigel Harding, an estate agent. He was dressed in a black leather motorcycle outfit that had seen better days, and peering out of the gap in the visor was a wrinkled face with a bushy moustache. "Let me introduce my friends. This is Grease." He indicated the next one to pull up beside him. He rode a battered old bike and was wearing ancient, well-worn leathers. Perhaps 'worn out' would be a better description.

"Hi," he said. "Pleased to be of service." Not exactly the sort of voice that fitted the image. It seemed he was a stockbroker, but had been a bit of a tearaway in his youth.

"And this is Dingle McClaren," said Nigel, indicating the final member of the group. It turned out that he wasn't Scottish and was now a retired teacher. He was dressed in more orthodox motorbike attire.

It was only then that Alan noticed two horses being ridden down the track towards them. These were the two women from the riding school – Nancy Green and Jocelyn Welsh, a very horsey pair. Weasel lifted a crate of beer out of the boot of his car and handed round the cans.

Alan hadn't noticed that Knuckles and Kevin had disappeared until they returned with arms full of branches and set about building a fire.

"You seem well-organised," said Alan.

"Of course," said Weasel. "Let the fire get going and we'll start the barbecue."

Alan wasn't sure whether he was joking, but soon found out that he wasn't.

Eventually, they all settled down around the fire, munching on chicken legs, lamb chops and sausages.

"So what's this all about?" asked Jocelyn.

"Well, I was working on some special software for a government department," said Alan. "And a senior member of this department decided they wanted to take over this project and tried to steal it from me."

"Did they succeed?" asked Nancy.

"Of course not," said Alan. "They thought they had it but it was booby-trapped. So they didn't get it. They also tried to kill me, or at least someone did, but they got the wrong person. However, I am now officially dead but recognised as the person they killed. Anyway, they are still trying to find me to get hold of my software, or at least Sir Malcolm Birch is – possibly for his own ends. I don't know. He has delegated the search to his niece, Annabelle Pringle, who I believe is recruiting people to keep an eye out for me. This makes it difficult for me to move about.

"There is also a group from the CIA who would like to get their hands on it. Weasel and his friends have sent him on a wild goose chase to France, but it's only a matter of time before they twig."

"So what do we do, then?" asked Grease.

"Watch out for the enemy, whoever they may be," said Alan. "Anyone who seems to be looking for us. I'll leave it to you how you organise yourselves, but basically Weasel is in charge and he will report to me."

"Leave it to me," said Weasel. They continued eating, drinking and chatting before dispersing.

Alan and Kirsty set off back to the lab.

"Do you think they'll be of any use?" she asked.

"Better than nothing, I suppose," said Alan. "At least we will be able to get out a bit more, knowing someone is looking out for us."

*****

The moment Magnus had been given his instructions, he went round the others and made sure they knew he was in charge. He had seen Annabelle taking people aside for a chat so knew exactly who they were. He gathered them all into a huddle and explained that Annabelle had put him in charge and that they were to take their orders from him.

"But she said we were to work alone," said Billy.

"Change of plan, old chap," said Magnus. "As I am a major and have experience of this sort of thing, she decided that it would be better if I took charge. So from now on you report directly to me. Understood?" They all nodded reluctantly. "Good."

From then on they moved around the moor like a small battalion on the lookout for the enemy. At times they would get together in small groups and grumble about Magnus bossing them about.

"I don't know why he should be in charge," said Billy.

"Thinks he knows everything," said Daphne. "Do you really think Annabelle put him in charge?"

"I very much doubt it," said Giles. "I think he just likes being in control. Anyway, might as well go along with it for the time being, but let's keep Annabelle informed of everything he does and says."

*****

Alan and Kirsty were kept busy producing more vaccine for Justin. There was a herd of highland cattle that could possibly have TB and he wanted to try out the new vaccine on them before the ministry ordered them to be destroyed. It would probably mean that they would have to travel up to Scotland, themselves, to administer the vaccine. Actually, it wasn't a vaccine at all, as Alan kept telling Justin, but the term seemed to have stuck so it was generally referred to as a vaccine.

"I wish he would get it right," said Alan as they worked on the next batch of the anti-virus, as he preferred to call it. "You give a vaccine to a well animal, or person, to prevent them getting the disease. It's of no use if they already have the disease. The anti-virus can be administered to a sick animal, or person, to fight the infection."

"You don't have to tell me," she replied. "I am quite aware of what it is called and how it works."

"Sorry," said Alan. "I've just got a bee in my bonnet about getting things right. It's a bit like someone calling a car-boot sale a car-boot. It's not a car-boot, it's a sale. Anyway, you know what I mean."

"I think you need to get out a bit more," said Kirsty.

"I think you're right," said Alan. "Let's finish this batch then go for a walk on the moor."

"Good idea."

It was a good climb to the top of the spiral staircase that led up to the surface, where it terminated in a small room fashioned out of a natural cavern in the rock.

Observation equipment had been installed to allow them to check that all was clear before they emerged onto the open moorland above.

Alan flicked the switch to activate the equipment, and a large screen sprang into life, showing the vista visible from the exit door. A control enabled the camera to be rotated to give an all-round view outside. All was quiet and there was no sign of anyone or anything moving out there. "All clear," said Alan. He switched off the monitor and followed Kirsty up the iron ladder that took them to the next level, which was sealed by a round bulkhead in the floor. This was counter-balanced so that it was easy to open it from below.

They left it open while they were up there, as there was an automatic system that blasted compressed air at the floor to stir up the dust, so that it would settle on the floor, concealing the outline of the hatch, and it wasn't a good thing to be there when it happened.

They opened the outer hatch and stepped out onto the moor, closing it behind them. Looking at it, you would never believe there was a door there as it looked just like rock with various plants sprouting from it. Also the area outside the door was fairly well hidden from view by the rocks to either side.

They peeked round the rocks to make sure there was no one around and then strode up the slope onto the moorland. It was a beautiful day and the heather was in full bloom. It was quiet, with the exception of the constant drone of the bees in the heather.

"The sense of freedom is how I would imagine it when someone is released from a long prison sentence," said Alan, stretching.

"So being with me is like a prison sentence, is it?" said Kirsty.

"No, being with you makes it bearable," he said. "It's just being cooped up all the time."

"Well, we'll be having a nice jaunt out soon," she said. "When we take that anti-virus up to Scotland."

"As long as we're not followed," he said. "I don't know how effective Weasel's lot will be. Still, we've got another week before we set off." He looked around. "It really is lovely up here."

They reached the top of the rise where they could see for miles in all directions. Straight ahead and slightly to the right, the ground dipped down into a narrow valley with a winding stream at the bottom with patches of gorse on either side.

"What's that down there?" asked Kirsty, pointing to the bottom of the valley about half a mile away.

"I can't see anything," he replied. "Where?"

"There's someone down there by the stream," she said. "And look, there's another over there."

As they watched, several people emerged from the gorse and started walking up the slope. They were well spaced out and each carried a gun.

"Oh, panic over," said Kirsty. "It's just the local shoot. They'll be heading off over there." She pointed into the distance.

"That's OK," said Alan pointing to the left. "We'll go up there." But just as they were starting their upward climb, a group left the line of guns, went into a huddle, and headed in their direction.

"I don't like the look of that," said Alan. "If they wanted to warn us away from the shoot, why are there five of them heading this way?"

"Perhaps we should make a strategic withdrawal," said Kirsty.

"Good idea," said Alan and headed off back towards the exit from the lab. "Problem is that by the time we get there, they will be in sight and will see us going in, and that will be no good."

The five people with the guns were moving fast and slowly catching up.

"If they didn't have guns, I would consider talking to them," said Alan, but at that moment there was a great roaring sound as three motorbikes crested the hill and roared down towards the five approaching guns, who stopped and gaped. They seemed to be arguing before four of them turned and walked off down the hill while the other one stood his ground and raised his gun to fire at the charging motorbikes. Just as he was about to fire, a horse galloped by behind him, knocking him off his feet. He cursed, picked up his gun and aimed a second time. The bikes were almost upon him and he couldn't miss, and wouldn't have done had a second horse not come galloping by, knocking him off his feet again just seconds before the motorbikes roared past right over his gun, which lay on the ground. He crawled to his feet and picked up the gun, but realising it was damaged and he could not use it, turned and stomped off back down the hill as the horses and motorbikes raced back past him, whooping with joy. All he could do was swear at them and wave his fists.

It was no use his joining the shoot again as his gun was damaged and could not be used. This was what made him most angry, as it was a very expensive gun of which he was immensely proud, and it would cost a fortune to have it repaired, which was something he could ill afford.

Alan and Kirsty had reached the entrance to the lab and slipped inside, out of sight of anyone. They went down to the observation room below and switched to the outer cameras just in time to see Weasel's gang heading off back up the hill, and the last of the guns retreating back down the hill.

"That was close," said Alan as they continued down the spiral staircase to the lab and their living quarters. "But at least we know what we are up against now."

"Not a lot, it would seem," said Kirsty. "I don't think five people with shotguns are going to be of any danger anywhere but up here on the moor."

"No," said Alan. "But they have eyes and ears and could be looking out for us anywhere. I didn't get a close enough look at them to be able to recognise any of them again."

"I think I might recognise the one who stayed and made a fool of himself," said Kirsty. "He looked as if he might be a retired military man. All we have to do is find out which one of the shoot members is ex-military."

"I suppose we could get Justin to ask a few questions," said Alan. "After all, he mixes with that lot from time to time."

"Good idea," she said. "He'll be in this evening, I believe."

"Good," said Alan, "I would like to sort out when we're going to Scotland."

*****

That weekend, they drove over to the Drovers Inn, which had become their new meeting place as it was more central. Weasel and his crowd were already there, each with a pint, so Alan had to get his own.

"Well, I'd like to thank you all for a timely appearance the other day," said Alan. "I think that gave them something to think about."

"No trouble at all," said Weasel. "It was fun. So I was told."

"Too true," said Grease. "We do all the work and you get the credit."

"Yes," said Weasel. "Management perks, and if it all goes terribly wrong, who do they blame?"

"Well, we're very grateful for your prompt action," said Alan. "Now about our trip to Scotland..."

"We'll all be there," said Knuckles. "Won't we, lads?

"We'd like to be there too," said Jocelyn. "But we'll have to come in the car. Bit far for the horses."

"Of course," said Alan. "Now the thing is, I want to know you are all around, but I don't want to see you and I don't want anyone else to be aware that you are there. Is that clear?"

"Sure is," said Weasel. "Leave it to me."

Thirty-four

A few days later, Alan and Kirsty set off for Scotland. It would be a long journey so they decided they would have several stops on the way, as if they were on holiday.

The first part of the journey took them across the A66 from Scotch Corner towards Carlisle, then on to the M6 northwards. On several occasions they were passed by three motorbikes.

"So much for invisible," said Kirsty.

"Well at least they are not staying with us," said Alan. "So no one could associate them with us. I don't know what sort of car the girls are driving, or how Weasel and his mob are travelling."

"Probably just as well," said Kirsty.

Their first stop was to be in Stirling, where they had booked a bed and breakfast for the night, but they stopped every couple of hours for a coffee break. Each time, they looked at every other car suspiciously, and studied any lone person carefully, but saw nothing to worry them.

After booking into the bed and breakfast, they went out into the town to find a cafe for something to eat. After they had been there for a while, three bikers came in and sat down at a table at the other end of the room.

"I don't suppose anyone would associate them with us," said Kirsty.

"Not just this once," said Alan. "But if someone is following us, they might think it strange that wherever we go, three bikers appear at the same time. I think I'll have a word with them as we leave."

*****

Devlin Johnson had arrived at Sir Malcolm's office in the early morning and was let in by the duty officer and ushered to the waiting room.

"I don't think Sir Malcolm is due in until ten," said the duty officer. "But you are welcome to wait."

As it happened, Sir Malcolm arrived shortly after Devlin had been shown into the waiting room and was taken straight up to his office.

"I have a major problem," said Sir Malcolm. "There is someone I need finding and apprehending, urgently."

"Apprehending?"

"Exactly," said Sir Malcolm. "I don't want him harmed. Is that clear?"

"Perfectly," said Devlin. "But, of course, that doubles the cost."

"As long as I get results, I don't care what it costs," said Sir Malcolm, knowing full well this fellow would never get paid anyway.

Devlin set off to find Annabelle, who was to fill him in with all she had manage to find out to date, which wasn't much. However, she did know on which road to lie in wait for him and it was agreed that her little group would watch out for any movements and report immediately to Devlin.

So, when Alan and Kirsty had set out for Scotland, word had been passed to Devlin and from then on he was on his own. The last thing he wanted was to be tangled up with a bunch of amateurs.

He had followed Alan at a discreet distance and noticed that a group of bikers seemed to keep appearing. At first he put it down to coincidence, but as time went on he realised that they were actually with him.

The cafe at Stirling clinched the matter. He would have to keep an eye on them, but they could make things difficult when he came to the point where he had to capture Westbrook and take him back to Sir Malcolm.

He waited until Westbrook and the girl left the cafe then followed them back to their bed and breakfast so that he knew where they were staying. It wouldn't be very convenient to try to capture him there as it was too public. It would have been much easier to have eliminated him, but that wasn't to be.

There was another bed and breakfast across the road, so he took a room there for the night. The next morning he was able to keep a lookout from the window in the breakfast room to see when they were leaving.

At about eight thirty, they set off again in a northerly direction on a road that would take them along the western bank of Loch Lomond. There wasn't any other likely route they could take, so Devlin followed them until he was sure that was the way they were going, and then overtook them and went ahead. There was a likely place that they would stop for a break, so he stopped there to wait for them.

*****

"Stupid idiot," said Alan as a fellow in a sports car shot past them. "Typical of people who drive that sort of car."

The fellow in question wore a tweed jacket and cap, and a scarf, as it was a little cool for an open-topped car that morning.

"He won't get there any quicker," said Kirsty. "The road gets narrower a bit further along and you end up going at the speed of the slowest."

"Unless he takes his life in his hands and overtakes everyone like he just overtook us," said Alan.

They were in no particular hurry, so they cruised along at a comfortable speed so they could admire the scenery as they drove along. At least they didn't see the three bikers, so it was obvious that they had taken note of Alan's instructions as he left the cafe in Stirling, and there had been no sign of the girls or Weasel and his gang so far. Alan hoped that they would all be on hand if needed.

The drive along the banks of Loch Lomond was very pleasant, but there were few places to stop for a rest and a cup of coffee, so they had to stop at the one place where they knew there was a cafe. By the time they reached it they were ready to stretch their legs.

"Isn't that the car that sped past us way back there?" asked Kirsty, pointing at the red sports car parked in the car park. "It didn't do him much good, did it?"

They got out and stretched their legs, then headed for the cafe. As they sat down, they noticed the fellow in the tweeds leaving.

"Looks as if he has more money than sense," said Alan. "At least we haven't seen the bikers. I hope they haven't got lost. It would be bad if they were nowhere to be seen if we got into trouble, and I don't like the look of that fellow in the Audi. Perhaps I'm just getting paranoid."

"Just because you're paranoid doesn't mean they aren't after you," said Kirsty with a giggle. "How much further is it from here?"

"About another fifty miles," said Alan. "The last bit might be on foot. I don't know. Maybe they've got tractors or something. We'll just have to wait and see."

After they had finished their snack and coffee, they set off again.

"I don't understand why Sir Malcolm still wants to find you," said Kirsty. "I would have thought he would have decided that the software was destroyed when they used the wrong password."

"He can't be sure, I suppose," said Alan. "But I don't know why he is so interested in it personally. If it were the department, they would have brought in the military or MI6 or someone like that, not Weasel and his lot or his niece. It doesn't make sense."

"Well we can't go on like this indefinitely, can we?" she said. "Hiding from everyone? It's like being in prison. But I don't know how we can throw him off the scent and make him think we are dead or gone to some distant land. Do you?"

"Not at the moment, no," said Alan. "But I'm working on it. At least we seem to have lost the Yanks, at least for the time being. But if Sir Malcolm is working on his own, for some reason, if we can eliminate him we might be OK."

"Eliminate?"

"One way or another," said Alan. "I'm not proposing hiring a hit man. In fact I'm not sure what I'm proposing. We'll just have to see how things pan out. Anyway, I think this is our turning."

A farm track led off to the left and it was fairly difficult going. The recent rain had made it very muddy, but they managed to keep going until they reached the farm buildings.

A dog came out and barked at them, followed by a man who shouted at the dog.

"Sorry about that," he shouted. "You the ones come with the vaccine?"

"That's right," said Alan. "Where are the cattle?"

"Up on top meadow in the barn," he replied. "Wanted to keep them away from the other animals."

"How do we get there?"

"On foot."

It was about half a mile along a muddy track. If it hadn't been so hard going they might have been able to admire the marvellous scenery.

The barn, as he had called it, had seen better days and had partly collapsed. All the cattle were penned in at the better end of the building.

"Better get started," said Alan and put a halter on the first beast to be injected, while Kirsty prepared the syringe. They applied it when the beast was standing still enough.

This was repeated for each of the cattle, before releasing them into the field where they would be kept away from other animals until the official vet had tested them in three weeks' time.

When they had finished, they made their way back to the farm; the farmer had gone on ahead to put the kettle on and prepare a nip of Scotch to go with it.

The route back to the farm first crossed a boggy field, then went through a small copse, before winding down to the farm.

"It's very quiet," said Alan. "There were birds singing when we came up."

"The farmer must have frightened them when he went through," said Kirsty.

All of a sudden a figure in tweeds stepped out from the undergrowth and pointed a gun at them.

"I thought we had lost you," said Alan, wondering what to do next. Perhaps it would be best to play along with him and then try to attract the farmer's attention when they got down to the farm.

"And if you are thinking the farmer will help you," said Devlin, "you can think again. He's a bit tied up at the moment." They put up their hands and Devlin prodded them into motion towards the farm. "I have someone who would like to speak to you rather urgently."

"I have nothing to say to him," said Alan.

"Oh, I think you have," said Devlin. "And don't think of trying to escape in the notion that I won't shoot you. I might have to shoot the girl instead."

"That would be a mistake," said Alan, trying to sound unruffled, though he felt sure his knees were knocking. "She holds part of the information your boss would like to get his hands on."

"A bullet in the legs won't prevent you talking," said Devlin. "Now walk!"

They walked and headed towards the farm where they found the farmer tied to a chair. Devlin untied him and herded them out into one of the barns. There he secured them to a central pillar. "We'll stay here tonight. I'm expecting more appropriate transport in the morning."

Luckily it wasn't a cold night, though it was rather uncomfortable. It was impossible to sleep and if they settled down for a while, they would hear rustling and squeaking in the straw.

"They won't hurt you," said the farmer. "And by the way, my name is Hamish. Now perhaps you would like to tell me why we are all tied up in my barn."

"I'm Alan and this is Kirsty," said Alan. "And it would seem this fellow works for someone who would like to get his hands on a project we're working on. This vaccine is the product of it so far."

"He wants to make vaccine?"

"Oh no," said Alan. "If you can make vaccine you can also make viruses."

"Germ warfare, you mean?"

"That's about the size of it," said Alan.

"Well wouldn't that be better in the hands of the government?" asked Hamish.

"Probably," said Alan, "but this fellow may not be working for the government. Well, he is working for the government, but it is possible that he wants the project for his own ends, whatever they may be. We just can't take the risk."

"So what do we do now?" asked Hamish.

"There doesn't seem to be much we can do," said Alan. "I can't loosen my ropes. How about you?"

"No, mine are tight," said Hamish.

"Mine too," said Kirsty. "Looks like we're stuck here."

"So what happens in the morning?" asked Hamish. "I know they're taking you off somewhere, but what happens to me? I can't see them wanting me around to tell people what has happened."

"You have a point," said Alan. "And you wouldn't be the first innocent bystander to get hurt."

"Thanks," said Hamish. "That's very encouraging."

"We need to get out of here tonight," said Alan. "We have people who are supposed to be looking out for us, but they seem to have disappeared. Has anyone got anything sharp they can get their hands on?"

"I have a penknife in my pocket," said Kirsty. "But I can't reach it. Maybe you can."

"I'll try," said Alan. "Which pocket is it in?"

"The left hand one," said Kirsty. After a great deal of twisting and turning they decided that it wasn't going to be possible, so they decided to try and think of some other answer to their problems.

The night wore on and it began to get colder. The wind was getting up, rattling the loose boards in the walls of the barn. Suddenly there was a creaking noise and the door swung open.

"Now what are you doing in here?" asked Jocelyn as she and Nancy walked into the barn.

"Waiting for you two to untie us," said Alan. "And a little less noise, please. We don't want to wake the gunman."

"Thought we'd better save your skins before we set off back home," said Nancy.

"Yes," said Jocelyn. "We're overdue back at the riding school. Thought it was just a trip up here and straight back."

"It was supposed to be," said Alan. "But we were waylaid by a gunman. We've got 'til tomorrow morning to get well away from here, but we can't head home because that's what they'll expect. Anyway, thanks for your help."

Before leaving, Kirsty tried to lift the bonnet of the gunman's car, but it was locked and she didn't want to make any noise and wake him. She went to their car and took out a wrench from the boot, reached under the sports car and undid the sump drain nut, letting out all the oil.

Alan got into their car and the others pushed it slowly down the track until they were well clear of the farm, then they all got in and drove the rest of the way down to the road where the girls had left their car.

"Thanks for the help," said Alan. "Have a good journey home." They got into their car and set off southward.

"Do you think he put a tracker on our car?" said Kirsty. "He seemed to find us rather easily."

"Could well have done," said Alan as he walked round the car feeling under the wings for anything that shouldn't be there. "Are, here it is." He pulled the tracker out and was about to throw it into the undergrowth when he had a better idea. He walked across the road and waited. He had heard a vehicle coming. It sounded like a lorry, which would be ideal, and sure enough a large lorry with an open back trundled round the corner heading south. As it passed, Alan threw the tracker into the back of the lorry.

"Bon voyage," he said and walked back to their car and got in beside Kirsty. Hamish was in the back. "Where can we take you?"

"Head north," said Hamish. "I'll tell you when we get there."

When they got to Inverbeg, Hamish told them they could drop him off there and he would contact the police. Maybe they would be able to catch the gunman still at his farm.

They pulled in and Hamish got out, waved them goodbye and disappeared into the darkness.

"Where to now?" asked Kirsty.

"I think we should carry on up this road and then head inland and back to Stirling. Hopefully it will throw everyone off our track."

There was a roar of motorbikes from behind and the three bikers pulled up beside them.

Thirty-five

Devlin woke with a start. He didn't know what had woken him but he lay listening for any further sounds. Then he heard it again, the sound of a door banging somewhere outside. He leapt out of bed, pulled on his overcoat and boots and picked up his gun.

Outside, all seemed normal until he realised that Westbrook's car had gone.

"Blast!" he said. Then he noticed the barn door swinging in the wind and banging shut every now and then. He rushed to the barn and as soon as his eyes accustomed to the dark, he realised that his captives had gone. After a few more pungent expletives, he dashed to his car and checked his tracker. He soon got a reading on them; they were heading back south, the way they had come. His car roared into life and he set off down the track at a breakneck speed. At the main road, he turned right and sped off in pursuit. They couldn't have been going long, as they were not too far ahead and he was catching up fast. There was virtually no traffic on the road at that time of night so he could break all the speed limits with impunity, and he did.

His monitor showed that his quarry was just ahead and he was closing fast. Then, for some reason it seemed to be speeding away from him. Then he realised that he had passed them. They must have parked somewhere off the road, so he stopped and retraced his tracks until he passed a transport cafe just off the road, but he couldn't see their car anywhere in the car park. There was just a large lorry parked there.

He took the monitor and scanned the car park and homed in on his target, which to his horror, turned out to be the lorry.

"Damnation!" he shouted to no one in particular, but a light came on in the cab of the lorry, so he dashed back to his car and sped off back the way he had come, as it was obvious that they were trying to throw him off the scent.

About a mile up the road, there was an almighty bang and clouds of smoke from under the bonnet. His car skidded to a halt at the side of the road. The air turned blue with his outpouring of cursing. There was nothing he could do but get out and walk. He would have to find alternative transport. He was adept at hot-wiring cars, as stealing expensive cars was a major sideline of his. The problem was that there didn't seem to be any cars around, so he just kept walking.

*****

The next morning, Sir Malcolm sat fuming at his desk with the telephone in his hand. He seemed to be struck dumb by what he had heard and Devlin was waiting at the other end for his response.

"Well it's your problem," said Sir Malcolm. "But don't come back here without him. And, if you don't come back, you had better keep looking over your shoulder for the rest of your life, which I can assure you will be very short." He slammed the phone down. "Can't I depend on anyone any more?"

He picked up the phone again and dialled.

*****

Alan and Kirsty set off again in convoy with the three bikers. As they had lost him previously, Alan thought it best if they kept together. After all, it wasn't a secret now that they were all together, and perhaps it would deter the gunman.

They drove on until it was quite light and then stopped at the first opportunity for breakfast.

"So what happened back there?" said Nigel. "Did we miss all the fun?"

"If you can call it fun, yes," said Alan. "We were lucky that the two girls hadn't lost us. We had a tracker on the car, but we got rid of it, so hopefully he has set off in the wrong direction, but he'll cotton on eventually."

"So he'll realise what has happened and set off after us again?" said Grease.

"Well, maybe," said Alan. "Kirsty emptied the oil from his sump, so he won't get too far before he wrecks his engine."

They were all ravenously hungry so they ordered a full Scottish breakfast all round and a big jug of coffee. While they were eating, two youths sitting across the room kept glancing at them. Alan thought it was the sight of the three bikers that fascinated them, but then they seemed to be more interested in Alan himself and Kirsty. They both sat with their mobile phones, texting madly.

"I can't imagine what they find so absorbing," said Kirsty.

"Oh, you noticed them too," said Alan. "They've been looking at us, on and off, the whole time we've been here."

"Perhaps they haven't seen real people before," said Kirsty.

After a while the two youths were joined by two girls who looked like hippies, or the Scottish equivalent. After a bit of hushed conversation, the two girls took sly peeks at Alan and his group.

Grease had been watching them and slowly got up, stretched to his full height, and strolled over to the group of youngsters. Before he reached them, they had decided they were late for an appointment elsewhere and rushed out.

"I wonder what their problem is," said Grease returning to the others.

"Perhaps they didn't like the look of you," said Alan.

"What's not to like?" he said.

"At least having you lot with us," said Kirsty, "you take the attention off us."

When they had finished their breakfast, they set off again, but a little way down the road there seemed to be a large gathering. There were groups of bikers and several others with vans and other ancient vehicles. They slowed down as the crowd was taking up half the road, and stopped when they couldn't get through without hitting someone.

Alan wound down the window. "What's happening?" he asked the nearest group.

"It's them," shouted one of the crowd and the others all crowded round their car. Even the sight of the three bikers didn't deter them.

"Will someone tell me what is happening?" demanded Alan.

"You're him on the net, aren't you?" said someone.

"Don't know what you're talking about," said Alan. "Now can you clear the road and let us move on?"

The crowd parted and a huge man in leathers strode towards them. He had a bushy red beard and a broken nose, which made him look quite aggressive.

"You," he said pointing at Alan. "Get out."

"I don't think so," said Alan, winding up the window, but the man with the red beard walked up to the car and bent down as if to lift it bodily, and he almost managed it.

"Now get out or I'll tip you over," he shouted.

"OK," shouted Alan and opened the door to get out. The three bikers moved in to back him up. "Now, what do you want with us? We're not here to steal your sheep."

"Don't try to be funny," said the brute. "This is not a laughing matter."

"I haven't a clue what you're on about," said Alan, as Kirsty joined him. "Perhaps you would like to explain."

"It's all over the net," he said. "You have been exposed."

"What's all over the net?" said Alan.

"All about you and your germ warfare experiments," he countered. "So, what have you been doing up here in Scotland? Spreading plague, is that it?"

"No," said Alan. "We've been vaccinating cows against TB. I don't think you could call that germ warfare, do you?"

"He's lying," shouted someone nearby. Grease turned and picked the fellow up by the front of his jacket and pushed his ugly face into his, and the fellow screamed, so Grease just dropped him on the ground.

"So it's GM, is it?" asked the brute.

"You don't even know what that means, do you?" said Alan. "You haven't a clue. You lap up all the rubbish you read on the antisocial media, and think it is gospel. Well it isn't. It's vicious spouting of idiots with no brains. And it's idiots like you, with no brains, that lap it up. Anyway, who are you?"

"Me? I'm Donald McIntosh."

"Well Mr. McIntosh," said Alan, squaring up to him, "I'll tell you what GM is. Genetic Modification, and you are a perfect example of that."

"What's that supposed to mean?"

"It means that you are not the same as your parents," said Alan. "Their DNA is modified randomly so that all offspring are different. This is nature's way of protecting itself. If the mod is beneficial, the creature prospers and passes on some of the improvement to its own offspring. If not, it doesn't do as well, and probably doesn't pass on its deficiencies."

"That's not the same as tampering with genetics," said Donald.

"Well, actually it is," said Alan. "Except that controlled modification is more likely to achieve the desired result than the random modification that happens in nature. Nature is more trial and error."

"Well, they said you were into germ warfare," said Donald.

"Well I'm not," said Alan. "I am fully against that, but there are people who would use GM technology for that purpose. That is why I am keeping anything I do completely secret and out of their hands so they can't misuse it. The people who posted those things on the internet are the ones who would like to get their hands on what I am doing, so they can misuse it. Do you believe everything you read on the internet or read in the papers or hear on the news?"

"Well they wouldn't say it if there wasn't any truth in it, would they?"

"They will say anything that is in their financial interest," said Alan. "Like this global warming nonsense."

"Well that's scientific fact," said Donald. "Everyone knows that."

"Actually no," said Alan. "In the last ten years there have been eighteen thousand scientific papers published that dispute that. The whole idea is riddled with errors and false suppositions."

"Then why is it getting warmer?"

"Natural cycles," said Alan. "There's nothing anyone can do about it. But actually, it will start to cool soon. We are on the edge of dropping into the next ice-age. But don't worry. It will take several thousand years to really make a difference."

"How do you know that?" said Donald. "You can't read the future."

"Well actually, I can," said Alan. "If everything is controlled by cyclic phenomena you can predict where it is going."

"But not everything is down to money," said Donald. "What about pure science – astronomy for instance?"

"Well if that isn't down to money, I don't know what is," said Alan.

"Rubbish!" shouted someone.

"Not rubbish," said Alan. "They are paid very good salaries to play with very expensive toys paid for by the tax payer who gets not a penny in return. And it doesn't matter what ideas they come up with. No one can dispute them because no one will listen. They say there was a big bang when everything appeared from nowhere. Can you believe that? I can't, but it doesn't matter as long as we keep handing out the money."

"But what about this doomsday machine that you've got?"

"I have some software that can manipulate DNA code so that we can produce anti-viruses to combat diseases," said Alan. "The thing is that if you can do that, you can do other things also, like create specialist viruses, or special genetic codes to create new human beings. It's all possible, but extremely difficult. I am trying to make sure that no one else gets their hands on what I have achieved so far so that they can't do these things, and you aren't helping in that respect."

"I see what you mean," said Donald, then he turned and shouted at the assembled crowd, "False alarm. It's all a scam."

The crowd looked disappointed, but drifted off in ones and twos until only Donald was left. "I find what you say quite interesting. Why don't we go and have a drink?"

"Sounds like a good idea," said Grease, and the other two bikers agreed wholeheartedly.

"Where do you suggest?" asked Alan. "I haven't seen any pubs around here."

"That's because there aren't any," said Donald. "But I have a wee cottage just down the road. If you give me a lift I'll show you the way."

*****

Devlin decided that his car was more important to him than doing a job for Sir Malcolm, so he found the nearest garage and got his car towed in for repair. The garage attendant looked at it, sucking his teeth, and gave him an outrageous price, which Devlin accepted, much to the surprise of the Scotsman. Devlin knew that he would never pay that price so told the garage man that he would be back for it in four weeks, and would like to hire a car in the meantime.

The car was hardly up to the standard he was used to, but it was a car and it went, at the moment, though it was doubtful how long it would continue to go.

So he set off in search of Alan Westbrook and his entourage. He stopped at every cafe and petrol station along the way to ask if anyone had seen them. He discovered that the three bikers had joined them, so they were quite easy to follow, until he came to a place where people had seen them, and had confronted them, but hadn't a clue where they had gone. Further on no one had seen them at all, which was rather puzzling.

*****

The cottage was small but cosy, and was rather cramped with them all squeezed into the little sitting room.

"A bit like when the old shepherd brought his sheep in out of the winter's cold," said Donald with a grin as he opened a new bottle of Scotch. "Now, who's going to join me in a wee dram?"

The three bikers were keen to try it. Alan and Kirsty told him they would only have a small one as they still had a long way to drive.

"Now I really am interested in this machine of yours," said Donald.

"Not really a machine," said Alan. "I use a lot of standard lab equipment, but it is the software that is the key. Without that, there would be nothing."

"So it's the software they are after, is it? So how can you protect it?"

"Easy," said Alan. "There are many ways to protect software."

"Such as?"

"Well I'm not going to give away all my secrets," said Alan. "But there are ways of encoding the source code, and then it can be password protected. Or you could keep it on a remote computer or parts of it on several computers where you would need several passwords to access it. Or there are dynamic passwords; they are very difficult to crack. Or you can set booby traps, or some of each. Why are you so interested anyway?"

"Oh, I used to do a bit with computers once," he said.

"Programming?" asked Alan.

"Yes," he replied. "But I have left the tech side now and prefer the simple life in the hills. I work as a gillie sometimes now."

"Is there much hunting in this area then?"

"Oh, yes," he replied. "But I travel all over. I work freelance, you see."

"So what computer language did you use when you did your programming?" asked Alan. "ALGOL, COBOL, C++? I use BLUCOL."

"I've used most of them at some time or other," said Donald.

"Look, it's been nice talking to you, Donald," said Alan "But we really must be on our way."

"I don't think these three should be on the road in their state," said Donald.

"Can I leave them with you 'til they sober up?"

"That's fine," he said. "Are you sure you can't stay for a bit?"

"No, we must be on our way."

They left the three bikers happily drinking Donald's whisky and set off south again. Without the bikers, they were harder to identify so there were no more hold-ups.

"Seemed a nice chap," said Kirsty.

"Yes," said Alan, "but he was lying through his teeth. He'd never had anything to do with computers or he would have known that BLUCOL wasn't a computer language."

"Perhaps he thought it was a new language that he hadn't heard of and didn't want to sound ignorant," said Kirsty.

"Hmm," said Alan. "I don't think so. I have a feeling he is more involved than he would like us to realise."

*****

Devlin decided that the only course of action left to him was to sit and wait, so he stopped at the next roadside cafe he came to, bought a cup of coffee, and waited.

He wasn't sure what he was going to do if he saw them, but decided to take things one step at a time.

The day wore on and nothing came past that he recognised, certainly no car with an entourage of bikers, until just after he had had some lunch and told the cafe owner he was waiting for friends to catch up with him. He saw a car he recognised go past. But there were no bikers to be seen. He dashed out to his hired car and set off to follow them. If he could find out where they had been hiding, *that would be good enough*, he thought.

*****

Alan pulled in to a bed and breakfast in Stirling and took the cases into the hallway.

"Did you see that car pull up behind us?" he asked Kirsty. "It has been behind us for ages. I thought he might overtake or turn off somewhere, but he just followed along about fifty yards behind, and now he has pulled up across the road."

Kirsty peeked out of the door. "He seems to be staying at that B & B across the road," she said. At that moment three bikers pulled into the drive. "Our friends are here."

After booking into their rooms – the bikers had to share – they all congregated in the sitting room downstairs.

The landlady poked her head round the door. "I hope you aren't going to be rowdy," she said.

"Of course not," said Grease in his best public school accent. "Whatever made you think that we would?"

"Oh, I'm sorry," she said. "I just thought… ". She left quickly, closing the door behind her.

"So what do you make of our Scottish friend?" asked Alan.

"Seemed nice enough," said Nigel. "Why?"

"You mean his whisky was nice enough," said Alan. "No, I don't think he rings true at all."

"You just have a suspicious nature," said Dingle. "I think he was OK."

"But then you are Scottish," said Kirsty.

"My ancestors were, yes," said Dingle. "But I'm not. I was born in Surrey."

"Well he talked as if he knew a lot about computing," said Alan. "But he made a few bloopers."

"Perhaps he was just trying to impress," said Grease.

"That's what I said," said Kirsty.

"Perhaps that's the case," said Alan, "but I still think we shouldn't assume it is. We must keep our eyes open. Then there's that fellow who locked us in the barn back there. He's just turned up and is staying across the road. It looks as if he has found himself a new car. Well, when I say 'new' I mean different. You can see it in the drive if you look out of the window."

Grease peered out. "That green Ford?"

"That's the one," said Alan.

"Leave it to me," said Grease, getting up from where he had flopped down in the easy chair. "And no one pinch my chair, or else."

Thirty-Six

As soon as the bikers had left, Donald sat down to have something to eat. He had drunk quite a lot of whisky, to keep the bikers company, and felt quite drowsy. He was just settling down when there was a knock at the door.

Who's that now, he thought. He wasn't expecting anyone and felt quite annoyed at being disturbed.

The knock came again, a little louder.

"OK, OK, I'm coming," he shouted, getting up and staggering to the door.

As he opened it, the sunlight dazzled him for a moment and all he could see was a slender figure standing in the doorway.

"What is it?" he demanded, none too politely. "Can't a fellow get a little peace around here?"

"Sorry to bother you," said a posh female voice. "But I need to talk to you rather urgently."

Donald was intrigued. "You had better come in," he said, and showed her into the cosy little sitting room. "Sorry about the mess. I've had some friends in and haven't got round to tidying up yet."

"That's perfectly OK," she said. "It's them I want to talk to you about, or at least one of them. By the way, I'm Annabelle."

"Hello Annabelle," he said. "Welcome to my humble abode. Now what can I do for you?"

"Well, you had some visitors today," she said. "I was in the crowd when you stopped them, and I recognised one of them as an old friend from my college days, but I didn't get a chance to speak to her. I was distracted by someone and when I looked for her, you had all gone. I asked someone where they had gone and they directed me here. I couldn't follow immediately, so I missed them again."

"So how can I help?"

"She was with a man called Alan Westbrook, and her name is Kirsty Williams. I believe they are living together, but I don't know their address or where I can contact them and wondered if you could help?"

"They didn't give me their address," said Donald. "But I got the impression it was down in Yorkshire or somewhere like that. But I did give my email address to one of the bikers. If he gets in touch, would you like me to give him a message?"

"That would be great, if you would," she said. "The thing is, I would like it to be a surprise, so if you could, get her to meet him somewhere to suit them both, but don't let them know why. Try to make it as intriguing as possible. Then let me know where and when so that I can surprise her. I'll give you my email address also."

"Well, it all depends on whether the biker contacts me, but I think he will," said Donald. "But that is a bit complicated, seeing as I don't know him that well. When he emails me, that is, if he emails me, I'll email his address to you and you can contact him directly. I think that would be better. Now, how about a dram of my best whisky?"

*****

The next morning Annabelle woke with a terrible hangover, and wasn't sure where she was. The room looked strange, what she could see of it, and when she turned over she realised that she wasn't alone. She let out a strangled cry and leapt out of bed, only to find that she was naked. Her clothes were scattered around the floor, so she gathered them up as quickly as she could and dashed out to find the bathroom.

When she was dressed, she went back to the bedroom just as Donald was emerging. She let out another cry when she realised that he was also naked, and dashed downstairs. That was also a mistake as her head throbbed worse than ever. So she slumped down on the settee. After a few minutes, Donald appeared, bright and breezy.

"Hope you slept well," he said. "Now, how about a fry up?" Annabelle felt a great feeling of nausea sweep over her, but she managed to keep the contents of her stomach where they were.

"No thank you," she gasped. "Just an Alka-Seltzer."

"You English," he said. "No stomach for the hard stuff. I'll get you something to settle your stomach. Works every time." He disappeared into the kitchen and returned a few minutes later with a glass of something fizzing. "Swallow this in one."

She looked at it uncertainly, then gulped it down.

She gasped. "Ugh, what was that?"

"Better not to know," he said. "But it usually works well."

"Well, it certainly took my mind off the hangover," she said. "In fact I think I feel better already, but I can't remember a thing about last night."

"You can't?" he said, surprised.

"Not a thing," she said. "Did we … you know?"

"Best not to ask," he said. "All I can say is that you seemed to be having a good evening. Now how about breakfast?"

"Perhaps some toast?"

"I make fine porridge," he said. "That'll get you back on your feet." He disappeared into the kitchen and after a short while, appeared with two steaming bowls of porridge.

Much to her surprise, Annabelle found she rather liked it.

"Now," said Donald, "if you give me your email address, I'll contact you as soon as I hear from that biker, and let you know where you can find him."

"That would be great," she replied. As soon as she had finished her porridge and downed a large mug of black coffee, she said goodbye to Donald and set off on foot to find where she had left her car.

As she walked off down the road, his neighbour, Dougie McGee, looked over the fence. "Had a good night, have you, Donald?"

"Not really," he replied. "I must have gone a bit heavy on the whisky and she fell asleep on me as soon as her head hit the pillow."

"Maybe you're just a bit boring for a young lass like that."

"No," said Donald. "I'm sure it was the whisky. These southerners just can't hold their drink."

*****

The following morning, Alan and Kirsty went down for breakfast and found that the three bikers had already left.

"Hope they haven't left us to pay the bill," said Alan.

They had a leisurely breakfast before going out and putting their bags back into the car. Kirsty was staring across the road. "Look at that," she said, grinning. Alan followed her gaze and burst out laughing. Grease had left the car with four flat tyres.

"That should slow him up," said Alan.

The rest of the journey back was quite uneventful and they were back in the company of Justin in time for a hot evening meal.

"So how did it go?" asked Justin.

"Well we got the cattle vaccinated fine," said Alan. "It was after that that we had trouble." He outlined what had happened.

"It seems that someone is still after you, then," said Justin. "And it is obvious they want you alive or they could have killed you rather than just lock you in the barn. I assume he was waiting for a backup team to take you back to whoever sent them."

"I can't think what they would want me for," said Alan. "Originally the department just wanted the project for themselves, as did the Yanks. But then Sir Malcolm seemed to want to get his hands on it for some reason, and I'm sure it wasn't for the department. I can't think why he would want it though."

"Perhaps he wants to sell it to the Americans," said Kirsty.

"Do you think he would risk it?" said Justin. "There'd be hell to pay if the government found out. Do you think he'd risk it?"

"I just don't know what to think," said Alan. "Someone had gone to the trouble to put those entries on Facebook and Twitter telling everyone we were in Scotland, spreading the plague. Luckily we were able to convince the ringleader that it was a hoax or we could have been in big trouble. I wonder what happened to Weasel and his lot."

"Must have got lost," said Kirsty.

"We'll have to go and see him and find out," said Alan. "There's always the possibility that Sir Malcolm has made him a better offer and he has shifted his allegiance again."

"The bikers still seemed to be with us," said Kirsty. "This is all getting rather confusing."

"Well, there's always the financial aspect," said Justin. "After all, my company stands to make quite a bit out of these vaccines, as do you. Maybe Sir Malcolm has the same idea."

"I don't think so," said Alan. "If he has, then he is going about it in a very strange way. Why didn't he just make us an offer for it?"

"I rather doubt whether he could afford it," said Justin. "I would want rather a lot for my involvement, and there's no reason why you should just give it away either."

"Even if he did make an offer that most people couldn't refuse," said Alan, "I wouldn't like to just hand it over to anyone else for fear that it might get into the wrong hands.

That's what the Americans were worried about – the bacterial warfare element. They would be quite happy for it to be in their hands, but are scared stiff of it getting into the hands of someone who doesn't like them, and there are plenty of those in the world."

"So, what can you do with this software that would be so bad?" asked Justin.

"Well, in theory, you could engineer a new type of virus that could wipe out half the world's population," said Alan. "Or you could tailor it to just affect a particular race or even a single person. I don't know how easy it would be to do that, but in theory it is possible. And going into the realms of science fiction, you could tailor human beings to be workers, soldiers, scientists, or anything you liked."

"Would that be possible?" asked Kirsty. "Surely people choose what they want to do. How can you programme them to be workers or anything in particular?"

"Well, in nature we are already programmed to do different things," said Alan. "Each person has a different set of natural abilities they are born with. For instance, I am good at science and engineering. I like doing these things because I am good at them, but I don't like learning languages because they don't come easily to me. Some people just can't get their head around maths or science, so just think they don't like them. It's just the way their brains are wired. We arrive with our brains only partly wired. The rest we learn and our brains wire themselves to optimise what we have to do to survive. It's that initial wiring that counts. Your DNA is like a computer programme that controls the way cells grow together to make an animal or plant. So if you can modify the programme, you can alter the resulting creature. But, as I said, this is theory only and will be extremely hard to achieve in practice."

"Sounds a bit like Dr. Frankenstein," said Kirsty.

"It does, doesn't it?" said Alan. "But he used lumps of bodies to try and do that. A rather primitive idea."

"So if it is just conjecture," said Justin, "why worry if he gets his hands on your software?"

"Because it is possible to engineer viruses," said Alan. "That's what I have been doing to produce these vaccines, and that is why we have been doing the trials in isolated places in case I have got it wrong. We don't want to start a worldwide epidemic that might wipe out all the cattle, do we?"

"Could that happen?" asked Justin.

"Theoretically, yes," said Alan. "But in practice it is most unlikely. If it did happen, there is less likelihood of it spreading."

"I'm glad I didn't know that when we started doing these tests," said Justin. "But I have just heard from the people in Scotland that your latest tests seem to have been successful."

*****

Justin wondered if he had been a bit hasty in allowing Alan to develop his products in his lab, but on the other hand, it looked as if there was a lot of money to be made with his new vaccines. What he didn't like was the chance that someone else could get hold of this technology and use it in an unscrupulous way, but he didn't know what he could do to prevent that except to continue to let Alan work in secret in his lab.

Justin had started out as a wheeler dealer and had gradually built up his empire until it was the successful pharmaceutical giant that it had become. He had plants all over the world, but his main one was in Cardiff, where he spent most of his time.

In the earlier days he had worked from the secret lab that he had set up in the disused bunker that no one had wanted. It had taken him a long time to get it to the state it was in now, and had been quite difficult to do, as he didn't want outsiders to know about it. He had had to do most of the work himself – hiring machinery which he had to operate himself. But now it was finished he had little use for it except to dabble with new ideas from time to time, so he was pleased that Alan could make good use of it.

His niece, Kirsty, had a degree in pharmaceuticals, and he had let her have access to the lab for some research she was doing for a higher degree which she gave up before finishing. Since then she had done a bit of this and a bit of that and had drifted rather aimlessly.

When Alan had come along, it had given her a focus, though she wasn't sure in which direction it was actually going, but as she got more involved with what he was working on she found it was giving her life a little more direction, though she wasn't sure in which direction it was actually going. For now she was quite happy to drift along wherever it took her. At least there was a bit of excitement.

Thirty-Seven

Grease was a little surprised when he got an email from a strange young lady, and at first was of the opinion that he should ignore it. But the longer he left it, the more it gnawed at him. What would be the harm in answering her? It would be interesting to know what she wanted. It appeared that she was a friend of the Scotsman, Donald, whom he had met on their foray into Scotland, but he couldn't imagine why she would want to speak to him.

Eventually he gave into the gnawing at his mind and replied to her email in a non-committal way. It didn't occur to him to mention it to the others, as he thought it wasn't any of their business and obviously had nothing to do with their involvement with Alan Westbrook. How could it? Now he would have to wait for her reply. He hoped it wasn't one of those Russian women who email people at random to try and get them to send money so they could come over from Russia to meet them. Surely it couldn't be, after all she knew Donald and knew his name, or at least the name he used when in his leathers. At the moment he was in his grey suit and tie, sitting in his office with his secretary sitting across the office typing frantically on her keyboard. Even she wasn't aware of his weekend persona.

*****

Devlin noticed that Alan and his friends were getting ready to leave, so he picked up his case and crept out to his car, making sure they couldn't see him. He was about to put the key in the lock when he realised that he had a flat tyre. *Just my luck,* he thought. *I'll have to change the wheel and then try and catch them up.* He waited until they had driven off before walking round to the boot to get the spare wheel. If the hub nuts weren't corroded on, he could do it in less than ten minutes, a bit slower than the F1 support teams who changed all four wheels in about five seconds.

It was then he noticed that the rear tyre was flat as well. He walked round the car to find that all four tyres were flat. It was then that he wondered why he hadn't just put a bullet in each of them when he caught up with them. It would have been worth losing his payment from Sir Malcolm. Anyway, he had lost that already, so what to do now?

He decided he'd get his tyres re-inflated and go back to get his own car, which he hoped would now be ready for him.

Half an hour later, after frantically pumping his tyres with a borrowed foot pump, he set off back north to retrieve his car. He was silently fuming and hoped he would have the chance to get his hands on Alan Westbrook at some point in the future. He didn't care what Sir bleeding Malcolm thought. He could get his revenge and still leave enough of Westbrook for whatever Sir Malcolm wanted.

After half a day's driving in the hired rattletrap, he arrived at the little garage where he had left his car. He drove round to the back and parked the car where it had been when he collected it, and went into the office. The place was deserted but he could hear sounds of activity in the workshop, so he went through to find the mechanic, hard at work on an old car. There was no one else about and the place seemed deserted.

When the mechanic noticed him, he straightened up, rubbing his back and putting the spanner he had been struggling with back on the table.

"So you've come for your car?" he said with a grin.

"I hope it's ready," said Devlin.

"You can drive it away the moment you have paid for the repairs," he said. "Come into the office." He headed for the office. Devlin picked up a large wrench off the bench and followed him.

"Some of the parts were very difficult to get hold of," said the mechanic. "And it hasn't been that cheap, I'm afraid." He passed the invoice to Devlin who looked at it and tensed when he saw the figure of £1500.

"Surely you're joking?"

"No," said the mechanic. "I've done it as cheaply as I could. It would have cost you twice that in England."

"Well, it's a bit of a shock," said Devlin, letting the invoice slip from his fingers to float to the floor. The mechanic bent to pick it up and that was when Devlin brought the wrench down on the back of his head. Then he picked up his keys, went out to his newly repaired car, got in and started the engine.

As he edged it out of the yard, a police van screeched to a halt in front of him and four Scottish policemen leapt out and surrounded his car. A senior officer climbed leisurely from the cab and strolled over to look down at Devlin in a rather superior way.

"Well Mr. Johnson," he said. "We've been waiting to have a word with you. Perhaps you would be so kind as to accompany us for a ride to the station."

Devlin began to think that someone up above had it in for him, and to make it worse, the mechanic appeared from the workshop holding his head.

*****

Sir Malcolm picked up the phone. "Yes?" he snapped. It was a policeman from somewhere in Scotland wanting to know if a Mr Devlin Johnson was a member of his staff on a secret mission.

"Never heard of the man!" he replied. "Certainly not a Government employee. If he were, he would have the relevant documentation to prove it."

He slammed the phone down. Why had he trusted this idiot to do the job? He was obviously an amateur and he could take whatever was coming to him. If the police were involved, Sir Malcolm really didn't want to know.

There was a knock at the door. "Come!" he shouted irritably.

The door opened and Annabelle poked her head round the door. "Is this a good time?" she asked.

"It depends what you have to tell me," he replied. She came in and shut the door.

"I think I may have a way of trapping Westbrook," she said.

*****

Alan and Kirsty arrived at the pub that Weasel was now frequenting and found him sitting in the corner with Knuckles.

"So here you are," said Alan. "Where did you get to when we needed you?"

"Sorry mate," said Weasel. "But we lost you. We drove up and down the road for ages but couldn't find you. We met the biker lads and told them we were heading back home as we were no use if we didn't know where you were. They said they would stay and wait for you."

"Yes, we met up with them later," said Alan. "But it was the girls who saved the day."

Alan told him the story. "I don't know what happened to the gunman. We left him with four flat tyres when we set off home. I don't think Sir Malcolm will be very pleased with him. I don't suppose he has been in touch with you, has he?"

Weasel looked a bit sheepish. "Well, now you come to mention it, yes he did, but I told him we had no idea where you were and didn't think we could help him any further."

"Why did you say that?"

"Well, he is a difficult person to work for," said Weasel.

"You can say that again," said Knuckles. "Last time we were involved, the Americans came after us and one of our friends ended up dead. I think I'd feel safer sticking with you."

"Well, that's very good of you," said Alan. "I'll let you know if there's anything you can do. But at the moment we are going to keep our heads down."

"Do you believe them?" asked Kirsty as they drove back again.

"I think so," said Alan, "but it depends how much pressure Sir Malcolm applies. He may not be interested in them now. We'll just have to wait and see. I don't think the bikers would do the dirty on us though. We'll have to meet up with them and sound them out."

*****

When they arrived back at the lab, Justin was waiting for them. "I have some good news and some bad news," he said. "Let's go inside and I'll tell you all about it."

They followed him into the farmhouse and made themselves comfortable while Justin poured the coffee.

"So which would you like first?" he asked, handing them the steaming mugs of coffee.

"The good news, I think," said Alan.

"Well, we have a contract to supply a hundred thousand doses of your latest vaccine."

"Well that is good," said Kirsty. "What's the bad news?"

"They want it in a month."

"It's going to take that long to set up a production line," said Alan, "and these things can't be rushed. You'll just have to tell them it isn't possible in that timescale. With a bit of luck we could start delivering product in a month but it would take a further six weeks to complete the full batch. Anyway, they couldn't administer all the vaccine in that time."

"They intend to send out batches to each area and let them administer the doses," said Justin.

"Well, I've been in this sort of position before when the customer wanted some electronic equipment first thing on Monday," said Alan. "We worked all weekend and I set off at five o'clock on the Monday morning to drive up to Edinburgh to be able to put it on his desk by nine o'clock. Then later that week, Thursday I think it was, I rang them to see how they got on with it, and they said they hadn't had a chance to look at it yet but would get round to it next week. So after that, when people demanded something by an impossible date, I told them that I was sorry but due to unexpected demand it would be another two weeks at least, and they just accepted it. When I delivered a week earlier than I had said, they were over the moon."

"We could try it," said Justin. "After all, they can't go to anyone else, can they?"

"Exactly," said Alan.

"Now, the other thing is that you will be needed down in Cardiff to oversee the installation," said Justin. "How long do you need here in the lab to prepare everything?"

"About two weeks minimum, I should think," said Alan. "If Kirsty can help me."

"Of course," she said.

*****

The next two weeks were hectic. They had to work all hours to get things ready. After two weeks they were both exhausted.

"I don't care how urgent this is," said Alan. "We both need a rest before I go down to Cardiff."

"Aren't I coming with you?"

"Well, not immediately," said Alan. "I will need you to stay here to finish assembling all the fittings. I'll take the first lot down and you can join me with the rest of the gear after about a week – if you can finish it in a week, that is."

"I'll finish it."

Much to Justin's consternation, they set off for Whitby the following morning and said that they wouldn't be back until late that evening.

It was just what they needed – a leisurely drive over the moors, past the early warning system and down into Whitby. At Eller Beck they stopped for a cup of coffee from the flask and a pork pie.

"This reminds me of the time I did the Lyke Wake Walk," said Alan. "Forty-three miles across the moors in fifteen hours. I did it three times. I must have been mad."

"Three times?"

"Not one after the other," said Alan, laughing. "Once each year. The first time, I went with a small group from the firm where I was working. It was quite amusing really. About halfway across there is a flat area of boggy ground and we were walking along, chatting, as you do, and when we came to the very wet bit I instinctively stepped onto the tufts of spiky grass that grow in marshland, as it is firmer there. But the lad walking to my right didn't know this, and stepped into the soft boggy bit and disappeared up to his waist in stinking mud. After we pulled him out, we insisted that he keep well downwind of us as the stink was awful. He didn't see the funny side of it. I don't know why."

They set off again and found the car park in Whitby and set off on foot to find the Magpie fish and chip shop. After that, they climbed the hundred and ninety-nine steps up to the abbey.

They didn't arrive back at the lab until late that evening and went straight to bed.

They spent the following day loading the van ready for the drive down to Cardiff.

"I wish I was coming with you," she said.

"So do I," said Alan. "But you can come down with the next load. Anyway, I'll be up to my eyes with the installation of this lot until then."

It was late afternoon when he finally set off and Kirsty went back into the lab to get on with the assembly work that had to be done before she could join him in Cardiff. She thought that if she kept at it, the time would pass more quickly and she would finish it sooner as well.

After ten days, she was nearing the end of her task when her mobile rang. She was surprised, as not many people had that number, and Alan wouldn't be ringing during the day. He always rang in the evening and she would lie in bed talking to him.

She picked up her phone, answered it and was surprised to hear the voice of one of the bikers. *What on earth could he want?*

"Hello," said the voice on the phone. "Grease here." After a few pleasantries, he got to the point. "I need you to come over and see me," he said. "I can't talk about it over the phone, so I'd hoped you could meet me at the Dog and Grouse tomorrow at about lunch time."

"Well, actually it's not very convenient at the moment," she said. "Alan is away and I'm up to my eyes. I have a deadline to meet and I can't afford any time off."

"Oh, I see," said Grease. "I'd hoped you could both come, but if you could manage it that would be OK."

"I'll have to ring Alan this evening," she said. "Ring me again tomorrow morning and I'll tell you if I can make it."

"Well if that's the best you can do," he said. "It is rather important."

That evening when Alan rang, she told him what had happened.

"It does sound important," he said. "Why not tell him you'll meet him in two days' time. That'll give you time to finish the work and make sure it is on its way. Then you could call in to see him on your way down here. It won't be much of a detour."

"That would seem better," she said. "He'll be ringing in the morning, so I'll tell him that's what I can manage. Surely it can't be that important?"

*****

Thirty-Eight

The work had been going quite well down in Cardiff and Alan was waiting for the rest of the equipment to arrive. Kirsty had told him it was finished and had dispatched it the previous day before setting off to join him. He expected her to arrive that evening, and was looking forward to seeing her again. It had been a long fortnight, but he had kept his mind occupied with his work. However, this hadn't helped in the evenings when he had returned to the hotel. There isn't much to do in a hotel except eat, drink or sleep, or perhaps watch a bit of television.

He thought she would be hungry when she arrived so decided to wait for her before eating. He had booked the table for eight o'clock, thinking that should give her time to shower when she arrived before going down to eat. So, to fill in the time, he went down to the bar and had a drink. There were others, most likely in the same situation, sitting nursing their solitary drink, and Alan thought what a terrible life they must lead if this was their everyday routine.

He was roused from his dreaming by the sight of Justin wending his way through the throng to join him at his table in the corner. "Thought I'd come and welcome Kirsty when she arrives," he said, pulling up a bar stool. "In the meantime you can buy me a drink."

"Oh, thanks," said Alan, signalling to the barmaid. "I thought she would be here by now. Hope she isn't long. I'm getting hungry."

"So am I," said Justin. "I suppose she managed to set off on time?"

"As far as I know," said Alan. "She said she would be stopping off on the way to meet an old friend, but I didn't think she would be delayed for long."

"Well you know what girls are like when they get yakking," said Justin. "If she's not here by eight we might as well go in and get started. She can join us when she arrives. I can't leave it much later as I've things to do this evening."

By nine-thirty they had finished their meal and Kirsty still hadn't arrived.

"I'll have to go now," said Justin. "Perhaps she's been delayed."

"I would have thought she'd have phoned if she was going to be late," said Alan.

"Well she probably forgot to leave her phone on charge last night and it's given out on her."

"But there are landlines," said Alan. If she has had to stay over somewhere she could ring from the hotel phone."

"Well, don't worry about it," said Justin. "I'm sure she will turn up tomorrow morning and wonder what all the fuss was about."

*****

When Kirsty arrived at the Dog and Grouse, she parked in the car park at the back and went into the bar. She looked around but couldn't see anyone she knew, so she bought a drink and sat down at a table to wait. She hoped that this wouldn't be too long as she wanted to get back on the road again.

When she had finished her drink, time was getting on, so she ordered pie and peas at the bar and a large coffee, thinking she might as well have some lunch while she was waiting rather than have to stop again further down the road.

Half an hour later she had finished her pie and decided that she couldn't afford to wait any longer. If Grease wanted to see her so urgently, why wasn't he here? He'd just have to contact her at a later date. If it was so important, he would have been here waiting for her.

The bar had filled up while she had been there, but there was no one she knew or recognised, so she put her coat on and made her way out into the car park.

A Transit van was parked right next to her car, so close that she would have great difficulty in opening her car door. She looked around for the owner, but couldn't see anyone. Then she heard a noise from the back of the van. Someone had opened the doors. Perhaps they were loading or unloading something. She walked round to the back.

"Do you think you could move your van, please?" she said. "I can't get into my car."

******

When Kirsty hadn't arrived the next morning and there was no answer from her mobile phone, Alan told Justin he would have to drive back to Yorkshire to find out what had happened.

"Of course," said Justin. "The technicians here know what to do, so you can leave it to them. Keep me informed."

It was a long drive back and Alan hoped he hadn't passed her going the other way. Anyway, if he had, Justin would let him know.

His first stop would be to see Weasel. He would be sure to know if she had called in there, so he was pleased to see him sitting in his usual seat in the corner with Knuckles.

Alan explained things to them, but they looked bemused.

"Don't know anything about her visiting here," said Weasel.

"But I thought one of your biker friends asked her to pop in as he had something important to tell her."

"News to me," said Weasel. "Which one was it?"

"Grease, I think," said Weasel. "Do you want me to phone him?"

"If you would," said Alan.

"He'll be at work at the moment," said Weasel, taking out his phone. When someone answered he asked for Charles Harding. "OK," he said and rang off.

"Charles Harding?" said Alan, grinning. "Is that his real name?"

"Sure is," said Weasel. "He's busy at the moment with a client but he'll ring back when he is free."

"She was just going to pop in to see him on her way down here," said Alan. "But she didn't turn up. I just want to know what time she left him."

"I didn't know he wanted to see her," said Weasel.

"Nor did I," said Knuckles. "Didn't she say why he wanted to see her?"

"No," said Alan. "She said he didn't want to give details over the phone. Maybe it was something to do with that chap we met in Scotland."

"Don't know anything about that," said Weasel. "We were back here by then. We'll just have to wait until he rings. In the meantime, it's your round."

"Mine?" said Alan. "I've just got here."

"Exactly," said Weasel. "We've each bought a round." Alan got up, went to the counter and ordered the drinks.

About an hour and two rounds later, Grease rang. "I didn't see her," he said. "I was asked to set up a meeting between her and an old school friend. It was to be a surprise."

"So who was this old school friend?" asked Alan.

"I don't know," said Grease. "I just got an email from her, so I set up the meeting for them."

"Did Kirsty know who she was supposed to be meeting?"

"No," he replied. "As I said, it was to be a surprise."

"I think it was more of a shock," said Alan. "You really are an idiot, Grease."

"Sorry," he said. "Just trying to be helpful."

"How did she get in touch with you?" asked Alan.

"That chap in Scotland, Donald, gave her my email address."

"You didn't get her name, then?" said Alan.

"No," said Grease. "well, yes, but I can't remember. Ann or was it Annette?"

"How can I contact this Donald in Scotland?"

"I can give you his email address," said Grease.

"Stupid idiot," said Alan after the phone call was terminated. "And he is supposed to be a solicitor."

"Takes all sorts," said Weasel.

Alan sent an email to Donald from his phone and they waited for a response, which came about a quarter of an hour later. He only knew her first name and that was Annabelle, he did give a pretty good description of her.

"Sounds like that woman Kirsty came to see, a while back," said Weasel. "We were here, if you remember. She sat over there. Quite a stunning looking woman. I wouldn't forget her in a hurry."

"Nor would I," said Alan. "And you know who she works for, don't you?"

"Sir Malcolm," said Weasel. "So what do we do now?"

"Not much we can do," said Alan. "If they've got her, we'll just have to wait until they contact us. But in the meantime, you can get your lads and lasses to keep an eye open for that woman, or anyone else you might recognise as being one of Sir Malcolm's employees."

"What'll you do now?" asked Weasel.

"There's not much I can do," said Alan. "Except get hold of Grease and cut off bits of his anatomy."

"I know how you feel," said Weasel. "I'll have some hard words to say to him later."

"However, I'll have to get back to Cardiff. There's a lot of work to do. Let me know as soon as you hear anything."

"Will do."

Thirty-nine

"You have done well," said Sir Malcolm as he passed Annabelle a cup of Earl Grey tea. "The thing is, what do we do now? How will Westbrook react now we have his girlfriend? Will he give in to us to save her, or will he sacrifice her for the greater good, as he sees it?"

"Difficult to say," she replied. "He is very keen to keep his work secret from anyone and everyone. Still, there is no rush, is there? Perhaps we should just let him stew for a while before contacting him."

"That sounds good," he said. "Then perhaps we could tell him we will send her back to him bit by bit, depending upon how long he takes to cooperate."

"Would you do that?"

"If necessary," he said. "You have to think of the greater good, don't you?"

"What is the greater good?" she asked.

"The project being in the hands of a responsible authority," he said.

"You, in fact?"

"Precisely," he replied. "I think when it comes down to it, he will give us what we want. Perhaps we will have to do it in easy stages."

"How do you mean?"

"Get him to do a little job for us first and keep the project to himself," he said. "And then when he has been responsible for something which turns out to be illegal, we can put pressure on him to hand it all over to us rather than take the blame himself."

"What sort of thing?"

"You'll have to wait and see," he said, tapping the side of his nose."

*****

Kirsty regained consciousness somewhere cold and dark. At first, she had no idea where she was or why she was there. She had an itch on her nose, but when she tried to scratch it, she found that her hands were fastened behind her back.

"I see you are back with us," said a gruff voice nearby.

"Where am I?"

"Never mind about that," said the voice, closer now. Then she felt someone close by and it was suddenly light. There was a rough-looking man holding the blindfold which he had just removed from her eyes. It wasn't actually as bright as she first thought; her eyes accustomed themselves to the dim light.

She was in some sort of deserted military shed – a Nissen Hut perhaps? There was little in the space, except a pile of old sacks on which she had been dumped.

"Who are you?" she demanded. "And why am I here?"

"All questions," he said. "Just keep quiet or I'll have to gag you." She kept quiet, as she didn't like the look of this fellow. Had he kidnapped her for his own pleasure, or was he acting under orders from someone else? She came to the conclusion that he was under orders, or she thought he would have molested her by now. He looked the sort.

"Now I've got to go and report that you are back with us," he said. "So keep quiet. Anyway, there's no one around to hear you so you might as well save your breath."

He went over to the door, unlocked it and went out, locking it again behind him.

Where could she be? If this was a Nissen Hut, it could be a disused military establishment, which meant that there would be no one about to hear her or help her. She wondered who it was that had kidnapped her and what they wanted. Could it be Sir Malcolm? Or perhaps it was the Americans? Or maybe it was nothing to do with any of them. Perhaps she had been kidnapped for ransom because she was related to Justin. She had no idea. She also had no idea how long she had been unconscious or how she had become unconscious. Then it slowly came back to her – the sight of a man behind the van, turning with a cloth pad in his hand, which he forced onto her face. That was the last thing she remembered.

What would Alan be thinking? When she hadn't turned up, he would have no idea where she had gone and wouldn't know where to start looking for her.

All she could do now was to lie there listening for any sounds that might give her a clue as to where she was, but all she could hear was the sound of the wind. She heard a clock striking in the distance, but that didn't help, so there was nothing for it but to lie and wait. At least she would be able to keep track of the time.

*****

The prime minister, George White, was not looking forward to the meeting. He had heard nothing from the Americans for ages, but now they were back on the scene. Walter Greenbank had demanded an urgent meeting with him and was, at this very moment, on his way up the stairs. He actually had a private lift, but decided the American could walk up the stairs. It wasn't much, but it was a small way of getting back at them.

The door opened and a breathless Walter Greenbank staggered in, walked over to the prime minister's large oak desk and sat heavily on the chair opposite him.

"Please have a seat," said the prime minister. "And what can we do for you this time?"

"You know damn well what I want," he said, gasping.

"Well, last time you seemed to want to take control of one of our projects."

"Which you have now lost," he said. "One of our agents followed that guy of yours until he lost him in France. So that project could end up in the hands of any of our enemies through your intransigence."

"That's a big word for an American," said George. "As far as we are concerned, the project was discontinued as it was found to be ineffective. It was a good idea, but impractical. So, you see, wherever our erstwhile employee went, he had nothing of value. If you don't believe me you could speak to our man at the MoD, Sir Malcolm Birch. You can contact him at Blakely House. Now if there is nothing else, I have a lot of work to do, so I'll wish you a good day. You know your own way out, I'm sure."

Walter Greenbank was rarely lost for words, but this was one of those occasions. Also he was completely breathless from his climb up the stairs, and now he faced the descent. He staggered to his feet and stomped out of the office without another word.

*****

Alan arrived back in Cardiff the following morning and told Justin all that he had learned.

"We'll just have to wait," said Justin. "I'm sure they will contact us soon with their demands. In the meantime, there is nothing we can do."

"Well, not exactly," said Alan. "I have got the lads in Yorkshire searching for any signs of her or where she could be. But until I hear anything, you are right. We'll just have to wait. But while we are waiting I'm going to spend some time on Google Earth looking for any likely places they could have taken her.

"I suppose that will make you feel that you are doing something positive, but I don't think you will find anything," said Justin. "On the other hand, I think we should inform the police."

"And say what?"

"I see what you mean," said Justin. "But when my niece's life is in danger I won't take any risks."

"Nor will I," said Alan. "But what do we say? That she has been kidnapped by the head of an important department of the MoD? I think we should wait until we get a demand from them. In the meantime, I'm going to search one way or another."

"I don't think you'll find much on Google Earth," said Justin. "Military installations are mostly not shown."

"Disused ones might be," said Alan. "Anyway, I'm going to look."

*****

After five days there was still no word about Kirsty, so Alan decided to go back up to Yorkshire. He had found several possible sites where a hostage might be held. By now he was getting really worried and felt he must be doing something, anything positive, rather than just sitting waiting.

He found Weasel in his usual haunt, sitting in the corner with a pint in front of him. He was talking on his mobile phone as Alan walked in.

"That was Knuckles," he said. "Still no sign of anything. The girls have been riding far and wide, and so have the bikers."

"I've found some possible places to look," said Alan, handing over a sheaf of papers. Weasel took them and glanced through, pulling several out and putting them on the table.

"We've checked all these," he said. "But not these. I'll get them onto it straight away."

Several phone calls later, they had set everything in motion and just had to wait and see. Alan ordered himself a large black coffee and another pint for Weasel.

"I see you have taken the difficult job," said Alan.

"Someone has to do it," said Weasel. "And as I have the brains, I thought it had better be me."

"Can I get a room here for a couple of nights?" asked Alan. "It would be more convenient than travelling back and forth from my base."

"Don't see why not," he replied. "Have a word with the girl at the bar. You can get me another pint while you're at it. It's thirsty work, all this thinking and organising."

The next day Weasel got word from Knuckles that one of the bikers had checked an old disused MoD site that Alan had found on Google Earth, and reported that there were signs of habitation there. He had seen a Land Rover leaving and thought that there was someone in one of the huts.

"Get everyone together near the site and we will go in together and see who it is," said Alan. "If it is just a farmer making use of the empty sheds we'll feel a bit stupid, but so what?"

Alan took Weasel in his car; they set off just after lunch and were at the meeting point by two o'clock. By three, they had all arrived and Alan gave them all their orders.

The three bikers were to go in from the other side and Alan, Weasel and Knuckles would go in from the near side. They would all converge on the group of huts at the centre. The two girls would ride round the perimeter and keep watch for approaching vehicles. Grease was carrying a twelve-bore shotgun, which had seen better days, and Alan hoped he didn't have to use it, as it would probably kill them all.

They synchronised watches; that's what they did on the films, so Alan thought they had better do it too. Then they all went to their allotted places.

Weasel cut the wire and opened up a hole big enough for them to squeeze through.

The place had been allowed to return to nature, the once tended grass was now at waist height and there were bushes, brambles and nettles in patches everywhere, causing Weasel to curse and swear every few steps he took.

They arrived at the back of the main hut and then made their way cautiously around to the front where they met the others. There had been no sign of life, so they assumed they had not been spotted.

Grease stood in front of the door, while Knuckles threw it open.

"Don't anyone move," shouted Grease, stepping in through the open door.

He must have been a terrifying sight, had there been anyone in there, but the place was empty. The others followed him in and looked around.

"There have been people here," said Alan. On the pile of sacks in the corner were pieces of cord lying around that had been cut with a blunt knife, and the sacks had a depression where someone had been sitting or lying recently. "But it looks as if we are too late. They must have been aware of people around the place and decided it was too public. We'll just have to continue looking."

Back at the pub, they sat round a table in the corner, discussing what they should do next.

"I can't think of anywhere else to look," said Grease. "Unless they have taken her off to the south. She could be anywhere, but we'll ask around and see if anyone in the area saw anything unusual. I don't think much of our chances as people seem to walk around with their eyes closed these days."

"Or staring at their phone or iPad," said Weasel. "As Grease says, all we can do is ask around and see if anyone has noticed anything unusual. But I'm sure they'll get in touch before long. Probably leaving it a while to soften you up."

*****

Alan drove back down to Cardiff to see Justin. "I just don't know what to do next," he said.

"There's nothing you can do," said Justin. "Unless you put it in the hands of the police."

"You know I can't do that," said Alan. "And I don't know how long I can put up with this waiting."

"Well there's a lot of work to be done here," he replied. "Things have got a bit behind while all this has been going on."

What do you expect me to do?" replied Alan, a bit more sharply than he had intended. "Sorry, I'm a bit on edge."

"I fully understand that," said Justin. "And so am I. But running around like headless chickens gets us nowhere. They will get in touch with us in due course so we might as well get on with things until they contact us. The more we panic, the more we play into their hands."

Alan agreed, reluctantly, and tried to concentrate on his work, which was difficult as his mind kept wandering. He wondered if she was terrified and kept in appalling conditions, whether she was being badly treated. He tried to console himself with the fact that they were obviously using her as a bargaining chip, so wouldn't want to maltreat her.

It was two days later when he got a phone call from Weasel to say that he had been contacted by Sir Malcolm. The only information that Weasel had was that Alan was to meet Sir Malcolm at a location in Yorkshire, but first he would have to travel to his normal meeting place with Weasel when he would be given further details. Sir Malcolm had insisted that no one else must be informed, or his hostage would be killed. He felt sure that Sir Malcolm would have no scruples about that, but only as a last resort. So he set off again for Yorkshire.

Forty

Weasel was waiting for him in his usual seat.

"Doesn't look good," he said as Alan walked over to him.

"Have you heard any more yet?"

"No, but he said he would contact us when you arrived," said Weasel. "What are you planning to do?"

"I have absolutely no idea," he replied. "Wait and see what he wants, I suppose, though I have a pretty good idea what that is."

"Your software, I suppose," said Weasel.

"Exactly. The choice is saving Kirsty but condemning possibly thousands of people to some dreadful disease."

"Is that possible?" asked Weasel. "Making a disease that can wipe out a selected race or group of people?"

"Theoretically, yes," answered Alan. "I might even be able to do it, but I haven't tried it as yet, and don't want to."

"Is there nothing we can do to stop him?"

"The problem is that he has Kirsty and I don't want her harmed," said Alan. "I'm working on a possible solution, but it will be difficult, and I don't even know if it will work."

"Well let's hope that it does," said Weasel. "Whatever it is."

"You don't want to know," said Alan. At that moment Weasel's phone rang.

"That was them," he said. "They want you to drive north from here for about a mile to just before the crossroads where you will find a lay-by. Pull in there and wait. If you have anyone with you or if you have anyone tailing you, it will be the worst for the hostage. She will be returned to you piece by piece, starting with an ear."

"Doesn't look as if I have much choice," said Alan. "Make sure none of your people follows me. I can't risk Kirsty being harmed."

"Well there's just you and me here," said Weasel. "So no one else knows."

"Right, I'll be off then," said Alan. "If all goes well, I'll be back here shortly."

There wasn't much traffic on the road and when he arrived at the lay-by, he found it empty, so he pulled up and waited. After a while, a battered white van pulled in behind him and Alan wondered if this was it, but no one got out. After about fifteen minutes, the van pulled away again and disappeared down the road. When it was out of sight, he realised that another car had pulled up behind him. This time the door opened and a man got out and walked towards his car. The passenger door opened and Sir Malcolm got in.

"Nice to see you again," said Sir Malcolm. "You're looking well Alan, or should I call you Peter Finch?"

"Alan will do," he replied tersely. "I want to see Kirsty. She had better be in good health."

"Of course," said Sir Malcolm. "Of course. As soon as you have done a little job for me."

"No," said Alan, "I want to see her first."

"If you insist," said Sir Malcolm. "I want you to do a little genetic engineering for me. Nothing too difficult, and you'll have to collect the genetic sample before you can get started. I have a little facility not far from here. I'll give you the details later and arrange for her to be there for you to see."

"So what is it you want from me?"

"I'll give you the details when we meet at the facility," he replied. "I'll be in touch."

He got out and walked back to his car and drove off. Alan sat for a few minutes, wondering what he wanted him to do. Then turned the car round and drove back.

Weasel was still sitting there. "So," he said, "did they turn up?"

"It was Sir Malcolm himself," said Alan.

"What did he want?"

"He didn't say exactly," said Alan. "Some genetic engineering, he said. I'll have to go to some facility he has near here to get the details. They said I would be able to see Kirsty."

"When do you have to go?"

"He didn't say," said Alan. "We'll be hearing from him in due course. I think I'll book a room here again until we hear from him."

"Is there anything the lads can do?"

"Not at the moment," said Alan. "I don't want to prompt him into doing anything rash."

That night, Alan phoned Justin to let him know what had happened.

"Keep me informed," said Justin. "And let me know if there is anything I can do."

"We'll just have to be patient," said Alan. "There's nothing anyone can do at the moment, but I'll let you know if there is."

*****

Of course I'm grateful to you," said Sir Malcolm to his niece, Annabelle. "But that doesn't give you the right to dictate terms to me."

"I think it does, Uncle," said Annabelle. "Without me, you would still be bumbling around with those idiots that you hired. Don't forget that I know what you're doing, and I'm sure you wouldn't want that information to get into the wrong hands, would you?"

"I hope that's not a threat," said Sir Malcolm. "I really hope it's not, for your sake."

"And what's that supposed to mean?"

"Exactly what you think it means," said Sir Malcolm. "And don't think that because you are my niece you are completely fireproof. Certainly I felt duty-bound to give you certain opportunities, and will carry on doing so. But if you think you can blackmail me into giving you everything you want, you can think again."

With a face like thunder, she stomped out of the room, slamming the door behind her.

"Temper," he said. *She's getting out of hand. I'll have to watch her*, he thought. He picked up the phone. "Send in Mr. Blackwood, please, Shirley." He put the phone down. A few minutes later, there was a knock at the door and a short but very overweight middle-aged man staggered in, puffing heavily.

"We have a bit of a problem," said Sir Malcolm. "My niece seems to be getting a bit above herself, John."

"Must be a family trait," said John. "I did warn you."

"There's no need to rub it in," said Sir Malcolm. "What are we going to do about it?"

"What do you normally do when one of your minions gets out of hand?"

"Yes, but this is my niece," said Sir Malcolm. "It's far too near home for a simple accident. I just can't risk it."

"Perhaps there are other ways she could come to grief without anything pointing to you," said John.

"Well," said Sir Malcolm, "I would be happy to hear any suggestions you might have."

*****

It was three days before Weasel received the next phone call, telling him to instruct Alan to be at their previous meeting place the following day at noon, but it wasn't until later that day that Alan came into the bar.

"Where have you been?" asked Weasel. "I've had another message for you."

"I got up early and had a drive round," he said. "I know it's futile, but it's better than just sitting here twiddling my thumbs. So what's the message?"

"Same place tomorrow at noon."

"Same conditions as last time, I suppose?"

"Of course," said Weasel. "I wish there was something we could do to help."

"So do I," said Alan. "But I just daren't risk it at the moment. I've got a few ideas buzzing around in my head, but it all depends on what he wants me to do and whether I can use it to my advantage."

"You've lost me," said Weasel.

Just then, Knuckles came in with the three bikers. "Any news?" he asked.

"Another meeting tomorrow," said Alan. "But I want everyone to keep clear. I don't want to risk any danger to Kirsty. However, I may need your help later. I don't yet know how or when, but I'm working on it."

"Well, lads," said Weasel. "You've just timed it right. It's Alan's round."

"How is it always my round?"

"Well, you're never here when it's my round."

*****

Alan spent the next morning pacing around the bar, waiting for the time to set off.

"For heaven's sake sit down," said Weasel. "You're driving me mad."

"Sorry," said Alan. "Just nerves."

"Well, it's another hour before you need to set off," said Weasel. "Why don't we have a bite to eat? You may not get anything later. I don't think Sir Malcolm is much of a host."

"You're probably right," said Alan. So they ordered bacon butties and a large jug of coffee and sat down to fill in the time before he had to leave.

"Will you agree to anything he asks you to do?" asked Weasel.

"At first, yes," said Alan. "We'll see what happens later though."

At last it was time to set off and he said goodbye to Weasel and went out to the car. When he arrived at the lay-by, there was a Transit van parked there, so Alan pulled up behind it to wait. However, when he stopped, a man got out of the van and walked back to where Alan was parked.

"You Alan Westbrook?" he said bluntly.

"That's me," said Alan. "Who are you?"

"Just the driver," he said. "Lock your car and get in the van." Alan got out and locked his car and walked over to the van.

"No, in the back," said the driver. "The boss doesn't want you to see where we're going."

"Fair enough," said Alan, climbing in. The van was quite comfortably furnished; there were no windows, but there was electric lighting so he didn't have to sit in the dark.

When the van set off, Alan decided to see if he could remember the turns it took so that he might get an idea of where they were going. It turned left at the crossroads, which cut down the possibilities tremendously. It was actually more difficult than he had imagined, as he didn't know if a sharp turn was a road junction or just a sharp turn in the road.

The journey took about twenty minutes, but Alan didn't know whether they had gone directly to the destination or had gone round in circles for a while.

When the van stopped and the driver opened the back door, he found that they were in a large barn, or some such building, so he didn't even have an idea what the place looked like from outside.

"Right, follow me," said the driver and set off across the barn towards a door on the far wall. It appeared that this was actually quite a large complex of buildings, though there didn't seem to be many people about.

Through the door was a long corridor of a style reminiscent of a military building. The brown and cream paint work rather gave it away. At the far end was a pair of double doors with two guards standing on each side of the door. When they saw Alan and the driver approaching, they stood to attention. Obviously, with not much to do, they had been a bit slack and Alan noticed one of them drop a cigarette stub onto the ground behind him.

The driver showed his pass and the guards opened the doors to let them through into a medium-sized room which had some rudimentary furniture in it. Sir Malcolm was sitting on a battered armchair with a plastic cup in his hand, which he threw into the bin as Alan entered. Sir Malcolm thanked the driver, who then took his leave.

"Please make yourself at home," said Sir Malcolm, pointing to another chair that had seen better days.

"Funds must be tight," said Alan, looking around. "The cuts must be biting."

"Always the comedian," said Sir Malcolm. "Now let's talk business."

"I would love to," said Alan, trying to appear cool and relaxed, which was not how he was feeling. "But first I want to see Kirsty."

"I thought that would be your first demand," he said. "So I've already had her transported here. You can have five minutes with her but no more."

"Alone," said Alan. "I don't want anyone listening in."

"Of course," said Sir Malcolm. "I don't think there is anything either of you could say that would be of any importance to me, and it's no use trying to plan anything between you as we have several other contingencies in place which I won't go into."

Sir Malcolm got up, and went to the door on the far side of the room, which he unlocked and ushered Alan through into a small cell-like room, before closing and locking the door behind him.

It was rather dim, but he could soon make out a figure sitting against the wall. "Kirsty?" he said.

"Alan?" she replied. "I didn't think I'd see you again."

"Have they been treating you all right?"

"Well they haven't hurt me, but they led me to believe that they would if things didn't go their way," she said. "And there's this thug who keeps guard of me all the time. I really don't like him, and I think he is just waiting for the chance to get his filthy hands on me."

"Look," said Alan. "I've only got a few minutes so can you give me any idea where you are being held?"

"Not really," she said.

"Well, firstly, how long did the journey take from there to here?"

"About half an hour," she said. "They let me keep my watch, so they must be quite sure of themselves."

"Well that's a start," he said. "Now, can you hear any sounds round about your prison? Anything at all that we might be able to identify?"

"Not much at all," she said. "No traffic noise. Just the wind, but there is a church clock that strikes every fifteen minutes. It drives me mad, mainly because they haven't put it back an hour when the clock went back. So I keep thinking it's an hour later than it actually is. I keep having to check my watch to make sure."

"Well that could be quite useful," he said. "I'll see if I can see you again next time I come, but I don't know what his nibs wants me to do yet. But don't worry. I'll not let him hurt you."

"I hope you're right," she said as the door opened and Sir Malcolm appeared in the doorway.

"Well, that's enough for the moment," he said. "If you're good I may let you see each other another time. Depends how things go."

Alan gave her a quick kiss and then followed Sir Malcolm out into the larger room.

"Right," said Sir Malcolm. "Down to business. I have here a sample of a rather virulent virus, and here," he produced a stoppered tube, "is a DNA sample of a person whose identity you needn't know. I want you to re-engineer this virus to attack only this subject and no one else. Do you think you can do that?"

"Theoretically it's possible," said Alan, "but I've never done it before."

"But you have modified viruses to act against bovine diseases, I'm told?"

"That's a little different, though," said Alan.

"Well, it'll be a nice challenge for you," said Sir Malcolm. "With the added excitement of knowing that your little friend's life depends on it."

Alan's blood ran cold. He was expected to do something that might turn out to be impossible, and if that was the case, Kirsty would suffer for it. He was beginning to think he had been rather stupid to continue with this project when others had said that it would be better to scrap it for good. Why hadn't he listened?

He took the samples and stood up to leave.

"Well, it's been good doing business with you," said Sir Malcolm. "Now, I would like a weekly update from you, so be at the pickup point at noon each Friday until the project is completed."

"And when will you release Kirsty?"

"As soon as the project is completed satisfactorily," he said. "By then I won't need her, as I will have all the insurance I need." Alan didn't know what he was referring to so just walked towards the door, which opened and the driver appeared, to escort him back to the van.

*****

Back at the pub, Alan filled Weasel in with all the details.

"Do you think your friends could search around for a church clock that hasn't been set back an hour?" he asked.

"I would think so," said Weasel. "But I think they are due more expenses by now."

"Sorry," said Alan. "I'll see to it. I'll be spending most of my time back at the lab from now on. But I'll be back each Friday as Sir Malcolm wants a regular progress report. He can't escape from the civil service procedures even when he's working for himself."

Back at the lab, he started to set up the equipment to analyse the virus. This was difficult because he couldn't afford to release the virus into the atmosphere. However, he had a technique of scanning things contained in a glass file, which would be the safest way of working.

It would take all of the following week to get any results from the analysis, so he put the DNA sample to one side for the moment. He wondered who the poor victim was and whether he deserved such a fate. Then he had an idea, which he let go round in his mind.

It took several attempts to get a full scan of the virus, but he managed it before the week was up. He put the virus sample into a safe place in case he needed it again. When he was sure of his results he would destroy it.

He had just done that when Justin arrived back from Wales. "All set up and running," he said. "How are you getting on?"

Alan filled him in with everything that had happened and Justin looked more and more perturbed as he went on.

"Surely you can't be part of something that leads to the death of an innocent person, can you?" he said.

"That's what I thought," he said. "So I have another idea. It has obviously got to kill someone or Kirsty will suffer. So I thought I would choose my own victim – one who deserves to die." He explained his plan and Justin nodded.

"I suppose that is a reasonable compromise," he said. "Though I can't say I like the idea."

"Well if you can think of anything better," said Alan, "I would be very pleased to hear it."

"I'm afraid I can't," he said. "So I will just have to go along with it. If there's anything I can do to help, just let me know."

"Well there will be some more equipment needed for the synthesis," he replied. "I'll let you know what I need nearer the time."

*****

The three bikers went out that weekend and cruised around the area that Alan thought most likely for them to find the church with the summertime clock. It was surprising how many churches there actually were when you started looking for them. Some didn't have a clock, and those that did seemed to be correct, though there was one that had stopped altogether.

They were about to give up and go home when Nigel returned from his little foray.

"I think I've found it," he said. "Follow me." He sped off, followed by the other two. Soon they came to a sharp corner with a track branching off to the left. "It's down here," he said and set off.

About two hundred yards from the main road, they found this quaint little church surrounded by trees. There was another track leading off in the opposite direction.

"I think you're right," said Grease. "The clock is an hour fast." And to prove the point, it struck five o'clock when it was actually only four o'clock.

"So she is being held within earshot of this place, then," said Dingle. "I can't see anything that stands out, can you?" The others shook their heads.

"Anyway," said Grease. "Alan doesn't want us to make ourselves known yet or they'll just move her again. Time to go home. I'll ring Alan this evening and tell him what we've found.

*****

When Alan received the news he immediately fired up Google Earth and had soon found the church. There were several places that looked likely for holding someone without drawing attention to yourself. He printed out the map and then drew a ring round each of the likely places. There were only three candidates, so that would work out well for the three bikers as they could split up and watch all three. All he needed was confirmation that one was disused but there was someone visiting it occasionally. He wasn't sure what he would do about it when he found out, but that was for another day.

The next day he set off back to meet Weasel before going to the rendezvous point. It was a miserable November day with a low mist, making everything wet. There wasn't much traffic about so it was an easy journey and he arrived in time for an early lunch before setting off to meet Sir Malcolm.

Weasel was sitting in his usual corner, and Alan wondered if he had actually taken root there. Unsurprisingly, he was ready for another drink when Alan walked up to the table.

"The lads have been watching those three sites," said Weasel, "but no sign of activity yet."

"Well keep watching," said Alan.

"How are your plans progressing?"

"Slowly," said Alan. "But I've had an idea that might solve all our problems."

"Oh, and what's that, if I may make so bold?"

"I'd rather keep it to myself for the moment," said Alan. "But there will be work for you later, I'm sure of that."

Alan ordered a steak pie from the bar and a cup of black coffee, and then went and sat with Weasel again.

"I can't think of any way of getting that monster off our backs," said Weasel. "I know he's left me and the lads alone for now, but you never know when he might decide he wants us working for him again."

"And would you?"

"Not willingly," said Weasel. "But you know him. He has ways of applying pressure."

"Well stick with me for a while and I might be able to solve all our problems."

He finished his pie and then put his coat on again. "If it was snowing you'd be able to follow my tracks," said Alan. "But it isn't, so don't."

The journey took about the same time as previously, ending up in the closed barn. Sir Malcolm was waiting in the same room as before and smiled when Alan entered.

"I hope you have good news for me," he said.

"Well, things are progressing quite well," said Alan. "I've got a good scan of the virus and I'm now in the process of identifying all the relevant parts ready for modification. That's the tedious bit. As soon as I've done that, I'll get on to the mods and then I'll be able to start the synthesis."

"And how long is this going to take?"

"Difficult to say," said Alan. "But if everything goes well it could be another two to three weeks. If there are problems, a little longer."

"Can't things be speeded up?"

"Not really," said Alan. "It's not like the old arithmetic question where one man can dig a trench in three days, so how long will it take five men. In this case it is how long the process takes. More people wouldn't help."

"Well, I'll take your word for it," said Sir Malcolm. "Anyway, you seem to be making progress, so perhaps we should drink to the success of the project." He picked up another plastic cup and poured some champagne into it and handed it to Alan. "To a successful outcome."

"A successful outcome," echoed Alan, thinking that his outcome might be different to Sir Malcolm's.

They both downed their drinks and Sit Malcolm threw his plastic cup across the room at the bin, but missed.

"Allow me," said Alan, picking up his own cup and walking over to the bin. He scooped up the fallen cup with his, making sure not to touch the rim and dropped his own cup into the bin with a clatter. As he turned round, he slid the other cup into his pocket and strode back to the table.

"Next time," he said, "I would like to see Kirsty again."

"Sorry," said Sir Malcolm. "Not until the project is finished."

"It will take about three weeks, as I said, so I'll let Weasel know when it's ready and I'll be at the meeting place the following Friday at noon, ready to be picked up." It was obvious from his expression that Sir Malcolm didn't like having the law laid down for him, but as he was getting what he wanted, he didn't say anything. "It'll be quicker in the end," said Alan, getting up ready to go.

Alan didn't see how Sir Malcolm did it but the door opened and the driver appeared again. "No longer than three weeks then," said Sir Malcolm. "It can't be good for your little friend having to be cooped up all that time, can it?"

Alan said nothing but followed the driver out to the van.

*****

When Sir Malcolm arrived back at his office, he found Annabelle waiting for him.

"I don't like being left out of things," she said. "After all, I set it up for you."

"And I'm very grateful, as I said before. So you can come with me to see the results of the trial in about three weeks' time. After that you can ask whatever you like and I'll do what I can to oblige you. I can't say fairer that that, can I?"

"I suppose not," she replied. "So what do I do in the meantime?"

"Well, if you remember," he said, "I hired a hit man to bring Westbrook in for me, and he failed where you succeeded, and he is now being held by the Scottish police and is due for trial next week. I would like you to go up there and let me know what happens. I wouldn't like to think that he was on the loose, so do whatever is needed to make sure he isn't."

Annabelle had mixed feelings about driving all the way up to Scotland in November, but thought it best not to grumble. After all, it looked as if she might be going to get her own way. She could be back in time to be in on the completion of the project, whatever it was, and she was quite excited at the prospect.

She had been brought up as an only child and had been quite spoilt by her parents, who really hadn't had the time to spend with her, so gave her whatever she wanted to keep her happy. Now she thought she could demand whatever she wanted and it would be given to her. People brought up in this way eventually get brought down to earth with a bump.

Forty-one

Alan carefully extracted the plastic cup from his pocket, where he had left it for the whole journey home, and placed it, using a pair of tongs, into a sterile container.

"I'll see to you later," he said. In the isolation of his lab, he had taken to talking to himself.

He was jolted out of his thoughts when Justin entered from his farmhouse through the concealed door. "How's progress?" he asked.

"Going well, so far," replied Alan. "But we'll know better when I have extracted the DNA from the plastic cup."

"Better get it right," said Justin. "Or all the plastic cups in the world could be wiped out by that plague virus you have there."

"The green people would like that, though," said Alan. "No, I just hope I can get enough DNA to be able to use it in the synthesis, and that there is no contamination from anyone else. I can check that it isn't mine easily enough, but if anyone else has handled the cup it could be a problem."

"Is that likely?"

"I don't think so," said Alan. "The packet of cups would have been packed by machine and remained sealed until Sir Malcolm opened it to have his champagne."

"Let's hope so," said Justin. "Well, I won't keep you from your work. I have got to get back to Cardiff. By the way, the vaccine line is working fine. It'll make us both a fair sum, and I'll have another project for you soon."

"As soon as this project is completed," said Alan. "Until then I can't think about anything else."

"I know what you mean," he replied. "But I have to keep going just to take my mind off it. Good luck. I'm relying on you." He went back to his living quarters in the farmhouse and left Alan to get on with his work.

Alan set about extracting the DNA from the plastic cup and hoped it would work first time, as he didn't want to have to try to get another sample. He had been lucky to get this one and he didn't think it would be so simple next time.

It was a slow process, as he had to line the sample precisely with the scanning electron microscope, and as he couldn't actually see the sample it was just trial and error.

The first five scans gave a good result for polystyrene. But the next one got only part of a DNA string. Further adjustment found the whole string, but it would have to be left to run through the night to complete the scan, so when he was happy that it was running correctly, he went through to his living quarters to make himself a meal.

The place seemed strangely empty without Kirsty. There were reminders everywhere. Alan was fastidious about having a place for everything and everything in its place, but Kirsty put things anywhere and everywhere and was always having to search for things. Alan used to tell her that if she had a place where she always left her keys, she would always know where to find them, but she just laughed at him and said he was too fussy.

Alan had told her that if she had to run a development facility, she would never finish a project as she would spend all the time looking for things. She just laughed and said that it was as well that she didn't run a development facility then. However, when she had helped him with his work, she had seemed more organised.

His meal was cheese on toast, one of his specialities. He took it through to the sitting area and sat down to watch the television, but it didn't seem there was anything worth watching. Now there were dozens of channels, they were all filled with reruns of old programmes which he thought were better that most of the recently made ones. However, there was a limit on the number of times you could watch the same episode of 'Midsomer Murders' or 'Endeavour'.

He finally settled for a so-called science programme where a good-looking young woman tried to give the impression that she knew what she was talking about. He ran it on fast forward as it went so slowly; they assumed everyone was as thick as two short planks.

He switched it off in disgust. *How many people are there being paid by the taxpayer to do all this research? What a waste of money. If these people had to live in the real world, they would starve,* he thought.

He picked up a book and tried to read, but his mind kept wandering, so he eventually decided to have a shower and go to bed.

He slept fitfully and got up once or twice to check on the progress of the analysis, but it was plodding along nicely, so he went back to bed again.

******

In the morning he slept in, as he was tired due to not getting to sleep earlier. After getting washed and dressed, he went out and fried some sausage and bacon, and made a large butty and a mug of coffee, which he took through to the lab. The computer was still plodding, though Alan thought it looked as if it was almost finished, so he sat and watched it as he ate his butty and sipped his coffee.

He had finished eating and was just about to take his coffee mug out to the kitchen, when the computer finished its night's work. The sudden silence startled him, so he put his mug down and set the computer to work again checking the new sample against his library of DNA samples. He had his, Justin's and Kirsty's DNA profiles plus several others of no relevance. Obviously Justin's wouldn't be on the cup, so he just checked it against his and Kirsty's. This would take most of the morning, so he decided to get a breath of fresh air up on the moor.

The wind was cold on his face as he stepped out onto the open moor, but he didn't mind that as it woke him up and made him feel alive. In the lab it was as if the rest of the world didn't exist.

He walked up onto the ridge and looked out across the moor, and for a while all his problems seemed to disappear into the mist.

When he returned to the lab, he made a cup of coffee to warm himself up again while the computer completed its machinations.

By lunchtime it finished, and told him that the DNA was not his or Kirsty's, which meant that it almost certainly belonged to Sir Malcolm.

Now we start the difficult bit, he thought, but he wasn't in the right mood just then, so he decided to go out to the local pub for a bite to eat. Justin had left for Cardiff, so he went on his own.

He didn't know anybody in the pub, but the barmaid knew him by sight and gave him a welcoming smile as she pulled him a pint. There was an empty seat in the corner, so he settled down to wait for his food to arrive. He could have cooked something for himself at the lab, but preferred to get out. It was strange though, that even in this busy pub, he still felt alone. He realised that he was missing Kirsty more than he had thought he would and wished that the project could be hurried along a bit more. He knew that wasn't possible as things had to be allowed to take their time and couldn't be rushed.

After he had finished his lunch, he drove back to the lab and set about analysing the data ready to engineer the structure of the virus. This was something that he daren't rush and he only had one chance to get it right. One mistake, and he could wipe out half of Yorkshire, including himself. The way he was feeling, this might not be a bad idea.

*****

Weasel, Knuckles and Kevin took it in turns to watch the three buildings that might be where Kirsty was being held, and it was during one of these sessions that a van drove down the track to one of the buildings where Kevin was on watch. He quickly phoned the others who immediately drove over to join him.

"The van's parked behind the building," said Kevin. "What should we do?"

"Well, Alan gave strict orders to do nothing," said Weasel. "Just to identify the place where Kirsty was being held and let him know."

"But it seems a pity to miss the opportunity to rescue her," said Knuckles. "I say we should go in. We've been pussy-footing around for far too long."

"I agree," said Kevin.

"Well, I'm not so sure," said Weasel.

"OK," said Knuckles. "If you're scared, we'll go in without you. Ready Kevin?"

"Ready," he replied.

"All right," said Weasel. "I can't let you two go alone. You're sure to muck things up. Anyway, the more the merrier."

They started to make their way towards the building, trying to keep concealed behind the hedge as they went. There didn't seem to be any sign of activity, so they assumed the van inhabitants were inside. Knuckles had brought his shotgun, which Weasel considered to be more of a threat to them than to the enemy.

They made their way round to the back, and found the door wasn't locked, so they crept in as quietly as they could.

They found themselves in a small kitchen, but could hear sounds from the next room.

Weasel got ready to throw the door open, while Knuckles stood with his gun ready. He nodded his head and Weasel threw open the door and Knuckles stepped forward.

"Don't nobody move!" he shouted. There was no one there, or so they thought, until something moved in the corner. Weasel pushed the gun aside and stepped forward.

They found that it was Kirsty, tied up and gagged, so Weasel started to untie her wrists and then undid her gag.

"Where did they go?" asked Weasel.

"Behind you," said Kirsty. They turned to find two handguns trained on them.

"Bugger," said Knuckles.

"My sentiments entirely," said Weasel. He looked round and realised that Kevin wasn't with them, but said nothing.

*****

When Alan got the call from Kevin, he was beside himself with rage, which was unlike him, as he usually took things quite calmly.

"The idiot," said Alan. "I distinctly told him that under no circumstance was he to make a move or even let them know he had seen them. It's lucky you got away or I'd never have known where they were. What on earth was he thinking?"

"Well, to be fair," said Kevin, "it wasn't his fault. Knuckles was hell bent on going in, and I'm afraid I went along with him. Weasel just went to try and make sure nothing untoward happened."

"So how did you manage to escape then?"

"I got caught on a bramble bush in the garden," he said. "And by the time I had untangled myself I heard shouts and realised they had been caught, so I thought it best if I got away to tell you what had happened."

"Well, I'm glad you did," said Alan. "At least we now know where they are. Now I want you to keep your head down until I contact you. Understand?"

"Yes," he replied, a little sheepishly.

"Can you contact Sir Malcolm when I'm ready to meet him again?"

"Yes," he replied. "I can do that for you. Just let me know when you are ready."

Alan went back to his work and made gradual progress. It was slow and tedious, as there were thousands of molecular groups in the chain and he had to identify the appropriate one before replacing it with the one from the target's DNA.

He had developed a sub-programme to search for similar groups, but when they were found he had to decide whether they were the ones he wanted.

Forty-two

Nearly two weeks later he had finished the work, and had cultivated a reasonable amount of the virus. He really wanted to test it, but didn't want to try it on just anyone at random. He could have released it in the pub to see if everyone was immune, but knew that he could never do that, even if he was there and would take the same risk as the others. No, there was only one option, and that was to try it on himself.

He put on a protective suit and took one of the samples into the clean room, which was well insulated from the outside world, and emptied it onto a piece of cloth. He waved it around to spread the virus into the air, and to make sure he gave it a sniff, then sat down to wait.

It should be a very fast acting virus and he would feel the effects within half an hour at the outside. He felt that if he were wrong then no one else would suffer, and if he were right then he could continue with the project in the knowledge that no innocent people would get hurt.

As he sat there, he thought that he was getting hotter. Was he getting a temperature? It was difficult to tell. He stood up and walked around. Was he feeling a bit light-headed or did he just stand up suddenly? He felt his pulse and that seemed to be racing. He must have got it wrong and now he was going to die. He hoped it would be quick and painless. He had heard such terrible stories of people dying of plague.

After half an hour the ill effects, if that was what they were, seemed to have subsided, so he decided he must be all right after all. He made his way into the decontamination chamber, where he could take off the protective clothing and make sure none of the virus was taken out of the cubicle. Decontamination took about half an hour, and when that was finished he still felt no ill effects, so had to assume that his work had been successful.

Back in his flat, he took a shower and then decided to have a fry-up as a form of celebration. While things were cooking, he phoned Kevin to arrange the next meeting.

"I'll contact his nibs," said Kevin, "and let you know when he wants you there. I think he'll have to travel up from Blakely House."

"OK," said Alan. "I'll wait for your call. The sooner we get this over and done with, the better."

"Will it be over and done with?" asked Kevin. "I get the impression that once hooked you're never released."

"Not this time," said Alan, "if all goes to plan, and I have every hope that it will."

Alan just had to fill in time until he heard back from Kevin and hoped it wouldn't be long.

That evening, Justin arrived back from Cardiff. "Your vaccine line is going splendidly," he said as Alan joined him in his sitting room. "I hope you're going to join me for some dinner."

"I'd love to," said Alan.

"Then you can tell me how things are going with your project for Sir Malcolm."

"As far as I can tell," he replied, "it's going well. At least it didn't kill me."

"You didn't try it on yourself, did you?"

"Well, I had to try it on someone," said Alan. "I'll probably be exposed to it when I take it over to him, so what the hell?"

"I suppose you're right. When are you going?"

"I'm waiting to hear from them," said Alan. "Sir Malcolm seems to like Fridays, so probably this Friday."

"Want any company?"

"I would like some," said Alan. "But orders are that I go alone. But you could come with me and wait at the pub with Kevin."

"Kevin?"

"One of Weasel's crew."

"So why Kevin and not Weasel?" said Justin.

"Weasel got himself and Knuckles caught," said Alan. "I specifically told him to keep well out, but would he listen?"

"Many a battle has been lost due to the minions trying to think for themselves," said Justin. "That's why the Norman conquest was successful."

"Well, thanks for the history lesson," said Alan.

*****

Friday found Alan and Justin motoring out to meet Kevin at the country pub. They arrived mid-morning and ordered coffee, much to Kevin's amusement.

"Got to keep a clear head," said Alan.

He was to be at the meeting point at midday, as usual, so they had time to eat a meat pie and chips before Alan had to set off.

"So, what's the plan?" asked Kevin.

"It depends what Sir Malcolm wants me to do," said Alan, trying to avoid explaining his plan. "However, I expect it all to pan out OK."

"And what if it doesn't?" asked Kevin.

"Then we'll probably all be dead," said Alan and he had to smile at the expression on Kevin's face. "But I am confident that won't happen."

"You sound like the captain of the Titanic just before they hit the iceberg," said Kevin.

"That's what I feel like," said Alan. "Anyway, I'll have to be off. I don't know how long it will take, but I'll ring if and when there is a satisfactory outcome."

*****

The driver arrived spot on time, as usual. He didn't speak but just signalled to Alan to get in, and they drove off. Anyway, Alan wasn't in any mood to chat, so it suited him fine. He kept feeling his pocket to make sure the container was still there and in one piece. There was no chance of it breaking or coming open, as it had been designed for the specific purpose of carrying toxic materials.

When they arrived, he was shown into the same room as usual to find Sir Malcolm waiting for him.

"Are you confident that you have it right?" he asked, without turning to face Alan as he entered the room.

"As confident as I possibly could be," he replied. "But I would like to know, before I kill someone, who that someone is."

"Does it matter?" asked Sir Malcolm.

"It does to me," said Alan.

"Well, I don't suppose it will make any difference if I tell you," said Sir Malcolm. "It is my niece, Annabelle."

Alan was stunned. "Your niece? What has she done to deserve this?"

"She's getting above herself, and I will not be threatened by anyone, not even a relative," he said. "Anyway, she is dispensable. Also, to make sure you aren't trying anything stupid, your little friend, Kirsty, will go in with her. That will prove that the virus is selective."

Alan was shocked. "Let me go in instead."

"No can do," said Sir Malcolm.

"Well, let me speak to your niece," he said. "I'd like to apologise to her."

"Very noble," said Sir Malcolm. "But no. I don't want her forewarned."

"If that's your final word," said Alan. "But I would like to speak to Kirsty. I haven't seen her for several weeks now."

"If you must," said Sir Malcolm. "The others will all be in the sealed room by now. I'll give you a few minutes before she has to join them. I can't see what harm it can possibly do at this stage."

Alan was shown into the next room, where he had met Kirsty previously, and found her sitting there looking haggard.

He went up and embraced her quickly and told her what was happening. She looked shocked.

"There's nothing to worry about," he said, hoping that was true. "But I have a message for you to give to Annabelle."

"Annabelle?" she said, surprised. "What's it got to do with her?"

Alan explained, gave her the instructions to pass on and insisted she carry them out to the letter. Just as he had finished, the door opened and they were ushered out into another corridor. At the end they went into another large room with an isolation chamber in the corner.

Kirsty was taken over to it and pushed inside. Alan looked through the viewing window and was surprised to see Weasel and Knuckles there as well. Kirsty found herself pushed against Annabelle and the two of them disappeared from sight behind the others. Alan hoped that Annabelle would play her part. Everything depended on it.

"Right," said Sir Malcolm. "I think we are ready to start. Introduce the virus, please."

Alan moved to the window and everyone inside moved back away from the window.

There was a panel with a handle on it that Alan pulled out. He reached into his pocket and took out the virus carrier, which he opened, and took out the glass capsule it contained and fitted it into the clip in the tray. He then carefully slid the drawer back into place and locked it with the handle on the front.

Above it was a push button. "Well, press it," said Sir Malcolm. Alan pressed it. There was a loud click from inside and a hissing noise. Everyone inside tried to get as far away from the hissing noise as they could. After a few seconds, it stopped and everyone waited. It was obvious that everyone inside had held their breath, and they were going rather red in the face. Finally, they had to give in and breathe.

Sir Malcolm stared through the window. "Nothing's happening," he said.

"Give it chance," said Alan. "The victim won't be aware of anything for about ten minutes."

They stood and watched. It was the longest ten minutes that any of them had experienced. Finally, Alan took out his handkerchief and mopped his brow. This was the signal for the dramatics to begin.

After another minute, Annabelle swayed a bit and then sat down on the floor holding her head in her hands. The others all looked alarmed and stood as far back as possible. She started to shake, then she started to writhe around on the floor. It was either a very good act, or something had gone badly wrong. Could it be that as she was related to Sir Malcolm, she was also susceptible to the virus? He certainly hoped not. At least everyone else seemed to be all right.

"We'll leave it a bit longer, then it should be safe to go in," said Alan.

Sir Malcolm went and poured himself a plastic cup of champagne and sat down to wait. Alan thought he could have offered him one, but that wasn't in his nature. He hoped that the virus wasn't completely harmless to everyone, including Sir Malcolm, or he would have a lot of explaining to do. Everything depended on him getting this right.

"We've waited long enough," said Sir Malcolm, struggling out of his chair and walking towards the sealed room. "Open it up."

Alan went to the door, neutralised the fail-safe and opened the door. Everyone poured out, leaving Annabelle lying on the floor. Kirsty rushed to Alan and threw her arms round him. "I don't want to go through anything like that ever again," she said.

"Me neither," said Weasel.

"Well, you're not getting a hug," said Alan. "What're you doing here anyway?"

"I know, I know," he said. "But it seemed like a good idea at the time. I just thought…"

"That's the trouble. You didn't," said Alan. "In future, just leave the thinking to me."

Sir Malcolm had dashed straight into the room and was looking at the prostrate body on the floor. He wasn't sure what to do so he just prodded her to see if she was still alive. Suddenly she sat up. "Boo!" she shouted, and Sir Malcolm leapt back in alarm.

"What's the meaning of this?" he shouted, marching out of the room.

"Surprise!" shouted everyone. Sir Malcolm went red in the face.

"Are you telling me that there was no virus in that sample?" he said. "Someone will suffer for this."

"That is quite true," said Alan. "And the recipient will deserve everything he gets."

"And what's that supposed to mean?"

"You'll find out very soon," said Alan. "Why don't you sit down? You don't look too well."

"What are you talking about?" he shouted. "Has everyone gone mad?"

"I don't think so," said Alan. "Annabelle, why don't you pour the champagne? Let's celebrate a successful project."

"Successful?" shouted Sir Malcolm. "How has it been successful?" He swayed a little and had to hold on to the table to prevent himself from falling. He had become very red in the face.

"Well, it's like this," said Alan. "I replaced the sample you gave me with your DNA, so the virus will only attack one person – you."

"What are you talking about?" he said. "How could you get my DNA?"

"Easy," said Alan. "You leave samples of your DNA on every plastic cup you drink from. Now, how are you feeling?"

"I need some fresh air," he said, and staggered out of the room.

Annabelle started passing the champagne round.

"Better go and keep an eye on him," said Weasel. "Come on, Knuckles." They dashed out in pursuit of Sir Malcolm.

"I think I owe you a debt of gratitude," said Annabelle. "I was acting like a spoilt kid, thinking I could get whatever I wanted from that man, but I never thought he would try and kill me."

"I'll go and see what has happened to him," said Alan.

"I'll come with you," said Kirsty. They headed for the door, followed by Annabelle.

"What's happening?" asked one of the guards, who found themselves surplus to requirements.

"I think you are all redundant now," said Alan. "But I'm sure the police will want to speak to you all shortly."

Outside, they found Sir Malcolm lying in a sea of mud with Weasel standing over him.

"Think he's had a heart attack," said Knuckles.

They all stood round looking at him. Alan rang the police and ambulance before carrying the body of Sir Malcolm inside. Then they all went into the room Sir Malcolm had used as his office and waited for the emergency services to arrive.

"Seems a pity to waste all this champagne," said Weasel, pouring himself a cupful and then filling Knuckles' cup.

*****

The paramedics examined Sir Malcolm and came to the conclusion that he had died of a heart attack, and Alan didn't comment on that. He was put in a body bag, put in the ambulance and driven away. The police then took them all into the office to take statements. No one mentioned the virus or the fact that Kirsty, Weasel and Knuckles had been taken prisoner. They had already advised the guards to say nothing, as they could be arrested if Sir Malcolm's activities came to light. They all agreed that this was a good idea. They all waited in the next room, while individuals were taken in to give their statement.

"So did the virus kill him, or what?" asked Weasel.

"Well, that we will never know," said Alan. "There were no obvious signs of an infection on the body, and there won't be now he is dead. Who can tell what would have happened if he had not had a heart attack?"

"If he hadn't," said Kirsty, "and nothing had happened, we would all have been in bad trouble."

"But he did and we're not," said Alan. "In fact, we would all seem to be off the hook now. I can't say I'm not relieved."

When the police had taken all the statements, the guards disappeared, leaving them on their own.

"Well, seeing as our transport has disappeared," said Alan, "perhaps someone could give us a lift back to the pub. Justin will be wondering where have got to."

"I think we can all squeeze into my van," said Weasel. "It's just down the lane."

It was a tight squeeze, but they managed to get everyone in.

"What is that smell?" said Knuckles.

"Look," said Kirsty. "If you had been kept prisoner all this time, you wouldn't smell so sweet. Come to think of it, you don't."

"Sorry," said Knuckles.

*****

As soon as they had arrived back at the farm, Justin set about making a meal for them.

"I think I've got time to get a shower," said Kirsty. "Come on Alan, you can give me scrub down." Justin seemed to be concentrating on peeling some potatoes and didn't look up as they left.

After she had showered and was putting on clean clothes, she asked Alan, "Were you worried about me?"

"Of course," he said. "I was frantic. I could think of anything to do except what was demanded of me. Initially I was prepared to cause some unknown person to die of a terrible disease to save you, but then I had the idea that if I could get the DNA of Sir Malcolm, I could make him the recipient. I felt that at least he would deserve it. I didn't know what the virus was that he gave me, so I didn't know what to expect would happen. I knew it would be fast acting. We were remarkably lucky that he had a heart attack."

"So we don't know for certain that he would have died of the virus, if he hadn't had a heart attack?"

"No, we don't," said Alan. "And I'm glad we don't have to do anything like this again. I'll let it be known that the software that enabled this to be done has been destroyed. I'll carry on using the analysis programme that allows me to produce vaccines. That is beneficial and something to be proud of. I'm glad that we can now go out without looking over our shoulders all the time."

"That will be a relief," she said. "Where shall we go to celebrate?"

"I'll let you choose," he said. "But now we had better get back through to the farmhouse. Justin will be wondering what we've been up to."

Forty-three

Life returned to normal and they had a day out in York to celebrate. The following week, they decided to meet up with Weasel and all those who had helped in the previous months. When they arrived, they found Weasel in his usual chair in the corner, with Knuckles and Kevin. Alan bought a round of drinks and sat down with them in the corner.

"Well, I'd like to thank you all for all the help you have given us over the past months," said Alan.

"Think nothing of it," said Weasel. "But we now seem to be unemployed, unless you can think of any way we can be of assistance."

"Now you mention it," said Alan, "I think we could use you now and then to take vaccines out to farms for the local vets to administer. I used to do it myself, but it is really a waste of my time. I'll get Justin to put you on a monthly retainer with extra payments for each job you do. How does that sound?"

"Seems good to me," said Weasel, and Knuckles and Kevin concurred by nodding their heads and raising their glasses, which were now empty. Alan took the hint and had them filled again.

"I can't think of anything for your other friends, though," said Alan.

"That's OK," said Weasel. "They've got day jobs anyway, but I'm sure they would be willing to muck in any time you wanted them. They'll be here soon so you can tell them yourself."

The five of them ordered steak pies and chips, tucked into those and generally indulged in idle banter.

"So what else can you do with computers?" asked Kevin, who dabbled a bit himself.

"Oh, I've written all sorts of programmes, from general business applications to machine control programmes."

"What about AI?" asked Kevin.

"Ah, well that's a fascinating topic," said Alan. "Having done a lot of work on genetic molecules, I have come to realise what a marvellous organ the human brain is. The thing about artificial intelligence is that it isn't really intelligent. It uses the equivalent of the subconscious part of the brain that learns how to do physical things like playing games, riding bikes, or in the case of birds, flying. The neural network in the brain adjusts its parameters automatically each time it tries to do something until it can do it perfectly every time. But it has no consciousness at all. People tend to confuse this with it having a mind of its own and deciding for itself what it is going to do."

"Could you create a system that actually thinks?" asked Kirsty.

"In theory, yes," said Alan. "That is if you could simulate the part of the brain that thinks, I don't see why it would not be able to think."

"So it would think it was a person, then," said Kirsty.

"That would be creepy," said Weasel.

"And dangerous," said Alan. "A machine or creature of that sort would be like another species and would do its best to be better than any other species. In other words, it would want to take over, if not wipe us out altogether."

"Surely you could programme it not to think like that," said Weasel. "Then you'd have the best of both worlds, wouldn't you?"

"Probably," said Alan. "But it would be difficult to do, and even if you did it, it would be possible to persuade it otherwise. That's the thing about the human brain, it adapts to the circumstances it finds itself in. That's why people can be brainwashed. If enough pressure is applied, the brain will change its thinking to adapt. This can be an advantage and also a disadvantage. I think the best possible scenario for a servant robot would be to have the prime motivation hard wired into standard computer programming, which can control neural networks that learn how to do jobs efficiently."

"But it would be possible to simulate the whole human brain in theory at least?" said Kirsty.

"In theory, yes," said Alan. "But it would be much easier and cheaper to make a human one in the normal way, and a lot more fun. The Romans did what you are suggesting though. They called them slaves. The other problem with the human brain is that it has a herd instinct, a bit like sheep. One is frightened by something and makes a dash for it and all the others follow without thinking."

"Yes, but surely we don't have that any more?" said Kirsty.

"Oh, we do," said Alan. "It's fed by the social media. Someone posts something and all the sheep bleat in sympathy.

Look at climate change. In this case a lot of people shout something enough times and everybody believes it. Ask anyone who thinks we are all going to cook to explain why, and he can't, yet there are literally thousands of technical papers showing that this isn't the case. Not only do the herd have a herd point of view, they will suppress anyone who tries to argue against them because that means they are not of the herd."

"You make humans sound very stupid," said Weasel.

"Well, it looks like that, doesn't it," said Alan. "En masse, we're not any brighter than chimps. Anyway, what I am saying is that an artificial version of the human brain is not what we want, but a combination of the best bits with some artificial bits."

"Are you working on AI then?" asked Kirsty. "You haven't mentioned it before."

"I've been working on it, on and off, for a while, but my mind has been on other things recently."

At that moment the two equestrian girls arrived, followed by the three bikers. Alan thanked them for all their help and asked them if they would be willing to help in the future, if the need arose.

"Well, my life as a solicitor is pretty dull," said Grease. "And you have managed to spice it up a bit over the last few weeks. So if you need our help again, I'm sure we'd all be happy to oblige."

"Yes, it was a bit of fun," said Jocelyn, and Nancy agreed. "Give us a call if you need us."

They all had a drink and then the bikers and the girls left.

"I'm glad they thought it was fun," said Kirsty. "I can't say I did."

"Nor me," said Alan. "Don't look now, but someone has just arrived that I hoped we wouldn't see again." Walter Greenbank had just strolled into the bar and was ordering a drink. They all looked away from him, hoping he wouldn't see them, but it seemed he already had and had picked up his drink and was heading their way.

"Well," he said. "What have we here?"

"Mr. Greenbank," said Weasel. "How nice to see you again."

"I don't know how you did it," he said, "but we followed him all across England and Wales and finally lost him in France. I don't suppose you know where he is now, do you?"

"Of course I do," said Weasel. "But it will cost you a round of drinks. We're all on double whiskies."

"Seems a cheap deal to me," said Greenbank. He went and ordered the drinks, and when they had been brought to the table said, "OK, give."

"Let me introduce my friend, Alan Westbrook," said Weasel, indicating Alan.

"Westbrook?" said Greenbank. "Well, you are a slippery customer. First you're dead, and then you're not and then you disappear in France. Now, don't you think you should hand over that software before it does any damage?"

"I really would," said Alan, "if I could. It has caused me enough grief already, and led to the death of several innocent people. But unfortunately you are too late. I have already handed it over to Sir Malcolm Birch, so you had better ask him for it."

"And you didn't keep a copy?" said Greenbank. "Alan, you disappoint me."

"I tried that and it only brought me grief," said Alan. "So I thought, enough is enough."

"I can't say that I believe you," said Greenbank. "But if we can't get the damned software off you, I don't suppose anyone can. I'll wish you good day. Enjoy your drinks."

After he had left, the barman came over with the bill. "American bloke said you were paying."

"Never trust a Yank," said Weasel.

Forty-four

Back at the farmhouse, Justin, Alan and Kirsty were sitting down to a meal.

"You haven't destroyed the software or given it away, have you?" said Kirsty.

"Of course not," said Alan. "But as far as anyone else is concerned, that's the story."

"So what have you done with it?" asked Justin. "Don't forget we are relying on you to produce our range of vaccines."

"I have broken it down into modules," said Alan, "so that the work I'm doing for you will have its own programme that can't be used for anything else. The other parts of the programme have been rearranged and given names that sound quite innocuous. This means that I don't have to hide them, but they'll need a password to open them. If you don't give a password it'll open the cover programme. It won't ask for the password so you need to know that it requires one."

"Sounds as if you've just made yourself redundant," said Justin.

"I thought I'd play around with AI for a while," said Alan. "I'm sure that'll be required in all sorts of fields soon."

After eating, Alan and Kirsty went back into their flat next to the lab and sat down in front of the TV to relax.

"We seem to have reached the end of an era," said Kirsty.

"I hope not," said Alan. "I enjoy being with you and hoped we could make it more permanent."

"I don't do permanent," said Kirsty. "But I'm in no hurry to move on. Perhaps you can get me interested in this artificial intelligence stuff. After all, I did study mechanical engineering, for a while."

"I didn't know you were a qualified mechanical engineer!"

"I didn't say I was qualified," she returned. "I said that I had studied it. I didn't take the exams as I wasn't out to impress anyone."

"You're always full of surprises," said Alan. "I think there could be a future for us."

"I hope so."

*****

The next day, while they were eating breakfast with Justin in the farmhouse, there was a knock at the door.

"Who the hell is that at this time in the morning?" said Justin, getting up and going to the door. There was the sound of voices and Justin returned, followed by two men in suits.

"Mr. Westbrook?" said suit one. "Or is it Finch?"

"Westbrook will do," said Alan. "How can I help you?"

"We are from an intelligence service attached to the MoD," he continued. "We are carrying out an investigation concerning Sir Malcolm Birch and think you and this young lady can be of assistance to us."

"I thought he died of a heart attack," said Kirsty.

"Oh he did," said the agent. "That's not the problem."

"Perhaps you had better explain," said Alan. "And as you know our names, perhaps you would be so kind as to supply us with yours."

"Certainly," said the agent. "I am Wilf Wilson, and this is my assistant Michael York. As I said, we're from a department of the MoD which is not well known publicly, and we would rather it remained that way. I don't have to remind you that you are still bound by the Official Secrets Act, do I?"

"No," said Alan.

"But I'm not," said Kirsty.

"Well, we can soon rectify that," said Wilf. "Michael will get you to sign all the appropriate papers when we've finished."

"Excuse me," said Justin, "but we're in the middle of breakfast, so if you don't mind, perhaps we can talk while we eat. If you would like to have a coffee with us, there's a jug on the side and some cups, so please help yourselves." Michael went to the sideboard and poured two coffees, and Wilf sat down in a spare chair opposite Alan.

"So what's all this about?" asked Alan.

"Well, for one thing," said Wilf, "there seem to have been some irregularities regarding your death certificate. From what I can gather, when Peter Finch died, the death was registered in your name. Why was that?"

"Well, Sir Malcolm seemed to think I was in danger from some unknown agency who had tried to kill me and had accidentally killed Peter Finch instead. He said that if they thought they had been successful they wouldn't be looking for me any more."

"And you thought that this was a bona fide MoD procedure, did you?"

"I must admit it seemed a bit unusual, but where matters of national security are concerned, it seems they can do whatever they like," said Alan. "But as it turned out, it put me in a rather difficult position. Alan Westbrook was officially dead and I was now Peter Finch. This meant that I no longer had any rights over my own software."

"Didn't that bother you?"

"In some ways, yes," said Alan. "But not as far as the software was concerned."

"But they had your memory stick containing all the software, didn't they?"

"Yes," said Alan. "And they thought they had the password."

"And didn't they?" said Wilf. "I was under the impression that your erstwhile colleague, Jim Stanley, had the password."

"He had the password for the previous day," said Alan. "It was too important to have a simple password, so I used a day of the week and month combination, so the next day when he entered the password it was for the previous day. A wrong password would then wipe the programme from the memory stick."

"So that's why Dr. Stanley came looking for you?"

"Yes," said Alan. "He thought all the data had been wiped off the computer also; I told him that was not the case, but that he should go back and do it himself. I gave him our new address, but I unfortunately got the number wrong. Well, fortunate for us but unfortunate for the people down the road. Both of them were killed the following night. We think that was meant to be Maggie and me. It was then we realised that it was Sir Malcolm who was behind it. Jim was a very clever scientist, but very naive and gave our address to Sir Malcolm. Then when he kept probing, he came to grief too. I suppose that was Sir Malcolm too?"

"What we are trying to find out is whom he was working for," said Wilf.

"You mean he wasn't working for the MoD?" said Kirsty.

"Well he was in a position with the MoD," said Wilf. "But he was trying to get your software for himself. What we don't know is whether he was intending to pass it on to another power, or if he had plans for it himself."

"Have you asked the people who worked for him?" said Alan. "I suppose you've rounded them all up?"

"Yes," said Wilf. "We have them all in custody, though they don't seem to know anything. Most of them were of the opinion that they were working for the MoD. They seemed quite upset when we told them they weren't and that they wouldn't be paid."

"I'm sure they were," said Alan.

"The thing is," continued Wilf, "we can't find any trace of the software that you handed over to him. Could you tell us what form it was in?"

"I always keep a copy on a memory stick, so that I can use it on any computer without leaving a copy for anyone else to use," said Alan. "But I didn't actually give him a copy."

"So you have the only copy in existence, do you?"

"I had," said Alan. "But I decided that it was too dangerous to keep. So I dismantled the programme and only kept the parts that I use for creating vaccines. The rest I have wiped."

"Can you prove that?" asked Wilf.

"Not really," said Alan. "I keep all my software on this memory stick. You are welcome to have a look at it." He passed it to Wilf, who passed it to Michael, who took it out to their vehicle where Alan assumed he had a computer.

"We may require you to come with us to some of the locations we know Sir Malcolm used. Some are MoD locations, and some aren't," said Wilf. "And we would really like to inspect your lab, just to confirm that you haven't got a copy of the software on one of your computers."

"We would rather the location of the lab were kept secret," said Justin. "We carry out a lot of work for various government departments and we are required to keep the locations secret. We would have to get full clearance from several departments before we could give you access."

"Well, I'll just have to take your word for it until we can get full clearance," he replied.

Michael returned with the memory stick. "Nothing on here except utility routines," he said, handing it back to Alan.

"As I said," said Alan, "I thought it better to get rid of all the contentious material. After all, it really is of no use to me, and I certainly wasn't thinking of selling it to the highest bidder. I wasn't going to let Sir Malcolm get his hands on it either, though after our last tests, I'm not sure that it worked, anyway."

"Well we'll leave it at that for the moment," said Wilf. "But we'll be in touch in due course." Justin showed the two visitors out and returned to finish his breakfast.

"I thought we were finished with all this," said Justin. "And I certainly don't want to let them know the whereabouts of the lab."

"Is there somewhere else that we could tell them is our lab?" asked Kirsty.

"That is a distinct possibility," said Justin. "Leave it with me and I'll see what I can set up."

*****

That evening, Alan and Kirsty were sitting in their living room next to the lab, drinking a cup of coffee and winding down.

"Have we heard the last of those men?" asked Kirsty.

"I very much doubt it," said Alan. "I think they'll root out all the places Sir Malcolm has used. For all I know, he may have some secret laboratory somewhere trying to synthesise viruses. They'll want to get rid of them, or at least take charge of them."

"But why do they want you to get involved?"

"To make sure they aren't using my software," replied Alan. "I know they're not, but they don't."

"But what if they find out about the virus?"

"I can't see how they could," said Alan. "If any virus was found in his body, who's to say how he got it?"

"What if one of his employees said something?"

"I'd just say it was all an act and there was no virus used."

"Will they swallow that?"

"Probably not," said Alan. "But they can't prove anything one way or the other. I'm sure it will all fizzle out eventually."

"So what'll you do now, work-wise?" asked Kirsty.

"Well, there'll always be work coming in from Justin," he said. "But that won't take up all my time. We could take a holiday I suppose, but work-wise, I would like to continue my work on artificial intelligence."

"Have you done much on that?" asked Kirsty. "I find that quite interesting."

"Quite a bit of the ground work," said Alan. "I have based it on my analysis of brain cells and cell structures. I had once thought of creating an artificial organic brain, but thought better of that."

"Why was that?"

"Too hit and miss," he replied. "You know how unpredictable people can be."

"So it will have to be made up of hardware then?"

"That's right," he said. "I can simulate it on the computer, but that would be too slow and cumbersome for the final version, so I'll have to reduce the whole thing to microchip."

"Can you do that?" she asked.

"No," he said. "I can design it but I'll have to get one of the large semiconductor companies to produce the chips for me. I'll have to break the whole thing down into several individual chips. In that way, there is less chance of someone pinching the design."

"Would they do that?" asked Kirsty.

"If they knew the significance of it, there's no knowing what they might do," said Alan. "That's why I will put the separate parts in with names that would lead them to think they were control circuits for a camera, or a washing machine, or something like that."

"I'm dying to see the computer simulation," said Kirsty.

"So am I."

Forty-five

Three weeks later they got another visit from the government agents, wanting them both to go to a place in West Yorkshire, where they had discovered an old abandoned government building that had been used by Sir Malcolm. So they set off to drive over to see it.

On the way, they called in on Weasel to see if he knew anything about it.

"No," he replied when asked. "The only place I went to was his office in London. Do you want me to come along too?"

"Could be useful," said Alan. "I don't want this to go on longer than necessary. It's a complete waste of time and money."

"Funny you should mention money," said Weasel.

"Well, there's none in this, I can assure you," said Alan. "For you or for me. This is just to get the security services off our backs."

"If you say so," said Weasel, looking disappointed.

It was about half an hour's drive to the site, which was surrounded by a high wire fence with 'Keep Out' notices all round. Inside, the undergrowth had grown to reach overhead height. At the gate, there were two guards who looked a lot more official.

After showing their identification, they were let through to drive up to the group of dilapidated buildings in the centre of the site.

"A haven for wildlife," said Weasel.

"That's exactly what's been using this place," said Alan. They pulled up in front of what looked like the main building. The door seemed to be the only solid part of the building and was standing open, so they went in.

It was dark inside, and at first the place looked empty. Then Kirsty pointed to the far side. "There's a light through there," she said.

They walked over to find a door left ajar. Alan pushed it open and they went through.

"Glad to see you could make it," said a voice. They spun round to find a group of men in uniforms, emptying some filing cabinets, and recognised one of them as the man who had come to the farm.

"I didn't think we had a choice, Wilf," said Alan.

"Mr. Wilson, please. This is official," said Wilf.

"Sorry, Mr. Wilson it is," said Alan. "Now, how can we help you?"

"Perhaps you could have a look through all this and see if you can find anything of importance," said Wilf. "Now I know Miss Williams, but who is this other fellow?"

"This is Weasel," said Alan. "He used to work for Sir Malcolm before defecting to help me."

"Weasel?" said Wilf. "A very colourful name."

"Just call me Nigel," said Weasel.

"Nigel?" said Alan, surprised.

"OK, OK," said Weasel. "Don't tell everyone."

They looked at the pile of dusty folders on the floor where the agents had thrown them, and started to look through them. There was so much dust that it made them sneeze, causing clouds of the stuff to fly in all directions.

"There's nothing of interest here," said Alan. "Most of this stuff's older than I am."

One of the agents appeared from the next room. "There's some newer stuff through here, sir," he said. They all followed him through into the next room, which turned out to be a room within a room and was quite clean. On the bench was a row of fairly new computers.

"Over to you, Mr. Westbrook," said Wilf. Alan walked along the row of computers and then settled on one to start with. He switched it on and waited for it to boot up.

"OK," he said. "Leave it with me. It may take a while to find anything interesting. I'll yell when I find anything."

The others reluctantly left, leaving Alan, Kirsty and Weasel. Alan opened up each folder in turn, revealing nothing of interest.

"What about that one?" asked Kirsty, pointing to the icon of a folder that was hidden down at the bottom right-hand corner of the screen. He double-clicked it and found that it contained dozens of notes between Sir Malcolm and various people he employed, plus a few between himself and the MoD. He did a search for any file containing his own name and found that there were about fifteen in all, so he copied them all onto his memory stick and then put it back into his pocket.

"We'll look at these later," Alan said and then erased the files from the computer. He then opened up some of the other notes and printed out any he thought would be of interest to the security people.

They checked all the other computers but couldn't find anything of interest on any except the last one, where he found a long proposal for a plant to produce robots with artificial intelligence, though they made it clear that the AI part of the project was still in its infancy. Alan copied this to his memory stick and then erased the original.

When they were sure there was nothing else of interest, he called Wilf back again and gave him the printouts. "Nothing else of interest," said Alan. "But you might like to take these computers back to your labs and let someone go through them in detail. There may be things that have meaning to you but not to me."

On the way home, Kirsty asked Alan if the MoD people could restore the files he had erased.

"No," he replied. "I used a deletion routine that cleans the record off completely. I keep it on my memory stick.

*****

They dropped Weasel off at his local pub, much to his disappointment; he would have liked to have seen what was on those other files. Then they continued home to the farm, where Justin was waiting impatiently for them. "Well, what did you find?" he asked as they took their coats off and sat down in the living room.

"There were a number of files with my name in the text," said Alan. "But I haven't had the chance to read them yet."

"Well, you'd better have something to eat first," Justin said. "Then you can settle down to go through them."

"Yes," said Kirsty. "I'm dying to know what they say."

"These are all the notes concerning me," said Alan. "So I removed them from the computers, as I didn't want the security people asking too many questions. They may not be incriminating, but it's better to be sure."

After they had eaten, Alan and Kirsty settled themselves on the settee and started to go through the papers. They were quite enlightening. There were messages to and from the different people Sir Malcolm had hired to track him down.

"This one will interest Weasel," said Alan. "He has hired some fellow to get rid of our friend and his colleagues. I hope they're not still out there looking for them."

"Better tip him off," said Kirsty. "I'll ring him and let him know, then he can be on the lookout. If the killer doesn't know that his employer is dead, he may still be going to carry out his orders." She picked up her phone and rang Weasel.

"Apparently that fellow that caught us in Scotland has been arrested by the police," said Alan. "I don't think he'll be a problem any more."

"There seems to be a lot of correspondence with Annabelle," said Kirsty. "It would seem she was getting a bit above herself."

"Yes," said Alan. "And Sir Malcolm had had enough. That's why he used her as a target for the virus trial. Kill two birds with one stone, as it were."

"Have you looked at that one about AI?" asked Kirsty.

"No, I'd forgotten about that," said Alan. "Let's have a look at it now." It seemed that they already had a facility somewhere for building robots, but they were still waiting for the software to be developed, and there was no mention of who was doing it. "I wish I knew where this facility was," he said.

"Perhaps there's a mention of that in one of the other files," said Kirsty.

"Maybe," said Alan. "Keep digging."

"There's this old folder here," said Kirsty. "We didn't look at it properly as it seemed to be irrelevant. But I have just noticed that there is a map in here. I can't make out where it is though." She handed it to Alan.

"It's quite a large scale map," said Alan. "We'll need to find a grid reference on it so that we can find out where it is on an Ordnance Survey map."

"Maybe Weasel, or one of his friends will recognise it," said Kirsty.

"That's a distinct possibility," said Alan. "Perhaps we should pay him a visit."

*****

Weasel was sitting in his usual seat in the corner with Knuckles and Kevin.

"You timed it just right," said Weasel.

"I know, I know," said Alan. "It's my round."

"Well that's mighty magnanimous of you," said Weasel, handing him his glass. Alan went and bought the drinks and handed them out.

"I'm a bit worried about that memo we found," said Alan. "You know, the one hiring a killer to tidy up some loose ends."

"I didn't know I was a loose end," said Weasel.

"Oh, I don't know," said Knuckles.

"It's no joking matter," said Alan. "If he's still planning on carrying out his orders, we've got to stop him. But we don't know what he looks like or where to find him."

"Well, if he's trying to find me," said Weasel, "all we have to do is wait."

"The trouble is," said Alan, "that you may not know he has arrived until you feel a knife in your back or a bullet in your head."

"Nice," said Weasel.

"The thing is," said Alan, "you need to have someone watching your back at all times."

"Could be a bit awkward," said Weasel. "You see, there's this pretty barmaid at the Old Swan."

"OK," said Alan. "I get your drift, but you need to have someone looking out for you all the time. Anyway, the reason we're here is that we have this map, but we don't know whereabouts it is." He opened the map and they all looked at it.

"Looks like somewhere up on the moors," said Knuckles. "Not quite sure where though."

"I suppose if we could identify some obvious features," said Weasel, "it would give us a starting point. Leave it with me and I'll see what I can find out."

Knuckles and Kevin took their leave and left them talking until Weasel decided that he had other places to be. They all walked out into the car park. As Weasel was getting into his car, Alan leaned forward. "I think there's someone sitting in that car opposite," said Alan. "It's possible he is waiting to follow you home. Perhaps we should have a word with him."

"Leave him to me," said Weasel, and got out of his car and walked over to the other car and opened the door.

"What do you think you're doing?" shouted the occupant.

"I've seen you before," said Weasel. "At Sir Malcolm's office."

"So what?"

"Well, you obviously don't know that Sir Malcolm is dead."

"What are you talking about?"

"Any orders you have concerning my demise are now obsolete," said Weasel. "You are unemployed."

"I'm employed by the MoD," he said.

"I don't think so," said Alan. "The MoD doesn't send killers after its erstwhile employees. As of now, you haven't committed a crime, at least that we know of, so I should quit while you are ahead."

"How did he die?"

"Heart attack," said Alan. "And we are working with the security people to sort out what he's been up to. Perhaps you can help us. In which case we may say nothing about this little incident."

"How can I help you?"

"We are trying to find a secret facility which is somewhere up here on the moors," said Alan. "It would be useful if you could pinpoint it for us. Here is the map." Alan thrust the map at him.

"Oh yes," he said. "That's High Moor. It's shown on any standard tourist map. You'll find it about thirty miles in that direction." He pointed in a general westerly direction. "Now, what are you going to do about me?"

"Well, you haven't actually done anything yet," said Alan. "Have you?"

"No," he replied. "I worked for him for a few years doing odd jobs, but nothing like this. I'm not sure I could have gone through with it anyway."

"So, what's your name?" asked Weasel. "It'd be nice to know who was trying to kill me."

"Frank Wilson," he replied.

"Not the name of a deadly killer," said Weasel. "So how did he get you to do this?"

"Blackmail," said Frank. "He said he had a folder on me with a record of all my crimes."

"What crimes?" asked Alan.

"Well, there weren't any but he had compiled a folder in the MoD," said Frank, "with a whole list of crimes which he attributed to me. He said these would be released to the security department if I didn't cooperate."

"We didn't find anything like that in his possession," said Alan. "I think he was having you on, and if you had done what he wanted he really would have had something on you. Now, can you lead us to this place?" He waved the map.

"I think so," he replied.

"Well no time like the present," said Alan. "We'll take you in our car. Weasel can follow in his own car."

"What about my hot date?" Weasel said indignantly.

"Phone her and tell her to keep it warm," said Kirsty. Weasel looked a bit bemused but took out his phone and made the call. Three quarters of an hour later they found themselves high on the moors with no sign of habitation in any direction.

"An ideal place for a secret installation," said Alan. "I doubt if it is on any of the MoD records. Most of these cold war installations were either sold off or just sealed up and abandoned."

"I was told that it was an MoD lab," said Frank.

"I'd be very surprised," said Alan. "Sir Malcolm had quite an agenda of his own. We don't know exactly what it was, but we know that he was up to no good. Now, how do we find it, and then how do we get in?"

"Just take us over the brow of this hill," said Frank. "Then look out for a track off to the left." Alan slowed right down and just crept over the brow of the hill until he could see a rough track leading off to the left.

"Doesn't look as if it goes anywhere," said Alan. He turned left onto the track, closely followed by Weasel. The track was easier going than it looked, though it didn't seem to be overused, which Alan mentioned to Frank.

"I think Sir Malcolm would arrive by helicopter," said Frank. "And there didn't seem to be many permanent staff here."

"I hope that's still the case," said Alan. "Now, what am I looking for?"

"Well this, if I remember correctly," said Frank, "is the car park. So pull up and we'll continue on foot."

Weasel pulled in beside them. "I hope this isn't a wild goose chase," he said. "This is a very wild place where would-be assassins might meet their end if they've been having us on."

"I can assure you that this is the place," said Frank emphatically. "Just follow me." They set off along an almost invisible path, which would have been difficult to see in broad daylight, but as the sun was beginning to set, was almost invisible.

Suddenly Frank stopped and said, "We're here."

"Where?" said Weasel. "We're in the middle of nowhere."

"Look in front of your feet," said Frank. They looked and soon realised that a square of the heather looked a bit different from the neighbouring heather. Alan bent down and found that it was artificial. Frank bent down and pulled a metal ring out of the undergrowth and gave it a good tug. The whole metre square section opened like a trapdoor. There was a metal ladder that took them down about ten feet into a corridor. Alan went down first and when he reached the bottom, lights came on all the way down the corridor.

When the others had joined him, they set off along the corridor, which turned out to be about fifty yards long and tilted downhill at a shallow angle. At the end there was a large metal door which looked more like a bulkhead.

"Wind the wheel clockwise," said Frank. "It's to keep the place airtight." Weasel started turning the wheel. It seemed fairly free, as if it had been used a bit recently.

There was a click and the door swung open to reveal another corridor. Alan checked to make sure the door could be reopened from the inside, and when he had satisfied himself that this was the case, he closed the door behind them.

Like the first corridor, this one was also lit by electric lamps spaced out along its length. After about another thirty yards, there was an iron staircase leading down into the depths. After four flights, they came to the bottom to be confronted by a sturdy looking steel door. There was a handle on it but no sign of a lock. Weasel turned the handle and the door swung open to reveal a large scientific workshop. They looked around but the place was empty.

"Well, lads," said Alan, "let's investigate." They all spread out and started opening drawers in filing cabinets and looking through the contents. There were many files with scribbled notes, but nothing that looked to be of any value.

"There seem to be quite a few that mention robotics," said Kirsty. "But nothing very specific."

"Yes," said Alan. "I'd noticed that. Do you think he was looking into creating some sort of artificial intelligence?"

"There's another door over here," said Weasel from the far side of the room. "And there are lights on." He opened the door and disappeared from sight. Alan and Kirsty set off to follow him.

Through the door, everything seemed more modern and less run down, as if this was the area that had been in use most recently.

"Where's Weasel gone?" said Alan, looking around. "Weasel!" he shouted. There was a scuffling noise from one of the rooms a little further down the corridor. "I think he's in there," said Alan, heading for the door. When they arrived at the room, they were surprised to find Weasel on the floor, with an attractive young woman standing over him, brandishing a chair.

"Stay where you are," she shouted at them. "Or your friend gets it." Alan couldn't help bursting into fits of hysterical laughter.

"It's nothing to laugh at," said Weasel from the floor. "She's lethal with that thing."

"Perhaps we should introduce ourselves," said Alan. "I'm Alan Westbrook, this is my partner Kirsty, and the unfortunate fellow that you have floored is affectionately known as Weasel, due to his upright and honest dealings."

"Cheek," said Weasel, scrabbling to his feet while the woman still threatened him with the chair.

"I assume you think you work for the MoD?" said Alan, "Under the control of Sir Malcolm Birch? Well, I have to inform you that you used to work for Sir Malcolm, but not the MoD. He was doing a bit of freelance work, it would seem. However, he is dead now, so you seem to be working for no one at the moment, so perhaps you would like to tell us what you are doing here. We do work for the MoD, you see."

"My name is Professor Diane Crouch," she said. "And I specialise in robotics."

"Does anyone else work here?" asked Kirsty.

"Well, I did have a backup team," she said. "They haven't been in for a few days, but it was always a bit like that."

"So what exactly has Sir Malcolm had you designing?" asked Alan.

"Well, if you would like to come through here," she said, "I'll show you." She led the way into the next room, which looked a bit like an operating theatre. In the middle of the room, on what looked rather like an operating table, was what looked like a partially dissected human body, but when Alan looked more closely, he found that it was not human at all.

"Doesn't look much like a robot," said Alan.

"Well, it wouldn't," said Diane. "We have been trying to simulate all the muscle and tendon structures that you'd find in a human body. That way we hope to get much more realistic movement. Servomotors are so slow and ponderous that the robot would fall flat on its face before it could react to make a correction. We've developed some artificial muscle material which behaves very like natural muscle. You apply a small electric current to it and it immediately contracts, pulling the artificial tendon attached to it. Here, let me show you." She turned to a control panel next to the robot and flicked a switch. The arm instantly made a fist, before relaxing again when she switched it off.

"I see what you mean," said Alan. "But it does seem a bit violent. OK for a fighting robot, I suppose."

"That's the open circuit response," she said. "There are also hundreds of microwires from all parts of the skin to sense pressure and movement. The 'brain' would have to combine its required movement with the feedback from the 'nerves', if you see what I mean."

"I most certainly do," said Alan. "That's pure genius."

"Obvious if you think about it," she said, dismissively.

"You are right, of course," said Alan.

"So which department of the MoD do you work for?"

"Well, actually, we're not employees of the MoD, as such," he said.

"So this has all been a scam to get me to talk, has it?"

"No, not at all," said Alan. "I used to work for them until Sir Malcolm did the dirty on me. I now work freelance and do a lot of work for my friend Justin Williams who is involved in many government and international projects. Kirsty is his niece. I think Sir Malcolm was trying to get me into a position where he could blackmail me into doing whatever he wanted me to do. I don't know what that was, but I don't think I would have liked it."

"He talked about growing an artificial brain to link in with this robot," said Diane. "He seemed to have someone in mind who he thought could do it."

"It's amazing how simple things look to the uninitiated," said Alan. "It could well key into your artificial nervous system, but even a preprogrammed artificial brain might have ideas of its own. No, I think a cortex of artificial neurons could control the movement of your robot. It could also process visual and audial inputs, but all decisions would be made by standard computer circuitry. Now, I would like you to continue your work on this robot, but as an employee of The Cymru Corporation, which is Justin's baby. I will work with you and develop the software. But first we would need to move all this lot to one of Justin's premises. Where do you live at the moment?"

"I'm in temporary accommodation in the village, so I can move at any time," she replied.

"Well, if you can give me your present address," said Alan, "I'll OK everything with Justin and then we'll send some transport out here to remove everything you will need to carry on with the project. Then you'll have to find some more convenient accommodation local to where you'll be working."

*****

On the way back, Kirsty seemed a bit quiet and Alan wondered what was bothering her. "What's the matter?" he asked.

"Why should anything be the matter?"

"You just seem unusually quiet," he replied. "Especially when we have a new project to work on."

"Well, it seems that you'll have a nice new project," she said. "But I don't see anything of interest for me."

"Why's that?" he replied. "I would have thought that you'd be in your element, working on a new robotics project."

"You may have overlooked the fact that you already have a glamorous assistant, who is already pretty well involved with the mechanical design of the thing, and what's more she's going to get her own facility. I still don't see where I fit in. I'm certainly not going to work for her. You know what these university types are like. They don't live in the real world."

"That's why I need you," said Alan. "We'll leave her to get on with all the ground work, laying out the muscles and tendons and nerves and so forth, then we'll take one of her prototypes and try to make it work. I'm sure that'll be the more interesting bit."

"But who would be in charge?"

"I would," said Alan. "She would be in charge of her bit in her new premises, and you would be in charge of your bit, which is making it all work. As you said, these academics tend to be a bit impractical, so between us we need to modify what she has done to make it work."

"Wouldn't it just be easier to let me do all the mechanical design? It'd be a lot cheaper."

"Not so sure," said Alan. "She'll have her own ideas as to how this is going to work. If you were working with her on the design you'd be at each other's throats all the time. Anyway, I'm leaving her with the tedious bit. She's already designed the basic muscle and tendon structure, so she's basically done her bit."

"Then why keep her on?"

"Well, as an employee of the company, all designs that she produces are the property of the company," said Alan. "If we gave her the boot and just pinched her ideas, we'd find she'd be throwing writs at us from all directions. So we keep her on and let her do all the donkey work, we make it work and everybody is happy. Anyway, I think Sir Malcolm owes us this."

"If you say so."

"You know," said Alan, "for a moment I thought you were jealous."

"Me?" said Kirsty indignantly. "Of course not."

"Well that's fine then."

*****

Once Justin had moved Diane and all her equipment into a small factory unit in the Vale of York, life returned almost to normal for Alan and Kirsty. Alan worked day and night on the software he'd need for the robot, while Kirsty set up the testing jigs ready for when she received the first artificial limb to work on.

One day, Justin came through to the lab while they were working. "Someone to see you, Alan," he said. Alan looked surprised as he didn't think anyone knew about this place.

"She's waiting in the farmhouse. She doesn't know about this place."

Alan followed him through to the farmhouse, but Kirsty stayed where she was. In the living room of the farmhouse, Alan was startled to see Maggie sitting on the settee.

"I'll leave you to it," said Justin, and went into the other room.

"So, to what do we owe the pleasure of this visit?" he asked, rather more coldly than he need have.

"I've missed you," she said. "And I thought it might be possible for us to start again where we left off."

"You didn't come to Blackpool Tower," he said. "I went, only to find that there was a spy watching my every move. Luckily, he wasn't very good so we soon lost him. At that point I think I might have said yes to you, but a lot has happened since then, and I was quite hurt by the way you just decided to abandon me. I'm with someone else now," he continued. "Someone who I can trust to stand by me whatever."

"I'm sorry if I gave away our meeting at Blackpool," she said. "But I didn't know it was to someone who was after you. I just didn't think…"

"No, you didn't," he said. "But I've had plenty of time to think and have realised now that it would never have worked. I should have realised the moment you said you were happy to be rid of Peter. That was rather unfeeling, wasn't it?"

"Well, I'm sorry, but that was how I felt about him, but I feel differently about you."

"It's taken you a long time to come to that decision," he said. "But I'm afraid the decision has come far too late. So, I'll wish you well and say goodbye."

"I didn't think you would be so unfeeling," she said, standing and reaching for her coat. "So I'll say goodbye and be on my way."

At that moment, Justin appeared. It was obvious that he had been listening. "I'll see you out," he said, showing her to the door. There was the sound of conversation outside before Justin returned.

"I've given her directions to the inn in the village," he said. "I'm glad you gave her her marching orders. I wouldn't trust her with any knowledge of our work. She'd be a real liability."

"I quite agree," said Alan. "She was very useful to me when I first got into difficulties with Sir Malcolm, but that was more for her own ends than mine. No, I've made the right choice with Kirsty."

"Glad to hear it," said Kirsty, coming into the living room. "She certainly had a cheek."

"So you were listening too?"

"Of course," she said. "But just so that I could rush to your aid if she got difficult."

"Well, in that case," said Alan, "perhaps we should move our relationship onto a more permanent basis."

"Now let's not get too far ahead of ourselves."

"Maybe you're right," he said, leading her back into the lab.